An Unsuitable Duchess

by

Kathleen Buckley

An Unsuitable Duchess

Cover Art by *RJ Morris*

The Wild Rose Press, Inc.
PO Box 708
Adams Basin, NY 14410-0708
Visit us at www.thewildrosepress.com

Publishing History
First Tea Rose Edition, 2017
Print ISBN 978-1-5092-1424-2
Digital ISBN 978-1-5092-1425-9

Published in the United States of America

The lock was old and not very complex,
much like the one on the pantry door at home. Mrs. Bowman would insist on locking it and then misplace the key. In Fletching, Anne had kept an L-shaped length of stiff wire. Here…she pulled a long hairpin out of her hair, causing a lock to fall free to her shoulder. The pin was a pretty one, with a filigree head, but not expensive. She contrived to bend it by holding the greater part down on the rough table, pressing the end of it over the edge with the knife handle. It was easily bent. Anne hoped it would be strong enough. "Were there many people about downstairs?"

Prue shook her head, watching in a fascinated manner, rather as creatures were said to be paralyzed by the gaze of a snake. The lock resisted; it was rusty and certainly not as well oiled as the one on the pantry door. Anne was unpleasantly aware of perspiration breaking out all over her body. If she could not open the door, they must see if it were possible to depart by the window. Would the bed sheets be strong enough to make a rope, and would it be long enough? She thought she would have little difficulty getting down, though it would be a longer drop than the rope in the barn which she had slid down as a child. Would Prue be able to do it? Or even be willing to try? She could hardly leave the girl behind.

When the lock at last yielded with a grudging *snick!* Anne's knees felt oddly weak.

"Come. I fancy this is our best chance in a house of this sort. You won't want to stay?"

"I'm afraid to go, mistress, but I'm more afraid to stay."

Dedication

For my mother and father,
and in homage to
Georgette Heyer
and
Sir Walter Scott

Prologue

September, 1739

The ladder teetered as she clung to the tree with one arm and stretched to hook the loop of rope over the highest branch she could reach.

"Have a care, Mistress Anne," the gardener's lad warned, fixing his eyes on the rung in front of his nose, lest he should catch a glimpse of her green stockings— or worse. "You should of let me climb up instead. Remember the time you fell out of the hayloft? And—"

"I was reading a book at the time and not paying enough attention, Seth. It was the merest coincidence that the edge of the loft was there. But with your lame leg, you have no business on a ladder. And I couldn't steady it for you. I'll be done as soon as I hang this broken meat spit." She had already attached other items to different branches, hoping that the towering clouds that had blown up would indeed produce lightning at the right time and place. Given the unsettled weather they'd been having, it seemed likely. Distant thunder had rumbled half a dozen times already, and the storm was coming nearer. It had been a startlingly loud crash that sent her scurrying to set up her experiment. Which substances would attract the lightning: the iron, the long silk ribbon (the color in streaks from an inadvertent wetting, which over-dyeing had not helped), the copper

1

pan? She had also pierced a turnip with a skewer and suspended it with a length of wire. If the lightning hit the wire, would the electricity cook the turnip? Experiments had been carried out, she understood, but it was not always easy to get accounts of them. Her grandfather, acquainted with various members of the Royal Society, passed on to her whatever news he could glean, and ordered scientific works on the subject, but it was not the same as actually doing it oneself.

Plump old Mistress Bowman came panting up, puffing and weeping at the same time. Both actions were so unlike her usual placid cheerfulness that Anne dropped the spit and stared at her.

"The doctor," she gasped, clapping her hand over her generous bosom. Her cap was askew and her kerchief coming loose. Anne stared back over her shoulder at her, amazed that her first words had not been, "Now, Mistress Anne, get you down from there before you fall."

"What's amiss, Joan?"

"Oh, the doctor…" She sat down with a thump on the bench by the tree and began to weep in earnest.

Anne wondered whether she should fetch the smelling salts from the house; there would be no sense to be got from Mrs. Bowman until the tears dried. Before she made up her mind, Jem came running up and stopped short at the ladder's foot. He avoided looking at the housekeeper—reluctant to approach a sobbing woman, no doubt, even if he claimed to be tough as the old roots he very much resembled.

"Me and Sam have brought the doctor home," he said.

Grandfather had set out to visit several of his

patients. A case of dropsy, an ague, and a gouty foot.

Without a word, she began to climb down. Whatever had occurred, with Joan Bowman weeping and Jem's flat statement, it must be bad.

Helping to steady the ladder, Jem said, "You shouldn't be a-climbing of ladders, Mistress Anne. Hoydenish ways, that is."

When she was on the ground, she asked, "What happened?"

"Sam's boy said a thunderclap startled the horse. It sent the gig into the ditch and threw Dr. Sinclair free. Might be he'd have been right enough—well, Mistress Anne, you know him! Never sick, and that time he fell down four steps and landed on his feet…"

"How badly is he hurt?" If it were serious, it would be necessary to send for the nearest doctor, ten miles or more away, assuming he was at home. If it were no more than a broken bone, she could see to it herself, of course. She'd helped Grandfather set bones a dozen times.

Jem looked down at the grass, and Mistress Bowman let out a yowl.

"Dead?"

"Ay." After a moment, he said, "It happened at the bend in the road by the stone wall. He hit his head. We've laid him in his bedchamber, miss, and Sam's gone for Parson."

So the storm broke without Anne being able to see lightning lured from the clouds, and it was some time before she could again think of any scientific endeavor.

Chapter 1

"Mistress Anne? Should I return another day?" fussy old Henry Morland asked. "I am sure Dr. Sinclair would not wish me to cause you additional distress, today of all days, by discussing certain matters."

"What might those things be?" she inquired. "My grandfather would not have expected me to give way to weakness and vapors."

"Regarding your late guardian's Will…"

She could hear the capital letter when he spoke of it. "I would rather be done with it, sir. And I would not put you to the trouble of returning another day, as bad as the weather has been." Those who had attended the funeral and come to the house to tender their sympathy had partaken of hot drinks and a light collation and had taken their leave, all but the attorney, old-fashioned in his long, curled wig and snuff-colored velvet coat.

"Then, in short, let me reassure you that you are not left penniless, if you had any apprehension of that being the case…even though it would have been more usual for him to have left his estate to his daughter." Mr. Morland paused to contemplate the unconventionality of the situation.

"I did know he meant to provide for me," Anne said apologetically, as obviously Mr. Morland was unused to dealing with females. Her adoptive grandfather had spoken occasionally of finances, as freely as he had discussed medicine and science.

"I recall the doctor telling me your father was his second cousin's son, on the Sinclair side. Hence, you shared the same last name. Is my understanding correct? Dr. Sinclair did not go into much detail, considering the distance of the connection."

"That branch of the family was extinct except for my father, who was wounded at the battle of Sheriffmuir in 1715 and never fully recovered his health. I was born shortly after he died, and my mother did not survive my birth."

"Neither, I take it, had any independent income, and your mother was also without family."

Anne inclined her head. "So my grand…my guardian told me. He told me to call him Grandfather when I was old enough to call him anything."

"It was good of him to give you a home."

"Yes. I had no real claim on him, which makes his generosity all the more admirable." She could almost imagine Grandfather exclaiming, "Humbug! Playing the mealy-mouthed milk-and-water miss, are you?" But it was what Mr. Morland would expect, and in spite of what Mistress Bowman said, Anne did not set out to put people in a bustle. She only did so by accident. It was so hard to know what would make them stare and think her a bold, outrageous creature.

Mr. Morland contemplated his glass of sherry. "I wish you had not been left without male guidance, apart from mine. I cannot like having to discuss financial matters with a young lady. Or even an older lady or widow. The fair sex should not have to deal with such things, even had they the necessary training and…er, so forth."

"Grandfather always said money is not an indelicate topic, and there was little he scrupled to discuss with me."

"Most improper," he sighed. "He did say you had more sense than most men. Here it is, then: you are left an income which will keep you in modest comfort and also this house." He steepled his fingers and gazed at them sternly. "He felt his daughter had no need of this house or his income, her husband being a wealthy man. In most families, it would be quite different. If Mistress Saltstall's husband had only a genteel income, she would naturally expect her father's estate to pass to her for the benefit of her children. Although, as it happens, I believe she has only one, and in any case, her husband can afford to provide for that one and I suppose, for half a dozen more. A pity he's in trade."

Anne expressed her gratitude again, since it seemed to be expected, and let him hem and haw at some length. Even she knew that men disliked being interrupted by ladies.

"You are hardly out of girlhood—" he began.

"Two and twenty, Mr. Morland."

"Indeed, and never been out of Fletching, I think. May I ask if you have a prospect of marriage?"

"No." When she had been a child, she had been friends with all the boys in the neighborhood, exploring the woods and fields with them, climbing trees to find birds' nests, and the like, very much to the detriment of her dresses. But they grew up and went to school, and left the neighborhood to pursue careers—or now spent their time with young ladies who had never climbed a tree or flown a kite or ridden a horse bareback. And had families and dowries.

"You should be married," Grandfather had remarked several times, the first not long after her eighteenth birthday. "It's damned difficult," he'd added, almost to himself. "For how are you to meet a suitable man? There's not many here to choose from. Most of 'em want a rich or well-connected wife anyway. Your portion won't be large..." And once, he'd gone on to say, "The right kind of man, the husband I'd want for you, wouldn't care a button for that, but the other thing..." But that was the night he'd had a third glass of port, which he seldom did, and although she inquired what "the other thing" might be, he would say no more. She had ventured to suggest that they might visit London, where surely she could meet educated men.

"London? No...no...Perhaps Bristol or York, however..." he'd responded. She found his indecisiveness puzzling. Dr. Sinclair's opinions were more commonly positive. Too positive, some said.

Mr. Morland sighed again and took a pinch of snuff. "Unfortunate! Although you could scarcely wed while in mourning in any case. Meanwhile, you cannot live on your own. It is a pity Dr. Sinclair made no suitable arrangements for you. Of course, one does not anticipate one's will being executed in the near future. No doubt he expected to have time to see you settled."

"As you know, his death was the merest mischance," Anne reminded him.

Chapter 2

Being some eighty guineas to the good, with the night yet young, Lord John Anniscote was not best pleased to be interrupted at the table. If one is obliged to eke out one's resources by gambling, it is necessary not only to limit one's play to games in which skill is of more importance than luck, but also to maintain one's concentration. Therefore when a footman murmured, "My lord, an urgent message for you," Anniscote was disinclined to bother with it.

"The fool should have left it at my lodgings."

"My lord, he says it is a matter of great importance, and he was instructed to find you, wherever you might be."

"Does he await a reply?"

"No, my lord."

"Well, then, tell him I have it and send him on his way."

Anniscote made to drop the letter by his place, then looked at its heavy wax seal and the quality of the paper.

"Gentlemen, if you will give me leave to glance at this? I misdoubt it will take long."

His companions assented and saw him frown a little as he read it.

"A love letter from a discarded lady?" one of them suggested. Only his closest friend, Thomas Jeffreys, noted that Anniscote seemed unwontedly disconcerted.

"No. It comes from an attorney. Nicholas is dead."

"Your luck holds, Anniscote. Not only have you emptied our pockets, but you sat down a lord and rise a duke." Hurst laughed.

"For God's sake, have you no sense of propriety?" Jeffreys snapped. "You speak of his brother, after all."

"I expect propriety from my wife and daughters," Hurst replied. "Beyond that, it seems overrated and best left to curates. Nick was my good friend, but we must all die, and the sooner if we are intrepid riders to hounds or essay stairs when we are in drink. Better perhaps to take our leave while we can still mount a horse. Or a filly."

Far from being offended, Anniscote smiled thinly. "I believe I can survive his loss. Let us continue."

But the table broke up soon after, to his annoyance, some going to join other games, some to spread the news. Mixed condolences and farewells concluded, Anniscote and Jeffreys donned cloaks and hats and stepped out into the cold. After the overheated and airless rooms of the hell, the freezing night was not unpleasant.

When they had walked for a while in silence, Tom said, "If you felt no family affection for your brother, I wonder you are not pleased to take his place. Most men would be happy to have Guysbridge and the title."

The new Duke of Guysbridge glanced at him. "You noticed, did you? But you are so observant, Tom. May I say, ofttimes inconveniently so. Do you know, I cannot tell you why I am not as happy as a grig. Perhaps because I am reluctant to owe anything to someone I disliked, and because I am glad he is dead. My noble

9

brother was unfit for the position to which he was born. Did you know him at all?"

"I met him once or twice."

"My brother was a gamester—"

"As are you."

"But I do not play deep, and I win. And a sot—drunk when he fell on the stairs, celebrating his good fortune, no doubt."

"You've drunk your share of wine and brandy."

"Oh, without question. But you've never seen me reeling drunk. And certainly there was debt when he inherited the title and estate. I cannot name you the last member of our family distinguished for probity and thrift. My father was one of the old, roaring sort. He spent, gambled, and drank freely, and paid little heed to his lands. But he was beloved by all the Guysbridge folk—if not by me. Nicholas was much like him, except that Nick had less care to his lands and tenants and piled up more debt, with never a thought for tomorrow. He was not popular. My sire was a gentleman, however careless of the family's honor and interests he may have been."

"I understood your brother made a good marriage not long since."

Anniscote laughed wryly.

"If by 'good,' you mean a rich marriage, certainly—to a foundry owner's daughter. The best thing Nick ever did was to die before he had time to get into debt again. I would wager his bride's father would have thrown away no more money on him."

"And no heir but you?"

"In addition to being one generation from a crofter's cottage in Scotland, my brother's bride has failed to breed. Although Nick's preference for London and sport may have had something to do with that. She's awkward in company, too, which has the benefit of keeping her in residence at Guysbridge, rather than showing herself in town, where she might forget her elocution lessons and admit that 'ma hoosband is awa' the nicht.' She was no sort of wife for Nicholas. Except, of course, for her dowry. Ah…have I mentioned she's her father's only child?"

Jeffreys said, "She sounds more to be pitied than despised. So the title has passed from your brother to you. Most would consider it a stroke of good fortune."

"It's hard to believe, given my brother's pastimes and his style of riding, but it never crossed my mind that I might succeed him, in spite of my standing as his heir until he should get a son." Anniscote discovered that he felt neither sadness at his brother's death or pleasure at gaining the title. "To inherit a title is no doubt a fine thing—if it is not accompanied by the responsibility of setting to rights years—decades!—of neglect of the estate. As well, perhaps, that I have the soul of a clerk, as my late, unrevered father once said."

"He cannot have meant it. There is nothing ungentlemanly about you, except perhaps…"

"Don't spare me. What offends you in my conduct?"

"Your pursuit of married women seems to me lacking in delicacy."

"My dear fellow! I only cast out lures to those who have shown themselves interested in dalliance, never to virtuous wives. And it would certainly be unprincipled to court any woman seeking a husband. Their families and friends would not consider me an eligible suitor."

Jeffreys sighed. He understood the algebra of suitability. An impoverished duke with ancestral acres was desirable, any gentleman with enough money was eligible, even a tradesman with a fortune was acceptable, but a man with no money or title was not, at least to careful parents or guardians.

"And yet the young ladies find you fascinating."

"Very likely because I do not court them."

"The Puritan simplicity of your clothing has something to do with it," Jeffreys mused. "'Tis the contrast with your usual behavior and reputation."

Fortunately, when he had removed his unwelcome presence from Guysbridge by going to live in town, he'd been well provided with clothing, and he had made it last. With lace wrist ruffles and silk stockings at nearly a pound the pair, breeches at one pound ten or twelve shillings, and brocaded satin for a waistcoat as much as eighteen shillings the yard, it was necessary to affect a certain austerity. And dark fabric showed wear and dust less.

"I prefer to think of it as being in advance of the mode."

"It also makes you stand out in a crowd."

"'Twas not my intention, but if it brought me into fashion in spite of myself—and for no great outlay, neither—why, what harm?"

"And will you now make a show in embroidered waistcoats and gold-laced coats?"

"All now expect to see me in sober raiment, without a quantity of embroidery or lacing, and with only a signet ring. To change my style would be to suggest that I had dressed plainly only from lack of money." With a faint smile, Anniscote added, "At all events, I would not wish to emulate that popinjay this evening, in his striped peach-colored suit with its excess of gold lace."

"God forbid," said Tom, piously. "And the sea-green waistcoat with it. Such a roly-poly has no business getting himself up like that. I hardly knew how to keep a straight face. A fellow with no taste should let his tailor design his clothing, not try to set his own fashion. With that complexion, too, to be wearing peach."

"That is why you see me only in blue and red and such colors as do not turn me quite yellow. And black, of course. Machiavelli had somewhat to say about choosing the colors of one's garments."

After a pause, Jeffreys said, "I never realized you were estranged from your father. Although I should have guessed, I suppose, as I have never known you to visit your home."

"I ceased considering it my home years ago. Our resources were inadequate to meet the calls upon them, even with my sister and brother having died young, and my mother having breathed her last petulant breath before I left Eton. And, as my fond papa pointed out, his heir must be supported in a manner suited to his future position. He offered to buy me a commission, for what else can a second son do when there's no money to make him an adequate allowance?"

"I suppose, when an estate is so burdened…" Jeffreys let the sentence trail off.

"Most fathers would say the same? Very likely."

"But you did not take the commission."

"No. Only imagine me, Tom, in some wretched garrison town, or at the ends of the earth, living in squalor, perhaps slaughtering Red Indians in the American colonies or capturing rioters here at home. Many of our officers are excellent fellows and a good number contrive to amuse themselves agreeably, but can you really envision me as one of them?"

"Well…no. Yet many younger sons go into the army or the church. Or if one studied the law…"

"I would have liked to study at Oxford. I would say, 'as my brother did,' but he was sent down in his first year. My father said the money to educate me would be wasted, because what profession could I practice but that of a soldier? I had no turn for the church, I assure you. If my father could have made it possible for me to begin as a bishop or a judge, he would have had no serious objection to either but it was not in his power to buy me preferment in either field. And our family's reputation would have made it a matter of scandal."

"To live like a gentleman without the resources is difficult. If I had not inherited a competence from my uncle, I must have asked my father to buy me a commission. It's a gentleman's profession, after all."

"Belike your father would have done so happily."

"And yet, what else could you do but accept? Though, somehow, you've made shift to live."

Anniscote laughed softly. "Oh, ay." He would not divulge even to Jeffreys what economies he had learned to practice. "The fact is, my father and I never dealt well together. I refused out of anger, and pride kept me from apologizing later."

"One must have one's pride, certainly, but I fear you carry it to a fault. Is it not one of the seven deadly sins? I mind my old nanny telling me that a high pride goeth before a fall. It's like to get you into difficulty one day." A sedan chair accompanied by a gentleman on foot and a link boy crossed their path.

"Oh, I'm not so easily provoked these days. Remember, I was young at the time."

"Best take it," the old duke had said. "I swear I'll not give you a penny more than twenty-five pounds a quarter—and I wish I might see you survive on that pittance. If you find yourself in debt, you must take the consequences. You won't last a month before you come home with your tail between your legs."

Anniscote went on, "I was a disappointment to him. You might have taken my brother for my father, thirty years younger. They both looked much like my grandfather, too, and all three shared the same tastes. You can imagine what they were. They never opened a book, had no conversation but that of sport, drink, and women, and the devil fly away with tomorrow. Unlike them, I was not of a frank, open nature. My father said I must be a changeling. He could not, however, blame my mother for getting me of some other man, as I am very like the portrait of the founder of our house. Did you know that our family is descended from a Spanish duke? Our ancestors had been fighting the Moors for two hundred years or more when William the Conqueror landed in England. I consider it cause for pride, and a reason to conduct ourselves with more dignity than if we were no more than a rabble of hard-riding, hard-drinking squires."

"This is a high pride indeed," Tom remarked. "I believe I understand your feelings, although the squire is the bedrock of England, surely?"

"The best of them are. But my worst offence was

that—like most young men—I was critical of my elders and dared to suggest certain amendments to management of the estate and income."

"How maladroit of you," Jeffreys said with a grin.

"Yes, I wanted tact. However, the advice would not have been well received however tactfully put." The old duke preferred not to think of anything which might trouble his repose or distract him on the hunting field.

They were nearly to Jeffreys's street when he said, "It will make a great alteration for you."

"Hardly! What should I change?"

Jeffreys laughed. "Why, most things! You will take your place in the House of Lords, you will own Guysbridge and a house in London, you will have servants and tenants and dependents and the business of managing your estates, you will make a fine marriage to provide yourself with an heir—"

"Damn you, Tom!" His Grace stopped on the flagway. "I could have done without this tedious list of responsibilities. No doubt my brother's…my attorney…will bring them all to my notice when I see him. Oh, and I shall have to arrange the obsequies, too, no doubt."

"It seems a tolerably easy chore for the benefit to be received."

They walked on, and presently Anniscote said, "I must have my brother's body sent north, and I will leave for Guysbridge tomorrow to see my brother's agent and inspect the estate. Nick never spent a groat on maintenance. No doubt there are repairs to make. And pay my respects to the widow, of course. Would you care to come along? I expect to stay a week or ten days. I'll call for you at noon, if that is not too early, in my brother's travelling coach."

"Noon today?"

"No, no." Anniscote laughed at Jeffreys's tone. "Tomorrow. After all, it's already four in the morning. One must sleep some time. And today I must visit the attorney and also Nick's…our family's…my house."

"So I am to provide you a card partner at Guysbridge? I don't mind bearing you company. Is there a stream to be fished?"

"There is. I beg you won't expect me to sit mumchance on a damp bank, waiting for a fish to rise, however. But you are welcome to emulate Izaak Walton to your heart's content. Your only chore will be to attend the funeral—there should be at least one gentleman there. I only hope," Anniscote said, as they reached Jeffreys's lodgings, "that my sister-in-law has not replaced all the furniture with those newfangled pieces that are now the fashion. I rather liked the old dark oak my great-grandfather bought out of the largesse he acquired with my great-grandmother. That would have been a few years before Cromwell rose and Charles I fell."

"A hundred years," Jeffreys mused. "Is it Anniscote tradition to keep one's old furnishings, or sentiment?"

"Neither, my dear fellow. My great-grandfather was the last of us to be able to afford to buy new furniture. Since, it's all gone on clothing, horses, and gaming. Oh, ay, and wenches. Until Nick brought home his little Scotch Elspat."

Chapter 3

Anne was polite to the Reverend Mr. Ott, who made it his business to call on her regularly in her bereavement. Grandfather had held a very poor opinion of his understanding, with which Anne found herself in agreement after his second pastoral call. Grandfather had also been known to say that he found much of the Bible difficult to reconcile with scientific principles or even gentlemanly conduct. She managed to keep her composure through the cold, gray, boring days with no company but Mistress Bowman, the kitchen maid, and Jem, but the lack of occupation wore away at her patience. Worse still was Joan Bowman's repeated question, "Whatever are you to do, child?"

She did not know how to answer. "There will be time to think about that in the spring," she said rather curtly, or "What anyone would, I suppose." She would not let Joan or anyone else know how uncertain she felt. Perhaps Mr. Morland shared that uncertainty, for it was not until late February that he called upon her one afternoon

"On the day of the funeral, I did not feel I could intrude any longer upon your grief," he said. "Has…er…anything occurred since?"

Anne shook her head, wondering what sort of occurrence the lawyer might mean: her grandfather's ghost visiting his surgery? "Except that Grandfather's valet left a day or two after the funeral, of course. I gave him a year's wages and Grandfather's better coats and waistcoats. He'd been with Grandfather since I was a baby. I believe his eyes filled with tears as often as mine did."

"A year's wages! Twenty or thirty pounds, I imagine. Hmmmph! You should have asked my advice as to a suitable amount, not that it was necessary to give the fellow more, as Dr. Sinclair left him a hundred pounds." He accepted Anne's offer of claret, and added, "The doctor had a fine palate for drink. However, I was not thinking of household matters as much as whether you had perhaps had any gentleman callers."

"Only Sir Randolph and Lady Beaton. And the Reverend Mr. Ott."

"Ah. I had hoped that perhaps, hmmm, hmmm…"

"Oh! You thought perhaps someone might make me an offer, now that I have inherited a competence and a house."

"It would be quite improper to propose marriage to a young lady in such recent mourning," he said, austerely. "Particularly when she has no family or friends around her. But a man might begin to pay calls upon her, to, er, lay the foundation for an offer to be made after a reasonable period."

"There are so few eligible men in the neighborhood."

"But no doubt someone you know has a friend or nephew or some other relation for whom he might wish to promote a match."

"Evidently not," Anne replied.

"A pity. It might have provided a satisfactory solution to an awkward situation. While ordinarily a lady should not marry during the mourning period, in your case, young and unprotected as you are, marriage after the first six months might be thought acceptable. However, if no one has shown an interest, we must find some respectable older lady to live with you. I could advertise for some suitable female, perhaps an elderly governess in need of a less taxing position, or—"

"But Mr. Morland, surely that cannot be necessary. I have Mrs. Bowman. It is not as if I were living here alone."

"A housekeeper is not an adequate substitute for a companion. She has her own sphere of work. It's well enough to rely on Mrs. Bowman's chaperonage for a few months during deepest mourning, as you are naturally not going out in company. But once that is past, until you marry you must have some suitable older woman companion. A genteel lady in straitened circumstances would provide you with company, as well as being able to escort you when you go out."

Anne opened her mouth to reject the idea out of hand. The prospect was not an appealing one: the idea of a companion who had no interests beyond needlework, gossip, and the latest novel or book of sermons fairly made Anne's blood run cold. Probably, too, she would flutter and titter and protest against Anne's interests. She supposed she should have anticipated that Mr. Morland would try to foist someone upon her. Young, unmarried women did not live alone except for their servants. While she was ready to flout some of society's rules, there were limits. If she defied convention by refusing to engage some lady to live with her, it would set the neighborhood in a stir. Not that she had much in common with any of them, but she had been largely dependent on her guardian for company and now found herself often lonely.

She sorely missed Grandfather's frequently acerbic wit, his interest in a dozen branches of learning, his talking to her as if she were an intelligent, reasoning being. She missed real conversation: discussions of whether it was possible that fever, catarrh, and phtisis might be prevented by inoculation, as was apparently the case with smallpox. What a pity that the Turkish method of preventing smallpox, brought back to England by Lady Mary Wortley Montague, was so little known.

"…a retired governess would perhaps be the best choice," Mr. Morland was saying, "as Dr. Sinclair took some pains with your education. I will advertise at once, if you wish, and by the time you are ready to emerge from seclusion, I am sure we will have secured someone appropriate to act as your chaperone."

A prim, proper companion, though easy to obtain, would drive her to distraction.

And she found she missed hearing a masculine voice raised to demand, "Damme, where are my boots?" She thought she might quite like to be married. To the right man, of course. He would have to be more sensible than the heroes of fiction and not as boring as the men she knew (with the exception of her Grandfather, who had not been boring at all). Given that there must be other men like Grandfather, somewhere gentlemen of wide interests and inquiring mind existed, even if not in her immediate neighborhood. The squire was an excellent landlord, and she believed him to be a good husband to Lady

Beaton and a fond father, but his conversation was largely limited to horses, dogs, hunting, and agricultural matters. Lady Beaton seemed to like him well enough, but my lady's interests were largely limited to her home and servants, the tenants, and parish matters.

Sometimes, reading a novel of the more frivolous sort, she could not help but imagine meeting a man who would want to press kisses on her hands (and lips). The novels, of course, did not describe what came after those ardent kisses. However, the behavior of the young country folk she had seen courting suggested that it was more interesting than some of Grandfather's medical books made it sound.

Marriage was the most sensible, indeed the only, course for her. However, to have any chance of meeting a suitable man, she would have to go where men were more numerous and more varied. In London, there would surely be men with an interest in scientific matters. Among them, a husband might be hunted out.

But if she could locate a suitable potential husband, could she attract him? That might be more difficult, in light of a remark she had overheard in church soon after Grandfather's death. She might have stayed home: it would not have been considered remarkable if she had been too prostrated by grief to attend. It would have been counted in her favor, Anne supposed, as many found her self-possession and lack of tears unnatural. The squire's lady said, not realizing that Anne was within earshot, "Really, what is to become of her?" unconsciously echoing Mistress Bowman. The answer was inaudible, but its import was clear enough from the next remark.

"I don't say she isn't a good, well-mannered girl,

but she really is worse than merely bookish, and that would be bad enough. The doctor taught and spoke to her as if she were a young man. She has not a notion how to go on in society! Even with an inheritance, and I misdoubt it amounts to much, anyhow, I cannot think how she will marry. And on top of all, she dresses badly, and her hair is a veritable bird's nest. A man may be careless in his dress, but a lady cannot be so unless her beauty or wealth outweighs the fault."

My lady was correct, Anne admitted. She had no feminine artifices or talents, and had to conceal boredom at the local ladies' conversation: the unreliability of modern servants, Mr. X's especial interest in Mistress Y, whether last Sunday's sermon was aimed at that dreadful Landry woman. She could suture a wound but not embroider, read Latin and German, but not sing or play music. Assisting once at an amputation—fascinating!—did not make for conversation on the occasions she and her grandfather had dined with the squire's family or the few other members of the neighborhood gentry.

Looking down at her plain mantua, Anne admitted Lady Beaton was correct in saying that she did not dress well. Grandfather had never seemed to care or notice, and her ordinary activities were not suited to dainty gowns. As for her hair, well, she had not the knack of arranging it tidily. Joan Bowman, having lived all her life in the village and never having served in any but a middling sort of house, and then only as a kitchen maid, cook, or housekeeper, had none of the skills Lady Beaton and her daughters had learned without thinking—or relied upon a ladies' maid to supply.

It made the task of finding a husband seem quite

daunting. She must undertake to correct her faults, but the first thing was to set her plan in motion.

"I am not sure I wish to continue to live here," she said to Mr. Morland. "Do you think you can find someone to rent this house?"

"But…but…"

"Would it not be possible? Holly and Ivy House is leased to Colonel and Mrs. Ferris, as the former owner's heir did not care for country life, so people do rent country properties."

"Yes, but no matter where you live, Mistress Anne, you must have a companion."

"This is the eighteenth century, Mr. Morland, not medieval Spain. However, I grant you the necessity."

"The world is a censorious place, Mistress Anne. I suppose you are thinking of Lincoln? It is but thirty miles away, so you would not be far from your friends here. "

"I have lived a very retired life, Mr. Morland. Grandfather several times said I should marry and was concerned about the lack of choice hereabouts." It was an argument likely to appeal to Mr. Morland's notions of what was fit, while citing Grandfather's opinion could only support it. "At the risk of seeming unmaidenly, I would point out that in London, with its much larger population, I may contract an eligible match. As I am of age, and have no family, I can live where I choose. I think I shall remove to London." Even if she failed to get a husband, London had the advantage of many book sellers, lectures, and who knew what more?

Mr. Morland seemed to ponder. "I see Dr. Sinclair's boast of your sense was not idle." He bit his lip. "It would be best if you lived with someone able to introduce you to the right sort of company. I think, if you do not object, I will write to Dr. Sinclair's sister. She may be able to advise us."

Chapter 4

The afternoon was well advanced when His Grace rapped at the door of the townhouse. The proceedings at the lawyer's office had been tiresome but not prolonged; fortunately, the same firm had handled Anniscote business for fifty years or more and had not been of Nick's choosing. The same was not true of the staff of Guysbridge House. It proved necessary to knock—hard!—three times before a footman opened the door.

"Sir?"

Anniscote surveyed the fellow from the toes of his slightly scuffed shoes to the top of his head. His wig was crooked, and his livery coat appeared to have been thrown on in some haste.

"I am Guysbridge. Ah…the brother of your late master and his heir," he added, lest further explanation be required.

The man goggled, but before he could speak, the butler tottered into the hall.

"Peters," Anniscote greeted him. "So you are still with us."

"Forty years, Your Grace. And a few more yet, I hope. May I offer both my condolences and my felicitations, sir?"

"You may, I thank you." He smiled. At least one longtime retainer remained, even if he was somewhat sunk in age. Peters had run the house well, he remembered, and perhaps was still capable of it, though it must have been disheartening to serve Nicholas.

"I fear Your Grace will find the house and staff in a sorry state. "

"I am sure of it. I wish to discuss the necessary changes with you, Peters."

Some three hours later, a glass of brandy in hand— for of course there was brandy, in a place Nick had inhabited—Anniscote contemplated the repairs needed, and the staff to be replaced. Fewer servants were employed than in the old duke's time, as Nick had not entertained beyond an occasional party of gentlemen, or sometimes gentlemen and their lights o' love. According to Peters, the groom and stable lads did their work well enough, the late duke having been interested in his horseflesh, but only one of the footmen was satisfactory. The maidservants were such as one might expect in the home of a libertine with no wife in residence.

"If they were decent girls, they'd have left," said Peters. "The ones we have are at best lazy and slatternly. The scullery maid does her work, at least, and gives the cook no sauce, and the cook has no complaint about her. Will you be wishing to replace Cook with a chef? 'Tis only the middling sort have a woman to cook for them as a rule. Though I do not hold with these finickal Frenchmen in the kitchen. Unless you were to be partial to the French style of cooking, of course, Your Grace."

"I'll decide after I've sampled her dinners, Peters."

"Very good, sir. And His late Grace's valet?"

"My brother's attire and appearance hardly spoke

well for his man."

"If I may venture an opinion, sir, the late duke's manner of dress was as displeasing to Mulley as to yourself. He always kept his clothing in excellent order and repair and is very skillful with boots. But one can only do so much when the object of one's labor is unwilling."

"Then I'll keep him on and see how it goes. I'm certainly more particular than Nicholas, though no one could call me finickal."

Peters smiled deprecatingly. "Would you be wishful to dine here, Your Grace? His late Grace not being in the habit of dining at home, the pantry is not as well stocked as one would wish…and I fear his death has thrown some of the staff into confusion."

Correctly interpreting this apologetic admission to mean that his presence would be inconvenient and the dinner ill-cooked, Anniscote replied, "No, I have other plans. However, I will drink another glass before I go."

While he did so, he glanced over the dusty book shelves. Clearly, no one had troubled the volumes since John himself had been a school boy. He'd been something of a reader, yet another reason his father had found him unsatisfactory. Drinking, gambling, wenching, and the more disreputable forms of sport would have met with no disapproval. He had not carried bookishness to excess, but the old duke regarded it as a scholarly habit, and therefore suspect.

A small volume, the binding rather heavy and old-fashioned, caught his attention. It was on one of the higher shelves and required a reach to take it down, which no doubt accounted for his never having noticed it years ago, when he had access to the library—at least when his father was out.

He held it at arm's length, giving it a gentle shake to dislodge some of the dust, but ended by using his handkerchief as a dust rag. There was no title stamped on the spine. When he opened the book, Anniscote was surprised to find it was not a printed volume at all, but a commonplace book, filled with small, crabbed writing. He sat down in one of the threadbare chairs to leaf through it. Very likely it would be no more than a collection of recipes, remedies, and household notes compiled by some ancestress, perhaps of Queen Elizabeth's time, if the handwriting and spelling were any guide.

In this year 1598, I, Charles Anascote, Earl of Helter, write this account upon my creation as Duke of Guysbridge for certain services I was able, by the grace of God, to provide to Her Majesty, our Queen. This is the story of the founding of our house in England which my father, Don Diego Anascote, recounted when he lay dying. Although it is some ten years past, his words are fresh in my memory, and I have set them down as he spoke them:

I was born the second son of the Duque de Navalero. He had a great love of scholarship and educated all of his children well, believing that knowledge was always of use, whatever might befall us, and in particular, he was intent that we learn languages. He often said that if we understood a foreigner's language, we would also understand how he thought. So each of us learned modern languages, as well as Latin and Greek. His heir, my half-brother, was taught French, Italian, and German, I studied French and English, and my younger brother learned Dutch and the language of our Indian allies in Nueva España. As it befell, this latter was to determine Sebastian's future, as learning English set my course.

Anniscote had known their founder came of a Spanish ducal house, but apart from that, only a few family legends. Considering the matter, it seemed strange to find a Spaniard in England at a time when men like Sir Francis Drake were seizing Spanish ships and cargo whenever they could, and when Spain had sent its Armada to defeat England. Over the years, it had come to be considered merely exotic, even slightly romantical, if indeed anyone remembered it, to be descended from a Spaniard. After all, much of the flower of England's nobility were descended from Frenchmen, which now occasioned no comment. But surely at the time, it must have been otherwise.

He closed the book gently and enjoyed the irony. So Don Diego's son had been created the first Duke of Guysbridge. *I wonder for what unspecified services to the Crown?* Anniscote family legend had always maintained that the title went back through the centuries as perhaps the Spanish title had done, but to pretend that the Spanish title was in any way related to their English title was preposterous. Particularly as Don Diego had evidently been a younger son. Of course, he himself had been that and had still inherited the title.

He drained his glass. Well! Sufficient unto the day, as the preachers said. The attorney could deal with the inventory, and Peters could arrange for cleaning and repairs to the house while he himself visited Guysbridge. He tucked the book into his coat pocket.

Chapter 5

Mistress Anne was not used to time hanging heavy upon her hands. She had been accustomed to going with her grandfather on at least some of his rounds and helping in his surgery. Ordinarily, she rode every day in good weather, but the exceptional cold and frost discouraged outdoor pursuits. Even as she packed his medical equipment and books into a stout trunk, wrote letters to his far-flung friends, and oversaw a complete if unnecessary cleaning of the house, she found she had too much time to feel the loss of her grandfather. Waking in the middle of the night, she wondered if she were exchanging isolation in familiar surroundings for loneliness in a strange place, without even acquaintances.

In spite of the weather, Lady Beaton escorted her to a Lincoln dressmaker to order several new gowns, for as she said, "There is no knowing when it will be better, and at least the road is frozen hard, not muddy." Anne admitted her wardrobe was dreadfully shabby: worn, darned in places, and faded. It hardly mattered when she was studying, or picking berries, or working around the house, or attempting some experiment (in fact, old clothing was better; if a little acid dripped onto it, or some substance that would stain, no real harm was done). She found herself noticing what ladies were wearing in Lincoln. Now that she was going to London, she could understand why Joan Bowman had so often advised that she visit a dressmaker, instead of having a local seamstress copy one of her old gowns. New clothing was definitely required—though not black, as Mrs. Bowman perhaps expected. Grandfather had disapproved of excessive displays of grief, and besides, if she was to put her plans into effect, she must not be hampered by the conventional rules of mourning.

None of the books she possessed but had not yet read held her interest: *Love in Excess, or, The Fatal Enquiry*, Ockley's *Improvement of Human Reason: Exhibited in the Life of Hai Ebn Yokdhan*, *Robinson Crusoe*. The latter was a little better than the rest; Crusoe's problems were simple and straightforward by comparison. Also it was pleasant to read of a place that was warm.

"I do not have even a Man Friday for company," she murmured.

"Did you speak, Mistress Anne?" The housekeeper poked her head into the library.

"Oh! No, Mistress Bowman, only to myself."

"You learned that habit from the doctor," the woman said. "Many's the time I'd hear him, and no one else around."

"Anyone could have heard him." Anne smiled. "He bellowed."

They both laughed then, which was the pleasantest sound Anne had heard in many days.

"I wish you'd put on mourning," Joan Bowman said. "I know he hated the sight of it, but it doesn't seem respectful, somehow."

"I can miss him just as much in bright colors as in black," Anne replied. "At that, I'm not clad like a parrot. Brown and dark green and gray." Her new gowns, not yet come from the dressmaker, would be dark blue, rose, and light green. Just as well Mistress Bowman had not seen the fabric.

"But you always wore those anyway. People expect mourning, you know."

"You mean, obvious mourning. It seems hypocritical to me. The Parkers dripped black last year, and I swear they hated old Mr. Parker. Everyone knows it, too."

Mistress Bowman shook her head. "I've known you since you were a babe, and Dr. Sinclair never could abide missishness, but you should curb your tongue. It will run you into trouble one day."

"I wouldn't say it to anyone I didn't know as well as you, Joan…I think."

"Well!…it *was* funny to see Mistress Parker forever pressing her handkerchief to her eyes, like as if she was wiping away a tear."

****

Mr. Morland,

…My brother, James Sinclair's, ward is welcome to come to me for a visit or permanently, if she does not object to my quiet life. I am not so old as my brother, but my sight is very poor now (this Letter is being inscribed by a Friend, at my dictation). I do not go in society much, but I believe I may make shift to find suitable chaperons to introduce Mistress Anne to the sights and amusements of London. Many of my circle are (like Me) old and staid, but I know my Niece, Dr. Sinclair's daughter, having a lively girl of her Own, would be glad to include Mistress Anne in such activities as might appeal to a young lady (if mourning

does not prevent her; and I know my brother disapproved amazingly of mourning, believing that a rational enjoyment of Life facilitated recovery from loss, and also holding that no religious person who believes in resurrection and eternal life should repine overmuch at a loved one's death unless he or she thought the said loved one was actually D—d. Although, since dear James was rather a freethinker, I never knew whether he was serious about that last, or not. Not that it is a suitable subject for Jest). Pray send to advise me when Mistress Anne may be expected, though I realize that travelling in this prolonged Winter may disarrange the most careful plans...

****

"Sir Randolph and I will be going up to town to stay with my daughter and her husband, for Sophia is breeding and soon will make an addition to the family," Lady Beaton informed Anne. "I am set upon being with her, as it will be her first, and my first grandchild. As I understand you intend to make a visit to Dr. Sinclair's sister, perhaps you would like to come with us? We mean to leave next week, on Monday, unless it snows again, which I pray it will not."

Anne accepted gratefully. Traveling in their commodious coach would certainly be better than going by the stage or a post chaise. The prospect of a long journey, culminating in arrival at some busy London coaching inn disheveled, cold, and weary, with her trunks and bandbox, only to have to take a hackney coach to Mrs. Bradshaw's house, had been a little frightening, even for Anne. The Beatons' travelling coach would be more comfortable than a public vehicle, and also spared her having to hire a maid as she could not have gone unaccompanied. Better to get one in Town anyway, according to Lady Beaton, "for depend upon it, a raw country girl would be of no use in London."

And the benefit of Lady Beaton's advice was welcome. Anne feared that in London she would feel like a country mouse without Lady Beaton's suggestions on what kind of clothes to order, and her descriptions of London and fashionable life (for she had visited London many times, and even been presented at Court on her coming-out), and the pitfalls that awaited the unwary.

"I am sure that Mrs. Bradshaw will give you excellent advice," Lady Beaton went on, "but she is a widow with no daughter."

"I believe she lives somewhat retired," Anne agreed. "But she said in her letter that my...Dr. Sinclair's daughter would chaperon me, with her own daughter."

"Oh, well, then! Nothing could be better," said Lady Beaton.

****

To be lett, a convenient house situated near the church in Fletching, containing two parlors, kitchen, laundry, six bedchambers, dairy, wash house, six-horse stable, hay loft, orchard, and garden. Enquire of Mr Morland, Fletchingford.

Chapter 6

"You deceived me, John," Tom Jeffreys murmured as the travelling coach crunched over the frozen drive, away from Guysbridge.

"Why, how's this?"

"You led me to believe Her Grace was a plain, untutored Scots lass, with no charms or art of attraction beyond her portion. Instead I found her delightful. That is to say, for a lady in such recent mourning, of course. I don't say her behavior was not perfectly appropriate for the occasion."

"Had I been she, I might have danced a jig at the loss of Nicholas," Anniscote said reflectively. "And I don't think I ever implied she was not pretty, though her hair is prodigious red, and her face freckled. I've been told that salt and lemon juice will fade the spots, but one can hardly suggest it to a lady. However, I was pleasantly surprised. The burr was hardly in evidence, she bore herself with dignity, and conversed like a rational woman. She also plays piquet well enough. Have you a mind to my sister-in-law, Tom? After longer acquaintance, I concede she might make a tolerable wife for any gentleman. So long as he could endure the blazing hair, for one cannot expect her to keep it covered all the time."

"I thought it quite pretty. It seems to me she puts to shame most of the acknowledged beauties, by her intelligence, grace, charm, lack of artifice…" Here words failed him.

"I see you have fallen a captive to Her Grace, Tom. Pay me no mind; I could not admire Venus herself, if she were born Venus McJupiter."

"I despair of you, John."

The duke smiled gently and said nothing else, leaving Tom to his meditations, presumably upon Elspat. He rather hoped Jeffreys would marry the widow, for it would secure him a decent living, and sever Elspat's connection to the Anniscotes—for lady-like as she might be, and rich as her father was, she remained the daughter of a Scots tradesman. And now that Anniscote knew her better, he was pleased to think that as well as those benefits to Jeffreys and himself, such a marriage would provide the duchess with a good husband. Tom had embarrassingly few gentlemanly vices. He might almost have been a vicar, as he seemed to have no passion for gambling, seldom drank to excess, and was careful and discreet in his liaisons with women. If not for his wit and well-informed mind, he might have been boring. What more could a lady ask in a husband?

His own thoughts turned to the portrait of Don Diego. He had remembered it as having historic interest but no artistic merit. Studying it during his visit confirmed his opinion, though he now thought that Don Diego's expression, though ineptly rendered, was meant to express resolve, rather than bad temper.

Chapter 7

The sun was low in the sky when the Beatons' coach reached London, after three wearying days. Seeing the size of the metropolis and the streets, all full of vehicles, riders, and pedestrians, Anne could only wonder how they would find their way, even in daylight, and said as much, timidly, to Sir Randolph.

"Nay, nay, be at ease, Mistress Anne. I have been in town any number of times, and John Coachman, too. Last night we consulted a book I have often used, which lists every street, court, and alley in London, and in what part they may be found. We are tolerably sure of being able to find Mrs. Bradshaw's house, and to make our way from there to our daughter's. They are not so very far apart, neither, though I'm sure the place seems a maze to anyone visiting it the first time."

It did, indeed, though perhaps it was only because the day had been long and her body ached from three days' jolting and two nights' restless sleep in unfamiliar beds at the inns where they had broken their journey.

Perhaps if she had not been so tired, the smells, clamor of peddlers calling their wares, and other coaches, chaises, and wagons rattling along would have been interesting. It might seem quite fascinating tomorrow. But it was a relief when they creaked to a halt at Mistress Bradshaw's house near Golden Square. The neighborhood might not be in the first style of elegance, but clearly money was not lacking. Anne guessed, without Lady Beaton telling her, that those who lived here were gentlemen and professional men with comfortable incomes. Their daughters would not be presented at court but would make respectable marriages to merchants, bankers, or the second or third sons of gentlemen.

The postilion had not even dismounted when the door of the tall and narrow-fronted house was thrown open, and a lady of perhaps five and fifty years came out, one hand on the butler's arm.

"I have been so anxious!" she said. "The roads being what they are, and…but I forget my manners. Lady Beaton and Sir Randolph? Will you alight and take something to drink? Or eat?—dinner will be ready in a trice. There's a nice beefsteak pie and potted pigeons and lemon cream, and a few other dishes I thought my brother's ward might fancy."

Sir Randolph and Lady Beaton declined with thanks, Sir Randolph saying, "My good lady is eager to see our daughter, as I am, too, and we should not delay."

Thus once Anne was assisted to alight—and she found she needed the assistance, as stiff as she was—and her trunks were unloaded, the Beatons' coach rattled off, and she was left with her hostess, the butler, the footman, and a maid Mrs. Bradshaw had summoned.

"My dear! Sally will take you to your room so you may tidy up, and then, I pray, come straight down, for by then dinner will be ready. I long to have a comfortable talk with you, too, for my daughter died when she was only five and I quite miss having a daughter."

"Thank you, Mrs. Bradshaw. I would appreciate a chance to wash my face and hands." And use the chamber pot.

The lady tilted her head. "Now who is it you remind me of? That chestnut hair...I don't see detail well, but I do see color, and that is a memorable shade of brown. Your voice, too—but I must not keep you standing here. Sally, do you lead Mistress Anne upstairs directly."

The maid, a plain girl with a pleasant expression, brought her to a chamber containing a four-poster bed with dainty hangings and furniture with the graceful curved legs of Queen Anne's reign, purchased perhaps at Mistress Letitia's marriage to Rupert Bradshaw. Anne would rather have gone straight to bed, but it would be unthinkably discourteous—and anyway, she was rather hungry.

****

"I cannot say how pleased I am to have you stay with me," said Aunt Letitia—for Mrs. Bradshaw had immediately decreed that Anne must consider her in the light of a great-aunt, having been her brother's ward. "Only, you know, Anne dear, if you called me 'Great-Aunt Letitia,' it would make me feel old. Older than I am, I mean. So let it be 'Aunt Letitia' instead. How lively we will be! I shall invite a few old friends to dinner—some of them have eligible sons—but not, perhaps, until you have had a chance to replenish your wardrobe. For I cannot imagine that James gave a thought to what you wore, and in the country like that one could not expect the seamstresses and tailors to know the latest fashions, not that they would be suitable for country wear anyway. And I see you brought only two trunks. I suppose he still wore that horrid peruke, which must have dated to Queen Anne's reign, at least."

"Only for dress wear, ma'am…Aunt Letitia, I mean. He had a bag wig for everyday use, and when he was treating a patient, he took it off. I remember, after the amputation at which I assisted, he left it hanging on the back of a chair, and we drove all the way home before either of us recalled it."

Letitia stopped with a morsel of crawfish on her fork. "He let you see an amputation? What can he have been thinking of?"

"He needed an assistant, and no one in Mr. Wetherill's family was of any use in such a circumstance, so—"

"No, don't tell me. That man! Well, at least he regained his health, which much concerned me when he quit London and dragged his poor daughter around the Continent for a year. Indeed, I don't know how he survived, as low as his constitution was. I offered to keep Marianne while he toured the European spas, but he would not hear of it. But afterward, when he was better and returned, he agreed that she should stay with me. And I must say, I think it was partly due to me that she got such a good husband. She was very beautiful, of course, and still is, for that matter, but she did not have a large portion. However, Mr. Saltstall took a fancy to her, and to have a wife who was an earl's granddaughter, and certainly he did not need to marry for money. And it has done very well. She has every luxury, and he has a very pretty, elegant wife who is an ornament to his home and lends him gentility. Marianne could never have done as well, buried in the country as she was. I wrote James half a dozen years ago, yes, and after that, too, asking if he would not send you to me, but he would not be persuaded. He verily doted upon you, and claimed he would miss you too much, and that there was time enough for you to visit London. How sad that he should have had to die to bring it about, for surely he would have been glad to see you well married."

They were nibbling little cakes when Aunt Letitia said, "My friends are mostly of my late husband's circle: attorneys, judges, and the like. Now, if Marianne will take you about with her daughter, you will make the acquaintance of families with interests in the City. Bankers and merchants and that class, you know. There is sure to be some rising young man in one group or the other who will suit you. "

"I don't wish to put you to any effort," Anne said guiltily.

"While it will entail some exertion, I shall find it highly enjoyable, I promise you. And really, a young lady cannot expect to make a decent marriage without her elders bestirring themselves a little. There was no one in Fletching or Fletchingford for whom you had a partiality, I gather? Or, if there was, his interest was not engaged?"

"I was always used to fish and ride with the boys, but that was years ago, and they went off to school or developed other interests…" Like that simpering, blonde daughter of Mr. Sloan at Chesham Old Place.

"I hope you have left off such tomboyish ways," Aunt Letitia said. "Did James see to it you learned the really necessary things?—like dancing?"

"The Squire and his wife invited the Reverend Mr. Ott's girls and me to join their daughters for dancing and deportment lessons and even held some small, private dances so we could practice."

"Very good! Things have changed so much that one needs quite different skills nowadays. Ladies were not always going to balls and parties and picnics when I was young. I well remember my dear mother making caraway comfits and cordials, and overseeing the dairy maids, and she insisted I learn to do so as well. Of course, my mother spent most of the year in the country and came to London only for a month or so, although Papa came up more often, and I suppose she did not do any preserving while in town. When I was a new bride I used to make preserved fruit. But of course we lived in London and our cook did not like me to invade her domain, so I quickly gave it up. The world has quite changed, and while I think some of it is for the better, I fear many girls have far too much freedom now."

"Surely not, Aunt," Anne said, Mr. Morland's views on the supervision of unmarried ladies in mind.

"Indeed, yes. I hope that your presence will restrain Marianne's daughter. Marianne has great ambitions for her, as well she might, because she is a pretty thing, with engaging manners, and her only child, too, but I fear she is rather flighty. Mr. Saltstall should make every effort to arrange a marriage for her as quickly as possible. But Marianne hopes to see Mariah married with a title and an estate, which she was unable to accomplish herself. I do hope she does not let Mr. Saltstall see that she would rather have married a nobleman. He is a very worthy man—and no, I do not mean that he is boring. Apart from being extremely wealthy, he is not much older than Marianne, has pleasant features, good manners, and even perhaps a sense of humor. But I fear my niece cannot forget he is a merchant and has no title. She is determined to do better for her daughter."

"Would it not be difficult for her to meet a titled man?" Anne inquired doubtfully. Unsophisticated as she was, she could not imagine Mrs. Saltstall's social circle overlapping any in which members of the nobility might be found.

"It would not be impossible. Mr. Saltstall is an alderman and is likely to be Lord Mayor of London one day. He is friendly with many men of fortune and influence. And Mariah is his only heir, so some impoverished but noble family might well covet her dowry. Still, she is quite young yet. Which reminds me, we will certainly visit Vauxhall Gardens."

"Oh! A botanical garden? I am very interested in the healing powers of—"

"No, dear, pleasure gardens. Masquerades, fireworks, scenic vistas, paths, and grottoes. Everyone goes there. And St. James mall, too: it is very modish to walk there, although one must beware of clerks and apprentices dressed above their station." She seemed to reflect. "And since you need some things, I think I must order a new gown or two. One of the new sacques, definitely. And a hoop. The latest style is for width to the sides. You will need one, too, and oh, I daresay a dozen things."

Even a serious-minded young woman cannot fail to find some interest in the discussion of how the loose sacque would display to best advantage silk painted in the Chinese fashion, the rival merits of Brussels lace and Mechlin lace, and whether to bespeak a gown in quilted silk for the winter.

Before they went up to bed, Letitia said, "Dear, in case you should find it difficult to sleep tonight—or any night, of course—because visitors from the country do complain of London's noise, let me suggest you provide yourself with a book. There is a fine collection of sermons in the library. I am particularly fond of *The Necessary and Immutable Difference between Moral Good and Evil*, from the text Isaiah 5:20, by Samuel Chandler, and *A Sermon Occasioned by the Death of John Sladen*, preached by Dr. Ridgley. A sermon is so soothing. After my maid reads me a page or two, I am always ready to close my eyes."

"But ma'am, don't you then find that you drowse in church?"

"No, of course not. I used to pay attention to what everyone was wearing, but now that my eyes are so weak, and I go out less, it gives me a chance to meet old friends—after the service, of course. Really, Anne, one mustn't fall asleep in church."

"No, indeed." Her grandfather had seldom felt it necessary to attend church, and, after she reached a certain age, did not insist that Anne do so. She herself usually went, as she enjoyed it and often found it elevating. The idea that someone would spend Sunday morning at a divine service only to see and be seen struck her as being far odder than her grandfather's refusal to listen to a sermon.

But her first evening in London passed very agreeably, and Anne felt that in spite of her occasional misgivings, her removal to town had been a wise decision.

Chapter 8

On his return from Guysbridge, the duke bade his coachman set him down at Guysbridge House, that he might see how the work was gone forward, the hour being little past noon. Peters pressed him to stay, the new duke owing it to his name to take up residence in the ducal house immediately.

"I'll remove here tomorrow," Anniscote assured him. But when he emerged from the house intending to look in at a coffee house to catch up on the news, a young lady descending precipitately from a hackney all but fell into his arms.

She was a pretty armful, he noticed, very modishly gowned in a pink and white striped open gown over a leaf-green underskirt, and she peeped up under her eyelashes roguishly.

"Oh, dear! I beg your pardon, sir. I lost my footing on the step…"

"You should have waited for the coachman to assist you," he said, releasing her once he had set her upon her feet. However, she kept a hand on his arm, as if for support.

"I fear I am quite shaken."

"Are you visiting someone nearby? May I see you safely to their door?" he inquired. If she had alighted here, it must only be a few steps to whichever house she intended to visit; indeed, the hackney was standing even with the door of Guysbridge House, the coachman at his horses' heads, making some adjustment to the harness. Her voice and dress were those of a young lady, although her manners were more free than one would have expected. But her coach was hired and shabby at that, and the coachman, even less prepossessing, had not bothered to turn his head as his passenger had stumbled out. And she was without any maid or companion.

"...Oh, thank you, but I have turned my ankle a little and think I must forego my visit today. But if you could assist me in remounting the step? And in return, may I take you to your destination?"

Oh ho, he thought, here's a coil. Odd behavior for a young lady to invite a strange man into a closed coach. Some new form of robbery, perhaps: coax a gentleman into a hackney driven by a confederate and pick the victim's pocket while flirting with him? Or drive to some quiet location where her friends might attack and rob him?

"I thank you," he replied, helping her up into the coach, "but I am going only to the next street." Seeing the man had already regained his seat, he ordered, "Drive on," shutting the door and stepping back. The minx peered out the window and gave a little wave of her hand.

It was not until he reached his lodgings that it occurred to Anniscote that almost three weeks had passed since his brother's obituary had appeared, time enough for word to spread. He might now be considered lawful prey both by courtesans and by a young woman of decent lineage (if not decent behavior). It was yet longer before he thought, *Good*

God, can she have meant to trap me into marriage by waiting until we reached a busy street and then screaming out the window that I was abducting her? She would have to be daft to believe such a shift would answer: when has an Anniscote cared for public opinion? And she certainly could not bring a case to law. The notoriety would destroy her reputation without tarnishing ours more than it already is.

Chapter 9

Over a late breakfast the next day, Anne asked, "Ma'am, can you tell me where I ought to go to purchase shoes?—for I now realize mine are quite countrified. And some other small matters, as well: some ribbon and perhaps a headdress. My round-eared caps are well enough for wear in the house, but my straw hat is not modish."

"I am glad you broached the subject, for I meant to address it myself. Sally told me that only one of your trunks contained clothing. Can it be true that the other was packed with musty old books?"

Anne hung her head and confessed it was true. "You see, some of my clothes were so worn that I left them behind, so I had a spare trunk. And I really could not have left the books."

"Sally says some of your gowns would be scorned by an abigail on her free afternoon, although you have several that are not unsuitable for at-home wear, if a little old-fashioned. You will need new ones, suitable for—oh, visiting, and evening parties, and walking, and going to the theater, and shoes and headdresses to go with them. White stockings, both silk and cotton, are a necessity. Only country folk and the hopelessly unmodish still wear colored stockings, whatever the moralists may say. Sally can take you to the shops. Heed her advice; she knows what will be proper, and where it may be had at the best price. That is why I offered her to you. She was wasted as the upstairs maid. Look for some silk—not blue, I think, or at least not light blue, popular as it is, for I think green might become you better. And perhaps also pink. One will do for a robe *à la Anglaise*, and one for a ball gown. A golden shade would be pretty, too. Sally will know how many new outfits you will require. Thank goodness you do not insist on mourning. We really cannot waste months before setting about our work. The day after tomorrow, we will visit my mantua-maker."

"But I have a ball gown, Aunt Letitia. It's cream with—"

"Embroidered pink rosebuds, yes. I warrant you've had it since your first ball, and worse, the style might have been worn by…well, I hardly know. Queen Anne, perhaps. I don't say it in any critical spirit, I'm sure, but you must have a new one. I beg you will give the old one to Sally."

"Do maids go to balls here?"

"Of course not, but one's maid is given one's old clothing to sell, if it be above her station in life, as a vail. Is it different in the country? I recall my mother giving her dresser cast-off gowns."

"I never had a maid, and the subject never came up in my hearing," Anne said.

Upon finishing their meal (a light one consisting of toast, tea, and some strawberries and cream for Aunt Letitia, and eggs, ham, toast, tea, and strawberries and cream for Anne, who had always a hearty appetite in the morning), Anne said, "I should put on one of my new gowns, if I am to go shopping, Aunt."

Letitia frowned a little. "My dear, perhaps…for

this excursion, it would be best to go as you are…with, of course, the addition of a hat and shawl."

Anne looked inquiringly at her adopted aunt.

"I don't wish to cause you pain or embarrassment, but…" Letitia's voice trailed off.

"Have no fear, ma'am. I know I am no better than a green country girl. You know Dr. Sinclair was for plain speaking. "

"Too well do I know it! Then let me say, if you go out attired in your…ah, fashionable…country gown, it will be seen that you are but late come to town. It occurred to me but a few minutes ago, when thinking how to get you rigged out in good style, that you may shop for what you need at once, and no one the wiser, if you go out as you are." Noticing Anne's lack of understanding, she explained, "You are dressed no better than a maid—indeed, not as well as Sally. In your current raiment, if you and Sally go out and walk side by side, you will be taken for another maid. Which is to say, no one will take note of you at all. Fine feathers make fine birds, you know. By the next time you leave the house, you will be attired as a young lady."

"Aunt Letitia, that is very clever. I would not want people staring at me, as if I were a curiosity in a raree show."

"Well, dear, I am not clever, but I have passable common sense, and I know something of society although I do not now live in the same circles as when I was the young daughter of an earl. Do you have enough money with you for your small purchases? The silks I have told Sally to have billed to me. Your new shoes, too."

"But I cannot let you pay for my finery."

"Dear Anne, there is nothing I would enjoy more. I so much enjoyed dressing Marianne when she stopped with me, and I have missed the experience since she married. Once she was Mrs. Saltstall, she no longer needed my assistance or my advice. Though she hardly needed it by then, for she has prodigious good taste. Please, for my brother's sake, let me make you a gift of what you need most."

Put so, it would have been churlish to refuse.

Anne set forth with Sally, who, though a plain girl, would never have to worry about earning her keep, being clever at all forms of needlework and everything pertaining to dress. Anne was not above taking her advice. They had transacted very satisfying business with the silk merchant, who would deliver the many yards of goods to Aunt Letitia's home. They purchased ribbons of several colors to match—for Sally had a good memory for color—stockings, four pair of shoes, none of Anne's being suitable to be seen, except around the house, when no company was expected, according to Sally—and one or two other trifles: handkerchiefs, a lappet, and face powder.

They had wandered into a street with very fashionable shops ("Everything is terrible dear, but you can see the latest mode," said Sally) when Anne noticed that a gentleman outside a coffee house opposite seemed to be staring at her, almost as if he knew her. She affected not to see him.

"Do you see that man in the claret-colored coat?" Anne whispered.

"With black hair? Ay—but pray do not let him see you looking at him, Mistress Anne. Belike he's a rake. If you notice him, he's apt to accost you."

Perhaps it really was necessary to have a chaperon. "I do not think he admires me." She could not make out his expression, but something about the angle of his head suggested hauteur.

"If he is a rake, Mistress Anne, he's fine-looking gentleman for all of that."

Even after they passed, Anne fancied she could feel his gaze on her back. It was very rude of him, but she felt a little flutter of excitement. Or gratified vanity, she reflected.

Apart from that episode, the shopping expedition passed very well, with Anne able to look around her at the sights without making a spectacle of herself.

Chapter 10

"What's this, Anniscote? Or I suppose it should be Guysbridge now." Jeffreys, entering the foyer, found the duke amid a pile of trunks, portmanteaux, and boxes.

"I pray you, let it be Anniscote still. Whenever I hear 'Guysbridge,' I think my brother's entered the room and have a lively desire to leave it."

"But still—are you packing? Visiting Guysbridge again, perhaps?"

"If I do, be sure I'll invite you," Anniscote said with a sliver of a smile. "The widow must have some entertainment, after all. No, you may recall I had not time to arrange for the packing of my belongings before we travelled north. So I kept my lodging until the house might be cleaned and furbished. Come into the library. Peters and my valet can see to the disposition of these things."

"So this is the family townhouse," Jeffreys remarked, gazing around the library. It was dust-free, although the draperies at the windows and the upholstery of the chairs were still noticeably worn. "How do you like your new estate?"

"I begin to grow accustomed. But it is sometimes still startling. Have I mentioned the charmer who threw herself at my head?"

"Ah! I knew you'd realize, sooner or later, that

you'd become a very eligible prey."

"Indeed. Thus far, there is but one: a pretty wench but far too forward. I became aware of her on my return from Guysbridge. She tumbled from a hackney into my arms, and I could hardly let her fall to the pavement. Imagine my surprise when I found I could hardly stir outside without tripping over the chit. Another day, she dropped her handkerchief when she passed as I was strolling to my club, expecting I would pick it up. I did so but favored her with the coldest of bows. I would have thought she must live near my former rooms, but that our first encounter was outside this house, and the other times I have seen her elsewhere. On my way to my club, as I mentioned, or strolling in the Mall. She seems impervious to snubs." Anniscote's eyebrows drew together. "And her maid should be whipped at the cart's tail as a procuress, for she is all too willing to efface herself."

"This is ingratitude indeed." Tom laughed. "You have bribed any number of maids, have you not?"

"True. But the blatancy of it, Tom! I deplore the lack of subtlety. And it is one thing to give a douceur to the abigail of a married lady and quite another to be hunted like a fox by a brass-faced baggage in search of a marriage."

"Marriage? Most likely she is seeking a protector. How else is a damsel of that stripe to secure one?"

"Think you she is of that sort? By her clothing and speech you might take her for the daughter of a good family, or perhaps some well-to-do professional man's daughter. But she might be only of the middling sort. It is easy enough even for a clerk or milliner's apprentice to ape his or her betters." There was a flourishing market in secondhand clothing, as Anniscote well knew. "Indeed, when last I saw her she was dressed very simply and was with a different abigail. She gave me the cut direct, Thomas! It had not occurred to me she might be a tart, but no doubt you are correct. She tries to pass as a gentlewoman, to increase her price, I suppose, and that having failed in my case, she ignored me to pique my interest. She is convicted by her behavior."

"Well, it's only to ignore her, after all. She can't always be falling into your arms!" Swirling the sherry in his glass, Tom asked, "Have you given any thought yet to wedding? Now that you are His Grace of Guysbridge, you owe it to your name."

"I have not thought of any particular ladies, although I know what I must have and would not have. Thank God, I have no need of a rich dowry, which might require some Cit's daughter. She must be well-bred and have no flaws of face or figure. That is to say, I would not have a woman who squints or has no chin or too much nose. Nor will I have for my duchess a flirt, or an inveterate gamester, or a spendthrift. My father and my mother were a pretty pair, between them."

"As the Duke of Guysbridge, I think you may set your sights high. But I hope you will not settle for someone you cannot feel affection for, at least."

Receiving only a "Pshaw!" by way of reply, Jeffreys forbore to continue that line of conversation.

Chapter 11

No sooner had she entered the house than the butler informed her that her aunt wished to see her in the drawing room. Anne found Letitia Bradshaw with a remarkably pretty blonde lady, fashionably gowned, who gave a little start upon Anne's entrance.

"Anne, here is my niece, Dr. Sinclair's daughter, Mistress Saltstall, come to visit. Marianne, did you never meet Anne? I suppose not, as your father seldom stirred out of that village. And you never visited him, I think."

"No…" the lady said slowly. "My husband likes to have me by him, and his business affairs do not permit of his leaving London often. Why, I scarcely manage to leave it even in the summer."

Mistress Saltstall was not above the average in height, with neat features and a pink-and-gold prettiness. Her lips were full, and everything about her bespoke delicacy and grace. She was, Anne reflected, everything that she herself was not. What a pity she had so little animation in her face. Anne wished she had paid more attention to Joan's advice not to go out without a hat and gloves. If her own skin was not actually as browned as a ploughman's by exposure to the sun, it was not of the alabaster pallor required by fashion. Sally said she must use cosmetics to make her skin white and her lips red, but Anne was not yet reconciled to doing so, and she misdoubted even cosmetics could disguise her rudely healthy color. She supposed her own hair was well enough, being thick and glossy, but it was only reddish-brown. Yet, studying the visitor, Anne wondered whether she was in good health, for all her beauty. Her voice was leaden, her face expressionless, and yet she seemed nervous.

"Do you mean to make a long stay in London, Mistress Anne?"

"I think I may. There are so many more opportunities here than at home, that I believe I will make it my home once I have found lodgings."

"Opportunities?" Marianne Saltstall asked doubtfully, as Letitia repeated in tones of horror, "Lodgings?"

"Opportunities because of the booksellers and lectures," she said. "Lodgings because I won't need a house." And probably could not afford one in a convenient part of town and with the necessity for a cook and maid; not to mention that a house of her own would require having a chaperon, whereas in rooms there could be no objection to her living on her own, surely?

"My dear, you will of course live with me, if you wish to remain in London, and you are very welcome to do so. You cannot, absolutely cannot, live alone."

"If you think it would be really improper, rather than merely unusual…"

"Improper it would certainly be, and eccentric in the extreme, as well. A widow, or a married woman who has been abandoned, or whose husband is in debtors' prison, might do so. An unmarried girl, a gentlewoman, never."

"It would be most improper," Mrs. Saltstall agreed. "The world is mighty critical of young ladies. What is overlooked in a wife or an older woman would quite destroy your reputation. A young woman who defies convention invites unwanted attentions from gentlemen. Nothing could be more fatal to her reputation…" She had spoken with some energy, but the last sentence trailed away.

"I do understand that, ma'am. Also, of course, if one surrenders one's virtue, there is the danger of disease, not to mention p…other undesired consequences," Anne finished, remembering in time that delicacy forbade mentioning such things.

Mistress Saltstall gasped, and Letitia gave a little scream. "Anne! What will you say next?"

"I beg your pardon," she said contritely. "But if one doesn't speak of the consequences, how would an innocent girl know…?"

Letitia, deprived of the power of speech, merely shook her head and pulled her vinaigrette from her pocket.

Mrs. Saltstall smiled tightly. "Ladies may talk of such things, amongst themselves, but an unmarried girl does not. I hope I need not add, particularly to, or in the hearing of, a man. It is for a girl's mother to explain these things to her, privately, and…er…discreetly. Not that it does a groat's worth of good to give a girl reasons to behave, for not a one of them will believe such a misfortune could befall her," she added, acidly. "Not one girl in a hundred has the sense God gave a lapdog; some think that love and one hundred pounds a year will suffice, and even one sensible enough to hope for a title and money may not have the wit to see that no gentleman will pay with marriage for what he can get for naught but a few compliments."

"It sounds very cynical," Letitia opined, "but that is the truth of it."

"Cynical, aunt? No. Merely practical."

"Still, modern misses take such notions…" Letitia began.

"Their mothers must see that they do not ruin themselves, by whatever means are necessary. It's best to keep a daughter on a tight rein, and marry her suitably as quickly as possible."

"Anne, dear, Mrs. Saltstall means to take you about with her own daughter. You will be able to meet more young people than are found in my circle, and to go to the sort of entertainments I do not attend as a rule."

"That is very kind, ma'am. Thank you."

Mrs. Saltstall acknowledged the thanks a little absentmindedly, but said, "We should not begin until you are properly gowned. That is of the utmost importance. You must not look like some poor country relation, but you must also not dress too richly. Your circumstances will be known, of course, and to dress like a young lady of fortune can only appear as a sort of deception—and not a successful one. Very simple gowns will be best. I know you will agree, Aunt Letitia. You have such exquisite taste."

"But, Marianne, do you really think—we do not want Anne to look countrified."

"Her attire should be of the current fashion, but not in advance of the mode, in good but not extravagant fabrics. The effect will be of a girl who is pretty-behaved and modest. There is this, too: as she is past the age when most young women begin the dance of getting a husband, simplicity of dress and manner will give an appearance of greater youth. And you must not stir from the house until you are properly dressed," she said to Anne. "Your introduction into society will be more striking if you are ready. One must not squander the element of surprise by having you seen in your present rustic state. Perhaps dancing lessons would be advisable, too—let me arrange those. You may be well-schooled in country dances, Mistress Anne, but you must be able to perform the ones now done here in town. You curtsey prettily, so we need not concern ourselves with that, at least. But keep her close, Aunt Letitia. I would not want her to jeopardize a decent marriage by emerging too soon and making some embarrassing blunder."

"Thank you, Marianne. I agree that the correct wardrobe is of the first importance. I will be taking Anne to my modiste tomorrow. Anne and her maid have already purchased several lengths of material. Sally has as good an eye for color as I do, and far more endurance."

"I think," Mistress Saltstall said, "it would be wise to have your dressmaker come to you. I am very anxious that my father's ward make her debut unheralded by premature appearances. And I will secure a dancing master." She gazed at Anne searchingly. "You do know, I hope, that a great marriage is not to be hoped for. As…as I think my father wrote me, your father was an officer in a foot regiment and your mother came of country gentlefolk, with neither money nor connections. The little income you inherited from my father, and a country cottage, will not secure you a wealthy husband or a titled one.

Unless the man is perfectly besotted by your face or charm," she added.

"It certainly seems unlikely that any man would find either irresistible," Anne agreed. Mistress Saltstall's comment struck her as having been unnecessary, and probably meant satirically.

"That is very sensible of you, my dear. May I assume you will make no more excursions until I think you are prepared?"

"I had hoped to see something of London…"

"You shall see it after you have been introduced to society. You will enjoy it so much more then, with companions."

"Not the booksellers, surely. I know that not everyone enjoys books as much as I do."

"Please be governed by my advice in this. I do know rather more of society than you can, fresh come up from the country."

"Which is perfectly true," Letitia agreed.

Mrs. Saltstall took her leave soon after.

"I am passing fond of my niece," Aunt Letitia confided when she was gone, "but she is not of as warm and open a disposition as her father. I own I was surprised that she took so readily to my suggestion that she introduce you into such society as is available to her."

"I don't want to be a burden to her," Anne began but Letitia cut her off.

"It will do her no harm to include you with Mariah. And she is on visiting terms with a great many ladies and…well, women who are perhaps not what one would call ladies, in the strict sense of the word, but whose husbands are successful in the City, and whose sons are as gentleman-like as one could wish. If my son, James, had lived, he could have invited his friends to dine here, as well." She dabbed at her eyes with a handkerchief and gave a doleful sniff. "Well, it's been a long time, and no doubt he would have been married by now, and with no bachelor friends. Perhaps I should mention that Marianne has one little habit which you may find as irritating as I do."

"What is that, Aunt Letitia?"

"She refers rather too often to her grandfather, the earl. Which may be only policy on her part, for indeed she is in high favor with her husband's friends and fellow businessmen. She is as close to an earl as most of them are like to come—unless they are bankers," Letitia added tartly.

"Her grandfather the earl—but not her father the physician?" Anne inquired.

"Precisely, my dear. My papa was a good enough father and a decent man and I loved him, though he was rather annoying at times, but James was a delightful brother, quite my favorite member of our family. Papa would not intentionally do anyone harm, excepting poachers, possibly, for he especially hated poachers…where was I? Oh, of course, James. James would go out of his way to give assistance. Papa expected him to go into law or the church or the army. Those would have been respectable careers. Our elder brother, Hugh, followed no profession, of course, because he was our father's heir, but our brother Alan chose the army, and Roderick went into the church. They're both dead now, or I should certainly be enlisting their help in introducing you to suitable young men. Or Alan, at least, because men always show to good advantage in a trim-fitting uniform. I'm not at all sure a churchman would do for you, Anne."

"No, I'm sure you're right, Aunt Letitia." Before Mistress Bradshaw could wander farther from the topic, she said, "It's strange to think of my…Dr. Sinclair being of a noble family. Of course, I knew his father was an earl, but I never thought about it and he never used his courtesy title."

"Yes, it was so peculiar of him, and yet since he insisted becoming a physician, it was really the best thing. It would have been so embarrassing for Papa and our brother. James pretended that practicing as 'Dr. The Honorable James Sinclair' would disconcert his patients. When he had a practice in London, it seems to me it would only have been of assistance, as surely it would attract more patients, and of a better class. Of course, after he moved to the country, it might have made the yokels shy of him."

"Why did he go into medicine, ma'am?"

"He did not care for the idea of a military career, and he would have it that the law did not aid those who most needed it but instead was more likely to send them to the gallows or debtors' prison, and that the church…no, really, I won't say it. Some of his opinions were shocking."

"I would imagine he said that the church pays too little attention to the temporal needs of the poor but only encourages them to look for their reward in Heaven. Whereas more care to how they survived on earth might make them less likely to commit crimes that end on the gallows, with a parson in attendance, urging the poor devil to repent."

"Oh, dear," said Aunt Letitia. "He'd grown worse."

"But Aunt Letitia, Aristotle held that poverty bred crime and revolution, so the idea is not new."

"Did he?" she inquired vaguely. "But he wasn't a Christian, was he?—so surely his opinion cannot hold now. Pray do not say such things to anyone else."

****

As her new wardrobe was not yet ready, Letitia impressed upon Anne the impossibility of attending public functions or even private parties. "Let them first see you dressed like a modish young woman," she said. "Not like a country bumpkin. I quite agree with Marianne about that." Anne agreed, the less reluctantly because Aunt Letitia's late husband had collected a decent library, including a number of volumes dealing with natural science. "If you would like, Aunt Letitia, I could read to you in the afternoon or evening."

"How kind of you, my dear. Of course, Polly is perfectly willing to oblige, too—and ought to be, Heaven knows, considering I pay her such high wages—but I could not be comfortable permitting her to read some of these novels. I've longed to read *Love in Excess*, to find out what everyone was talking about, but I am afraid it is a little warm. Polly is a very superior young woman and I have no objection to her reading improving literature…"

"But one cannot call *Love in Excess* improving," Anne pointed out. "Interesting, yes, and exciting, but the fact remains that Count D'Elmont is a rake."

"I'm sure he will be reformed, and he must have very taking ways. But if girls like Polly are exposed to such tales, they will get an odd notion of what is permissible and will perhaps give their children utterly unsuitable names."

"Like Amena or Anaret? One would suppose the author did not know what names are used in France." Anne said no more, but continued to wonder whether it was not very foolish for so many of the ladies in the book to fall in love with a libertine and to behave so indiscreetly. Even she knew that a girl must never meet a man in private, except after their betrothal, and then only for short periods. When she and Letitia were immersed in the adventures of D'Elmont, Anne found herself imagining him as resembling the odious gentleman outside the coffee house.

"Well, it is a novel, and one cannot expect much more than amusement, perhaps. I am glad it is you who are reading it to me, and not Polly, for I do not think such stories promote virtue in the lower classes."

"Do they promote it in the upper classes, Aunt?"

"Well, perhaps not, but I am over the age of being corrupted, and I know I need have no concern about you, as much sense as you have."

****

Letitia was in her chamber, drinking her chocolate when Anne came in to say good morning.

"I had hoped we might go out in the carriage so you could see some of the sights, which I think Marianne would say was permissible, so long as you did not leave the carriage or lean out the window, but I fear I am not quite well today. The wind is coming up, and there will be rain. I can always tell because my head aches. We had better stay in today. Oh, and here is a note that was delivered this morning. Will you read it to me, please?"

Breaking the seal, Anne unfolded it and read, "*Dear Aunt,*

I am sorry to say that Mariah is suffering a trifling indisposition. The silly girl has felt tired and out of sorts for a week or more but refused to admit how worn down she was. I believe I must take her to the country to recover her strength, and so Mistress Anne's meeting her must be postponed. However, although Mariah will stay where she can rest and regain her customary spirits and vigor, I will be back within a week or two, by which time Mistress Anne will no doubt be suitably gowned and have had dancing lessons enough that she may be introduced to the amusements of the town.

Your affectionate niece,
Marianne Saltstall"

"How vexatious!" Letitia exclaimed. "And worrisome, too. I hope Mariah is not going into a decline. Or perhaps…"

"Yes, Aunt Letitia?"

"No doubt I'm wrong, but she is a very…lively…girl. I only wondered whether Marianne might be removing her from London because she has formed some unsuitable attachment. Girls nowadays have so much more freedom than we did when I was young. Though I will say that Mariah takes after her mother and is hardly likely to throw herself away on a man with no fortune. Or title. Not but what one's first love may overthrow one's reason."

"We must hope it's only some minor illness," Anne said. "If Mrs. Saltstall feels she is well enough to travel, she must not be seriously ill."

"You are quite right, my dear. However, it is too bad that she has to go out of town to recover," Letitia lamented. "It would be perfectly suitable for the two of you, and her maid, to go shopping or visiting. Well, we shall see. Do you go downstairs and eat your breakfast. After I've had my chocolate and perhaps a little toast, I may feel better."

"If you do not feel like going out, I may do so. I sadly miss my country walks," Anne said.

"Pray recall Marianne's advice about being seen before you are ready to be introduced into society, and stay within doors, Anne, dear. I am sorry to keep you in when I know you must wish to see all the sights. I promise you it will not be long before you can go out in company. "

"I am well able to amuse myself within doors, ma'am," Anne replied with a smile. "I have not yet exhausted your library, after all."

Aunt Letitia beamed at her. "You are fortunate to have such a happy disposition, dear. Marianne fell into melancholy so easily. Or not that, precisely. How can I explain it? Marianne counts it as one of the great disappointments of her life that she was never invited to Wemley Court or Sinclair House after she was of an age to marry. James took her to the Court when she was ten or eleven. Our mother was in failing health, and we wanted to see her one last time. Marianne sometimes refers to her stay there, without going into detail as to when it took place."

"Only the one time? I would think one would want to see one's children and grandchildren."

"James was reluctant to leave his practice and in any case did not get on with our father, who was very conscious of the responsibilities of his rank. You would have thought him very old-fashioned, which he was. Having a son engaged in a profession unsuitable to a gentleman was a sad embarrassment to him, and he also held that the different ranks should keep to their own kind and certainly not intermarry. Unless, of course, it was necessary for a gentleman to marry an heiress and he could not get one of similar rank," she added. "He would have felt it dishonest to promote a marriage for Marianne among his noble guests."

"How unfair!"

"While I do not agree with his attitude, there was some justification for it. While there was certainly nothing wrong with her birth, she was reared in a modest household. She acquired some of the necessary accomplishments, and I did what I could to fill in the gaps in her education when she came to live with me, but she had no experience of overseeing a large household or of entertaining members of the nobility. I quite understood, for I had no understanding of managing a small establishment like this, in which there is no footman who is in charge of the silver, and, when dear Rupert brought me to our first home, not even a housekeeper. Even here, where we moved when he became so successful, it would be impossible to have more than sixteen at the table. Not that I ever regretted marrying him, although at Wemley Court, we sometimes had as many as sixty guests sit down to dinner, and the house parties! You can't imagine. Neither could Marianne. She would have been at a loss as the mistress of such a house. However, she does very well in Mr. Saltstall's house in Soho Square, which is not much more elaborate than mine. She does complain that it is not truly a fashionable part of town, which is true. When it was built, any number of men of rank and title moved there, but now most of them, or their heirs, have moved to other parts. Marianne teases her husband to do the same, but Mr. Saltstall says he has no ambition to ape the beau monde or squander money on a residence where his neighbors would scorn his connection with trade. Well! Marianne is easily discontented with her lot, although she's grown good at concealing the fact. But I'm glad you are more sensible."

Later, Letitia having declared she still had the headache and intended to spend the afternoon lying down on her bed, Anne browsed the shelves in her library, in search of amusement, and found nothing to entertain her. Any number of good books, yes, that she would like to read…sometime. But today she wanted exercise, an activity foreign to Aunt Letitia. Yes, even with the wind blowing and some clouds scudding over, what she wanted most was to be striding out, feeling her lungs filling with air, even the often noxious air of London. Riding would answer, but her aunt kept no horses, and she would still not be permitted to go out. That chafed, too, because as the world knows, there is nothing more desirable than that which is forbidden. You would think some parson would preach on the subject, with reference to Eve and the apple.

She could work on the piece of embroidery she had been mangling at Aunt Letitia's direction. Aunt Letitia said that it was a ladylike pastime, and one she could work on without rudeness when boring company came to call. She could read in one of her grandfather's German texts, or one of the Latin volumes in the Bradshaw book room, to keep up her command of those languages. She could ask Sally to show her again how to apply the cosmetics so necessary to a lady of fashion and laugh at her own altered appearance! If she were to put on one of her older dresses, with a round-eared cap and her old bergère hat, she could pass as a maid, as she had when she went out with Sally to shop for necessities.

Her aunt's maid would be fully engaged in reading to Letitia and supplying her with compresses for her forehead and soothing tisanes and would be none the wiser. But Sally could not be evaded, so it would all depend upon her willingness to abet the plan.

She found Sally mending a lace sleeve ruffle.

"The mistress said you wasn't to go out until your new clothes was ready. Mistress Saltstall, too."

"But I went out that first day in town, and even Mistress Saltstall said it had done no harm, because no one really sees servants." Though it did rankle a little that she had taken one look at the gown Anne had worn (one of her better ones, too) and dismissed it as a maid's best gown.

"Except when there's somewhat to be done, or someone to be scolded," Sally said, practically.

"I'm so tired of being within doors. Don't you find it tiresome?"

"Sometimes, when the weather's nice. But I go out on errands two or three times a week, Mistress Bradshaw's abigail, Polly, not being as brisk as she used to be."

"Polly will be with my aunt, so she won't know. It would only be a matter of the butler and footman not noticing."

"Catch Joseph noticing anything! Mr. Mayhew…often as not he sits down for a few minutes this time of day. If you hurry into one of those plain dresses, we might do it. Getting back in, we'd have to go in through the kitchen and hope as Mr. Mayhew didn't happen to be there. Cook wouldn't say anything, nor Bess, either, poor little thing. I wouldn't want to be a scullery maid for anything."

****

The air was not, perhaps, as fresh as in the country, even with the wind, and soot and dust were everywhere, but the sun was shining between the clouds. There were houses and shops and churches to look at, and small squares, and Sally was not averse to walking, fortunately.

Then Anne saw books in a window. There was no resisting the joys of a bookshop. Besides, how could a young lady fall into trouble in a bookseller's?

"I will be some time looking at the books, I fear. Perhaps you should go to the draper to choose some ribbon," she suggested, taking several shillings from her purse. "Something to furbish up that green dress, and get some for yourself, too. Don't hurry back."

Sally agreed cheerfully.

Anne slipped into the shop, noting that the proprietor was assisting someone at the back, and apart from them, it was empty. So much the better. Anne settled her spectacles on her nose and was soon deep in *A Curious Herbal*, a reference of plants with medicinal uses and very fine illustrations by Elizabeth Blackwell. How her grandfather would have enjoyed it! She jumped a little when someone spoke at her shoulder.

"Who would have thought a fair damsel would stoop to wear eyeglasses? Indeed, who would have believed you such an avid reader?"

"I beg your pardon, sir!"

Anne blinked at the tall, loose-jointed man smiling

down at her. It was an odious smile—condescending, knowing, arrogant—the gentleman from the coffee house. He wore no wig, and his own hair was dark and without powder. His coat and breeches were of good plum-colored cloth but rather plain, except for the coat's handsome buttons. His waistcoat was fawn silk. She approved his style if not the man himself. Anne had noted that the extreme of men's fashion in London seemed to run to bright colors and excess ornament.

"Ah, Mistress Propriety! How well you do it, too, and no chaperon in evidence. Did it give you some trouble to find me here?"

"I believe you must have mistaken me for another," Anne replied, clutching the large volume to her breast. She glanced toward the counter, but the bookseller was paying no attention. Why would he? The gentleman's voice was low and would not carry so far. She could raise her voice, of course, which would attract the shop owner's attention. But she looked no more than a servant or a girl of the middling sort. The proprietor was unlikely to take her part rather than the gentleman's. And if there was a scene, she would never feel she could come back to the shop.

"Sir, I beg you will remove yourself, as your presence is distasteful to me." Anne did her best to mimic the frigid tone she had once or twice heard Lady Beaton use to insolent menials.

"What have I done to offend you, I wonder? Well, I would certainly not wish to give offense to a…lady." The tone in which the last was uttered was itself an insult. "Until we next meet."

He gave an ironic little bow and strolled out before Anne could think to retort, "Sir, we have not yet met at all."

It was a disagreeable incident, and almost distracted Anne from her orgy among the books. But by the time she had looked at everything and determined to buy *A Curious Herbal* and several other tomes and arranged for their delivery, she had concluded that such encounters were only to be expected in a big city—an ordinary hazard like watered milk, pickpockets, and filth in the streets. She did not think she had committed an impropriety by sending Sally off on an errand while she herself remained in the shop, but apparently the rakes in London were bolder than she could have imagined. She would not mention the encounter to Sally and certainly not to Aunt Letitia, who would just as certainly say she should not have gone out at all and should have kept Sally with her anyway. Well, it had been unpleasant—and infuriating—and in the future she must have someone with her, she supposed. Sally had been right about the obnoxious man: he must be a rake. He certainly looked it, with his sallow face and bold stare.

Seeing Sally approaching, Anne carefully enclosed the spectacles in their case. She needed them only for reading—and if her sight had been far worse, Letitia would still have said she should not be seen in public in eyeglasses. "For only think how odd it makes a lady appear," she imagined her saying. "And Sally would keep you from tripping, or stepping into anything disagreeable just as Polly does when I go out. Not that it is often a difficulty, dear, because I take my chaise or a chair, and am set down at my destination, so there are only a few steps to go."

Chapter 12

"There's rioting in Norwich," Harry Davies remarked to the table at large, conversation having lapsed as the men drank their coffee. Several had been glancing over newspapers.

"Rioting? I had not heard of it. From what cause?" Tom Jeffreys asked.

"The rabble need no reason." That from Hurst, who had met them by chance and joined them. "The dragoons will put it down, and those who are caught will be hanged."

Davies, who had rather too literal a mind and was heir to a large estate, replied, "They are angry at the high price of grain. It incenses them that wheat is sold abroad when there is want here at home."

Hurst snorted.

"It is hard to know how to address the problem," Jeffreys said. "Those who have wheat to sell naturally want the highest price for it. But at the same time, it increases the cost of food here. Some must naturally feel the pinch."

"I've noticed no increase in my household expenses. Let the improvident classes work harder, or emigrate. Or apply to their parish for assistance."

"But then, Hurst, the cost of bread would hardly affect you," Anniscote murmured. "I misdoubt you check your kitchen accounts yourself, or that a few shillings more for flour and bread would touch you."

"Hardly! It is my butler's duty to make sure my cook does not cheat me, else why do I pay him twenty-five pounds a year? Which is doubtless too much," Hurst added, discontentedly.

When he had first come to town Anniscote had paid almost thirty pounds per annum for his lodging, and his rooms were no more than fair. God knew how London's poor contrived to live on far less than what he had received for a quarter.

The conversation took another turn, to the high cost of evening entertainment. "Damn me if I didn't spend almost eight guineas the night before last, and for what? A good dinner, admittedly, and a few bottles of wine, but still—then a visit to a bagnio and a courtesan. Outrageous!"

Hurst laughed raucously. "Why pay for a used woman? There are untouched girls enough for the plucking, who will yield for nothing but a smile or two or a few trinkets. That puts me in mind of an amusing thing. At Ranelagh last week, I spied a woman I had some twenty years ago in another party—City men, by the look of them. She amused me the summer I stayed in town, dancing attendance at my father's deathbed. It would seem she went on to make a profession of lifting her skirt, as she was dressed very fine for a wench whose father was naught but an apothecary or some such thing, for all she claimed he was of a noble family. And the neighborhood was no more than passable for a merchant. She may have been some gentleman's byblow, but no more than that. The ripe little hussy must have thought me a fool to be taken in. She expected marriage, too."

"Do you know, Thomas, I find Hurst's company objectionable," Anniscote remarked later.

"Many do," Jeffreys agreed. "But what would you? He passes as a gentleman."

Anniscote gave a short laugh at Tom's barely noticeable stress on the verb. "So too did my brother. Am I wrong to feel there should be more to it than birth?"

"It's only the way of the world: if one is born to a good family, and does not cheat at cards, or enter trade, one is a gentleman. Hurst has done neither of those things."

"To boast of despoiling honest wenches hardly befits a man of honor."

"I don't suppose all of them were, John. And I don't suppose he rapes them. You yourself have said—"

"Yes, yes, I've said a vast deal of things, and some of them may have been foolish. They sound different, coming from Hurst's mouth."

"I believe you may be the salvation of your family, and a very estimable duke," Thomas Jeffreys said, grinning.

"The Devil fly away with you!"

"Speaking of young women of accommodating nature, have you seen your charmer recently?"

"I have. What an actress the baggage is. She was dressed like a tradesman's daughter or a maid, but assumed the air of a lady."

"That does not argue she belongs on the stage, John. If she had a talent for it, would she not have talked as an abigail would?"

Anniscote frowned. "I had not thought of that. It's

odd, too, that I found her in a bookseller's."

"Belike she knew you would be there, or followed you."

"How would she know? But never mind that. She wore a pair of eyeglasses, and I'd swear she did not expect me, for she leapt and squeaked when I addressed her."

"That is surely a strange way of catching your interest." Jeffreys laughed. "Clearly the girl is an original. I suppose 'tis like fishing with her: for some sorts of fish you employ one kind of bait, and with others, a different lure."

"But such lures, Tom! And how could it be anything but coincidence to find her there?"

"You have lived in lodgings too long. My mother is wont to say that in a gentleman's house, if one servant knows of a thing, all do—and so do most of the other servants in the neighborhood, within a day or two. It's likely she has her system of spies, to whom she pays a few pence for information concerning the men she hopes to ensnare."

"Your mother is prodigious wise and so is very likely correct. But I think I told no one I meant to visit the shop. My valet and butler knew I was bound for my club."

"Does the shop lie along your route?"

"Well...yes."

"Then she had but to learn of your intention to walk to your club, or even simply know that you often do walk to it from Guysbridge House. She might follow you, or linger along the way until you came upon her. Then she would accost you. After all, you are acquaintances of quite long standing by now, are you not? She was not in the shop when you entered, was she?"

"No…she must have come after me. I suppose that would explain all. Except the spectacles. What doxy needs them or pays to have them?"

"A mystery, true enough, but life is full of them. I assume you will offer her a carte blanche?"

"Why assume so?" Anniscote asked.

"She seems to figure largely in your thoughts. That is usually an indication."

Anniscote levelled a cold look at him. "She does not figure largely in my thoughts."

"Yet whenever we meet, I hear of her." He laughed at the duke's expression. "Will you call me out for saying so?"

"I'm not so quarrelsome."

"No? I hear Anglesey has never regained all the use of his arm."

The duke did not reply.

"No one seems to know why you called him out. There was some nonsense about spilled wine or jostling. It is assumed it was no more than a pretext."

"If you must know, Thomas, he mocked my brother's choice of bride."

"It becomes clear. You rushed to Her Grace's defense."

"My sister-in-law needs none. But for an upstart like Anglesey to laugh at my family…! No, I really could not let it pass."

"Oh, well, in *that* case!" Jeffreys added pensively, "But the others, John, the others. You have a reputation for being dangerous."

"I've been out only four times. If I am not mistaken

in my arithmetic, it comes to only one every three years or so. Though I will admit, I was in the wrong to call out that first one."

"We're all hot-blooded when we're young."

Anniscote glanced at him, eyebrows raised. "And we're so much older now, I suppose."

"Perhaps a little older, at least."

"Ha! I look to see you at dawn, breathing fire, if someone—Hurst, say—should speak disparagingly of Her Grace."

Thomas Jeffreys laughed ruefully. "An' it come to that, I'll ask you to be my second."

Chapter 13

Letitia kept regular habits. She had told Anne the very first week, "I spend Thursday afternoons with my husband's mother. But I do not expect you to join me. You are not obligated to visit her—I wouldn't, myself, but out of duty to my dear Rupert—and you would find her very tedious. Worse, you might easily send her into an apoplexy with your free speaking."

So Anne looked forward to spending some time with her books, and was engaged in trying to read *Don Quixote* in Spanish with the assistance of a Spanish dictionary for travelers and her grandfather's antique copy of Covarrubias's *Tesoro de la Lengua Española* when the butler announced that a Young Person was below, wishing to deliver a message to Mistress Anne, and wait for a reply.

"A maid?"

"I could not take it upon myself to say," Mayhew replied repressively. "I have put the Young Person in the morning parlor."

Entering, Anne could understand Mayhew's disapproval. If the young woman was a maid, her mistress must be decidedly low on the social scale. She had a sly face, and while her gown was dark and plain, it was not quite as neat as one would expect of a servant, and her fichu was slightly grubby. But she dropped a creditable curtsy, saying, "Bless you for seeing me, Mistress Anne. I was told to give this into your hand and no other."

The folded, sealed sheet was of excellent quality. Breaking the seal, Anne found the message short and written in a pretty, flowing hand.

"*Mistress Anne,*

There is something you must know, which will prevent your coming to utter Disaster. I cannot explain in writing. Can you slip out tonight and meet me? If so, you need only tell Prissy, who is the bearer of this message, and she will wait for you at eleven o'clock tonight outside the kitchen entrance, and take you to a coach. Conceal your face. You need not fear to be unchaperoned. Prissy will accompany you to a place where we may meet safely and secretly. Say to the butler, 'The Pearl Room' and he will lead you to me. Please do not fail me, for our meeting is essential to the happiness and safety of both of us.

One Who Has Your Best Interests at Heart"

Anne read the note twice over and thought, *How like something in a novel!* Not the best sort of novel, either.

The maid was watching her closely.

"Can you tell me anything more, Prissy? Obviously you are in your mistress's confidence."

"No, ma'am. It'd mean my position to say another word—except that I'll be with you, and it's not far off, anyhow."

Anne bit her lip. Aunt Letitia would undoubtedly condemn the suggestion that she slip out of the house to meet a stranger (because who did she know in London, after all, but her aunt and Mrs. Saltstall and a few of her aunt's elderly friends? And they certainly would not have to arrange a secret meeting) at some unspecified location. If someone had asked Anne's advice after receiving such a missive, Anne would have told her not to go, because it would be deceitful, and risky, and too unconventional even for Anne.

But it piqued her curiosity. She recalled her foster-grandfather's one unguarded reference to "the other thing" that might make it difficult for her to find a husband. There had been a few matters about which he had been reticent, and they had not all concerned his patients. When she was about twelve, she had asked if there were no mementoes of her parents. Other people possessed things their parents or grandparents had passed down to them; in novels, babies abandoned or orphaned always had some token with them. A locket, or a ring, or at least a note beseeching that the infant be cared for. Something to be a connection to her mother and father.

Dr. Sinclair was silent for several moments. At last, he said slowly, "Your mother, poor girl, was left very badly situated after your father died. Neither of them had any close family still living, and she was too proud to apply to more distant relatives, like my brothers and sister and me. When she knew she was like to die, she finally sent to me. I went north as quickly as I could but when I arrived, she had already died. There was nothing left in her lodgings but a little clothing and a few utilitarian items. The rest had been sold to pay for food and rent. If she had aught else, the landlady must have taken it before I came. It would explain why the woman did not ask me for money for the two or three days she'd taken care of you. Perhaps I should have tried to find something left to save for you. But my mind was wholly on the problem of what was best to be done."

At the time, Anne had accepted it unquestioningly. She was not normally sentimental, and so it had seemed to make sense. But looking back, her foster-grandfather's explanation had sounded rather unlike him. She could not have said what it was that rang a little false, only that it was not how she would have expected him to phrase it. Now she began to wonder if there was some mystery—and if the note's writer knew what it was.

Her aunt would be home and asleep in bed well before eleven, and her maid would not sit up, Anne supposed. She herself could retire early and dismiss Sally. Then it would be easy enough to slip out the kitchen door. Surely, accompanied by a maid, it would not be terribly wrong—especially if no one found out.

Chapter 14

Anniscote received a number of delicately-worded congratulations from men he had not seen since Nick's death while he and Jeffreys strolled in St. James's Mall that afternoon. It is not easy to combine condolences for the death of a man no one particularly likes with felicitations on the resulting good fortune of the heir. When they were clear of the well-wishers, Jeffreys remarked, "That isn't your charmer, is it?—coming toward us? I've noticed her once or twice before and thought she was looking at you as if she wished to approach."

Anniscote followed his glance. "What, the yellow-haired wench? Hardly. Some maidservant, I imagine."

She passed by with a slight smile and curtsy. A moment later, they heard a call and swift footfalls, "Oh, sir! You've dropped something!"

Jeffreys turned quickly and the duke languidly to see the girl hurrying back toward them with a folded, sealed sheet of paper in her hand. She held it out to Anniscote.

"This must be yours, I think, sir."

"I think not."

"I am quite sure it is," she said with a meaningful glance. Anniscote noticed that his friend was restraining a smile with difficulty and responded, "Then you must be correct." He accepted the letter, and fished a coin out of his pocket and held it out.

"Oh, I couldn't accept a reward for such a trifling service." The chit smiled, casting down her eyes.

"Oh, I expect you'll find you can."

"Thank you!" She dropped them a demure curtsy and tripped away.

"An intrigue, as I live," Jeffreys murmured.

Anniscote snorted and unfolded the billet. After a swift glance, he refolded and tucked it into his pocket.

****

The coach awaited around the corner in the next street. Like Prissy, it was down at heel, with a dull-coated, thin horse, and an air of not having been maintained. When she climbed in, she noticed that the upholstery was badly frayed, even torn, and it smelled musty.

"It's a hired coach," Prissy told her, noticing Anne's distaste. "My mistress couldn't send her own."

"Does the driver know where—"

"It's all arranged, ma'am."

Although Prissy had claimed their destination was nearby, the trip seemed endless. Which was ridiculous, of course; a journey always seems to last longer when one looks forward to the end with either apprehension or pleasure. It was a trick of the mind. The maid had drawn the curtains, explaining that her mistress preferred Anne not to know where they were meeting. Not that she would have seen much, judging by the quiet in some of the streets they passed (except for the sound of their own wheels, the horse's hooves, the creak of leather harness, and the jingle of metal) but in other places, she heard other vehicles, and occasionally voices. They were loud, and clearly not those of even drunken gentlemen. She felt a little worried, before recalling that quite nice neighborhoods in London were sometimes almost cheek-by-jowl with areas in which no lady could set foot. Gentlemen…well, they were another matter. They went where they would.

"There's no danger here," Prissy said. "The coachman'd take his whip to any as tried to stop us or bother us. Likely he has something besides the whip up there with him, too."

Then the sounds died away, and they were once again in a quieter part of town. The coach rolled to a stop.

"Here we are. Step out, please, mistress." Prissy hustled her up the steps to the door.

"The fare—" Anne started to say.

"Already paid," Prissy responded, as the door opened.

She felt foolish, telling the butler, "The Pearl Room, please," but he replied, "The maid will take you up, ma'am." He snapped his fingers, and a rosy girl, neat as a pin, whisked into view.

The house was certainly more prepossessing than the hackney carriage had been, or than Prissy, for that matter.

"Oh! Prissy—where can she wait?"

"She'll be made very welcome in the kitchen, ma'am," the butler said. He was a pleasant-looking middle-aged man with fair hair going white at the temples, and as neat and properly attired as the maid who was waiting by the stair, but not quite as refined as Aunt Letitia's butler, Mayhew. Something in his voice suggested he had somehow risen from very humble beginnings.

Outside, Anne heard a murmur of voices.

"If you would, ma'am?" The butler bowed her toward the maid and the stairway.

The maid led her up two flights of stairs and through a dimly lit hall to a door.

"I'll light the candles, ma'am, and if you'd like any refreshment, just ring the bell and I'll come right up, so you can be comfortable while you wait."

"Thank you," Anne said, a little faintly. The presence of an ornately-canopied bed made it clear that she had not been shown to the expected small parlor or library. The bed hangings and walls were a creamy color, perhaps why this was called the Pearl Room. She began to feel quite uneasy. Something was much amiss. If the note had come from a man, she would suspect an attempted seduction (ridiculous as that might seem), but of course, she would not have agreed to meet a man secretly, even during the day, much less late at night. After all, she was not some naïve chit just out of the school room. But there could be no such danger, when the message had come from a woman. And there was the fact that she had hinted at some information Anne should know. Besides, even if Prissy were not all that one could want in a lady's maid, her presence below stairs was reassuring.

After a few minutes, Anne began to explore the room and found that the windows overlooked a small yard at the back of the house. Light from the lower windows did not suffice to illuminate much, and she turned to searching for something to read while she waited. A book always took her mind off her worries. *Not that I am worried*, she thought. Not really. But there was not a book to be found. Finally, there was nothing for it but simply to sit in one of the upholstered chairs near the fireplace and wait upon events.

She was almost drowsing in her chair when she heard the maid's voice in the corridor. The door opened, and the maid dropped a quick curtsy, slipping something, a coin for her trouble, no doubt, under her apron, before closing the door. Anne fairly leaped from the chair.

A tall man, in a coat of rich blue, with an old-gold waistcoat, stood staring at her.

"Who are you? And what are you doing here?" she demanded. The light was dim, and his face was in shadow, but she thought, she was almost sure, that it was the same gentleman who had approached her in the bookseller's.

"I wonder you should ask, having importuned me so long and invited me here."

"I never did!" Anne gasped.

"Oh, insulted virtue! Then why are you here, if not to enter into an arrangement with me?" He moved to the fireplace and propped an elbow on the mantelpiece. Light from a sconce fell on his face then, and confirmed her suspicion. "I was in two minds about answering your…solicitation. On the one hand, I had thought you might be an innocent, if a very foolish and immodest one. I felt positively hunted. I had no intention of being cozened into marriage by such a forward little baggage. Then you wrote to me, and my doubts were at an end. A wench who invites a man to a house of accommodation cannot expect to insist on marriage or anything else. I hardly think I would even be willing to maintain you as my mistress, pretty as you are, and convenient as it might be. I expect a certain level of decorum even from a mistress."

"How dare you! I never wrote you. I don't even know who you are."

His lips curled. "As for how I dare, I have already addressed that topic. As for not knowing who I am, I dare say you saw the notice and made it your business to learn my direction. Would you like wine? Or negus? I suppose the kitchen could also supply ratafia, if you prefer." The odious gentleman turned toward the bell pull.

"I am leaving," Anne announced, hoping that a resolute manner would prevent any attempt to stop her.

"As you wish." He sounded bored. He pulled the cord.

It was almost insulting. Not that she wanted him to try to force his attentions on her. It occurred to Anne that she should wait for the maid to come and have her summon Prissy from the kitchen, rather than have to wait in the foyer while she was fetched. If this was a house of assignation as now seemed all too likely, that might prove embarrassing.

"Surely the letter you sent me was written by a woman," she ventured when he said nothing more. "It was an ungentlemanly trick."

"I write you a letter? My dear, to repeat your claim—but mine is true—I have no notion who you are or where I would send a letter to you. If you continue in your current way, however, your residence is like to be the Bridewell."

"If, as you say, I, or should I say, someone wrote you a letter, it must have been signed," Anne said, trying to match his cool, infuriating, tone.

A tap at the door intervened, and the maid entered.

"Your Grace?"

"A bottle of claret. And...ah, negus for the lady."

"No, thank you. I don't want negus. But please send for the maid who is waiting in the kitchen. I am leaving now."

The maid bobbed a curtsey and blushed, and fixed her gaze on the floor. "Please, ma'am, there's no one waiting in the kitchen."

"But the butler said she could wait there!"

"I'm sure I don't know about that, ma'am. I've been in and out all evening, and Prissy's never been there at all that I've seen." She was already backing toward the door.

"Get the wine and negus, and be quick about it."

"Yes, Your Grace, it will only take a moment..." The end of her answer trailed off as she whisked out of the room.

"Thank you very much for your offer of refreshments, but I am leaving."

The gentleman dropped into one of the chairs. "Wait. Did you not notice something in the girl's answers?"

"It is puzzling that Prissy is not there. And I think she was truthful about that," Anne replied slowly. "She was nervous, though, wasn't she?"

"There are other mysteries yet. You never mentioned your maid's name, and yet the maid knew it. Knew Prissy, too, it seemed to me. And she knew my title, as well."

"Good servants are supposed to remember guests." Anne blushed, realizing she had implied that the gentleman—the duke, evidently—had visited the house before.

"Indeed. But I've never been here in my life, and I certainly did not give my name on my arrival. It isn't expected, you know, and even if the servants in such a place know full well who their…clientele…are, they know better than to show it. One naturally wants to believe that one's little amours are secret."

This supercilious answer would have stung Anne to say something ill-considered, noticing the slight emphasis on the word "here." However, she had much else to ponder, and she remembered her grandfather warning her that men were different. "Men are not held to the same standards as women, my dear. I won't say it is right, but if a man does not debauch innocent girls, supports his by-blows, does not humiliate his wife, and avoids the sort of wench who may give him the pox, the occasional liaison should be overlooked."

"How was the letter you received signed?" she asked instead. "The girl came in just as I asked you."

He gave a derisive snort. "'Your Fair Unknown.' Immoral and inane of mind. I almost did not come tonight. Then I thought I would teach you a lesson."

"Well, really! I would never…the one I received was signed, 'One Who Has Your Best Interests at Heart.'"

"And so you came out late at night, in response to a letter from someone who did not identify himself?" Disbelief was writ large on his saturnine face.

"I was sure it was from a woman. I would certainly not have done so if it had been written by a man."

With another quick knock, the maid popped back into the room, bearing a tray with a bottle, a glass and a glass of steaming negus. She set it down on the table and retreated so quickly that she almost failed to receive the coin the duke held out.

"And yet surely the request for your presence here at night and in secret I assume, must have seemed odd to you," he said, passing her the glass of negus. "You must have had some reason for agreeing to it."

She took a careful sip. While the heat might have caused the alcohol in it to cook off, she did not care to risk becoming tipsy in such a place.

"She said there was something I must know, if I were to avoid disaster."

"And you believed such vague nonsense?"

"I know it sounds like something from a bad novel. I thought so at the time, but…you see, my grandfather, my adoptive grandfather, that is, died suddenly. Once he had referred to something that might make it difficult for me to marry. I asked him what he meant, but he would not say more, except that he would arrange matters somehow. So I wondered when I received the note. I was curious. I couldn't ignore it."

That won a slight smile. "Had it been a novel, she would have appeared and revealed that you were a royal princess, stolen at birth. Or that insanity had claimed every other member of your family, and you must get you to a convent so as not to pass on the taint. This, my dear, is real life." He frowned at her. "I really cannot continue calling you 'my dear.' What is your name, please? As we have not been introduced?"

"Anne Sinclair. And you are?"

"John Anniscote…Duke of Guysbridge."

She made a respectable curtsy, and he made her an elegant leg. The social decencies observed, he said, "It appears we were both brought here by a stratagem. It's plain enough that the intent was to ruin you, but I have no idea why I was involved. Any man would have done as well. Or no man at all," he added. "For with your maid gone—why would she have gone? Could she be bribed to assist in your ruination? And which is she? The plain one who looks decent or the fox-faced minx who accompanied you on several occasions and delivered the letter to me?"

The man was infuriating, she thought. He had fired a veritable salvo of suppositions and questions at her. It was hard to know where to begin to deal with them.

"Prissy is not my maid. She brought the letter I received, and said she would chaperon me to the meeting with the writer, who I took to be her mistress."

"Then she is part of the plot. So—"

"But I don't know why you say she was with me several times. I have only seen her twice. When she brought me the letter, and again when she met me tonight with a hired chaise. And this is only the third time I've seen you: once when you stood outside a coffee house and ogled me, then in that bookshop, and tonight. Prissy is rather foxy in appearance, however."

He stared at her thoughtfully, then drained his glass. "That explains much that previously baffled me. You certainly resemble her very closely, but you don't talk or dress as she did, and you carry yourself differently. And I really cannot imagine my Fair Unknown wearing spectacles. "

It took her a moment to understand his thought. "Do you mean there is some young lady in London who looks like me?"

"Oh, I wouldn't call her a lady, Mistress Anne. Say a young woman, rather. And yes, if you are not as alike as two peas, or identical twins, you are at least sufficiently alike to be mistaken for one another. Evidently, she is your enemy."

"How can that possibly be, sir? I have not been in town long, and I have no acquaintances here but my grandfather's sister. Well, not my grandfather: my father was a distant relation of his, but I called him grandfather, and now I am residing with his sister. But I have not gone out in company yet. Why should anyone want to ruin me?"

He gave a little shrug. "Perhaps I can determine the reason eventually. At the moment, we must decide how to save you from this contretemps."

"I must go. Please ring for the maid and have her send for the hackney coach. I must get home." Anne took up her cloak and wrapped it around her.

"I could ring for her but would you care to wager that Prissy isn't off in that hired coach?"

Anne stared at the duke. Of course if Prissy had left, so would Anne's means of leaving this place have gone. She did not even know in what part of town this wretched house was located. After a long pause, she said, "If you are correct, this is…is…"

"Damnable, I would call it. I congratulate you on not falling into a fit of the vapors, Mistress Anne. As evil as your situation is, we may still be able to avert disaster. I think our best course is to take the servants' stair and go out by the kitchen. I will take you to your great aunt's. Dare I hope you will be able to gain entrance?"

"I brought a key. No footman waits up at night, as my aunt's household keeps early hours."

"Then you may come off well enough. I fear we will have to sacrifice my hat and roquelaure, but that's a small loss, considering the alternative."

"Which is…?"

"Being seen by someone who might recognize you. Even if no one knows you at present, when you are introduced into society, someone might remember your face, and where they had seen you." He opened the door and glanced into the corridor.

"That's why I dressed as like an abigail as I could. No one notices servants or thinks about them."

"Come, then."

The hall was empty. Anne could hear muffled voices from downstairs, and a spurt of laughter from behind one of the doors. The duke led her away from the main stairway, moving quickly toward the back of the building.

The narrow servants' stair was in sight when a door opened a few steps ahead of the duke, and Anne caught sight of a bulky figure silhouetted in the dim light of the room behind him. His Grace pivoted slightly, cutting off her view. Anne heard a tipsy-sounding titter from deeper in the room.

"Blast you, where's my brandy? Hell, you're not the wench. Thought you was the maid."

"My humblest apologies. I am not the wench," the duke said with a slight bow.

Anne lowered her head, turning it away slightly, scarlet with mortification. If the man should see her, it would be a constant worry. How could she stay in London, wondering whether he would see her again and recognize her?

Anniscote thought, *I hope the girl has the sense to stay behind me so he cannot see her face.*

"Anniscote?" The hoarse, slurred voice inquired.

"You, here?"

"Indeed. Good evening, Hurst. Pray do not let me interrupt your amusements."

"Your amusements, too, I ween. You've a woman with you, I see her behind you. Is it anyone I know?"

"No, only a…a cast-off maid who took my fancy. If you will excuse me—"

Hurst blundered out into the corridor. "Mayhap she'd take my fancy, too. We might trade. My woman's as game as they come, but one wants change after all. Don't care to eat roast mutton every day, hah?"

As Hurst moved the duke turned to stay between him and Anne, but though he'd clearly drunk deep, Hurst was faster than Anniscote anticipated. Before he could intervene or Anne retreat, Hurst had a finger under Anne's chin and tilted up her face. The nearest sconce gave enough light for him to see her clearly for a few seconds before Anniscote took him by the shoulders and spun him around.

"Hands off."

Unless the night's drinking dulled Hurst's memory, he was likely to recognize her if he saw her again.

"So hot over a common wench, Anniscote?"

"My property, Hurst. I keep my property."

A squeak from the top of the stairs distracted all three. The maidservant stood agog with a tray containing bottles and glasses.

"You're slow, girl," Hurst said. "I've been waiting this half-hour. Come, bring it in." To Anniscote, he said, "We'll discuss this some other time, perhaps…Your Grace."

The maid passed, not looking at any of them, and Hurst followed her into the room. Anniscote took

Anne's arm and hurried her to the stairs.

They passed the kitchen, a hive of activity, with the cook and his minions preparing a late supper for those who wanted it, and bottles of wine standing ready to be taken upstairs. Risking a glance, Anniscote saw no sign of Prissy, which was no surprise. He led Anne out the door and through the alley to the street.

"You should have pulled your hood up before we left the room. It might have prevented Hurst from seeing your face. Thank God it's the custom for ladies to go to the rooms still cloaked. As chill as the nights have been, you'd be frozen if you'd come out only in your gown. This way. Where does your aunt live?"

"Near Golden Square."

"Too far for a chair, then. We should find a coach for hire in the next street." Of course, taking her home in a closed carriage with no chaperon might be thought improper, but given the circumstances, she could hardly be more compromised than she already was. And Hurst was a difficulty. On the other hand, from the aunt's address, it seemed unlikely that Hurst's path and Mistress Anne's were likely to cross.

"In what sort of company does your aunt move?"

"Her late husband was a judge, so the most of her friends are of the legal profession. Her niece married a wealthy merchant, although I don't think Aunt Letitia very often meets their circle." She had followed his thought with startling quickness, he noted. She added, "So I don't think I'm likely to encounter Mr…Hurst, was it? He was drunk. I shouldn't think he would remember me by morning." She sounded as if she hoped to convince herself as much as him.

"I trust you are correct." At least, he thought, not at

a private gathering. But the chit was too unaccustomed to London to realize that all classes of society (who could afford the admission) mingled at Ranelagh and Vauxhall Gardens. And there was no admission to the Mall, where one might see anyone promenading, from a laundress to a duchess. She would soon realize that she might at any moment encounter Hurst, who had no doubt of her immorality. "If your aunt should find out, is she likely to bear up and support you?"

"She won't find out. I can't let her know."

"Yet she may discover it in any case, if your maid reports you missing from bed, or someone hears you enter the house."

A hackney was standing near the corner, the coachman wrapped up in a blanket on the box.

"You, there! A fare for you," the duke called. "First to Golden Square, then to King Square."

"King Square, sir? I don't rightly know—"

"'Tis sometimes called Soho Square, for the neighborhood."

He handed her into the coach. Once they were settled, Anne responded, "She mustn't hear of this. Her nerves are not strong, and I would not for anything upset her."

"I think I should see you in a day or two, to find out if all is well," he said, after an uncomfortable silence.

She glanced up at him, and he could see with some pity that she was well aware that she might find herself in intolerable circumstances. "You can't call upon us," she pointed out. "Aunt Letitia might believe you'd known my grandfather, but she wouldn't leave us alone to talk."

"It would be best to meet at the bookseller's. We need exchange only a few words. If no one is the wiser about your—" He had meant to say "escapade," but it seemed too cruel. "Your absence tonight, so much the better." For the time being. She would find, soon enough, how difficult it was to keep such a secret. "If it becomes known, I may be able to help you somewhat."

Her apprehensive expression told him she was learning caution. Too late, unfortunately, but better late than never.

"Not by offering you a carte blanche."

"Oh! I beg your pardon. Of course, I never supposed…" Her voice trailed off, because of course the thought must have crossed her mind.

"And I certainly will not offer marriage to save your reputation," he added. "As I did nothing to damage it. I hope we can preserve that valuable asset for some other man." The thought of such an ill-conducted girl as a duchess! No, it did not bear thinking of. To give credit where it was due, she had not dissolved in tears or gone into hysterics at finding herself in such straits.

"I wouldn't marry you if…That is, I am convinced we should not suit," she said primly, adding. "Thank you for your assistance. Shall I meet you tomorrow?"

"The day after. At ten o'clock." Hurst was unlikely to rise so early.

At Golden Square, Anniscote escorted Mistress Anne to the door, to make certain she could get in. There was a candle burning on a console table in the foyer. "Will you be able to find your way upstairs?" he asked, very softly.

"Yes, thank you. There's a spare candle here in the

drawer of the table. I'll take that. Good night, and thank you again for helping me."

"I hope it may serve," the duke said.

****

After dismissing Mulley, Anniscote sat down with a glass of brandy and his ancestor's book.

I was studying at Salamanca when my father died, and Francisco took his place as Duque de Navalero. While I grieved for my father, his death made little alteration in my life. Francisco was some five years older than I and had always seemed more a full brother than a half-brother. It was when he began negotiations for the hand of the daughter of a very ancient and noble house, at about the same time that the marriage of Prince Philip of Spain and Queen Mary of England was being contemplated, that a mischance befell us.

One day Francisco sent for me.

"There is a rumor abroad that your mother's family was of impure blood," he told me. "No one can trace the source of this malicious talk, but I believe it began with a certain marqués, who as you know also aspires to wed Doña Mencía."

"The lying dog," I said. "The false, black-hearted—"

"Enough, Diego. To abuse the marqués will avail us nothing."

"But to say such a thing! And it is, it must be, untrue."

"Even its truth or falseness matters nothing—or very little."

"Will Doña Mencía's family refuse you her hand?" I asked.

"Possibly, but it is unlikely. There is no question

about my ancestry. Our father's lineage can be traced back six hundred years, and my mother was related to half the royalty of Europe. Also, a duke is preferable to a marqués, particularly if the duke is rich and the marqués is not. If they do refuse me, there are other suitable ladies. No, I am chiefly concerned for you, Sebastian, and Lucia."

I waited, but when my brother did not speak immediately, I said, "We must disprove it." I was young then.

"I have thought and thought but I see no way to do so, Diego. How can we prove your mother's grandmother was not Jewish? Sometimes records are lost or destroyed. And you know that the whispers, by themselves, are a danger. But I thank God that our father and your mother are dead."

"My mother was a virtuous Catholic lady," I said.

"And a woman of rare generosity of spirit, as well. From the time our father married her, I never missed my own mother. She treated me as if I were hers. If she were a heretic, I would still love and be grateful to her, and pray for her salvation. And," he added, "I would certainly keep her out of the hands of the Holy Office. Or remove her from thence, if necessary."

This might have seemed mere boasting from another man. My brother possessed our father's intelligence and integrity and though Francisco was but five years older than I, already he was a worthy successor to the late duke. The blood of the founder of our house ran strong in his veins. In the days when we fought against the Moors who ruled so much of Spain, the king's army lost several of their battle flags while crossing a flooded river during a hard campaign. To have no banners, with a great battle anticipated in a matter of days, was a serious thing. But in the next town, there was a tailor who undertook to sew new ones, although for lack of the customary silk, he had to use the wool fabric called "anascote." He and his apprentice sewed and painted for three days and nights, and when the banners were completed on the eve of battle, he borrowed a sword and fought under the flags he had sewn. If the twilled wool fabric did not fly as freely and snap in the breeze as silk would have done, still it was adequate to its task. The Moors were defeated, and the king rewarded him by granting him and his heirs the right to use the name "Anascote," and gave him other honors and privileges as well. I always thought Francisco must have been very much like him, immovable once he had settled on a course. It never occurred to me to doubt that he would have wrested our mother, or anyone else he cared about, from the Inquisition or the Pope or the devil himself.

He continued, "Our mother is in heaven. There is no suggestion that she herself was guilty of non-Christian practices or heresy. It is your futures which are in jeopardy. I have made arrangements for Sebastian to escort Lucia south, to a convent near Sevilla. There—"

I interrupted rudely, "Lucia to be a nun? No one was ever less suited to the religious life!"

But Francisco only smiled. "Have I known our little sister for fifteen years without noticing as much? They will not reach the convent. Their disappearance will be put down to bandits. Under different names, they will take ship for Vera Cruz. I have arranged to supply them with money and to ship such goods as will

Kathleen Buckley

give them a good start there. Sebastian is sensible and will have no trouble making a life for himself in Nueva España. And I believe they are not well-supplied with Spanish ladies. Lucia will make a suitable marriage."

"I will pray that it may be so." In spite of my faith in my brother, I was a little doubtful, and Francisco saw it.

"New Spain is distant. Those who go there do so to make their fortunes and waste little time wondering whether their fellow adventurers come of converso stock. And I believe not a few of those have gone for the same reason that I am sending our brother and sister. As for you, Diego, I believe you will go to England with Prince Philip's entourage. You will not return."

And so at England's court, I contracted a marriage with the cousin of one of Queen Mary's ladies-in-waiting. Prince Philip left England when it became obvious that Her Majesty was not with child and never likely to be so, and I retired to my wife's manor at Helter to learn to manage an English estate and English peasants.

Anniscote stared at his empty glass. His however many times great-grandfather's history had not had the soothing effect he had hoped for. Instead, that long-dead Spaniard's problems brought his own into focus, as Robert Hooke's ingenious magnifying lenses made it possible to see the hairs on a flea.

The immediate difficulty caused by Tobias Hurst's sudden appearance had driven the real danger from his mind. Not that Hurst was not a genuine problem. He himself had made it worse by implying that the girl was his mistress—he might yet have to wed her, for that alone. But if he had attempted to maintain her innocence in the circumstances, Hurst's curiosity would have been piqued, and he would have made it a point to try to learn Mistress Anne's identity.

However, the underlying mischief was that someone had deliberately tried, by a rather intricate scheme, to ruin Anne Sinclair. Who could benefit from destroying her reputation?

And who was the ill-bred hoyden for whom he had mistaken her?

Chapter 15

Anne scrambled out of bed the next morning even before Sally came in with her chocolate. She had had difficulty falling asleep and woke several times, remembering her folly. It had been exactly like a ploy taken from some novel, and she had recognized it as such—and foolishly taken the bait anyway, exactly like some witless heroine. But the writer knew some secret about her. Who else knew it? Her grandfather, of course. What had he said? "The right kind of man, the husband I'd want for you, wouldn't care a button for that, but the other thing…" Did he mean "the other thing" might make her ineligible to marry any man? Perhaps the duke's flippant suggestion of inherited insanity was correct. Nonsense, Anne told herself. I'm not mad. Or maybe it simply hasn't come to maturity yet. Some did not show signs of it until later in life, the seed growing inside them slowly, making the lunatic first only a little odd, then odder yet, until finally it was necessary to confine him. Or her.

No. Her grandfather had quite plainly meant her to marry eventually, as soon as he could find someone suitable. Had she carried the burden of hereditary madness, he would not have encouraged her to think marriage was possible. It must be some lesser thing.

Who else would know? Not Mistress Bowman, whose emotions were an open book. If she had known some dark secret about Anne, she would have showed it, if only by an air of mournful sympathy. Whenever she had seen or even heard of some unmarried man in the district, she had speculated endlessly on whether he would be just the husband for Anne. Too, she had once or twice mentioned to Dr. Sinclair that Anne should be sent to town where she could meet more men. No, Joan Bowman had no thought of any impediment.

Attorney Morland? No, he obviously had no concern about anything worse than the possibility of Anne's living without a chaperon. Sir Randolph and Lady Beaton? From what she had overheard in church, Lady Beaton's only doubts about her were for her bookishness and lack of social graces, her gaucherie.

That brought back memories. The thin, severe face of Mademoiselle…Mademoiselle…Bardes, that was it. "Bonne," Anne had called her at first, because mademoiselle was a *bonne d'enfants*, until Mademoiselle Bardes insisted that she say "mademoiselle" instead. She had not thought of her in years. When had Mademoiselle Bardes gone away? *I was six or seven*, Anne thought. *It was about the time Grandfather gave me a pony and taught me to ride.* She had not missed Bonne much; Mademoiselle was not the plump, jolly sort of nurse, always cooing over her charge and doting uncritically. Had Grandfather spoken with Anne, and told her Mademoiselle would be leaving? She could not recall it—but she definitely remembered his telling her she was to have a pony the color of cream. She still remembered dear little Custard.

Would Mademoiselle have known something? Anne could not think of anything to indicate it. But children can be both uncomfortably perceptive and oblivious at the same time. There was one thing which was perhaps a little odd. Mademoiselle spoke no English, or very little. Remembering her Bonne, it was possible she had chosen not to use a language she clearly regarded as barbaric. She had always communicated in French with Anne and Dr. Sinclair, and held herself apart from the other servants.

Could the dire secret be that I am half French? Anne wondered. But even a writer of novels could hardly make anything sinister of being French. English people did occasionally marry foreigners, and English society often visited Paris.

Sally came in then, bringing her chocolate.

"Did you not sleep well, Mistress Anne? You look a bit pulled, like."

"No, I kept waking up." She was very glad she had put away the clothing she had shed on reaching her bedchamber, tired and chilled to the bone, early in the morning. Sally would certainly have remarked upon a pile of clothing on the chair.

"If you would like to breakfast here…"

"No, I'll come down. I'm not ill." Anne did not look forward to facing Aunt Letitia with so much on her conscience, but she would have to do so eventually.

Chapter 16

"If I may mention, Your Grace," Mulley began. He was brushing Anniscote's black velvet coat while the duke drank his chocolate.

"Yes?"

"Your black velvet suit is growing a little shabby, Your Grace. You may wish to consider replacing it."

He himself had noticed that there were threadbare places, though not where they were likely to be noticed. Except, of course, by one's valet.

"I'm sure you are correct. Does the rest of my wardrobe meet with your approval?"

Mulley glanced at him. "Since you ask, sir, I would recommend buying more stockings. And wrist ruffles. Several of your coats and breeches…"

"Should be replaced, I know."

"Also you need at least two new waistcoats, and a new hat."

"Very well. You may see to the stockings and ruffles. I shall visit my tailor. If he meets with your approval?" Anniscote inquired satirically.

"While he is not a fashionable tailor, he appears to do very good work. No, I think you may continue to patronize him. The slight alterations to your fawn waistcoat are all but invisible, unless one is handling it and has a sharp eye."

As the duke had purchased it from the tailor when

the much heavier man for whom it had been intended had died unexpectedly, and Harris the tailor had taken it in to fit Anniscote, he gathered that Mulley had, indeed, a sharp eye. Probably he also recognized the signs that his new master's clothing had been bought or made with an eye to economy. How humiliating! but not surprising.

"Perhaps the new waistcoats should be a little less subdued. Nothing to catch the eye, you understand, Your Grace. Or some gold or silver lace on the coats."

"I hope you don't expect to dress me in pink and apple green, or to wear shoes with diamond buckles, Mulley."

"By no means, sir. The colors and fashions worn by men of less height or delicate face and figure would not at all suit you. Your taste and your feeling for color are excellent. I suggest only a slight increase in richness, to reflect your new station."

"Mulley, why did you stay with my brother? For I believe you served him for several years, and he cannot have done justice to your talents."

The valet smiled primly. "His late Grace didn't, of course, but he had a good figure, near as good as yours, if I may say so, and did not insist on tricking himself out in the extremes of fashion. He was untidy and careless, but in my opinion, that was a lesser sin than one often sees committed for fashion's sake. I could not like working for a man who needed to be corseted to present a decent appearance. Or who would be sent into despair over the choice of a waistcoat. There is also the matter of rank. It is an advantage to serve a duke rather than a mere sir." Helping Anniscote into the black velvet coat, he added, "By the way, Your Grace, your rocquelaure and second best hat have disappeared."

"Pray do not think of it," Anniscote replied. "They needed replacement anyway."

"Very good, sir."

"Mulley."

"Yes, Your Grace?"

"Do servants gossip about their employers? Among themselves, and to the servants of others?"

Mulley smiled. "Of course, sir. In that matter, why should they differ from ladies and gentlemen? However, I do not talk about my master's doings."

"Thank you, Mulley. After breakfast, I'll see Harris about new clothing."

"Do not forget you will require a suit for court wear."

"I suppose I will."

"And new shoes, Your Grace. With red heels."

"Must it be red heels?"

"Yes, Your Grace. It is the established mode."

"Very well, then, but no jeweled buckles."

"Jeweled buckles are quite unnecessary. But if the coat buttons were set with gems—"

"No, Mulley."

"Is there anything else I can do for Your Grace?"

The duke stopped with his hand on the doorknob and bit his lower lip. "I left my hat and rocquelaure last night at the Cantwell house. Do you know it?"

"I do, Your Grace." Anniscote read disapproval in Mulley's face.

"You needn't prim up like a deacon. It's the first time I ever set foot in the place, and I won't do so again. I would like you to retrieve them. Discreetly."

"Very good, sir."

"And you might gossip with the staff a little. I know it goes against your grain, but both I and a young lady were brought there by a trick. There was a wench posing as a maid who was sent to the young lady to escort her to a meeting with, as she thought, a woman who had some information for her. I had a sort of a feeling that the false maid was not unknown at the Cantwells', at least by the chambermaid. I am sure I needn't caution you to be discreet yourself, though if the servants there should be indiscreet, it would be gratifying. The young lady who was lured there is an innocent, and I wish to protect her name."

"Certainly, sir. Innocent young ladies are easily deceived, exactly because they're too innocent to suspect villainy."

"Precisely. I leave it in your hands, then."

Mulley gave a little bow, and the duke went downstairs to breakfast with more appetite than he had expected.

Chapter 17

Aunt Letitia was in a very cheerful mood, because, as she explained, the chore of visiting her late husband's mother was behind her for another week and she could be easy.

"Not that I consider it a chore, of course," she hurried on. "One must respect one's elders and particularly elderly relations, and Rupert was very fond of her. Although I expect she was never so disagreeable to him. I don't think she ever really approved of me, as I've heard she had set her heart on his marrying the daughter of a dear friend of hers. I heard it said, in confidence, of course, that she thought I lacked sense."

"That was very unfair of her, Aunt Letitia. But she must be rather old now, surely? Unless she gave birth to your late husband at a very young age."

"My dear, she's ancient! Which is my only hope of escaping eventually. Not that I would wish her to die, poor old lady," Letitia Bradshaw murmured, "but she must be ninety if she's a day, and perhaps it would be a blessed release, to look on the positive side."

"We should certainly do so," Anne agreed gravely, amused in spite of her worry about the previous night's adventure.

"But enough of that tedious subject. The dancing master is coming today. And I think you should wear your old ball gown, for the benefit of learning the steps while you are wearing a hoop. And by the way, Anne, my love, you must not mention giving birth. Unless you are doing so yourself, or at least are enceinte, and must discuss the subject with your husband or doctor or a close female friend. Did your governess not teach you these things? "

"No, Aunt. I had a nanny, but she left when I was quite young, and Dr. Sinclair must not have felt a governess was necessary."

"No, he wouldn't," his sister agreed. "He had no sense in some ways. I don't believe Marianne had one after she was fifteen. When hers left to keep house for her ailing sister, James said there was no need for another, as Marianne had probably learned as much as she was likely to do. She had, I'm sure, for she was not of a bookish nature, but that was not the point, and so I told him. They were living in London at the time, where a girl needs a governess as a chaperon."

"Won't a maid do as well?" Anne asked. "I thought a maid was an acceptable chaperon."

"For married ladies or older ladies, and for young girls with good sense, like you," said Mistress Bradshaw with a fond smile. "But a silly or headstrong girl needs a stronger-minded chaperon than a maid who is very likely no older than her mistress, and just as silly. Of course, I know I need have no concern that you would do something indiscreet anyway, and Sally is a sensible girl, too."

****

In the afternoon, Anne found she had rather too much time to think as she sat with Letitia.

"How intently you bend over that embroidery," the latter remarked. "Such a posture cannot be good for you. A young lady doing some pretty, ornamental stitching is an attractive sight, but one must keep a straight back to achieve the effect. Are you making good progress at it?"

"No," said Anne, baldly. "I am not clever with my needle." She meant to add that she could think of half a dozen things to do with her time which were improving and entertaining, but she had no opportunity. The butler announced Mistress Waller and her daughter and niece.

Aunt Letitia greeted Mistress Waller as an old friend.

"I fancy you have not seen Charlotte these half dozen years, Letitia. And this is my niece, Eugenia Giddings, up from the country to stay with us, while her parents are on the Continent." The older ladies soon put their heads together, leaving Anne and the two girls to make slightly awkward conversation. Charlotte was no more than seventeen and seemed younger. As Anne recalled, at that age, she had already been helping her grandfather with his patients. Charlotte seemed to have no interests beyond clothing and the beaux she expected to have after she was presented to society the following year.

"My mama means to present me next spring because my older sister's wedding was in May," Charlotte confided. "I didn't want to wait, but Mama was too busy to think about my coming out. My sister's new husband is a baronet and has an extensive manor. It is in Northumberland, however," she added in a flattened tone. "I suppose you must already be out."

"In the sense of being out of the schoolroom and going about in society in my own village, yes. But as yet I have attended no balls or assemblies or events here in town. I only recently came to stay with Mistress Bradshaw, and she wished to give me time to grow accustomed. Her niece has offered to chaperon me, as she has a daughter ready to make her debut."

Eugenia, whom Anne had disliked almost on sight, was listening with a slight, condescending smirk. She was of an age to have come out two or even three years since, but since she was unmarried, Anne thought that she had little reason for complacency.

Mistress Eugenia deigned to say, "You will find London quite different from the society to which you are no doubt accustomed."

"So I have already noticed."

"Men here have far more polish. Those who stay buried in the country but for a month or two a year lack sophistication and have few interests outside their own manor."

"That does seem to be true," Anne agreed, remembering Fletching and Fletchingford.

"I hope by my counsel to save my cousin Charlotte from such a fate," Eugenia patted Charlotte's hand. "She is too innocent by half and lacks the daring necessary to attract the right sort of suitor, having been reared in strict propriety. One really cannot depend on one's family to choose a husband."

"The right sort of suitor?" For the first time Anne considered that Eugenia might know something useful.

"One who does not wish to spend his life in the country, and knows some form of enjoyment beyond the hunting field and shooting. If one wishes to move in the best society, and attend balls and routs and have a cicisbeo, one must live in town, which means a husband who is not a bumpkin. And such husbands are seldom to be found in the country, unless they have repaired thence to avoid a temporary financial embarrassment."

"A cicisbeo?"

"A fashionable married lady must have a follower or two, to be available as an escort when the lady's husband is not. It is all the rage to see and be seen at the opera, for example, but sometimes men—by which I mean husbands!—prefer to spend an evening playing cards with their friends, or visiting some female of obliging habits. So one has a gentleman friend who will pay one pretty compliments and be seen to be enchanted with one's company. This is not my first visit to London," she said, taking note of Anne's quizzical look. "Though I wish I were in Paris with my parents, for the fashionable world there is marvelous sophisticated."

"How does one attract a gentleman whose interest one wishes to engage?" Anne inquired. She had not yet met any man whose attentions she would welcome, but sooner or later…She had never learned the art of flirtation, which was, in any case, condemned by all moralists. And yet, she had seen young ladies in Fletchingford and Lincoln draw gentlemen as flies are attracted to honey. Presumably, after a time, they were trapped, like the flies.

She doubted she could emulate the subtler encouragements: the casting down of eyes, the play with the fan, the languishing glances. She certainly could not hang breathless and wide-eyed upon some man's every word. However, Eugenia was full of advice for furthering any promising relationship.

"Charlotte, before you come out, you must contrive to rid yourself of your maid. A London maid, if you get on good terms with her, can often be persuaded to lose herself when she should be acting as a chaperon."

Anne already knew that was true. However, she had not dispensed with Sally's chaperonage to be alone with a man. She had expected to meet a lady, and only did it surreptitiously in the hope of learning the secret which had troubled her guardian. Still, it had been foolish and had ended in potential disaster. And now, she reflected, she intended to meet Anniscote privately. But that was quite different: it would be in a public place, after all.

She ventured, "But how can a gentleman respect a lady who is so lacking in modesty?"

"La, Mistress Anne," Eugenia trilled. "How can one let him know he is favored, but by such shifts? If one is stiff and proper, he will have no encouragement to pay one court."

Anne recalled that the requirement for a girl not to show partiality for a man until he declared himself had been a theme in *Love in Excess*, as had conniving maids. She was unable to feel that events in that novel had turned out well, as both the scheming young ladies had come to unsatisfactory ends, leaving the rake, ultimately, to marry a virtuous girl who should have had better sense.

"Surely it is for one's father or guardian to arrange these matters…?" Charlotte ventured.

"Oh, back in the Middle Ages, no doubt. But if one is to get a husband who is not dull, one must exert oneself."

"Although, if one should find oneself married to a boring or inattentive man, all is not lost," she continued. "In the best society, these things are understood. A married man may have a mistress, or visit houses of pleasure, or spend his evenings drinking and gambling, and a married woman may take a lover."

"But…"

Anne said, "I know nothing of the manners and behavior prevailing in London society. But an unmarried girl who dispenses with her chaperon so that she can meet a man alone runs the risk of losing her reputation or her virtue, and I believe that men cannot be counted upon to marry a girl who has lost either."

"Oh, these matters are concealed every day in the best families in the country." Eugenia shrugged.

"Not if the young woman gets with child—or the French pox," Anne retorted.

That silenced Eugenia, and Charlotte gasped, her eyes as big and round as shillings. After a moment she ventured, "I don't know about…about the pox…but a young lady near our home in Wiltshire suddenly went to visit some relation in Northumberland for months. A relation no one had mentioned previously," she added. "She had always been known as a very forward girl, and so it was whispered that she had to go away to have a baby. And when she came back, the young men who had fancied her before no longer paid her any notice. Eventually, she went to live in another part of the country."

Then Eugenia asked Anne how long she meant to stay in town, and the conversation drifted into more conventional channels.

Chapter 18

The duke was already browsing the shelves when Anne slipped into the book shop. The shop's owner, at the far end of the long, narrow space, gave her a slight bow and continued writing in a ledger, well aware that many of his clientele preferred to shop without assistance. Anniscote, having heard her enter, turned and made her a far more elaborate bow, before turning back to the wall of shelves. Anne went to stand beside him, automatically reading the titles on the books on the shelf at her eye level.

"I hope all is well at your aunt's, Mistress Anne?"

"Yes, thank goodness. No one noticed anything. Did you learn anything about"—she hesitated over choosing a word—"the other matter?"

"I did, or rather, my man did. I sent him for my hat and rocquelaure. Had I gone myself, it would have called attention to the circumstances of our leaving. And the inmates of that house would not have spoken so freely."

"Can he be trusted?"

"Mulley likes being valet to a duke. He could not, of course, ask very pointed questions. What he did learn is that Prissy is the daughter of the proprietor—he saw her there, and learned her name from the kitchen porter, pretending to admire her figure. Mulley is a sly fellow," Anniscote commented. "On explaining his errand, he made some remark about the quality's careless ways. The footman laughed and said, 'Careless wasn't the half of it. First there's some d—d nonsense about getting the gentry mort to the house to meet her spark, then when the cully does show his face, they only stay to order wine, then shab off, and the…' I beg your pardon, Mistress Anne, I'm quoting Mulley's account of what the man said, which I found diverting, but I should certainly not repeat it to you without editing it."

"I would suppose the end of his remark was 'the bed not even used.' " She might safely have made the remark to her grandfather, but she should not have done so to anyone else, she realized too late.

Anniscote's eyebrows shot up. "You really must not say such things. It would lead people to think you were loose in your morals. Although," he added, "you are correct. He also said, 'They've got money to toss away, hiring the room and leaving half a pound for the drink, and not hardly using neither and the cully leaving his cloak and hat, too.' "

"I'm sorry you should have been put to such expense," Anne said, feeling her face grow warm.

"I am out nothing but what I left for the refreshments and the douceur which I hoped would dispose the maid not to chatter about us."

"And that horrid Hurst?"

"I have not yet encountered him. When I do, I shall know whether he will be a problem; if he seems like to be, I can deal with him. But whoever wrote you that letter is the real danger to you. Have you any admirer who is perhaps coveted by some other lady?"

Anne gave a little chuckle. "I? No, for I came to London to try if I could get a husband, and as yet I have met no one. Except you," she added.

Anniscote said severely, "I believe I have never heard a young lady admit to seeking a husband. It is not at all the thing, you know."

"Even though everyone knows that almost all young ladies and wenches, too, are hopeful of marrying?"

"Everyone knows it, but it is not discussed, unless perhaps by the young ladies and their mamas. There is a polite fiction that young men do the pursuing. You make it sound like a hunt. With the lady as the huntress."

"But we all know that it is necessary for the lady to take some action to attract the right man. Further, there is classical authority of a sort. The Greek goddess Diana was a huntress. I suppose one might consider the maenads as huntresses, also. Not that I would wish to be considered a maenad." This was a most improper conversation, Anne knew, but could not resist the temptation to bait the duke a little.

"Particularly as they tore their prey apart. When you have been brought into society, Mistress Anne, you will either become a sensation or succeed in wrecking your reputation yourself."

"Why, because I am honest?"

The duke slid the volume of poetry he had been perusing back onto the shelf. "Honesty is generally a virtue not appreciated in society, where it is accounted at best tactless. Society prefers to have a good opinion of itself, and not to be brought face to face with its errors and sins."

"That is remarkably cynical," Anne said, though not in a critical spirit. "My grandfather might have said something like that."

'Did your grandfather have charge of your upbringing?"

"From my infancy."

"That explains much. But we have wandered far from the topic. Have you no idea at all who might hate you or fear you enough to attempt your undoing?"

"None at all. Why should anyone hate or fear me? I am not the least dangerous."

"Except for your tongue, perhaps. I have not had much time to think upon it yet. And there are one or two other lines of inquiry I could pursue."

"It is very good in you to try to help me, but I can't think why you should trouble yourself over my affairs."

"My dear Mistress Anne, it is partly my affair, also. Someone involved me in it. I regard it as a personal affront, an attempt to smirch my honor. I can hardly overlook it."

"Oh! Of course. I'm sorry. I fear I was seeing it only from my own perspective."

"So I gathered. Before we part, we must decide how we are to communicate. We cannot be meeting here always and your maid—where is your maid?"

"I told my aunt I needed one or two things to go with my new gowns. Sally is choosing them. She has a better eye for fashion than I and is happy to be given the responsibility while I come here."

"Do not make a habit of going around without your maid. Especially under the circumstances. Is there a possibility I might have known your grandfather?"

"He almost never travelled after I came to live with him, although he spent nigh upon a year on the Continent before that time. You must have been a child then. But he corresponded with a great many people. Some were old school friends of his, but a number were scientific men. If you take any interest in science or the arts or history, you might have…well, not met him, but written to him. He would have written back. I wrote to any number of his friends and correspondents, to let them know of his death."

"That is very good. You wrote to me to advise me of the sad event. Naturally I will come to call upon you now you are in town. When I do, remember we have never met before."

"That is well thought of, Your Grace. It is a perfectly respectable way to meet, but how are we to communicate in my aunt's presence?"

"After the first time, I will bring a book for you, knowing you to be a very learned young lady. There will be a note inside. If it is a book of history or science, I suppose your aunt will not open it?"

"No. Even if it were a novel, it would be quite safe, as her sight is very bad. I or her maid read to her."

"Well enough, then. I trust you will take care not to go out without either your maid or your aunt or someone your aunt trusts. I will make it a point to pay my respects in a few days."

****

"Anne, dear," Aunt Letitia said, as Anne entered her aunt's boudoir. "Mistress Waller called upon me while you were out shopping. Whatever did you say to Charlotte and Eugenia?"

Before the question was out, Anne knew, with a sinking sensation, what prompted it. It was not as if she had not been warned repeatedly about the freedom of her speech. Mortification robbed her temporarily of the power of speech.

"Why…we discussed…that is…"

"I inquire because Charlotte asked Blanche Waller about the French pox. She claimed you had mentioned it, and Eugenia confirmed it. Not that I would trust that girl not to lie, but I don't think Charlotte would. Which makes me think you must have said something, quite innocently, of course, because you do come out with the most startling things sometimes." Aunt Letitia peered at her, in the manner of a small bird studying an object which may be edible—or not.

The culprit wondered whether she had any duty to shield Eugenia and decided she did not. "Eugenia was giving her cousin advice about how to encourage gentlemen and meet them privately, and then she said that a married lady might take a lover, if she was bored with her husband. It seemed wrong to me to let Charlotte think such behavior was acceptable, which even I know it isn't, so I…ummmm…pointed out the risks of such actions."

"French pox," Aunt Letitia murmured. "And…?"

"Pregnancy, of course," Anne agreed. "And I wasn't inventing the dangers, though I feel sure that Eugenia was talking nonsense when she claimed that losing one's reputation or taking a lover was without consequences."

Mistress Bradshaw sighed deeply.

"Some women, for I will not call them ladies, do cast decency to the winds," she said. "Sometimes at house parties when I was young, we all knew Lady This and Mr. That were…never mind. Sometimes these things are ignored, if conducted discreetly, and if the husband is either oblivious or does not care, which I must say, I would consider very insulting. But one cannot count upon its being condoned, and the penalty can be very high. And certainly no unmarried lady can afford to ignore the possible consequences."

"Yes, that is what I thought. That's why I mentioned the pox and pregnancy."

"I understand your reasoning, dear. To be sure, it may seem only sensible to caution girls, many of whom—most of whom!—know nothing of such things. But it is generally held that the less a girl knows, the better. For if she begins to think of such matters, she may begin to be curious, or she may show that she knows more than is appropriate, if she chances to hear an indiscreet word, which would make her appear less innocent than she is. It would have been acceptable to say to Charlotte that such behavior is not safe and is ruinous to the reputation, as well as being immoral, but not to explain why. I told Blanche that it was all James's fault for having neglected to provide you with a governess and for failing to censor his words when you were present. I trust she will not spread the tale, which would certainly rebound upon Charlotte and Eugenia as well as you."

"I'm sorry, Aunt Letitia. I will try to think before I speak in the future."

Aunt Letitia gave her a mock-stern glance and said, "I should try to impress your folly on you, but I'm convinced you are aware of it—now that I've brought it to your attention. But oh, you remind me so of James. The things he used to say!" And she laughed a little.

Chapter 19

The duke's bookroom was pleasantly warmed by the fire on the hearth, for it was a chilly, damp afternoon. After considering all that Mulley had told him, he was at a standstill. The most important fact was that Prissy was connected with the Cantwell establishment. Indeed, that was the only fact they possessed, beyond the existence of a young woman who looked so much like Anne Sinclair. Of course, similarity in height, figure, and hair color, wearing their hair in the popular style, and dressing in whatever sort of gown was favored in their level of society could lend a resemblance to many young women.

No, by God! It was more than an apparent similarity between Mistress Anne and the "Fair Unknown." When he considered it, they had not been attired alike. Anne dressed like a dowdy up from the country. Her reddish-brown hair was worn in a fashionable but simple style (the only fashionable thing about her; it argued a skillful maid). The other gowned herself in the height of fashion. Anne's eyes were gray, the minx's were blue. However, the shape of their faces and their noses and chins were amazingly alike, enough to be related. That might be a thread worth following. If she had been left in Dr. Sinclair's guardianship, she must have no near family. He would have to ask her about her family with more particularity. And the existence of the wench who looked like Anne and the plot to ruin her could not be coincidental. But no other insight followed that thought. Anniscote picked up the old book and opened it.

Don Diego: To accustom myself to English country life was hard at first, but it was eased by the tenants' regard for my wife. Also, at court I had learned to suppress my pride so as to avoid giving offense to the English. I came to realize that it was founded on belonging to an ancient and honored family, which was no doing of my own. I was well-educated, reasonably skilled with arms, and not ill-looking, but so were many other men. I had no cause to think myself much out of the common way.

Interpolation by Charles Anascote: I marveled at this, as my father was a proud, reticent man, who seldom spoke of himself. My father smiled a little, seeing he had struck me speechless which was not usual for me, and for which he had often rebuked me, very justly. We had heard, as a cradle tale, that he met my mother and fell in love with her, although she was not a great beauty (being somewhat scarred by the smallpox), but as we grew up, we all supposed that he had given up impoverished nobility in Spain in favor of a comfortable living in England. It was a sensible marriage: her portion was small but included a tidy manor, in spite of which she could not easily have made a good marriage because of her face, and perhaps because of her extreme shyness as well. But we children loved her dearly, and my father often praised her for her modesty and discretion and treated her with great kindness. I know he was deeply saddened when she died a few years since.

My father continued: I found myself faced with a dilemma. I must remain in England, and on Queen Mary's death, her half-sister, Elizabeth, became Queen of England. Our new Queen being of the Protestant persuasion, we had all to conform to the English church's doctrine. My lady wept and pleaded that we should continue to practice what we had been taught to think the True Faith, even if we had to do so in secret. I can recall no other occasion on which she so vigorously opposed my will. Finally, in spite of my shame, I told her why I had come to England. Before my birth, Queen Isabella and King Ferdinand forced the Moors remaining in Spain to convert or depart, and the Jews also. Still, however devoutly they practiced our faith, they and their children were always under suspicion. When I was young—before the rumors of my mother's mixed blood began—these things seemed reasonable to me, both the mass conversions and the subsequent doubt. And now this new religion in England has done the same to those of the True Faith and the most extreme Protestants as well. It might be that the English would hold my former beliefs against me, as well as my being a Spaniard, or it might not.

I do not know whether it was wifely loyalty, her own good heart, or perhaps only that she was English rather than Spanish, but when she had heard me out, she exclaimed, "But you cannot help who your ancestors were! And in any case, our Savior was a Jew, wasn't he?" I looked afresh at my little sparrow of a wife, with her disfigured face, and realized that God— or perhaps the Blessed Virgin—had sent me a better wife than I deserved. And she gave way on the question of our religious practice, whatever her private prayers may have been.

Giving up the religion of my birth pained me, but by the time my sons attained manhood, the matter might be forgotten, a thing more likely in England than in Spain, where memories are long. And I have no enemies or rivals to profit by my fall, as our house and lands are small, though with the money my brother had supplied me, I had bought a fine manor ("of sticks and mud," as one Spaniard described the new English style of building) at a far remove from the court, and let it at a reasonable rent, through an agent. My lady and I lived in the old stone-walled manor house which was her portion, and if it did not have as many sparkling diamond-paned windows or as much oak paneling as my property, it was very comfortable by reason of long occupation and my wife's housewifely skills. Thus I did not appear to be worth plucking. And I saw to it you were raised to be English, and I believe it has answered well.

Now you have rendered assistance to England, and Her Majesty has rewarded you by making you Earl of Helter. I trust you will continue to deserve her favor.

Anniscote closed the book gently, put it aside, and went to the bell pull to summon Mulley. When his man appeared and the door closed, the duke said, "I would like to know a great deal more about the Cantwell enterprise than either you or I are able to learn. Have I a servant with wit who might be willing to undertake a task outside his own duties? And discreet, of course?"

"As it happens, Your Grace, the most junior footman is my cousin's son. Matthew is a coming lad, but there was no money to apprentice him suitably, so when many of Your Grace's staff were replaced, I took the liberty of speaking to Mr. Peters on his behalf."

"Then I will leave it to you to sound him out, to see if he would be willing."

"What is the task you had in mind, sir?"

"It might be useful to have Matthew become familiar with the staff at Cantwell's. The Cantwells themselves may be close-mouthed, but surely not all of the servants belong to the family. I confess I have no idea how he might scrape acquaintance with them, but perhaps you can suggest something."

"Matthew will think of something," Mulley said.

Chapter 20

Anne found her aunt very busy at her writing desk, and the tranquility of the house broken by servants bustling about on various tasks.

"Oh, Anne, I've had such a good idea. Come sit with me and help me plan it."

Anne was very willing to do so.

"I received a letter from Marianne this morning. She does not feel Mariah is regaining her bloom as quickly as she hoped, and has decided to take her to Bath, to try if a course of the water there will serve. So I think I really must begin to introduce you to my friends. I have decided to give a little dinner party. While all are older couples, except for young Mr. Hodgehead, Mrs. Reeves and Mrs. Snow and the judge's wife will invite us to dinner or some entertainment, and so you will meet other young people. The Merrills may possibly have some young relatives, but I invited them chiefly because they are old friends and play whist well. There will be cards afterward for those who like to play. Do you play, Anne?"

"No, Dr. Sinclair did not greatly care for card games, though he played when we went out to dinner at the Squire's, where that was the usual entertainment. I play very badly, I'm afraid."

"Then you shall play the harpsichord or sing, or

both, of course, to entertain the ones who do not play. Perhaps some of your new gowns will be ready."

"I am sorry, Aunt Letitia, but I can't play the harpsichord. Or sing, either, except hymns and a few old tunes. And those not well."

"No matter. This dinner is by way of introducing you gradually into society. Fortunately you have a very easy flow of conversation, which is always helpful." She added in an unusually acerbic tone, "I am quite out of patience with Marianne. It would have been so easy for her to introduce you, for Mariah has a vast number of young friends. And she could have taken you to Bath, to bear Mariah company while she recovers, for it is not as though she had a disease, like smallpox. I am sure she is merely tired from so many late nights and activities."

****

The dinner was not an unqualified success. Aunt Letitia had invited her late husband's cousin, an old, rather deaf bachelor, to act as host, and the rest of the party consisted of Judge Hodgehead, his wife and son, two attorneys and their wives, and Mr. and Mrs. Merrill, an elderly couple. "I do not expect that you and young Mr. Hodgehead will find each other's company enthralling," Letitia sighed as they prepared for their guests' arrival. "The judge has molded his son into a pattern of propriety and thereby removed any vestige of spontaneity or gaiety. You will terrify him, and I hope you will not express any of the opinions you learned from dear James, as we do not wish to give the judge a bad opinion of you. Or an apoplexy," she added. "That would end the dinner on such an awkward note, wouldn't it?"

Anne felt she was behaving with great circumspection, until, fatally, someone remarked on having been delayed the previous day by the crowd at the hanging of a thief.

"One must be willing to tolerate some inconvenience for the sake of justice," the judge said.

"I had not thought of it in that light," Mr. Snow said. "You are correct, sir, of course."

"It seems barbarous to treat a hanging as a...an entertainment," Anne said.

"The poor have little enough amusement," the other lawyer replied.

"I regard it as the majesty of the law made manifest, and a deterrent to those who may consider turning to crime." The judge drank from his glass before adding, "Although I do feel that the execution of highwaymen should be carried out within the prison, not in public. They are often treated as heroes by the mob, if they go to their death with dignity or a jest upon their lips."

"This is very distressing conversation for the dinner table," the judge's wife said timidly. "Mistress Anne will get a sad notion of London life."

"We must not permit it," the older attorney, Reeves, said. "I hope she will bear in mind that the law, though it may seem harsh, has been much mitigated and is tempered with mercy. The thief's young helper, who crept into the house through a small window to let him in by the door, was pardoned. To hang a lad of ten would be almost unthinkable. It has been half a century since the last execution for witchcraft took place, and several years since, witchcraft ceased to be a crime. The law has made great strides, this century."

"But it is still a crime to be a gypsy, is it not? And how can one be held responsible for who one's parents are?" Anne asked.

"It's not the fact of being born a gypsy," the judge said, "but the refusal to settle in one place and do honest work. To be a vagabond and live by theft and frauds perpetrated upon the public—"

Young Mr. Hodgehead interrupted his father, a transgression Anne felt certain he would pay for later.

"Yes, but there are other terrible injustices. Burning is the penalty for a woman who murders her husband. Surely it would be enough to hang such a female."

"Peter!" his mother snapped, "that is quite enough."

"Do not speak of what you do not understand. The law is just. If it were not, it would have been changed."

Though the only ones who could change the law were those who benefited from its harshness, as no women sat in Parliament. Anne thought that if she were the judge's wife, she might be tempted to risk it…she would simply have to be very careful not to be suspected. She gave Mr. Hodgehead a slight smile, by way of approval.

After the gentlemen finished their port and rejoined the ladies in the drawing room, the judge, Aunt Letitia's cousin-in-law, Mr. Reeves, and Mr. Merrill formed one table and played ombre and Mistresses Reeves, Snow, and Merrill and Aunt Letitia played whist. This left young Mr. Hodgehead, Mistress Hodgehead, Mr. Snow, and Anne to converse. Mistress Hodgehead kept darting imploring glances at her son, who showed signs of casting off his father's direful influence and speaking in a very bold manner.

"Do you intend to follow a career in the law also?" Anne asked him.

"Yes. After I finish at Cambridge, I will be clerking with one of my father's old friends. But eventually I mean to enter politics."

"My dear!" Mrs. Hodgehead expostulated.

"I do. I would be a very bad judge, but I might help to make better laws."

Overhearing this, the Judge interposed from his table, "Such laws as you would support spoil the rabble. We have seen what happens when the lower classes take the bit in their mouths. Without firm governance, we would have chaos."

Anne supposed that the judge had had a great deal to say to his son on their arrival at home, and she did not escape a mild scold from Aunt Letitia. "Ladies— young ladies in particular—should not express strong opinions. Not that yours were unreasonable, and of course you couldn't have known that the judge would have such strong views himself, although you might have supposed it, as he is a judge. Not but what I think it a great shame to hold executions in public because it does block the streets and sometimes there are riots. But all the same...oh, I've lost the thread of my thought. But you must confine your remarks to things which are not controversial and will not set people against you."

This must be what the duke had meant by his remarks about society disliking honesty.

****

When the butler announced the Duke of Guysbridge, Aunt Letitia went into a flutter which hardly subsided until refreshments had been brought.

She must, Anne supposed, have come into contact with a duke or two before her marriage, having been the daughter of an earl, but the intervening years having been dukeless, she had evidently lost the habit of consorting with them. Anne herself was perfectly at ease.

"…and so, as I did not know if Mistress Anne was yet in residence here, I thought I had best see you in person, rather than simply leaving my card, as you could not have known I was acquainted with Dr. Sinclair. And Mistress Anne I know only from the letter she sent to inform me of his death."

He was looking very elegant and even quite friendly, in a proud, austere fashion.

"It is so good of you to call," Aunt Letitia quavered. "So kind. My brother had many friends, although he saw them seldom, buried in the country as he was. That is…well, you know what I mean, even if it sounded a little odd, sir. And I am afraid you may think it a little peculiar that Anne has put off mourning—not that she ever—oh, dear, I hardly know what I am saying. Pray forgive me."

"I understand, Mrs. Bradshaw. I fancy I know Dr. Sinclair's opinion of mourning clothes."

The surprising thing was that he probably did know, though how he could, Anne had no idea. In spite of his criticism of her free speaking, he did not appear to suffer from excessive conventionality himself.

The visit was short, as good manners required, and, as expected, Aunt Letitia pressed him to visit again.

"And Her Grace would be very welcome, too, of course."

"My sister-in-law is at Guysbridge, still in

mourning. When she comes up to town, I will bring her to call upon you."

After he had departed, Aunt Letitia exclaimed, "To think of a duke coming to see you! It is an excellent thing, Anne, for you may be sure word will get around, and his condescending to pay a call on you will do no harm. It is a shame, I admit, that society values a plain, worthy gentleman less than a rather rackety nobleman, but so it is and we must resign ourselves to it. Although he seemed respectable enough. Perhaps it was not Guysbridge who was rumored to be a…well, an unsatisfactory example."

"A rake, you mean, Aunt?"

"If you must know, that is what I had heard. A very deep gambler, too. Although," she added, brightening, "as he only recently came into the title, perhaps it was his brother who was the rakeshame. Not that you should be talking of such things, dear. And how fortunate that he is not married!"

Anne, who had taken a sip of tea, choked. "Aunt Letitia! Really, you are refining too much on a simple courtesy visit. If you mean what I think you mean."

"Yes, I fear so, for a duke will be the target of every matchmaking mother in London and out. Besides which, he may look as high as he pleases for a wife and will probably want one from a noble house. It is too much to hope for, so you mustn't be thinking of it and turning up your nose at some decent young attorney or merchant, or plain country gentleman, if you should be so fortunate as to attach one."

"Ma'am, I am not hoping for an offer from the duke, I assure you. And I would not marry him if he did make me an offer," Anne retorted.

"Whyever not? His manners were pleasant, and while I could not see his features clearly, he seemed well set up, and I particularly noticed that his movements were graceful. Granted, his face appeared somewhat swarthy, but his coat was a suitable color and complemented his complexion. Of course, you have only met him, so you have not had time to form a partiality, but that's no cause for such vehemence. You aren't thinking him too old, I hope. I take him to be about thirty years of age."

"It never crossed my mind to think of him as a possible husband." As her aunt did not know of their earlier meetings, she could not be aware that Anne considered him rakish, haughty, censorious…if he had helped her out of a very bad situation, it was only because it reflected on his own honor.

"Then it should have," her aunt said briskly. "Any unmarried gentleman, unless he is poor, or too much a rakehell, or has insanity in his family, is to be considered a prospect. Men will have their affaires, and as long as they are not blatant, and they do not spend excessive amounts of money on their *petites amies*, a prudent woman will ignore them. And His Grace has much to recommend him. What a pity he will probably insist on a lady from a noble or wealthy family."

Chapter 21

Calling on Jeffreys, the duke found him refolding a letter. Jeffreys looked a little embarrassed and tucked it into his pocket.

"A love letter, apparently," Anniscote murmured, raising his eyebrows.

"No, no! Not at all. It's just…just…"

"An invitation to play cards, no doubt. And you such an enthusiastic gamester that you have colored up for sheer excitement."

Jeffreys laughed. "Enough, John! If you will know, Her Grace wrote to me."

"Oh, ay?"

"It must seem very strange," Jeffreys said hurriedly. "I wrote to her expressing my gratitude for her hospitality so soon after her bereavement when we stayed there after your brother's death, of course."

"And she took so long to acknowledge your letter?" the duke inquired gently. "Tsk-tsk. How inattentive to her correspondence she must be."

"No, not at all. She responded in a reasonable period after, and…ah…"

"Jeffreys! Can you have been carrying on a clandestine correspondence with my widowed sister-in-law? For shame!" Anniscote exclaimed, and burst into laughter at the guilty expression on his friend's face. "I'm roasting you. I do recall you seemed quite taken with Elspat."

"I wrote to her, as I said, and she replied, and her letter was as charming as she, and I wrote in response."

"And then she wrote again, no doubt."

"Yes. If you have no objection?"

"None at all, if you feel inclined to court her. I'm not her papa, and she is of age. Only I trust, if she is willing to exchange a title for a plain 'Mrs.,' you will wait until she is out of mourning."

"Faith, yes! To do otherwise would be outrageous."

"I would not be put about by it, but the decencies ought to be preserved when possible. My own house has such a reputation as could hardly be damaged, but she comes of stock which values the proprieties. You and she should suit admirably."

"I hope she may think so, when it is appropriate for me to address her upon the subject. You are correct, I found her delightful when we were at Guysbridge. And then, when she wrote to me—I would I could write such letters as Els...as Her Grace does. It is yet another of her attractions that she can describe the most commonplace daily activities and imbue them with humor and interest."

"Tom, I fear you are deep in love."

"I confess 'tis true. And how she has borne up under blows which must have cast most ladies into despair, I do not know."

"Marrying my brother being chief among them, no doubt."

"You might think so, but her life was not easy before. Mind you, I know it only by the most oblique references. Her father seems to have had little interest in her until the second of his sons died. The first ran away to sea, but his father, though vexed, did not think the worse of him for it. Rather, he boasted of the boy defying his father's plans to raise him to be a gentleman. The second son obligingly finished at Harrow and attended Oxford, and was bidding fair to appear to be a gentleman and a credit to his family but was carried off by some ailment. Then the first son was killed in some shipboard accident."

"Neither with a son?"

"Alack, no. Elspat's father must not even have waited until he was out of mourning before he married a girl younger than his daughter. Hoping to beget another son or two, you know."

"I suppose it is understandable." The duke felt little interest in his sister-in-law's family.

"Elspat spent much of her childhood in a ladies' academy, and after being released from school, acted as her father's hostess until her new young stepmama stepped into her place. The bride then died in childbed and the babe with her. So nothing would do but to marry Elspat to a nobleman, the higher the better. And of course, it had to be one who was…"

"In need of any wife who would bring him a great deal of money," Anniscote finished. "Tact is not required. Not from you, anyway. You know how it was with my brother. With our family. And my poor sister-in-law was willing to marry Nick?"

"I think," Jeffreys said carefully, "that her father veritably forced her into the marriage. He must be devilish unpleasant, although she doesn't say so, of course."

"But since your hearts beat as one, you understand each other," the duke said, smiling a trifle cynically.

142

"No, it's not that—damn you, John! You make me sound like a smitten boy! No, it's not what she said. It's what she did not say. I complained of my father at times, when I was a lad, and that in spite of respecting him. I don't quite know how to explain it."

"I think I know what you mean. From things you have mentioned, I know your father is painstaking as a landowner and a magistrate, and can be relied upon for good advice and common sense. I felicitate you, Tom. I gather the courtship prospers?"

"It's hardly a courtship yet, given that she's in mourning. But I dare to hope that when the year is over, she will look upon my offer favorably. Have you given any thought to making some lady your duchess? You are now an eligible *parti,* whatever your reputation. I would present my younger sister for your inspection, but she is already betrothed to a very fine young man. She's too young for you anyway."

"I thank you for the thought, but it would be a shame to marry your sister to a rakehell like me. But I suppose I must get myself some young lady of decent birth, behavior, and dowry, not given to extravagance or tempers, who will take no notice of my activities, and provide me an heir or two."

"It sounds devilish boring. I want something more: a little vivacity and warmth and a passably pretty face." After a moment's thought, Tom added, "And under no circumstances a silly woman, which would be tiresome. As you have less patience than I do, I would counsel that you choose one who's not a fool."

"My family tree is already littered with clever, free-spending, shrewish women." With the exception, he supposed, of Don Diego's Lady Mary. Well, one exception in a hundred and fifty years hardly disproved the rule. "Lively manners are permissible in a mistress, but the devil in a wife. No, I am of Hurst's mind in this, if nothing else: give me a wife who's all propriety and silent, too."

"Have you never laid your heart at a lady's feet? I know I was in love several times when I was younger."

Anniscote grinned. "Speaks the graybeard! You're two years younger than I. But oddly enough, I have been in love. Once. My beating heart lay before her, rather like Sir Walter Raleigh's cloak before Queen Elizabeth, and it suffered the cloak's fate. Pardon me, I am inaccurate. The young lady herself did not tread upon it. When I applied to her father for her hand—he was an earl, but the earldom went back only two generations, I think, or possibly three—he told me that if he were willing to bestow his daughter in marriage on any man of so decayed and corrupt a house as ours, it would be to my brother, who at least was a duke and had a manor. He then went on to say that given our family history and proclivities, he would rather see Frances in her coffin than wedded to either of us."

Jeffreys winced. "How rude of him."

"Of course, at that time, my brother had not yet married little Elspat and recouped our fortune. Now, I dare say, our history and proclivities may not be so insurmountable an object."

"Is Lady Frances—"

"Married to a respectable marquess, these last ten years. Thank God! Belike I'd find her insipid now. These boyhood passions don't last."

"I feel differently about Her Grace than I did about the girls I fancied I loved when I was a boy, which is only natural. Youths grow up, and so do their minds and hearts. I hope you may be lucky enough to find some lady for whom you can feel some warmth, at least."

"I'm lucky at cards. I can scarce expect love as well."

"Lucky at cards, unlucky at love? Why not both?" Tom Jeffreys asked.

"What need of love? Do love matches turn out better than the other kind? I have not observed it to be so. I have not brought my mistress to live in the same house with my wife—not that I have one—as my grandfather is said to have done, and had his by-blows educated in the same schoolroom, too. I have not blown my brains out for love of a Covent Garden orange girl, as my uncle Edmond did, if you hadn't heard that pretty tale. He was unlucky at cards, as well, which gives the lie to your adage. But I disapprove of love matches only for myself. I trust you and Her Grace will be very happy. Well! I came to suggest we visit the *salle d'armes* and take a little exercise."

"I would be heartily glad of some sport. Do you intend to call someone out?"

"How blunt you are, my dear fellow. I hope it need not come to that."

"Best to be in practice, I suppose."

Chapter 22

"The weather is so pleasant I've a mind to take you to St. James's Mall to walk," Aunt Letitia said. "This is the first day I've really felt that it might be summer. If you agree, I will have Mayhew send for the chaise." Anne pronounced herself very pleased to go out for some exercise although she suspected her idea of a walk and her aunt's might be quite different things.

"Don't stare," Aunt Letitia hissed, when the chaise set them down at one end of the Mall. "You will look like some country cousin."

"But I am, ma'am. Do look at that amazing headdress. She must surely be a duchess or a marchioness at least."

"More likely a lady's maid—or housekeeper. No, don't acknowledge that young sprig's bow—he's probably no more than a clerk."

"But he's so well dressed."

"To make a showing, a young man in trade, or a young woman who wishes to dress above her station, can buy clothing a gentleman or lady has given a valet or maid, which the servant then sells. No valet could wear such a waistcoat. You must not seem to attract such upstarts, Anne."

"Oh!"

"Now, over there, in the sea-green coat, is a real marquess. A friend pointed him out to me at the theatre once, and I remembered him."

"I should think you might, Aunt Letitia. He has the face of a weasel. And is almost as tall."

"My dear!" Aunt Letitia exclaimed, smothering laughter. "Please don't say such things. Though, to be sure, he does look like one. Or a stoat."

"Of course, he may have a good heart, in which case, I'm truly sorry for judging on appearances."

"He doesn't. According to gossip."

The variety of folk on the Mall was amazing to Anne. They moved in eddies, like shoals of fish.

Two foreign-appearing gentlemen strolled past in the opposite direction, speaking French. When they were out of earshot, Anne laughed softly, and said to her aunt, "The one was describing to the other the freedom of Englishmen's conversation over the port, after the ladies have left the table. He said that the jests and stories were such as would be thought grossly indecent among men of similar status in France."

"I have always suspected as much," Aunt Letitia replied. "How fluent you must be in the French language! I caught a few words and phrases, but not enough to follow the conversation. Of course, my hearing is not as sharp as yours, and it is many, many years since I had occasion to speak the language. Rupert felt that foreign travel was too taxing for ladies, and of course he was busy with legal matters." She added reflectively, "I did enjoy visiting Paris as a girl before my betrothal. Our family used to have friends there. Poor Rupert did not care for travel and was not generally fond of foreigners."

"My French nanny only spoke French to me. After she left, Dr. Sinclair conversed with me in French almost every day and made sure I read books in French. And German, too."

"A French nanny! That is an original notion. Of course, James was an original, himself. Some prefer a Scotswoman, feeling that the usual sort of English nurses dote too much on their charges to discipline them."

One could not make that accusation of Mademoiselle Bardes, Anne reflected.

"I wonder how it came about that he engaged a Frenchwoman? Although I imagine he thought you would more readily learn the language if you began very young."

"That may well be true. And he taught me German, beginning when Mademoiselle Bardes left us."

"I wonder how he found her? He could have hired her when he was in France with Marianne. But no, he would not have known he would need a nanny, as he did not learn that you had been left an orphan until after his return. I am sure of that because he brought Marianne to live with me and went off to find a house in some town where he might set up a practice, then almost immediately wrote me that he was off to Scotland to fetch you."

"He could have placed an advertisement in the newspaper, I suppose. Aunt…would anyone else know of my parents and how Dr. Sinclair came to be my guardian? Would Mistress Saltstall remember anything from that time?"

"I suppose 'tis possible, although the young are often so wrapped up in their own concerns they do not take much interest in the affairs of anyone else. Also, she was rather worn down and low in spirits when they returned from the Continent. Perhaps my brother may have written her at greater length, but whether she would recall aught or kept his letters, I do not know. Why so curious about such ancient history?"

"I simply wondered. I have heard so little about my father and my mother. I don't know what they looked like, or how old they were when they died, or how they met. Until I came to town, I never gave it much thought, but now I begin to regret knowing nothing of my family."

"Was there nothing in James's papers?"

Anne caught her breath. "You are a marvel to think of that, Aunt Letitia. I have not gone through the documents from his office. When I cleared it out, papers which appeared to be essays or correspondence relating to scientific matters, I stored in the attic. His personal correspondence I kept but did not read."

"You say I am a marvel only because ordinarily I sound completely scatterbrained. James used to say that I wandered off on tangents—what is a tangent, by the way? I can never remember except that I knew what he meant, of course—because my thoughts outran my tongue. You could write the tenant of your house and ask him to have your servants send that box to you by freight wagon, if you can describe where you stored it."

"I have his personal letters with me. I brought them in my second trunk, with the books I particularly wanted with me and his medical equipment. Thank you, Aunt. When we get home, I will go through it and see what I can find."

****

Item: Fifteen letters from Mistress Marianne Saltstall to Dr. James Sinclair, containing nothing but descriptions of sights she had seen and balls and assemblies, though she wrote disparagingly of them as being small and attended only by men of law and business and their wives and offspring.

One sentence in the first letter, written not long after she came to live with Mistress Bradshaw caught Anne's eye:

"I hope all is well."

An unusual phrase, Anne thought. Most would write, "I hope everything is well with you," or "…that you are well." Most of Mistress Saltstall's correspondence was phrased as if they had been copied from some text on the writing of genteel letters. She might have left the awkwardly-worded part rather than cross it out or recopy the letter.

Item: Two letters relating to the purchase of the house in Fletching.

Both were directed to an inn near Lincoln.

Item: Twenty-eight letters from her grandfather's brothers and sister.

There must have been more, but evidently he had kept only those dealing with memorable family matters: betrothals and weddings, the birth of nieces and nephews, and the like.

Item: Six letters of condolence on the death of his father.

Item: Five letters from his wife, one dating from before their marriage.

Dr. Sinclair's wife seemed to have been an intelligent and kindly woman, which Anne supposed she might have guessed from the occasional references he had made to her.

Item: Ten letters of condolence on the death of his

wife.

Anne put down her quill and read through the list again, and disappointment washed over her.

There was no letter relating to Anne's mother's death or Dr. Sinclair's taking her in. She had been sure there would be something. It must not have been important enough to him to cause him to preserve it. She was tying up the bundles with ribbon when it occurred to her that he could not have destroyed her mother's letter to him, any more than he could have grown wings and flown. It might have been lost, or it might be among the other documents. She eyed the other pile, the one containing papers that looked more like business than family affairs.

When Sally came to tell her that tea was set out in the drawing room, she was ready to leave the project for a while. Only one thing of interest had come to light thus far: at the end of a letter from Dr. Sinclair's banker in London there was a paragraph of a more personal nature. "I do not know if you have heard of the recent Death of your late cousin Colin Sinclair's son, Captain Ewan Sinclair, which was followed by that of his Wife. I was only slightly acquainted with Captain Sinclair, who was a friend of my son Robert, but knowing he was related to you, and that you are currently travelling on the Continent, I thought it Right to mention this Sad circumstance. They are interred at Edinburgh." The letter was dated in April about a month before Anne's birthdate and had been sent to Mistress Bradshaw's address.

Anne went down to tea with a great deal on her mind.

When Aunt Letitia asked whether she had found

anything of interest in Dr. Sinclair's papers, Anne said slowly, "Not what I was hoping for. But I have not yet finished," she added, making an effort to sound more cheerful. Then she turned the conversation to the monstrous headdress they had noticed at St. James's Mall.

When a lull fell in their lively discussion of the way some women saw fit to garb themselves, Anne ventured, "I suppose when Dr. Sinclair and his daughter returned from their stay in Europe, it was to the chill and fogs of an English autumn." It was an awkward way to introduce the topic, but she needed to know.

"Why, no, dear, not at all. They returned in June. The weather was quite pleasant. I remember particularly because there were any number of things we might have done for amusement, like picnics and riding in the park, but Marianne was not in such blooming health as one might have wished, and would hardly leave her room for the first month or two. I blame it all on the foreign food. Some constitutions find it difficult of digestion. My Rupert suffered cruelly from it. But she improved quickly, though I think by the time she had regained her health, many people had gone to the country or the seashore or spas."

"Oh, I see," Anne said. Mr. Hale could not have written an April date on his letter, in error for June.

The only time she could recall her grandfather saying or doing something which had caused her a pang was when she was ten and he told her that she could not be a doctor. This was worse. Anne had thought that he had already been living in Fletching when he received a letter from her mother begging his assistance for her baby daughter. He had claimed to have travelled north immediately but been delayed by spring's muddy roads. But if Mr. Hale were correct, Dr. Sinclair had not yet returned to England when the death occurred. If her mother had written to him, why had he not kept the letter? He must have known it would be a cherished memento, Anne's sole connection to her. To learn now that he must have lied to her cut the ground from under her feet. Why would he lie? Everything about it was inconsistent with her knowledge of her adoptive grandfather.

She offered the best explanation that occurred to her for what might otherwise have seemed an odd question. "I would have wanted to spend the summer in France, even if it meant coming home to rain and cold. I have heard that France is lovely in the summer."

"Certainly the countryside is, but so is England, of course. And they'd been away for…oh, almost a year, I think, so very likely they had the pleasure of some summer weather there and were eager to come home."

Which led to a gently flowing monologue about the various places friends or connections of the Bradshaws and Sinclairs had visited and enjoyed, or disliked, or merely passed through on their way to someplace more interesting.

Later, alone in the bookroom, Anne took out a sheet of paper, dipped her quill into the inkwell and began to write.

Mr. Edward Hale
Child's & Co. Bank
Dear Mr. Hale:
I recently discovered while looking through my deceased guardian's, Dr. James Sinclair's, papers that in addition to being his banker, you were also a

personal friend…

Of course, Mr. Hale might be dead. It had been over twenty years, and there was no way of knowing whether he had been middle-aged or even old at the time of his letter. If he was alive, he might be offended by her suggestion that she call upon him, although she had hinted that there was estate business involved.

****

"Thank you for calling upon me, Mistress Anne. I do not go out much these days. Neither do my staff. Alack, we've all grown old together. My housekeeper will be glad to entertain your maid at tea in her own parlor."

"Thank you for inviting me to see you, Mr. Hale."

"It is a pleasure." He added with a twinkle, "Somewhat unconventional, I know, but unless he had changed, James Sinclair would have made nothing of that. Nor am I of an age to threaten the reputation of a young lady."

"He would probably have said, 'Devil take the conventions.' "

"And if no ladies were present, he'd have phrased it even more forcefully. So you are the child of whom he took charge." Mr. Hale looked her up and down. "You look like a Sinclair."

"I do?"

"Yes, something about the eyes and nose. That's plain, though I never heard what branch of the family it was you came from. As you may have guessed, although we were close friends in our youth, we did not stay in close contact after university, and especially after he moved to the country. We were busy with our own pursuits, he in medicine and scientific study and I in banking. When I wrote him about business matters, I would add a paragraph or two on personal subjects, and he did the same."

"I was going through some of his correspondence, and that was how I found out about you," Anne said. "You informed him of the death of Captain and Mrs. Sinclair, so I realized you must be a friend as well as his banker."

"Oh, I remember it. Later, I wondered if that was what made him think of becoming your guardian."

"I wondered, too, when I read it." Anne sipped her Bohea. "I know very little about the Sinclair family, except Dr. Sinclair's brothers and sister, naturally. Having grown up in his care, I never thought much about who my parents were. So he never mentioned anything about my...my antecedents?"

"If he did, I cannot call it to mind now. The Sinclairs are a large family, or were, and bred prolifically. Let me think for a moment." He nibbled a biscuit. "James's grandfather had four sons who lived to adulthood, I think, or maybe five, and at least two daughters. James's father succeeded the old man as earl. James's Sinclair uncles, ha, what became of all of them? Those were unsettled times. Robert was the youngest, but he went to the American colonies, I recall. Roderick now, he went to sea and, I think, married and had a child or two. Though his wife did all the work, of course. Zounds, I'm talking to you as if you were James, poor fellow. Most improper. "

Anne smiled back at the old man. "It reminds me of him. Thank you for not mincing words."

"Leaving Robert out, because he was out of England, there's maybe two generations since, and each

155

member of each generation might have several children—or none at all. I never heard much about James's great uncle Allen, but he was Captain Ewan Sinclair's grandfather. I only know that because my son received a letter from Janet Sinclair, Ewan's wife, when she was mortal ill. He went to see if he could be of assistance, and found she'd already died, and the child, too, poor little thing. Mrs. Sinclair had hardly a gown left, or any other thing except her Bible, with the family tree written in it. Neither of 'em, neither Ewan nor Janet, had a living parent or brother or sister. The closest kin Ewan had were cousins, and no telling at all where they were. Not in Edinburgh, at any rate, for Robert made inquiries."

"How sad," Anne said, and meant it. Here was substantially the story her grandfather had told her. Which meant he must have heard it from his old friend and banker, at some point after the letter. "I suppose you must have seen Dr. Sinclair on his return to England?"

"Oh, indeed. He'd financial arrangements to make, as he was going to buy a house near Lincoln. We had a merry reunion to celebrate his return. A long time ago, now, and I think I saw him only three or four times after that, when he came to London for his daughter's wedding, or on business." Mr. Hale shook his head regretfully, and Anne feared the movement would dislodge his old-fashioned wig.

Her grandfather claimed she was the daughter of Ewan Sinclair and his wife, but if they had no surviving child, that was not true. Who were her parents? Why lie about it?

The only thing she had learned which countered

the shock of discovering that Ewan and Janet Sinclair might not be her parents (assuming Mr. Hale was correct) was that she was at least descended from some Sinclair.

"Ah, well, does it matter what branch of the family? You come of the Sinclairs, and that's good stock. It must have been some other offshoot of the family with no close relatives remaining."

"I wonder how he found out about me?"

"James had a mort of friends or gentlemen he corresponded with, anyhow. One may have mentioned hearing of a Sinclair orphan. I am sorry I can be so little help to you. Would you pour out a little more tea, my dear? Have you been to the theater yet?"

If she had not learned much, she had at least discovered who her parents were not. But she had also enjoyed a pleasant chat with Mr. Hale, who recommended in the strongest terms that she see Lillo's *London Merchant* the next time it played. "Unless you have no taste for tragedy," he qualified. "But you should see it all the same, as it is a most improving tale."

Chapter 23

"Matthew, Your Grace," Peters announced.

Anniscote put aside his book.

The young man was slightly less point-device than is expected of a footman. In fact, the duke noted several smudges on his white hose. The scrutiny appeared to embarrass him. "I came straight from Cantwell's, Your Grace. I thought…"

"I would not have wanted to wait upon your report. What have you learned?" For something quite interesting must have come to Matthew's ears, to bring him so precipitately to Anniscote.

"It's taken a bit of time for that lot to trust me," Matthew said. "It was easy enough to meet the upstairs maid and get upon good terms with her, for she's new, one of the Cantwells' country cousins. Her parents would be right set about, I guess, to know the sort of place she's in service."

"Go on," Anniscote bade him.

"I mentioned as I was looking for work, as I'd lost my position. So Rachel told the others, and I've got to know them, too. Mr. Jones, the butler, says he'd be glad to hire me, but their fellows have all been there some time and not likely to give notice. But he'll recommend me to another place that's always losing footmen, because some of the menservants are no better than apes in livery and do not give satisfaction. But it's a requirement of that other establishment to be handy with your fists, as well as being well-trained in service. Which makes me think it's a low sort of business."

"I am sure you are correct, Matthew. A gambling den of the less genteel kind, or a brothel. Are you handy with your fists?"

"Yes, sir. I've four brothers."

"What else have you to tell me?"

"Mr. Jones is related to Mr. Cantwell as owns the house."

"Quite a family business, then."

"And Prissy is Jones's daughter. She's not employed there regular, as you might say, not being the stuff decent maids are made of. Too saucy and sly, and being Mr. Jones's daughter, she gives herself airs. Most times, she works at one o' the other businesses. Rachel don't know much about those, except one is an inn. She's not up to snuff, as the saying is, so they don't tell her everything. But she'll learn in time, sir, and I'm worried her innocence will wear away."

"I wouldn't be surprised if it did."

"She says they've a cousin in respectable service, and she wishes she might find a situation like that. The Cantwells' trade bothers her. She's not like that Prissy."

"You could not hear anything of why a virtuous young lady and I were tricked into going to that place?"

"They're tight-lipped," Matthew said. "Which in good servants is proper but…"

"But you might say the same of criminals also?"

"Ay, that's it, sure enough, Your Grace." He hesitated. "Your Grace is wishful to know who'd want to do harm to you or the young lady. I can't see why the Cantwells would, if they couldn't make money by it.

159

Which they could only do by blackmail, I'm thinking."

"Are they foolish enough to think I'd pay?"

"No, sir, they aren't. They're particular about the house's reputation, too, as the gentry wouldn't come there if they didn't think they could do so without scandal."

"Have you formed a theory, Matthew?"

"Well, sir, from what you told me, I'd guess it's someone of quality as got the Cantwells to do it. The only gentlefolks they meet are the ones that go to the house, so you might think it was one of them."

"But you are skeptical?"

"It's maybe the most likely thing, sir, but there's something Rachel told me that makes me wonder. You recall I said Rachel wanted a respectable place?"

"I do."

"Well, when she heard that one of the girl cousins was a lady's maid in a merchant's family, she asked Prissy if there was a chance she could get work there, too. And Prissy laughed and said no, but she wouldn't say why. Rachel thought it meant she wasn't good enough, which made her feel low. But to be an undermaid in a merchant's household is no great thing, and she's a good, hard-working girl. So why would Prissy laugh?"

Anniscote shrugged. "It is strange, but it's hard to see what bearing it has. Who's the merchant?"

"Rachel didn't know, for Prissy wouldn't tell her. Thought she'd go and ask for work there if she did, I guess."

"Would you be willing to take service with the Cantwells? You would still be in my employ but on…ah, detached duty. If you were working for them in one of those positions that require footmen who are good in a mill, you'd be better able to work your way into their confidence."

"As a spy, Your Grace?"

"It's an ill-sounding word, but yes."

"I'm honored to serve you, sir."

Chapter 24

"Anne," said Aunt Letitia, reading a letter as she drank her morning chocolate and nibbled at a slice of bread and butter, "my nephew and his wife have come up to town."

"Indeed, Aunt?" Anne offered, politely. "Which nephew?"

"Why, the earl, of course. The son of my older brother. Nothing could be better."

"I will be delighted to meet them. You and Mistress Saltstall are the only members of Dr. Sinclair's family I have met. Is the earl much like him?"

Letitia set down her cup and stared at Anne. "No, not in the least. Poor dear Hugh is rather…rather bland. But you do not take my meaning. His son has become engaged, and they intend to hold a ball and no doubt all sorts of other festivities to mark the occasion. The young lady comes of an extremely good family and has a large dowry. It is really a most desirable connection. And for our purposes, it will serve exceeding well, for naturally Hugh's family has entrée into a part of society I have not frequented since my marriage. You and I will be invited to the parties and ball. We may be what some would call poor relations, but I do not care a groat for that. You are a pretty girl and have an attractive vivacity, and I shall make sure that you are as well gowned as any girl there. And with more propriety than some," she added. "You need only be yourself, except that I hope you will not talk of amputations or dispute about politics. Or argue, particularly with gentlemen. Or talk about books unless someone else inaugurates the discussion."

"What may I speak of, Aunt Letitia?"

"The weather, music, and plays are safe topics. It may be best to ask the person to whom you are speaking about himself. Is he down from Oxford or Cambridge? Is he visiting London or living here? I don't mean you to stifle your liveliness, but you should temper it. I vow, I am quite excited. This is almost like having a daughter."

"Aunt, do you regret not being part of that world? I beg your pardon, I should not have asked."

"As it is between us, the question is permissible. It would not do to ask someone you did not know well such a thing. Yes, I always quite enjoyed the round of amusements and the dashing gentlemen and frivolous talk. I will enjoy it when we attend parties at Sinclair House. But I do not for a moment regret having married my Rupert. The legal set is not nearly as amusing, but that was a small price to pay for wedding a man I loved.

"My parents were disappointed I did not make a brilliant match, but they let us choose for ourselves. Not that my papa would have permitted me to make a bad marriage, of course, but Rupert came of an acceptable family and could support me decently. Bear these things in mind, Anne, for while I believe it is a good thing to love one's husband, it is even more important to be established comfortably.

"Now I think we should visit a silk warehouse. And you will have to practice managing your new hoop so as not to let it reveal more than your ankles, as some girls do."

Chapter 25

It was amusing that in spite of his previously ineligible status as a suitor, Anniscote had never lacked for invitations, even to the most exclusive parties. Unmarried men of good family and either fortune or good prospects were always welcome; unmarried men with libertine or rakish habits and without prospects (such as he had been) were welcome if they danced well and had pleasing manners. There were, after all, married ladies who needed entertainment and dancing partners. At Lady Waring's ball, Anniscote saw proof he was now considered marriage material, rather than merely an extra gentleman for the benefit of the wives and chaperons. Lady Waring kept him provided with a steady supply of young, marriageable dancing partners.

She would never have introduced him to the Honorable Cecilia Wingham before he inherited his brother's title. No doubt his hostess considered that she was benefitting both of them, for Cecilia was a tall, handsome girl, with a respectable if not lavish dowry. Her family was unexceptionable, tracing its ancestry back to a follower of William the Conqueror, through a succession of knights and barons to her proud papa, and thence to herself. Lord Wingham could take his pick of any number of suitors for her white, long-fingered hand. Perhaps it was not unnatural that both he and his daughter would prefer a duke to an earl or a mere baron, among Cecilia's other aspirants.

"Do you ride, Miss Wingham?"

"My papa is not in favor of the exercise for ladies," she murmured in her soft, well-modulated voice, "although I was taught to ride, of course, and I am sure I should be fond of it if I had more opportunity to do so."

When it was next possible to exchange words in the course of the dance, he said, "How do you occupy yourself here in town?"

"Why, much as other young ladies do, Your Grace. Balls, routs, visiting…"

"The theater? *The London Merchant*? "

"Oh…I have seen several plays since I came up. But Mama prefers them to be moral in tone."

Conversing with the Honorable Cecilia was certainly much heavier going than with the lively matrons who ordinarily were his partners. Or with Mistress Anne, whose opinions would have forced him to stifle a laugh. "I thought Lillo's play conveyed a very moral message. Certainly the crime, remorse, and punishment of Barnwell clearly illustrates the fate awaiting the dishonest."

"I am sure it does, sir…only Mama says that the main character is steeped in vice."

"I don't think I would put it in quite those words," Anniscote replied, wondering whether Lady Wingham might have applied the phrase to him before he inherited. She was certainly reputed to be an even stricter moralist than her lord.

"No doubt you are correct," Miss Wingham agreed. "Mama has not seen the play herself, but going on the report of others who have, she has told me that it concerns an immoral relationship with a female lost to all sense of shame. If I may refer to such a matter without incurring your censure."

"Certainly." Her last sentence was one he would surely never hear from Anne Sinclair.

After he led her off the floor and restored her to her mother and older sister, he encountered Tom Jeffreys on the way to the room where a few card tables had been set up.

"What's this, Jeffreys? You are failing to do your duty to your hostess, if you do not dance."

"It would be unfair of me to raise expectations in any young lady in search of a husband," Jeffreys answered with an air of conscious virtue. "My heart is given to Her Grace. But you have no such excuse."

"Yes, I do: this fox is looking for refuge."

"I saw you dancing with the fair Cecilia, and I take your meaning. Although she fulfills your requirements for a wife, being exceedingly proper, of good family, and silent, too."

"Pray do not remind me of my display of idiocy. Proper and of good family are certainly necessary, and I expect a girl who is passably pretty, but I must also have one who is not without conversation. She has no opinions, Tom. None! And she is a trifle too proper, as well. She is as embraceable as one of the Classical statues she rather resembles." He considered, and added, "The statue might be preferable, as it would not talk in platitudes."

"Oh, well, in that case, I see Mrs. Beaumont approaching. Was she not a flirt of yours a year or two past?"

"She was," the duke admitted. To call her his flirt

understated the matter somewhat.

"She is lovely, and she can carry on a lively conversation," Jeffreys went on, encouragingly. "And you must have heard that Mr. Beaumont made her a widow something over a year ago. She has now cast off mourning."

And if her year of mourning had not been quite over, she would surely have put away her black on hearing he'd stepped into his brother's shoes, Anniscote thought.

Eustacia smiled warmly at both of them and made a point of asking Tom about his mother's health and how his father and brothers and sisters went on, confirming Anniscote's good opinion of her manners. Then Jeffreys excused himself gracefully, saying he must pay his respects to a lady of his acquaintance. Who must be in the card room, judging from the direction he took.

She offered her sympathy on the death of the previous duke, avoiding hypocrisy by adding, "Although I know you and he were not close, and I cannot say I liked him, myself."

Good manners, beauty, pedigree, and she had two healthy children from her marriage. He realized with dismay he might have described a mare he meant to buy in almost the same terms. Well! She was charming and definitely embraceable. She would certainly do for a duchess, but he wished she possessed some more unique trait. She admired the correct paintings, plays, and books and could discuss them intelligently. 'Pon rep, he believed that she would not have cuckolded her husband had he supplied the affection and satisfaction she desired. All very admirable, no doubt, but he began to understand Tom's insistence on some other quality. Some little eccentricity—nothing too extreme, of course—would give her a piquancy. At table, he preferred a savory to a custard. If she were a bit more like Mistress Anne, in some quite undefinable way, she would be perfect.

Chapter 26

"So this is my Uncle James's ward," the Earl of Wemley said. Anne was sure he had been unaware of her existence until Aunt Letitia had taken her to call at Sinclair House a few days after his family arrived in town. "How are you liking the metropolis?" A pleasant but vague man, she thought. She guessed him to be no more than four-and-forty. He did not have the air of a man of fashion and admitted he spent most of the year in the country.

"Very well, Lord Wemley," Anne replied.

Letitia said, "Anne was to be introduced into society by Marianne, but now she is unable to do so, as her daughter is not well, and is taking the waters at Bath. It is slow work, bringing her to the attention of my little circle, in the hope that through them she will meet…younger persons."

She and the countess exchanged a look. "I shouldn't think that Marianne would be the ideal sponsor for Mistress Anne," Lady Wemley murmured. "Of course, she and Mr. Saltstall have a very large acquaintance, and it might be useful, but…"

"I do agree, but I ceased going about in the best society after my marriage. And one cannot simply shop for a husband as one shops for a hat."

"My dear aunt, have the men nothing to say to the decision?" Wemley inquired plaintively.

"Now, Hugh," his wife responded, "you know they do. But it cannot be left to them to find ladies; the ladies must go where gentlemen may be found. Any woman who is not a fool knows as much." She went on, "Of course I will send you invitations to the ball, and to whatever other events we hold. My sons have any number of friends who would be much more appropriate for one of our Sinclair connections than some City beau."

When they had left Sinclair House, Letitia said, "What a fortunate thing it is that Julia has no daughters. I think we need worry no more about Marianne not being able to take you about with Mariah."

"Aunt Letitia! You knew the countess would help launch me as soon as you heard she and the earl were coming to London!"

"I protest, I did not know she would be willing, but I had hoped the challenge of bringing out a girl and seeing to it she is betrothed to the right sort of gentleman would appeal to her. Of course, I've known her almost since her birth. She always was a merry, obliging little thing and with a good deal of sense, too. And she loves entertaining, so their stay in town will be busy, apart from the parties and assemblies they are invited to attend."

****

Ruffles of gathered lace falling from her elbows, with a hoop that was wide from side to side but narrow from front to back holding out her skirt, and a confection of lace, ribbons, and flowers on her head, Anne hardly knew whether she felt like a princess or a marionette. It was lucky that the closely-boned corset made it impossible for her to bend unwarily, as she feared that leaning forward too much might cause her bosom to escape. Impossible, of course. Probably. The corsage of the gown was cut very low.

"Dear Anne, you look lovely," Aunt Letitia said fondly, before they left for dinner with the earl's family and the family of Jeremy's affianced bride. "What a pity Marianne, at least, is not in town and able to be here to see how well the dressmaker and dancing master have done! Not that you were not very fetching before, but—"

"Aunt Letitia, I was a drab little sparrow before. You and Mistress Saltstall between you have turned me into some brightly-plumed, exotic bird. Although, of course, for suitability for cooking or egg-laying, plumage may not be the best guide."

"Anne, if you discuss such agricultural matters with gentlemen, I despair of you."

"No, I understand that most men would be bored by the subject. Although, if I were dancing with someone who was interested in estate management and progressive agricultural practices, would it still be inappropriate?"

Aunt Letitia sighed. "If he initiates the topic, you may respond. It would seem a boring conversation, but gentlemen will go on about their interests."

"Or if I should be with a medical man and he introduced the subject of amputation or wound treatment…"

Letitia laughed behind her fan. "Nothing less likely than his mentioning such a thing to a lady, believe me."

The Sinclairs had not invited so many as to make the ball a crush, but even so, a hundred or more gorgeously colored gowns, coats, and waistcoats, and a sprinkling of regimentals swirled around the ballroom. Anne thought she had never seen anything so pretty as the colors of the gowns and gentlemen's suits in the light cast by the ballroom's chandeliers and sconces. The colors changed with the movements of the dance, punctuated by the flash of gems. She had little time to admire the sight, however, as the countess saw to it she had a succession of partners for the dances. Thanks to lessons at the manor at Fletchingford and to the dancing master's recent tutelage, she was able to perform the steps and converse at the same time, except for one or two trifling missteps. During a pause between dances, she had one glimpse of Aunt Letitia and the countess standing together. They were gazing in her direction and looking immoderately pleased about something.

Anne and her most recent partner, a young man with very agreeable manners but not too much conversation were watching the next set and refreshing themselves with glasses of champagne when a strongly-built man in bottle green velvet passed them with a negligent nod. Anne had only a heartbeat to register his square, ruddy face before he stopped in midstep and turned back.

"Well, well. Sir, I believe I have not had the pleasure of making your acquaintance, but if I am not mistaken, I have met this lady, although I confess I have forgotten her name."

Her partner introduced himself with the shyness to be expected of a boy recently down from Oxford in the presence of a man old enough to be his father, and then presented Anne to Tobias Hurst.

Hurst was at least not the worse for drink this time,

but Anne feared that he remembered her as clearly as she remembered him.

"Now, where was it we met previously, Mistress Anne?" She could not mistake the mockery in his voice.

"I do not like to contradict you, Mr. Hurst, but I have no memory of meeting you before," Anne replied coolly, hoping she had not given herself away in the moment she had recognized him, as he had revealed a flash of surprise on seeing her. His slight smile made her blood run cold.

To her relief, two other gentlemen came up, and after introductions were made, haled him away to discuss some sporting matter. Then Anne was claimed for the next set, this time by a fashionable sprig who was very full of himself. His flow of inconsequent chatter made it unnecessary for Anne to do more than respond with an occasional "Oh! Really?" or "How interesting!" For once, empty social exchanges exactly suited her. What would Hurst do? What could she do? Good God, by morning it could be all over town that Mistress Bradshaw's protégée from the country had been seen in a place no virtuous lady would go.

A little later, Aunt Letitia sought her out and asked, "My dear, are you not feeling well? You have lost a little of your sparkle."

With an effort, Anne composed herself. "I believe I am a trifle overwhelmed by it all. I have never seen anything to compare."

"I suppose every girl feels the same at her first real ball. And it is always too warm in the rooms, especially when one is dancing. But are you enjoying yourself? I have been watching, and it seemed to me you were. Julia has exceeded my expectations in providing you with partners, too."

"Yes, indeed, Aunt Letitia. I've met so many people, I hope I can recall all their names."

"I hope you have met a number of pleasing gentlemen," Letitia said delicately.

"I have—and one I did not much care for. A Mr. Tobias Hurst, who seemed to think he had met me before."

"Oh, Hurst. He does not add greatly to a ball, but then, he's married, so it makes no difference. I hope he said nothing to disgust you. Even Hugh admits his manners are more suited to the stable or alehouse than to good society. He was at school with Hugh, and his wife is some distant connection of the bride's family, so they had to be invited." Then Aunt Letitia's attention was claimed by a woman she had known in her youth, and Anne joined a group of girls and young matrons. While she listened and contributed her own mite from time to time, she also surreptitiously watched for a tall, black-haired figure. She felt that the duke should know as soon as possible that Hurst had recognized her, in spite of realizing that Anniscote could do nothing about Hurst's discovery of her identity. But the Duke of Guysbridge was apparently not among the guests, or if he was, he was not visible. She certainly could not ask whether he was present.

She did not see Hurst again that night and so was able to put the matter out of her mind, though she hoped Anniscote would come to call again in the near future.

Chapter 27

"Why, you have a letter here from Mr. Hale," Aunt Letitia exclaimed. "I haven't thought of him in years. I wonder how he does. And how does he come to be writing you, Anne? Not that there's any harm in it, as he is an older gentleman and a friend of James's, of course."

"I wrote to him, as I did to Dr. Sinclair's other correspondents." She felt guilty about the equivocal answer, which Letitia would undoubtedly take to mean that the letter had been immediately after her grandfather's death, and added, "I did not learn that he was a friend as well as Dr. Sinclair's banker until I came to London, which is how he knew where I am staying."

"Oh, of course. It had not occurred to me." Sorting through the pile of letters, invitations, and bills, Aunt Letitia said, "Oh, my. I believe he has written to me also." And she became engrossed in reading it.

"My dear Mistress Anne,

It came to me only Today that I may be able to render some assistance after all, in relation to your Question. The only possession left to Mrs. Ewan Sinclair when she died, apart from a few pieces of clothing, was her Bible, which Robert ransomed from the landlady to assist his search for any remaining close relatives. I have written to my Son to request that he copy out the Family Tree. Your parents likely belonged to Captain Sinclair's generation. It is only a question of Locating the various branches and Writing to inquire. Some may be difficult to find, but they cannot have sunk quite out of sight.

I have also sent a billet to Mistress Bradshaw, whom I well remember from the Days when she was yet Mistress Letitia, inviting her and you to Attend the theater with me to see The London Merchant performed.

Your servant,
Edw. Hale"

"This is delightful, Anne. Only think, Mr. Hale invites us to see a play. We will accept—unless you dislike the idea?"

"I would love to see a play," Anne said. "He sounds like such a nice man, too."

"He is indeed. I could not tell you how many times I danced with him when I was a girl. If Rupert had not asked for my hand first, I think perhaps Edward would have done so. I will write to him and invite him to take a dish of Bohea with us."

She would have to write Mr. Hale, requesting that he not mention her visit to his home, which was a fact she would rather Aunt Letitia did not learn.

****

Nearly a month since her potentially disastrous adventure, with no sign of its discovery, Anne began to hope she was safe. She had been busy, too, which had kept her from brooding about it. Between the earl and Mr. Hale, she and Aunt Letitia had attended a rout, a ridotto, the theater, and a picnic. To her great pleasure, Mr. Hale decided he should stand as a sort of adoptive uncle and was willing to escort her to the booksellers' shops.

And the Earl of Wemley, whom Anne had thought at first only kindly and vague, proved more interesting on further acquaintance.

He seldom visited London, preferring his country seat (which sounded to Anne like a vast and inconvenient house), where he was happy to manage his estate, ride, hunt occasionally, and study the history of the Sinclair family.

"I am no scholar, as my uncle James was, nor especially clever," he admitted, "but with so many family records, letters, and diaries in our library, it requires only an interest and time to organize them."

"Are you tracing the Sinclairs' ancestry?" she asked. Here was another possible source of information about her parents.

"That, of course, but that is the easiest task and largely complete already. We've always been very good about keeping records of that sort. I don't say there haven't been one or two who were lost sight of, but not many. But the hardest part is what I am chiefly concerned with: I am writing up a little account of the accomplishments of each of our forebears. It's not always stirring stuff. For instance, my great-grandfather's sister was an extremely fine needlewoman, but it is almost forgotten that she also painted pictures, and very well, too. We have a number of the portraits she made of members of the family: great-grandfather, his first and second wives, their children…oh, we have quite a gallery of ancestors and connections. When we were children, I fear my brothers and I made up scurrilous stories about them."

"It must give such a sense of belonging to know so much about one's family and have pictures of them."

"I suppose it does," he agreed. "But you speak as if you felt you did not belong. You do, you know, even though we are only making your acquaintance now. Between my uncle's ruralizing and my own tendency to stay at home, our paths never crossed 'til now. Upon my word, we do sound dull, don't we? I only come to London to do my duty to the House of Lords and to visit the bookstalls in the Strand. Except this time, of course." Anne found herself laughing with him.

No one was close enough to overhear, as Lady Wemley and Aunt Letitia were having a comfortable chat on a bench in the garden and Lord Wemley had led Anne to inspect a planting of tulips which had come into bloom.

"I know so little about my parents and my father's connection to the family," Anne explained.

"My aunt told me that your father was Ewan Sinclair."

"So I believe."

"That is odd," he murmured. "I thought Captain Sinclair had died without issue."

"Oh." As she had already heard this from Mr. Hale, the fact was not a surprise, but the earl's also knowing it was, though given his historical and genealogical interests, it was only to be expected. It was additional proof that Dr. Sinclair's account of her birth was untrue.

Seeing her dismay, he went on, "But perhaps I was misinformed. I find that many persons are sadly unreliable. Someone, hearing that your mother died in childbed, may have assumed the baby died also."

"But…"

"You are obviously a Sinclair."

"How can you be sure, my lord?"

"Why, because faces like yours hang in our gallery, going back as far as the time of Charles I. The jawline and set of the eyes are distinctive. Three of my great-grandmother's children have one or both features. It is not surprising. These things run in families, you know, and she was a cousin of my great-grandfather, which I suppose must have doubled the odds of what I call the 'Sinclair face' showing up. Sometimes it skips generations. I do not have it, nor does Aunt Letitia, but I have a miniature of one of my sisters, painted when she was about your age, that might be you. So you must be a Sinclair. And I am heartily glad to have you added to the family. I am only sorry that we did not maintain a closer connection with Uncle James and his daughter. I should have made an effort after my father died."

Clearly, she was not the child of Ewan and Janet Sinclair, as it was unlikely that both Mr. Hale and the earl could be mistaken. But if she did not know how she was related to the Sinclairs, it seemed that she must be connected somehow. So what was the thing that had worried Dr. Sinclair?

"You mentioned bookstalls in the Strand, sir? Places that sell books?"

"Yes, and very cheaply, too. I can spend an entire afternoon turning over the books, in the hope of finding some curiosity."

She filed away the information but did not mention that she would certainly make an excursion to the Strand at the earliest opportunity. It would not do, she supposed, to display her tendency to bookishness.

****

There was a little rain the next morning and a chill wind, more like autumn than summer.

"It's too wet to go shopping today," Anne said while Sally was dressing her hair.

Sally sighed but agreed, and added, "I thought we might buy another packet of pins and another needle, when we went out. The one I use for ordinary mending is grown dull. But if the peddler woman comes round, I can get them from her."

"What peddler woman?"

"She's a poor old body that's been coming to the kitchen door most days of late with a tray of useful things. Needles and pins, thread, ribbon, a bit of old lace, a few trinkets, and the like. Nothing much for a lady, but she says she doesn't do badly, streets like this, where there's houses with a number of maids. The weather may not keep her away, for Cook always gives her a mug of ale and a bite of something, and the old besom's a mine of gossip, so it's well worth it. If she's as welcome in other houses, she can't need to buy food or drink, and it's cheap to keep warm by someone else's fire. In some houses she's let in as much for her tongue as her wares. She told our scullery maid that Mrs. Jervis, three houses down, is visiting Italy because she got with child by her lover, and Captain Jervis away on a voyage for months."

"Oh, dear! So she's gone to be delivered of it where no one will know? But what will become of the poor little thing?"

Sally shrugged. "Whatever happens to gentlewomen's babies that can't be explained. Sent to be raised by some poor woman as minds children of that sort for her living. A man's natural children, that's different. But for a lady, it's divorce, if she can't pass it off as her husband's. The ladies and gentlemen would be ill-pleased to realize the talk the old woman spreads. And if Cook ever heard how Betty the scullery maid lets her own tongue run on, the poor little chit would be out on the street. Not that she has any scandal to tell, but she will babble about anything—the kitchen cat bringing in three mice and laying them by the hearth, or the color of your newest gown and what it reminds her of, or what parties you and Mrs. Bradshaw are to attend."

"Well, whether the peddler comes or not, I mean to go out the next day that's not raining. With the earl and his family in town, Mistress Bradshaw says I must have two more dresses at least."

"And another ball gown. If you have two petticoats for it in different colors, I can change the trim on it so it's almost the same as two different dresses. A gown in ivory would be pretty, with one petticoat figured and the other plain."

"After we visit the mercer, I should like to go to the Strand," Anne said.

"Why, what's in the Strand, Mistress Anne?"

"Bookstalls, I am told."

Sally's eyes, seen in the mirror, twinkled. "Ay, there would be no point to going there unless the day was fine."

"It's not wrong for a lady to visit them, then?"

"I don't think so, Mistress. Might be it's a little unusual, but ladies read, some of them, and if you save money on books, you can spend it on shoes and lace and such."

"I think perhaps we should have a footman with us," Anne said. She had not forgotten the duke's advice. While she would have Sally with her, she suspected that it would be well to have a male attendant also.

"He'll be of use to carry the books," Sally remarked. "I think they don't deliver from the stalls."

Chapter 28

Two days later, the bookstalls were everything she could have hoped for. Dusty old copies of the classical authors for as little as four pence, histories, plays, scientific treatises…Anne sighed with pleasure and began to hunt for treasure. Sally and the footman hung back, not to be in the way of other browsers. She was deep in a copy of Sir Isaac Newton's *Opticks* when the shouting began.

"Stop, thief!"

"After him!"

A coach, driven fast, swung around the corner, and someone brushed past Anne, overturning the table at which she was standing and knocking her off her feet. Surrounded by milling people who did nothing to help her get up, she struggled to her knees, annoyingly hampered by skirt and petticoats. Then someone loomed beside her and bent to assist her. "Thank you," she began, and heard Sally call out, "Mistress Anne!" Then nothing.

****

She woke to an aching head. Was she recovering from some illness? She hurt all over, although her head was the worst, and she felt chilled. Her mouth was dry and her stomach felt uneasy, which was not made better by the smell of the room: musty with an overlay of other odors—cheap perfume, wine, a chamber pot left unemptied…Anne opened her eyes and blinked. The room was dim, with some gray light coming through a small window inadequately covered by thin curtains. Between their edges, she could see panes so grimy that they were translucent rather than clear.

Where on earth was she? Thinking was like trudging through thick mud, the kind that holds your shoes and weights them when you take a step. She managed to sit up on the rumpled bed and began to feel slightly better.

She stood up in cautious increments, first putting her feet to the floor and sitting on the edge of the bed for a moment before rising. Treading carefully, she made her way to the old-fashioned casement window. She unlatched it and pushed it open. Although she could not see the sun, to judge from the angle of the shadows, it must be afternoon.

She was about three stories above the street, which was no better than an alley, and the houses leaned precariously. It was not a familiar neighborhood, or one she would care to visit. A ragged man was lying beside the front of the house across the way and two doors down. From the heavy wooden sign that projected almost halfway across the alley, it was a tavern. In the other direction, she saw a space between two buildings with a mound of debris and a few huts cobbled together from timbers and canvas. The only other people she could see were slatternly women and rough-looking men.

Heart pounding, she went to the door. It would not open. Anne was on the verge of calling out when she heard a voice, very faint. Pressing her ear to the thin panel, she heard,"…yourself this time. Bit off more'n you can chew, I'd say."

A door nearby opened. From the sound, it came from the right—perhaps the next room. The wall would be too thick to enable her to hear anything. Anne returned to the window, hoping that the speakers would also find that room airless.

She must have missed a few words but was rewarded by hearing a creak, and then, "There! Gets hot up here, but that'll let a breeze in."

A lighter voice said, "It was a pocketful of guineas for the taking. The first try should've worked—would have, but for that man."

"Ay, the man was a mistake, right enough."

"Not mine, Ned. And we've got the money safe now. If only the sailing wasn't put off."

A male laugh.

"It's only to keep her close 'til then. 'Course, there's other places she could vanish."

"She wasn't to be hurt."

"There's no hurt about it, after the first, anyhow. I know a place as would pay well."

"You know my uncle'd be mad as fire if he found out—and he would! He's that careful of the reputation of the business. And if she got away and went to a magistrate, it'd come back on us."

"She don't know who we are. And she'd not likely want to advertise her situation. Mind, I'm only saying it'd be one way of dealing with it, if you're worried about the ship being delayed long."

"She's to go to the Colonies. Safer, that way. Who'd believe her if she said she was kidnapped, with the indenture all signed? She'd be out of the way for seven years and when she was free, she'd have to pay her way to come back here. And that's assuming she didn't die before her time was up or get married and settled. And if she did get back, she'd be ruined anyway and not fit for society. It's only the keeping her 'til then worries me. And getting her aboard."

"If you're set on her going to the Colonies, it's easy enough. A long drink of gin and I'll carry her aboard. Captain's used to passengers sailing with a full skin."

"But when she sobers up and tells him—"

"What, would he turn back to port? Not to save his soul. It'd make trouble for him, and he makes a fair profit on every indenture he sells, assuming the merchandise don't die before he gets 'em there. Priss, there's some captains I wouldn't try this with, but he's not one of 'em." A long pause.

"The rub is, we'll have to keep her here 'til the ship's ready to sail. Might be three or four days, might be a week or more—the captain wasn't certain sure. Which means her room and board'll have to be paid. The old woman won't house her for free. Are you willing to pay out for it?"

"The one that's paying will bear the cost. I'll explain as how otherwise you might have to make other arrangements."

"Oh, if there's money in it—" He laughed. "But I can't swear on a Bible that nothing'll happen to her here, Priss. This's no parsonage. There's no business done on this floor, just the bawd's and the servants' rooms, but…"

"Well do I know it, Ned. That's why it's settled that she'll have me with her o' nights and one of my cousins in the day."

187

"Then there'll be two of you pretty morsels if things get rowdy."

"Which is why I'll have a pair of pops with me, and trust me to shoot if I have to."

"You'd never!"

"I would. Pa taught me. Comes in handy sometimes. And you make sure the hackum helps, if there's anything going forward."

"Who'll stand watch during the day?"

"Prue. Her mistress turned her off. I didn't want to use her for this, but there's no choice. We've no one to spare, except me, and I can't do it all myself. I'm sorry for it, but I think Prue might have to go to America, too, if you can get another indenture written out. But she'd better go on to a different colony."

"Ho! So we'll be housing her until another ship sails? There's another charge for you."

"I'll get the money for that, too, never fear."

"Why would you lay out the gelt for her? A poor, discharged maidservant, what harm could she do? There's me and the bawd here to swear she's never been across the threshold, and you that's her cousin to swear she's not right in her mind, if need be. Any number of others, too, for a pennyworth of gin. Maybe she won't want to go to the Colonies."

"I'll see to it she's glad to go. Now, she'll be along to watch her until I come back tonight. We'd best go down to let her in."

****

Anne heard footsteps in the hall, one light and brisk, the other hesitating, and was not surprised when the door opened. Prissy entered, followed by a girl dressed like a maid, who was carrying a tray. Prissy now looked nothing like a servant, in a gown of yellow with green trim, over a silk petticoat of the same green.

"Prue, put those things down."

The maid set a laden tray on the small table and obediently came over. Her eyes were fixed on Anne and her lips parted as if to speak, but a single glance from Prissy silenced her and made her look down, biting her lip.

"Why have you abducted me?"

"Ransom, o' course," Prissy answered readily. "Your people will pay to get you back."

"Why did you lure me to that other place?"

"Same reason, only that went wrong," was the glib answer.

She forbore to pursue it; she would get no truth out of Priss.

"Now, you just wait quiet-like, until we get the money for you. Then I'll make sure as you get home safe."

When Prissy had gone away, Prue cut untidy slices of bread and cheese with a dull, point-less knife and poured out two mugs of ale.

"I'm sorry, mistress, it's not what you're used to, I'm sure," the girl said.

Anne, recovered enough to feel a little hungry, said, "No matter. I'm not so delicate."

The maid, leaving the one chair to Anne, perched on the bed. She picked at her own meal for a few minutes, then said, "Please, ma'am…"

"Yes?"

"I'm sorry about all this. It's not my fault, it's only that Priss is my cousin and gave me a place to stay when my old mistress turned me off. Prissy offered me money to stay with a lady for a few days, as a favor to family, like."

"Well, one cannot live without money. How did you come to lose your place? Talking will pass the time and you'll feel better." *And I'll know more.*

"Mistress claimed I'd taken a silk petticoat of my young mistress, but she wasn't inclined to turn me over to the magistrates, as she'd be sorry to see me hanged for one mistake. And she said her daughter needed an older maid, anyway, one who wouldn't let her fall into mischief. That's what she *said*."

"But you don't believe it."

"Well, it was true I couldn't control her. I don't know who could, as headstrong and hot at hand as she is. Mistress said I'd be all right, for I could go to my cousin, it wasn't like I'd nowhere to go. Only it wasn't like her, proud and hard as she is. She'd never forgive the theft of so much as a pin. She even let me keep the petticoat. I swear I never stole it. My young mistress give it me."

Anne nodded encouragingly.

"My ma brought me up decent, and her brother's family and connections aren't good folk. I didn't know that when I came to London, and my ma didn't either, or she wouldn't have told me I should go to my uncle when she died. Well, I didn't have to, then, as a lady at home got me the position with my mistress, who was a friend of hers. But being in London, I went to visit my uncle and cousins, and I saw what they was like. I don't know if you know how it is, mistress, but I missed having family, so I kept on visiting them on my half-day, and they acted glad to see to me."

"I suppose we all have to overlook some faults in

our families." She knew what it was like to be without family.

"Ay, 'tis truth. But the thing I did that was wrong was when my young lady took a notion to get to know a fine gentleman she admired." Prue blushed hotly. "She met him once or twice before, in the street, which was easy to arrange because he lived nearby. Well, it wasn't going on as well as she'd like, so she tells me she wants to hire a hackney, and she'll fall from the step just as he passes and hurt her ankle. Being a gentleman, he'll take her home and that will make it all respectable, and she thinks if she just has a chance, he'll fall in love with her."

It was a foolish and improper plan, but girls did practice wiles to attract suitors, as even Anne knew.

"She wanted to know how she could hire a coach without anyone the wiser—like the butler, the footmen, and the page boy, who would all tell her mother. It would do no good to say she wanted it to take her to the shops, because her mother would have sent her in her own chaise, and you can be sure the coachman would refuse to do what she wanted. Well, I knew it was wrong to help her, and I begged her not to do it. But she has such wheedling ways that at last I told her my cousin would know, and that if she arranged it, it would only be a matter of going out for a walk, and we could meet the coach somewhere away from the house. Priss sent a coachman she knew. It worked fine, as far as that went, except that when we met the coach, my mistress wouldn't let me come with her but bade me wait and she'd come back for me. She wanted to be private with the gentleman, so I don't know what happened, but he wasn't with her when she come for me and she was in a rage. After that, she wanted to write to Priss, though she wouldn't say what it was about, and I know I shouldn't have taken the letter, but she's got a temper like Mistress's when she's refused something she wants, and the only one can handle her is her pa, but he leaves her to her mother as a rule. And Priss wrote her back, and I carried that, too, but Mistress caught me with it before I took it to my young mistress. She opened it and read it and sealed it up again so you couldn't tell, and she swore that if I let on to her daughter, she'd have me charged with stealing the silk petticoat that my young lady had given me because she decided she didn't like the color—some other young lady had one too much like, I guess—and it had a little tear in it anyway. Mistress said it cost above forty shillings, and that meant I'd hang for it."

"You didn't learn what was in the letter later?"

"No, but it must have been bad, for I've never seen the mistress so angry, and she's like one of those lions as was given Christians to eat, a long time ago. Then she said I could make up for my wickedness by getting Priss to do a favor for her. So I took a letter of Mistress's to Priss because what else could I do? And Priss wrote her back, and I had to take another letter to her, a thick one. Priss wouldn't tell me a word. She just smiled and said she was helping my mistress."

Priss sounded like a young woman who might know how to arrange a number of things a lady of fashion might find useful but not wish to be known. Find a discreet midwife? A pawnbroker? Certainly she knew how to make illicit meetings possible. "After that, your mistress discharged you?"

"A little while later, Priss came to the kitchen door

one morning and said she had to see the mistress. We
pretended as how she was seeking a situation as a maid
and my mistress might know of one. Mistress spoke to
her in private, and Priss went away, and oh, my
mistress was in a rare taking, for all she tried not to let
on. That very day she went out, and the next day a
woman with a face like a hatchet come and said she
was my young lady's new maid. And Mistress gave me
my wages and some extra and said my young lady
needed a maid as would be strict with her and not carry
messages. And when I'd packed my things and was
leaving, one of the footmen told me that he'd been sent
to hire a coach to take my mistresses and their maids to
Bath and it was too bad I was missing the treat."

"What a pity," Anne said. "I've never been to Bath
myself, but I have heard that it's very pleasant,
although it rains a good deal."

"They do say so," Prue agreed. "I went to Priss and
explained how I needed a new place and asked if she
could get me one. She'd get me a better one, she swore,
and I could stay with the family and help her a little
while she was fixing it. When she said she needed me
to stay with a lady that was going to go off with her
lover, as soon as the ship was ready to sail, I agreed
because she offered me more than I'd earn in a year. It
didn't seem really wrong."

"I was abducted and brought here against my will.
I have no intention of eloping with anyone," Anne said.

"I begun to wonder when I come in, for you look
so much like the young lady I was maid to, I thought
you was her, so I knew Priss lied and there was some
deep plot."

"Do I really resemble your young mistress that

closely?"

"All but for your hair, because hers is just brown, and she wears it dressed very elegant, most of the time. And her eyes are blue. But they aren't blue as harebells, no matter what she says, so that's not a big difference, and you can hardly tell the difference between light blue and gray anyhow."

"That's very true," Anne agreed, "as my eyes aren't a dark gray, like some. But I still don't quite understand." So Anniscote's and her theory was correct, and she did have a double or near-double. And that was inconvenient for someone.

"I don't either, mistress, for a fact. But what's to do?"

What indeed?

"We must escape from here," Anne said. "If you help, it will be easy."

"Priss will be terrible angry. Now I've seen this place, I think my uncle must be worse than I knew, and Priss, as well. I think it's a place men go to visit women."

"I wouldn't be at all surprised. I'll see you don't suffer for helping me, for we must get away," Anne said. "I overheard something Priss and a man called Ned were talking about earlier. Do you know who Ned is?"

"He's Priss's spark. I only met him twice and I didn't like him much. He can be pleasant enough, but he's low. I can't make out what he works at, either, except it's something to do with my uncle's business."

"They plan to send me to America as an indentured servant, and you, too, but to a different place. It seems to me they don't want you here to testify against them, or to testify in the Colonies that they abducted me and indentured me against my will."

Prue turned white.

Anne abandoned her mug of ale and went to the door to listen. Not a sound. She tried the door knob.

"It's locked," she told her fellow prisoner. "But I think it won't stop us." The lock was old and not very complex, much like the one on the pantry door at home. Mrs. Bowman would insist on locking it—as if the maid or Grandfather's valet would raid the pantry in the night!—and then misplace the key. In Fletching, Anne had kept an L-shaped length of stiff wire. Here…she pulled a long hairpin out of her hair, causing a lock to fall free to her shoulder. The pin was a pretty one, with a filigree head, but not expensive. She contrived to bend it by holding the greater part down on the rough table, pressing the end of it over the edge with the knife handle. It was easily bent. Anne hoped it would be strong enough. "Were there many people about downstairs?"

Prue shook her head, watching in a fascinated manner, rather as creatures were said to be paralyzed by the gaze of a snake. The lock resisted; it was rusty and certainly not as well oiled as the one on the pantry door. Anne was unpleasantly aware of perspiration breaking out all over her body. If she could not open the door, they must see if it were possible to depart by the window. Would the bed sheets be strong enough to make a rope, and would it be long enough? She thought she would have little difficulty getting down, though it would be a longer drop than the rope in the barn which she had slid down as a child. Would Prue be able to do it? Or even be willing to try? She could hardly leave the girl behind.

When the lock at last yielded with a grudging *snick!* Anne's knees felt oddly weak.

"Come. I fancy this is our best chance in a house of this sort. You won't want to stay?"

"I'm afraid to go, mistress, but I'm more afraid to stay." They tiptoed out into the corridor.

Anne thought she could hear snoring from behind one door. Otherwise, all was silent. They crept along the hall and down the narrow stairs. They felt solid enough, though they squeaked in places. Anne held up her hand to stop Prue short of the first floor and listened. She descended the last two steps and peeked around the corner. The door to one room was open, and a broom and basket stood outside it. Someone was cleaning. Anne beckoned, and Prue followed her onto the flight of stairs that led to the ground floor.

Just short of the landing, they paused to listen. No sound came from the front of the house. Going as silently as they could, they continued down the last steps. Then the front door was in sight. Far off, a metallic rattling suggested someone in the kitchen, preparing for the night's business, but that would be at the back of the house, or maybe in the basement. Anne squeezed the maid's hand for encouragement, and whispered, "When we get out, we must make haste, but it would be a mistake to run. Can you take us to the nearest street where we might find a hackney coach?"

Prue nodded. "We go to the right once we're out the door."

Then they were in the narrow front hall, dim without any candles lit. Anne took a firm grip on the heavy bolt that secured the door and pulled hard. With a rustle of cloth and a squeak from Prue, a big, hairy hand closed on her wrist, and Ned growled, "What's this, missy?"

Chapter 29

Jeffreys, arriving to dine with Anniscote before Lady White's ball, eyed the duke's suit and remarked, "I perceive the hand of a valet at work."

"Yes, Mulley has had his way," Anniscote admitted, studying the silver lace edging the front of his coat. "You must see my court suit some time. Burgundy velvet, with the cuffs and waistcoat of ivory silk, embroidered with a design of gillyflowers of burgundy and pink in a lattice of silver thread. But I will not—not!—let him paint my face. He may powder my hair for formal occasions," he added, fairly.

Over the second course, Jeffreys said, "I like your chef. He has a neat way with chicken and a light hand with pastry. Not too many French kickshaws."

"I'll tell her you said so."

They had almost finished their port when Peters entered. "Your Grace, if I may have a word with you?"

"What is it, Peters?"

"Matthew is asking to speak with you. I told him you was at dinner and he'd have to wait, but he swore it was a matter of urgency. He's in your bookroom. "

"If you'll excuse me a moment, Tom."

The young footman was pacing the bookroom.

"What's amiss?"

"Your Grace, Ned, that manages the Cantwells' gaming house, told me he needed me at another place for a se'ennight or mayhap a bit longer. I wouldn't ha' thought a thing of it, but that Ned is Prissy's beau. See, he's not a Cantwell nor yet one of their kin, but sometimes they hire outsiders. He's a sharper and none of them Cantwells is much for games of chance. Like the sure bets, they do. Like enough Priss will marry him, for they're hand in glove. She was there this afternoon, talking with Ned, and I heard her say she wasn't easy about the arrangements, even though the wenches was locked in, as she couldn't be there, after all, nor him, either. 'It's pure bad luck the Swanhope House bawd's down with the colic, and I must take her place tonight. That girl's too clever by half, and too lucky, the way she got herself out. So locked door or no, we'll have a man on guard. Give me one that's reliable and has his wits about him,' she says. 'What about that new one? Here, you,' she says to me as I was passing, 'If you had two maids held prisoner, what would you do with them?'

"'Nothing but what I was told,' I answered her.

"'You wouldn't be tempted to sample 'em?'

"I have too much respect for the fair sex—even the ones that's not as clever and able to take care of themselves as you, Mistress Priss.'

"'And you cast off for a thief?' she asks me, laughing.

"'I stole, sure enough, but the way things are, how else can a fellow live? But I'm no rake, like some o' the gentry.' She liked that and told Ned to have me stand guard, nights. And after, Ned gives me the direction of a brothel o' Cantwell's and tells me to tell the bawd, he's sending me to see the two wenches don't get away. They're locked in a room on the top floor, and he claims they're servants as owe the family money, and so they're to be sold to a sea captain. I don't know it's anything to do with that other thing, but it seemed funny-like to me. If they owe money, why not put them to work in the house?"

"Why not, indeed."

"And Priss, before she went off, warned me not to believe anything they said, for they both could lie and sound like angels, and one of 'em could pass as a lady when she minded her speech. What would you have me do, Your Grace?"

"When must you be at your post?"

"I was to go there direct, but I figured by taking a hackney coach I'd just time to come here first."

****

"Tom, I do beg your pardon for that interruption. Pray make my apologies to Lady White. Something has arisen that requires my attention tonight."

"We'd do better to write her a note instead. You'll do well to have a friend with you."

"What makes you suppose I haven't been summoned to an assignation with a lady of obliging ways, Tom?"

"Your expression is not that of a man looking forward to an evening of pleasure with his mistress. What's afoot?"

"I believe I once said you were too perceptive. Really, you must have been annoying as a child."

"I may have been, at that. But don't try to put me off, John. The way you're fondling the pommel of your sword should be a warning to anyone who knows you at all. Do you intend to call someone out?"

"No…this would be more in the line of

investigating a nest of vermin, I think."

"Do vermin come in nests? I thought that was vipers."

Anniscote laughed wryly. "A pack of rats is closer to the mark."

"How are we spending the evening, then?"

"This is nothing to do with you, my dear fellow. I misdoubt it will be dangerous…or not very…but it might be extremely embarrassing. And you're so well conducted."

"Are we like to be taken in custody by the Watch?"

"No, that's the least of my worries."

"Then I'm with you. You'll not go alone."

"I thought to have one or two of my footmen dress in their own clothing and meet me…"

"If you thought of that, you should think of having a friend at your side as well. Come, I've known you for years. Tell me what we're going to do."

"I can't tell you all of it because I can't make a plan until I see the place. Is your sword for dress or for use? I've another you could borrow."

"My father gave me this when I left home for London. He said it would be serviceable for footpads or an affair of honor. It will do."

"Very well, then. It may be this will come to naught, or very little, and we may yet make a late appearance at Lady White's."

"It bids fair to make an amusing change from the usual entertainments," said Jeffreys.

****

"Try to look less like a hanging judge," Jeffreys admonished. "You'll terrify 'em, 'pon rep, you will."

A greasy-looking rascal opened the door at

Anniscote's heavy rap. The duke shouldered him aside, calling out, "Wine! We want wine!"

"'Ere, sir, this is no public 'ouse…" the man protested. "We got nothing for gents o' your quality to drink…"

"It's not a tavern we want. You've got women, don't you? That's what we're after. And I'll wager you've got something we can drink."

A thin little dame with a lined face and snapping dark eyes came forward. "We'll accommodate the gentlemen somehow, Sam. Come into the parlor and inspect the wares, sirs."

The "wares" were clad either in their smocks or in tawdry finery which must have been bought second- or third-hand. At least, since it was still comparatively early, the women did not look as tousled as they would later.

"We've a tolerable brandy," the bawd said. "Our wine, I confess, is not of the best. Or there's porter or ale or gin."

"Porter! Ay, that's a strengthening drink. For as Shakespeare says somewhere, wine increases the urge but takes away performance. Something like that."

"Oh, yes, porter," Tom agreed and began to laugh like a fool or a man already gone in drink. He had a lively sense of the ridiculous.

Anniscote heard the rapscallion who'd admitted them mutter to one of his fellows, "A pair of rum cullies, flush and ripe."Anniscote guessed the man thought they'd be easily plucked. The duke threw himself down on a chair, and Tom took another, beaming foolishly at the whores. They smiled back languishingly or pertly or mischievously.

Mugs of porter came and the bawd said, "If you've made your choices, gentlemen—"

"It bears thinking on," Tom said. "One mustn't make a hasty decision."

"And I'll drink the health of every one first," Anniscote said. "Beginning with you, madam. Tell me your name, dear lady."

"Get on with you now! I'm Susan, your hostess," the thin woman said.

"To Susan's bright eyes," the duke said, raising his glass to her, and drinking.

"To Susan," Tom echoed, a beat late. Anything to slow the proceedings down. Fortunately, the porter was drinkable—undoubtedly a better choice than either wine or brandy would be in such a place.

"And you, girl with the flaxen hair?"

"Bella, if it please you, sir?"

"And if it doesn't?"

"Then I'm Beth," she giggled.

"To Bella-Beth, good health."

Four toasts made and another four to go, someone slapped the door with an open palm and cried, "Open up!"

Thank God, Anniscote thought, recognizing the voice of Solomon, his second footman. There was a little banter as Solomon and Davy, one of the grooms, came in. The two girls seated on a sofa made room for Solomon, and Davy draped himself over the back of a chair, the better to look down its occupant's smock.

"Too crowded here now," Anniscote said. "Better choose before these fellows snabble the pick of the litter. I'll take the pretty Bella."

Susan murmured an amount deprecatingly in his

ear, and he pressed a guinea into her hand.

"Red-haired Kitty for me," Tom said.

Bella was already leading Anniscote to the stairs, her arm hooked through his. Solomon grinned at him as he passed. Behind him, Tom had his arm around his Irish charmer and (by the sound of it) pretended to stagger a little.

At the top of the stairs, Tom and Kitty close behind, Bella started to lead Anniscote toward the front of the house.

"Nay, I've a mind to see what's upstairs," he said, disengaging his arm and going up the next stairs two at a time.

"But there's not a thing up there," Kate called after him. "My chamber's down here." And she started up after him.

Glancing in both directions, the duke heard Matthew say softly, "Your Grace!"

Anniscote turned back to the stair and shouted, "Fire! There's flames at the back of the house!"

The signal given, Tom, still on the floor below, spun the Irish lass around and gave her a gentle shove. "For your life, get downstairs and warn the others—the house is afire!" although it was certain everyone in the parlor had heard at least Anniscote's bellow. Then the duke hurried back down a few steps until he was one above Bella, who stood frozen halfway up the stairs, and turned her around. "Go on down. I'll just make sure everyone on this floor gets out."

She fled down the flight of stairs, and Tom ran along the hall below, pounding on each door and yelling, "Fire! Fire in the upper storey! Save yourselves!" The Great Fire was three-quarters of a century past, but Londoners had not forgotten; the corridor filled with panicky half-clothed women and their stumbling customers, trying to pull up their breeches while keeping a grip on their coats and hats. They streamed toward the stair leading down, while Tom ran up the steps in Anniscote's wake.

"Have you the key?" Anniscote demanded.

"Ay, sir. They give it to me so's I could let the maid in with their dinner." He pushed open the rough door, and Anniscote hurried forward, his heart pounding with more than exertion. He hardly knew which would be worse: finding Anne within or finding only some debtor-wench.

One girl he had never seen before; her eyes were wide, and showing white around the edges. The other—

"Your Grace!" Anne Sinclair took the other girl's hand and pulled her toward the door. Anniscote found he was exhaling a breath half of pure relief and half of exasperation. 'Twould have been monstrous embarrassing to have freed only a pair of doxies, who'd likely have done better in the Colonies than in London. Her kerchief had come untucked, exposing the top of breasts like pink alabaster, though no doubt warmer. He scarcely knew whether he wished to strangle her or kiss her, not that he had time for either at the moment. How was it that Anne Sinclair found herself in such situations?

"Matthew, you take them out, keeping among the others who are fleeing until you get outside. I'll follow. I've a weapon, if it's necessary."

"Ay, Your Grace, but so've I." And he pulled a bludgeon out from under his disreputable coat.

"Your Grace," Anne started to say, but Anniscote

cut her off.

"We haven't much time before one of them notices there's no fire. Turn left when you go out. Davy and Solomon are downstairs. When they see you, they will set upon you and abduct Mistress Anne and her maid. Mistress Anne, your part is to allow yourself to be rescued. My coach is around the corner. If you are pursued, Jeffreys and I will delay them. Don't wait for us. My men will take you to your aunt's home. We'll come later to explain to her. Matthew, appear to put up a fight. Let yourself be knocked down. I don't want your employers to realize you're not their loyal man. Quickly, now!"

With a nod, Matthew herded Anne and the maid to the stair and down past Tom.

Anniscote grinned and ran lightly after them, saying, "Thomas, we will follow them. If anyone seeks to stop him, we will prevent them—but not as if we were doing so. We blunder into their way, trip them by accident, grab them and bawl 'Fire!' or what you will. But be ready to draw if you must."

"Well enough," Jeffreys said with an answering grin and followed.

The lower floors were deserted, as was the reception room where they had seen the women of the house. A manservant ran past, toward the back with no more than a glance at them.

The street was full of people, not only those who'd been in the brothel but also passers-by who had stopped to see what was happening and street sellers and pickpockets hoping to make a little money from the crowd. The bawd saw Matthew and the prisoners and began to push her way toward them. The occupants of neighboring houses had come out, trying to see what was on fire. Some, fearing for their own dwellings, were carrying their most cherished possessions.

Anniscote reached her first.

"The upper floors are emptied, we made sure of that," he assured her, remembering to sound fuddled. They were sure to realize eventually he was behind the escape, but the longer she took him for a harmless drunken reveler, the better. "Terrible thing, a house fire, terrible."

He caught a glimpse of Solomon and Matthew on the edge of the crowd; Davy, shorter than either, was invisible, as were Anne and the maid. Then Matthew disappeared from view and Solomon turned and hastened away.

"Ay," Tom added, giving the madam a buss on her painted cheek, "all your chicks are safe, and their gentlemen as well. Adzooks, it was funny to see 'em trying to pull on their breeches and shoes and run all at once."

"I thank you, sirs," the woman replied distractedly, trying to see around Anniscote and Tom, although she could hardly have seen over the mob anyway. "If you'll excuse me, I have much to see to…"

The duke saw Matthew pushing through the crowd, rubbing his jaw and staggering a little. He met Anniscote's eyes and gave a minuscule nod.

"We'll take our leave, then, and find some entertainment elsewhere tonight. Too bad, I fancied that Belle. Or Beth. Whatever the chit's name is." He supposed she hardly heard him, as she was trying to free herself from Tom, who had taken possession of her hand so that he could kiss it. Jeffreys clearly had a yearning for the stage.

"Susan, I can see naught amiss anywhere," a brawny brute shouted to make himself heard over the buzz of questions and exclamations. "There's no smoke nor flames showing."

She heard that, no question, and turned to him. By unspoken agreement, Anniscote and Jeffreys drifted away. They wove through the mass of onlookers, and once out of the press, made briskly for the next street.

The coach was gone, thank God. "This way," Anniscote said and led the way into a lane which was no better than an alley, and then into a wider street.

"The sooner we're out of here, the better," Tom remarked.

"That's my thought. I have hopes of finding a hackney this way."

****

"And that is what we were doing tonight, Thomas," Anniscote said as the hackney coach rumbled along.

Jeffreys looked appalled. "This is monstrous. The poor girl is ruined—and through no fault of her own, it seems. What's to be done?"

"First, we must reassure the aunt. Which means making some explanation which will not send her into a fit of the megrims and which must certainly not include the earlier episode."

"Errr…are you sure you want my company?"

Anniscote smiled thinly. "I did warn you this night's work might be embarrassing, didn't I? Yes. Your presence may make it seem more respectable—"

"I cannot imagine how.'

"Come, come. This involves only a little social difficulty, not the possibility of being set on by a pack

208

of unhanged felons."

****

The scene at Letitia Bradshaw's house proved to be one any rational man would wish to avoid at all costs. Which must prove that he himself was fit for Bedlam, Anniscote reflected. On the other hand, Tom's expression—that of a martyr going to the stake for his faith, a combination of tight-lipped resignation and the wish that he might be elsewhere—made it almost worthwhile. At least, the lady was past her first bout of hysterics. After falling on Anne with little cries of joy, Mistress Bradshaw had first fainted, then burst into tears when she had been revived with smelling salts. The room was still as full of women as could be: Mistress Bradshaw, her maid, Anne, the girl they'd freed with Anne, and another maid, Sally. Anne was white-faced from shame or exhaustion or reaction, but her kerchief was once again in place, he noticed with regret. He wished he could talk to her privately.

After Mrs. Bradshaw had recovered her composure and had her butler bring ratafia for the ladies (and the maids, too, which he thought amazing egalitarian of her, almost radical) and brandy for Tom and himself, she felt able to hear the story.

"So my footman, who happened to be passing, heard Mistress Anne and the girl—Prue, is it?—calling for help from the upper window and came to me, and I and my friend Mr. Jeffreys and my servants were able to release the prisoners." Knowing Anne, he had no qualms that she would betray the fact that he was editing the account somewhat, and little Prue was too timid to speak in such company. Better not to mention the nature of the building in which they had been held.

He did wonder how he should account for Prue's connection to the affair. If at all. Perhaps Mrs. Bradshaw wouldn't notice the omission.

"Poor Prudence was kidnapped, too," Anne volunteered before he had to decide. "They planned to send us to the Colonies as bond servants. I had no idea that there was such a trade. Apparently it is quite lucrative, too. I suppose, as I was dressed quite plainly, that they assumed it was safe to abduct me."

Anniscote regarded her with approval. It would be less worrisome to Mistress Bradshaw to believe Anne had been kidnapped at random. If she did not notice or question the gaps in the tale, why burden her with explanations which would not add to her peace of mind.

Letitia Bradshaw had quite enough on her mind to overlook the omissions and inconsistencies. "They say the criminal class has grown shockingly bold. I have heard of gentlemen robbed even in broad daylight in fine neighborhoods, yes, in their very coaches, but I had no idea—whatever are we to do? Oh, Anne, I am so sorry, but it will be all over town. I fear that you will be utterly humiliated and…and…" Then she began to sob again.

He cleared his throat. "I realize that some talk may be occasioned by her disappearance and subsequent return by my coach. It might be best to say that she met friends and went to visit them, then stayed for dinner. I offered to escort her home. Mr. Jeffreys was also present," Anniscote said, levelling a look at him.

"Certainly I was present," the latter agreed. "It would not have been proper for a young lady to share a coach with one man."

Letitia Bradshaw, who was not entirely bird-witted,

stopped sniffling long enough to retort, "That would be a very good story, Your Grace, if so many of my servants did not know it to be false."

"But our servants know all of our secrets already, don't they?" Thomas Jeffreys said. "We don't usually admit it to ourselves, but they do. Unless you have one you know to be dishonest—or at least unreliable—there is no reason to suppose they will not support any story you tell. I'm sure Sally would never say a word," he added, smiling at the young woman who was evidently Anne's maid. "Or your own woman, either, ma'am."

"Never, sir," Sally breathed, and Polly nodded as well.

"As to that…well, it is true. And most of my staff have been with me for years. The footman who was with you, Anne. He's only been employed for a year or two, and I'm afraid he's not very clever."

"I expect your butler will make sure he understands what he is to say, or not say."

"He's the housekeeper's nephew, ma'am," Polly said. "George is not needle-witted, but he knows when to hold his tongue. When he's told, like."

"So there is no reason to suppose it will become a matter for gossip," the duke said, after Mrs. Bradshaw had wiped her eyes and had another sustaining glass of ratafia.

"You may well be right about the upper servants, but still, some of the others may talk, not meaning to do any harm, but I know the kitchen maid at least gossips with the tradespeople who come to the kitchen door with deliveries. Even threatening to turn them off without a reference won't prevent them from making some slip."

"Then you must simply brazen it out with the help of any close friends or relatives you have who will support you. How many know Mistress Anne was missing?"

"My nephew, the Earl of Wemley, of course. When Sally and George returned and told me what had happened, I sent a note around to him, begging him to call upon me. I did not know what else to do."

"And what did he suggest?"

"At first he thought I should report the matter to the local magistrate, but his wife, who accompanied him, did not agree. She said and I think she was correct, that if they were acquainted, it might serve, but since Thomas de Veil is unknown to him, it would be better not to make Anne's abduction public. Instead, we sent the most reliable of my footmen to look for Anne and make inquiries. George did not see what happened. Which," she said, brightening a little, "may be all to the good. Sally said she thought she had been taken away in a hackney coach that stopped nearby. But none of the stall keepers noticed anything, being occupied with preventing theft or damage to their property. We made inquiries at the hospitals, too, and then we could do nothing but hope Anne was able to make her way home somehow. Although if she had not done so, I must have gone to Colonel de Veil."

"If your nephew and his lady lend their support to Mistress Anne, we may be able to weather any ill-natured talk. I will continue to call, certainly, and Mr. Jeffreys will do so, by your leave. If anyone says anything to either of us, we will give the rumor the lie."

"I'm sure my nephew the earl and his lady will help, and thank you for your kindness, and thank you, too, Mr. Jeffreys. We will be pleased to receive you. And there is an old friend of my brother, Anne's guardian, you know, who will also stand by us."

Mistress Bradshaw agreed to keep Prudence until Anniscote could arrange to send her to Guysbridge. As he rose to take his leave, Anne exclaimed, "Oh, wait a moment, please, Your Grace! I've a book you lent me that I should return. If you will excuse me while I fetch it?"

At home, he looked inside the book, which was quite definitely not one of his own, and found a scrawled note.

"*Come tomorrow at 3:00. My aunt rests in her boudoir then. I have things to tell you.*"

What a clever young lady she was! What a pity she was so unmaidenly. On the other hand, one would never be bored in her company.

Chapter 30

There was no impropriety in visiting her the next day in spite of her aunt's not being present: Mistress Anne had Prue with her. Anniscote found Prue's revelations particularly interesting, having himself been the target of her former mistress's schemes. Anne's look-alike had merely wanted to scrape acquaintance with him, in the hope of becoming his duchess. Ploys to secure an eligible man's regard were not unknown—although the girl had carried it further than most would—but after that, her mother had become involved and attempted to ruin Anne. Why? Because she resembled the other girl? Why should she care?

The trail from Prue's young lady mistress to Priscilla was clear. The mother had found out about her daughter's scandalous behavior and decided to scotch it by sending her daughter to Bath in the company of a stricter chaperon than her maidservant. That made sense. Very likely, she would have her husband arrange a suitable marriage before the chit could get into any more trouble. Having made use of Prue to employ Prissy, she had dismissed the former. Prissy would not have decided on her own to discredit Anne. Further, what Anne had overheard made it clear that Prissy was being paid to do so. He would not gamble on the source of that money being someone other than Prue's old mistress; such odds at the gaming table would ruin one.

The duke fixed Prue with a stern eye. "You have not told us your mistress's name, Prue."

"My mistress told me not to talk about the family, sir. She said it might hurt my young mistress's reputation if I blurted something out, and she give me a pound to remind me."

"Under the circumstances, Prue, I think you must tell us," Anne said. "As it seems that my abduction is somehow connected to your mistress."

The maid's chin trembled. "If I tell, it might be she'll swear out a charge against me for that petticoat."

"You need not worry about that. I will explain matters to the magistrate, if it becomes necessary. And she will not be quick to accuse you of theft, when she knows you could tell a tale that would harm her and her daughter. Who is she?"

She took a deep breath. "Mistress Saltstall, Your Grace. The master is Richard Saltstall, the alderman."

Anniscote saw Anne give a little start of surprise, but Prue did not notice; her eyes were fixed on her clasped hands.

"I think," Anne said, "that I would be the better for a walk in the square."

"Should you go out, Mistress Anne?" Prue asked hesitantly.

"With His Grace's escort, I daresay it will be safe enough. You will follow us, of course, which will make it perfectly proper."

When they were in the square and Anne and the duke were out of Prue's hearing, he murmured, "What is it?"

"Marianne Saltstall, the alderman's wife, is Mistress Bradshaw's niece—my late guardian's daughter."

"Well, we make some progress. Though I had hoped that when we knew who your enemy was, we would know why you were being persecuted. Unless you have some idea?"

"It's a mystery to me," Anne said. "I have met her only twice, and I did not perceive that she had taken me in dislike. Perhaps you know how it is: sometimes you meet someone and immediately conceive a distaste for him. Though it would have to be a strong emotion indeed, I would think, to lead one to such lengths."

"I do know, having abhorred one or two on sight, myself. What is she like? What is her daughter like?"

"I have not met Mariah, her daughter. She herself is rather cold, or at least aloof. She does not seem happy. I wonder if she is in poor health? For when she paid a call on Aunt Letitia soon after I arrived, she seemed overset. She did write to Aunt Letitia when she realized Mariah would have to go out of town to recover—"

"Or to be removed from temptation's path," Anniscote added.

"Yes, it does seem likely, doesn't it? Aunt Letitia said something that suggested she is rather flighty."

"You would not be—" He had meant to ask if she could have become the object of devotion to some swain of Mariah Saltstall's and then rejected the notion as ridiculous: Anne could not rival a beauty like the Saltstall girl. But if Anne so closely resembled her...He turned his head to study Anne's profile.

It was easy to see how a face he'd dismissed as no more than ordinary might actually be beautiful. The appearance of plainness came from its being bare of cosmetics and revealing lively intelligence and perhaps a streak of single-mindedness. A few tendrils of hair had escaped confinement. The effect was rather fetching. She had a very neat figure—quite embraceable, too. While not as fashionable as Mariah Saltstall's style of beauty, he found it more interesting. From the side, she might be mistaken for a depiction of one of the goddesses. Athena, perhaps, or Diana. If she painted her face and aped the ways of other young ladies of good family, she would be very pretty indeed. Or should that be "merely pretty"? One wouldn't call Athena or Diana pretty. Lovely perhaps or radiant, yes. But that left out the liveliness that distinguished Anne. How odd that powder and paint should be thought to confer beauty. And if she simpered, fluttered her eyelashes, and avoided all controversy, she would be as insipid as rice pudding, like the rest. If Letitia Bradshaw's circle intersected the Saltstalls' at some point, Anne might have been a rival to Mariah.

"Your Grace?"

Recovering himself, he said, "If you have not been going out in society enough to be a rival to Mistress Saltstall's daughter, you are inconvenient in some other fashion. I was merely trying to think what it could be. If they had attempted to murder you, I would wonder if someone coveted your inheritance."

Anne chuckled rather than tittered, Anniscote noted with approval.

"My house at Fletching, with six bedrooms and stabling for six horses, and my two hundred pounds a year income?" She sounded amused. Anniscote, who knew that among many middling folk such an inheritance would make her sought after, was not.

"In some parts of London, you might be killed for a shilling or two. I suppose you do not know what becomes of the house and money if you were to die unmarried?"

"Of course I do! I sat through the reading of the will, and then the attorney explained it all to me, clause by clause, as if I were too silly to have understood when he read it. If I should die unmarried, it passes to a foundling hospital in Lincoln."

"Ah! Then there can be no motive there."

"Unless the foundling hospital's directors covet my goods," Anne suggested. "Or, wait—someone among my limited acquaintance here desires my inheritance for his second or third or fourth son, and wishes to ruin me so that I will accept the first proposal made me, which would, of course, be the son's." She glanced at him, a gleam in her eyes.

"Yes, an excellent plot for a novel! But you forget that we know the author of your difficulties, and it is Mistress Saltstall, who has no son, I believe."

"Perhaps she has a lover she wishes to benefit?"

"Brass-faced little hussy!" he said. She had recovered her sense of humor. "Strive to be serious."

"Yes, I should be in hysterics, I suppose. What am I to do? Should I leave London and take up residence elsewhere?"

"I wonder if the intent was to remove you from London, and rendering you a social outcast was intended to accomplish that end? From the conversation you heard between Priss and Ned, some care was being taken not to harm you."

She turned and stared at him then. "Not to harm me! Your Grace, do you think social ruin is not harm?"

218

"Certainly, in the sentimental view, that is true. And yet we know that ladies sometimes elope, which is said to be social ruin, or have lovers, and are not the worse for it in the eyes of the world. By harm, I mean physical injury or death."

"Perhaps those things are overlooked in ladies of high rank, but would society be so forgiving of plain Mistress Anne from the country? Can a gentleman suffer no harm that is not physical? What if he is given an undeserved reputation as a rake or card cheat?"

The duke concealed a wince. Of course, his own family actually deserved their evil reputation, at least over the last century or so. "You're very earnest, Mistress Anne. But you are right on both scores. I beg your pardon. Rank does change the rules. To some extent, at least."

"And the rules differ for men and women," she continued.

"Agreed." They contemplated each other briefly.

She said, "I confess I have no idea how to discover why my ruin should be desirable, to Mistress Saltstall or anyone else."

"You do not wish to think she is to blame, do you?"

Anne sighed. "No. She is my late guardian's daughter and Mistress Bradshaw's niece, and for their sake, I wish it were someone else. But all the evidence we have is against her."

"I could pursue the matter from the criminal end, as we know that Priss and Ned were involved. We could have them taken in charge by the magistrate, and they might reveal their employer's name."

"That would be to make it public," Anne pointed

out.

"Yes, that's the rub. I might pay Mistress Saltstall a visit and ask her what she means by it. That might frighten her off."

"Or it might not. She might simply deny everything."

"I could then threaten her with witnesses. Prissy would not keep silent for the lady, do you think?"

"No, but again, that would make it all public."

"Which would harm Mistress Saltstall as much as you. I do agree such an approach solves nothing, Mistress Anne. When we learn why you are a target, we will know how to eliminate the danger."

"But how are we to find out?"

"I set one of my footmen to work in Priss's family business. The one who guarded the door at that house and escorted you out in the confusion. He is still in place, and I hope may yet discover something. It may take some time, and in the interim, you will have to be careful. For God's sake, no more excursions to the bookstalls! Or shopping, or…"

"In short, I should stay in Mistress Bradshaw's house and not venture out."

"Precisely."

"I suppose you are right." And they parted on terms of some coolness.

****

Brazen baggage, the duke thought. But she never gave way to vapors, and she must have the heart of a lion. Lioness. And how enterprising for a lady to pick a lock, as she had in attempting to escape that brothel! Not that such enterprise was at all suitable in a well-bred young lady. A pity that unexceptionable ladies tended to be so unexciting. By way of settling his mind, he took up his ancestor's book.

Charles Anascote: This account of my father's gave me much to ponder, as I never thought of my ancestry, though my father taught me the Spanish language when I was very young. My brothers and sisters learned Latin and French and some Greek, as I did also, but only I learned to speak, read, and write our father's native tongue. When I was grown, I asked why he required me to become fluent in a language that, apart from his lessons with me, never passed his lips.

"I was of two minds about it," he admitted. "On the one hand, you must all be true English, that you not be suspect, as I still am. On the other, there may come a time when fluency in my native speech may be useful." I gained not only a facility with the language but also learned a great deal of Spanish life, customs, and the like.

He must have expected that there would be war with Spain eventually. Later I realized it was not simply because I was the oldest son that I spent those extra hours closeted with him, listening to tales of long-ago battles and foreign customs. I favor my mother's family, with a ruddy complexion and hair the color of ground ginger. I think Don Diego felt that if one of his sons must needs learn Spanish, it should be one who was of the most English appearance.

So it happened that I came to speak and read Spanish very fluently and was therefore able to be of some assistance to our Crown in translating certain letters and dispatches which fell into the hands of Her Majesty's agents.

Chapter 31

Aunt Letitia had left earlier than usual to visit her late husband's mother, leaving Anne to spend a dull afternoon and look forward to an equally empty evening. When Mayhew announced Mistress Saltstall, Anne's first thought was to tell him that she was not at home. But Marianne Saltstall swept in in the butler's wake, giving Anne no time to deny herself. She had no choice but to receive her. She offered Aunt Letitia's niece refreshments but was refused.

"I cannot stay long. My excuse for coming is to bring you copies of two plays which I thought might entertain you to read, and my aunt to hear, as she seldom attends the theater. *The Provok'd Husband* is a comedy and *The Mournful Nuptials* a tragedy, the two together summing up virtually all of married life. However, my real reason is to offer you my advice and my help. My dear, my heart goes out to you. I have heard rumors that, when they become more widely circulated, will ruin you. I will do what I can to help you, but…" Mistress Saltstall gave a little shrug.

Anne raised her eyebrows slightly in polite inquiry, momentarily speechless.

"Oh, I know you cannot admit to having found yourself in a compromising situation—certainly not to one who is almost a stranger to you. Nor to anyone else, I hope! But it has come to my ears that you were seen in an establishment where apparently respectable ladies go to meet their lovers. I cannot imagine a reason for any lady to go to such a place for an innocent reason, and neither will anyone else."

Anne wondered how the duke would advise she respond, then thought, *I don't need Anniscote to rescue me. And I really cannot pretend now.*

"Mistress Saltstall, I know you arranged that 'compromising situation.'"

Her visitor sat frozen, all color draining from her face. Anne almost wished she were in the habit of carrying smelling salts with her. She really did not want to have to summon a servant. At last, Mistress Saltstall said, "I don't know what you mean."

"I have evidence that you conspired with a young woman called Priscilla to lure me to that place," Anne said. "Please take a deep breath. If you faint, I shall have to ring for a maid, and I am convinced you would rather this be kept between us."

Mrs. Saltstall swallowed visibly and took several breaths. "A virtuous young lady would not slip out to go to a clandestine meeting."

Anne stared at her coolly. "Certainly my behavior would be criticized, but yours would create a scandal. Everyone would want to know why you had done such a thing and would speculate upon it. Priscilla's testimony in court, and that of those who assisted her, would embarrass your husband the alderman and you and your daughter, whose own behavior seems to have been questionable, at best. I don't think I'd rely on Prissy keeping silent," Anne added. "I have no idea what the penalties may be for abduction and forging indentures, but I expect Colonel Thomas de Veil, the magistrate, could inform us."

Mistress Saltstall groped blindly in her pocket for a handkerchief and, finding it, pressed it to her eyes. As Anne had not noted the presence of tears beforehand, she assumed it was to gain time to think. It was a mystery to her how Dr. Sinclair's daughter could be so lacking in principle. Which reminded her of the odd way in which kittens sometimes did not resemble their mother at all. And what about family traits, like height or a certain shape of jaw or aptitude for mathematics or music. What caused such similarities and differences?

Marianne Saltstall folded the handkerchief. Anne's suspicion was confirmed; no one can weep without leaving the eyes reddened and puffy.

"I must apologize to you, Mistress Anne, and beg you to forgive me. Does my poor aunt know?"

"You mean, does she know you are responsible for trying to ruin me? No. She knows I was abducted but thinks it was for ransom. I did not wish to cause her more sorrow and anxiety than she already felt over the incident."

"I am glad of that. She was so kind to me when I lived with her, as I expect she is kind to you."

"Yes, and it's especially good of her, when I am only the remotest connection," Anne agreed.

"Then you would not wish to reveal my folly to her, either, out of consideration for her feelings. I have been wicked, but I hope you will understand the reason for it." She sighed deeply. "How can I make you comprehend it when I do not understand myself. It's so difficult…"

"Perhaps it will be easier if you simply tell me why you tried to destroy my reputation, and why you meant to have me sent to the American colonies as an indentured servant."

"You learned that bluntness from my father, I suppose. Ever since I was a girl, and he sent me to live with my aunt, I have been jealous of you. He took you in and kept you with him. Between that time and his death, I doubt I saw him half a dozen times, when he visited London on other business. Then he left you everything—no, I don't begrudge it you. I don't need a cottage in some little village miles from anywhere or his books or a few extra guineas. My husband is wealthy, and you had no other resources. But when I saw you and thought of all those years of abandonment by my father, it was more than I could bear."

"Were you angry?"

"Yes, furious."

Anne could not remember ever being jealous of another person. Except perhaps the squire's oldest daughter, who had a gray horse with a coat like watered silk and the smoothest paces. But it was not difficult to understand Marianne's distress over seeming to be supplanted in her father's affections. Only, it was odd that she did not sound angry. Nor had her face flushed, which would have been another sign of agitation. Anne had a sudden memory of one of the Beatons' visitors, a lady who complained she'd lost her balance and sprained her ankle. After Dr. Sinclair attended her, Anne remarked that it was too bad that she would be unable to enjoy her stay in the country. Her guardian said dryly, "You needn't pity her. There's nothing wrong with her ankle."

Knowing from personal experience that a sprain might show little outward sign of its existence, she asked how he knew.

"If that foot or ankle had been sprained, she would have winced when I was examining it. It did not really pain her. She'd turned it a trifle—damme, why will ladies wear such ridiculous shoes? She merely enjoyed being the center of attention."

"But surely it would be more pleasant to be able to ride and walk in the garden and go down to dinner and dance, rather than to have to rest in her chamber."

"Sometimes ladies depend upon ill health to make themselves interesting or hold their families' interest. Women of the middling and lower classes usually have too many responsibilities and too much work to take to their beds except for childbirth or actual illness. Be that a lesson to you, Anne, to keep your hands and mind occupied."

Mistress Saltstall's recollection of the jealousy she claimed she'd felt was strangely without emotion. An actress on the stage would have done it more convincingly, Anne thought. It did not mean she was lying—some people's emotions are shallow or well-controlled. But would nothing more than jealousy have led her to commit two well-planned attacks against Anne?

"Did it have anything to do with my resembling your daughter?"

The handkerchief came into play again. "You know about that?"

"His Grace of Guysbridge deduced it," Anne replied. She did not want to betray that poor Prue had supplied the confirmation.

"It would have been...it would have caused talk," Mistress Saltstall said finally. "I can't explain to you…"

"Why? The Earl of Wemley and an old friend of your father's both told me I have the Sinclair features that show up in some of the family portraits. Your daughter evidently does, too." Seeing her expression, Anne remembered something the earl had mentioned. "You didn't know that, did you? You only visited Wemley once, when you were a child, and I suppose paid no attention to the portrait gallery."

Mistress Saltstall's expression put her in mind of a stuffed fox she had seen in the home of one of Dr. Sinclair's acquaintances. The similarity was in the fixed, glassy eyes, perhaps.

At last she heaved a deep sigh. "My dear girl…I don't know how to tell you this," she began.

"Ma'am?"

"You are my father's illegitimate daughter. My half-sister."

"Oh!" Then, "Oh, good! Thank you for telling me. It explains so much."

This response appeared to stun her visitor. "How can you call it good? There is nothing good in the shame of your birth, the doors that will be closed to you, the whispers, the impossibility of making a decent marriage."

"I realize it must be an embarrassment to you, and I'm sorry for it," Anne said, a little guilty for not taking Mistress Saltstall's feelings into account. Considering it, she supposed that knowing one's father had a by-blow might be uncomfortable, even though everyone knew that men did have such connections. "That Grand…that Dr. Sinclair…that my father…took me in makes it more respectable, it seems to me." At least she now knew what the difficulty was and why he would not discuss it with her. "Who was my mother? What became of her?"

"She was a woman my father met while we stayed in France," Marianne replied. "She died, and her relatives did not care to raise her bastard."

"I wonder he did not marry her." Not to do so seemed out of character for James Sinclair, but men were odd creatures. Perhaps her mother had been of peasant stock so that making her his wife would be a greater handicap to him and to Anne than the stigma of illegitimacy. It was another mystery, but one she did not feel she needed to investigate. And it solved her problem and Mistress Saltstall's. Marianne's. *My half-sister*, Anne thought. How strange to think of it. After a moment, she said, "I don't see that it is any great matter for concern. It's always been believed I was a distant relative of the Sinclairs, so there is nothing amazing in my looking like a Sinclair. So you see, there is no reason anyone would suspect that I am not simply a member of a branch of the Sinclair family, and therefore, I should be no embarrassment to you. And you need not attempt to remove me now. Because that is what you were doing, wasn't it—trying to get me out of town?"

"Yes. If you can forgive me, there is no reason we should not be friendly. Indeed, it will cause talk if we do not appear to be on good terms. It would also cause Aunt Letitia distress."

"Yes, of course." The appearance of civility was necessary to smooth things over between them, though Anne doubted she would ever feel warmly toward Marianne. Her answer was not really a lie, either, as she had not said she forgave her. "Your actions have not had much effect."

"Even if there should be some gossip, my cousin the earl and his family and Aunt Letitia will make it plain there is nothing to any talk that does arise," Marianne said.

"There is only one thing that might pose a difficulty," Anne said, with a little hesitation. "When I was leaving that house, a Mr. Hurst saw me. At the engagement ball, he recognized me."

Marianne repeated, "Hurst?" and pressed her for details of the meeting, though there was little more to tell.

"He made me quite uncomfortable. It is hardly surprising he should have a false opinion of me, considering where he first saw me."

"If that man is showing an interest in you, you must—must!—leave London, and soon."

"Why? I go nowhere unchaperoned now."

Her newly discovered half-sister seemed to grope for words. "If Hurst spreads gossip about seeing you...or abducts you...no, you would be safest out of town." She twisted her pretty handkerchief so hard Anne heard the fine lace edging rip.

Before Anne could ponder the volatility of Mistress Saltstall's emotions, Marianne said, "I realize that moving to another part of the country will be an expense you can ill afford. You would have to hire a house or at least lodgings, engage a companion—not that that will amount to much! Some indigent but genteel older lady will cost you less than I pay my abigail. Still, it is an expense. For my father's sake, and to spare my aunt humiliation, and of course to save you from Hurst's advances, I will give you three hundred pounds. That should cover your moving to wherever you will, and leave a bit over."

Anne found herself speechless. Here was Mistress Saltstall, again trying to send her away. She could not help suspecting that Marianne had not given up her schemes and had struck upon the mention of Hurst as an excuse.

"I will also pay for the cost of the journey by post chaise. That would of course include the postilions, changes of horses, and lodging at inns, which will be a great saving for you."

"I really think there is no need for such extreme measures," Anne replied.

Mrs. Saltstall took a deep breath. "Hurst is a rake and utterly without principles. Do not underestimate your danger."

"I will be careful. I have learned something from your own efforts to rid London of my presence."

Marianne's rose-leaf complexion flushed pinker. "You are gracious to overlook my offense against you. But please consider my advice carefully. I truly believe the only course is for you to retire from London for a time at least. If you are not present, Hurst will forget you soon enough, and any gossip that has arisen will be forgotten when some new scandal occurs. You won't mention this conversation to my aunt, I hope? She does not know the truth about your birth."

"Of course not."

On the whole, Anne felt, her problems were at an end. If Marianne would still prefer her absence, at least she was unlikely to attempt anything further. The difficulties between them had been covered over, in the manner of a woman with a raddled complexion applying powder and paint—appearance, if not reality.

As Marianne rose to leave, Anne said, "Mistress Saltstall? The earl regrets that his father did not keep up the family connection and was sorry you were not in town for the engagement ball. He and the countess mean to invite you and your family to their other entertainments."

"Thank you, Anne, you are more kind than I deserve. And I believe you are correct to maintain a certain formality between us, rather than expecting a—a sisterly relationship." This time, Anne thought that Marianne was on the verge of tears. But she quickly turned to leave, so she could not be certain.

Chapter 32

For years afterward, Anne recalled her first visit to Vauxhall Gardens as a mixture of fairy tale and nightmare. The earl had arranged a party to visit the famous gardens, comprising Aunt Letitia, herself, the earl and his lady, a Mr. Dunham, the duke, the Saltstalls, and Mr. Jeffreys. "More would be awkward," he explained, "as the shelters in which our supper will be served hold ten handily."

It started out so well, with Anne relieved of her worry and certain that nothing else could mar her pleasure.

They went by boat from the Westminster Bridge stairs, the trip up-river being part of the enjoyment of visiting the Gardens on the south bank. The weather was pleasantly warm for a change, making the river breeze welcome. Disembarking at the Vauxhall Stairs, they strolled a few yards to the entrance, where the earl paid their entrance fee.

"I have only been here a few times, myself," he remarked. "I am pleased to visit the Gardens again. It is quite out of the ordinary."

Entering the central portion of the grounds, Anne thought she saw what he meant. The orchestra building occupied the center of the Grove, with the supper boxes ringing the area.

"There you see the statue of Handel," the earl said.

"I like it, don't you, Aunt Letitia? There's a charm to its informality."

"It is a fine piece of work," she admitted, "but to show him relaxing, as it might be in his own chamber, with no wig…I am not quite sure how I feel about it. And yet, it suits the setting."

"Those are handsome paintings, too, in the shelters."

The orchestra finished "Black Eyed Susan" and struck up "Nymphs and Shepherds," and the earl suggested they stroll around the grounds until it was time for supper.

"Oh, yes, let's do so," Anne said, "if Lady Wemley and Aunt Letitia do not mind? I would like to see everything while there is still light enough."

"Yes, indeed," the countess replied, good-humoredly. Anne thought that the earl and his lady and her aunt exchanged amused glances, and supposed it was because they viewed her as a child begging for a treat, which was a little embarrassing. But the gardens were lovely, and she was anxious to see them. Mr. Saltstall begged that they be excused on the ground that he wished to introduce his wife and daughter to a friend who was there with his own family, and they had been to Vauxhall Gardens many times. The duke and Mr. Jeffreys accompanied the earl's group.

They proceeded to the statue of Aurora, the notes of "Sally in Our Alley" behind them. Anne found the other attendees no less amazing than the views. It seemed that anyone who could afford the one shilling admission fee was there and in high good humor. Gentlemen and ladies, the nobility, merchants and tradesmen, and even apprentices. Families brought their children as well.

The sun sank, and it began to be rather dim under the trees.

"We should start back," the earl said. "They'll begin serving shortly."

"What a pity the evening is not longer," Anne said. "I suppose it is not open during the day? One would have more time to admire its beauties." She happened to be facing the duke and saw his lips curl a little. No doubt he was scornful of her enjoyment; ladies, she had observed, were expected to exhibit a genteel boredom with entertainments. Well, she would not pretend to be bored, and she did not care a farthing for his opinion, anyway.

"Ah, but one can visit again, whenever the weather permits," the earl said.

They were almost back to the Grove when a whistle shrilled. Everyone paused, not only their own group, but several people walking ahead of them on the path as well.

"What's…?" Anne began, but never completed the question, as suddenly the Gardens were nearly as bright as day. All around she heard "Ah!" and delighted laughter, and lamps were burning everywhere.

"How do they do that?" she asked.

"I understand that there is a system of fuses to the lamps and servants stationed all over, each of whom ignites his assigned fuse at the signal, which in turn lights a number of lamps. At least, so I've heard," the earl ended, dubiously.

"It is one of the marvels of Vauxhall Gardens," Mr. Jeffreys added.

They found the Saltstalls already returned to their

supper box and took their places as the waiters began to serve. There was ham sliced paper thin (a Vauxhall specialty, Mr. Saltstall told her) and roast chicken and a variety of custards and jellies. Mariah Saltstall had contrived to sit beside the duke. Knowing how she had hunted him, Anne wondered at her optimism; did she still think she could entrance him? From Mistress Saltstall's expression, it appeared that Mariah's mother considered it a possibility. Mr. Jeffreys sat beside Anne and conversed like a sensible man and without making any reference to the circumstances of their original meeting. Aunt Letitia and Lady Wemley appeared to approve of him. On her other side was Mr. Saltstall. Anne was rather surprised to find him well-spoken and with no sign of status-seeking in his manner. She had expected a jumped-up tradesman and a more foolish man, judging by his choice of wife. But he had made a substantial fortune, Anne understood, having come from modest beginnings. From something he said, she realized his father had been a vicar in a country parish, and that Mr. Saltstall had been taken into a cousin's business. Nor was he ill-looking; he had a grave, oblong face and wide-set brown eyes.

Her own gaze would stray to where Anniscote was listening to Mariah's prattle with half-closed eyes. He made occasional responses—when the flow of her chatter allowed—and no one could have seen anything discourteous in his behavior, but Anne thought his attitude was that of an adult to a child. Amazing that the chit thought she had a chance. Then it occurred to her that the duke had never listened so courteously to her.

Mr. Saltstall leaned toward her slightly, and said quietly, "I am not generally in favor of marriages between the nobility and merchant families. Expectations and standards of conduct are too different to lead to a successful union. I am considering a young man who has a bright future in a banking house as a possible husband for Mariah."

"I wish her every happiness," Anne said, wondering if Mariah was aware of her father's plans. From the answering twinkle in his eye, she decided she was not.

"I think," he went on, "that some contrast in personality is desirable, for a lively woman may leaven a rather stolid man, while he may restrain the worst of her fits and starts. Not that Peter Dunham is in need of much leavening," he added. "He is steady enough and very clever at his work. All he requires is a good marriage."

"I'm sure you are correct, sir," Anne agreed, with an inward sigh. They both gazed at Mariah, who was laughing merrily beside the duke, quite ignoring Mr. Dunham, and at Mistress Saltstall, on the duke's other side, whose attention was also fixed on her daughter. It was only by happenstance that a pair of men, strolling by the open front of their dinner box, caught Anne's eye. It was quite usual for visitors to Vauxhall to look into the boxes to admire the paintings on the back wall. Of course, it also gave gentlemen an excuse to study the ladies present, as well. One of the men stopped short, however, and stared rudely toward the other end of the table.

She saw Hurst's ruddy face and realized that he was looking at Mistress Saltstall. His gaze travelled on and encountered Mariah, and finally, herself. Then he smiled widely in a way that made her feel hot and oddly frightened. His enjoyment was unmistakable.

And the duke had seen him, too. Their eyes locked, Hurst gave a slight, mocking bow, and continued on his way, making some light comment to his companion.

Anniscote seemed about to rise, but then relaxed back into his seat with a visible effort. Anne thought the rest of their party had not noticed his movement or the faint, vertical lines between his brows. Mariah had not ceased to chatter. The incident was certainly a little unpleasant but of less importance than tripping over one's own feet or hem at a ball. But Hurst had seen her at that place. Yet he had said nothing since, except that one time. Besides, he had now seen her surrounded by perfectly respectable people and (she thought) noted the resemblance between Mariah and herself. With any luck, he might decide it was Mariah he'd seen at—what had Anniscote called it? A "house of accommodation"? Especially since she was sitting beside the duke. It would serve her right, the scheming cat.

By the time they left Vauxhall Gardens at the closing hour, all Anne's discomfort at seeing Hurst had been forgotten in happier memories. The delicacy and excellence of the meal, the almost magical lighting of the lamps, which Anne thought might be accomplished by means of electricity if only one could work out how, the beauty of the vistas and the statuary and the gardens, the knowledge that the question of Mariah's marriage was already settled.

Chapter 33

The incident was not recalled to her mind for several days until Aunt Letitia, in a burst of energy, decided they must take a little fresh air and exercise in the Mall.

"Mr. Grover seemed quite taken with you, at the ball," she remarked. "His money comes from his father's being in trade, of course, but importing silks and porcelain is not really objectionable, and of course, he's very gentlemanly and his uncle has a manor in the West Country. I would not be surprised if he is as successful one day as Mr. Saltstall. Do you think—"

"Oh, Aunt Letitia, Mrs. Colley and her daughter are coming up the path," Anne interrupted, glad to be able to change the subject. She knew her aunt did not care for Mrs. Colley, and she herself found Mistress Minerva Colley lacking in a sense of humor, but at least it was a distraction from the topic of Mr. Grover. Anne did not hold his connection with trade against him, and while it was not his fault that he had chubby hands and a moon face, his personality was no compensation for such drawbacks.

"Where? The blue-gray and the pink?"

"Yes, how did you know? For they are quite far off."

"While I cannot make out their faces, that steel gray is exactly the sort of color Mrs. Colley wears, and she has the same sort of peculiarly graceful gliding walk that I recall," she answered with some complacency. "I've always wondered how she does it. Why, how odd. Mrs. Colley's sight must be as bad as mine, or worse, for they have turned aside into another path. I would have thought they must have seen us."

"Certainly Minerva did. She recognized me and spoke to her mother, and then they turned away."

"Oh…" Aunt Letitia said, in fading tones.

"What's amiss, ma'am? Are you faint? Shall I send for the carriage?"

"They have given us the cut. I think, yes, I think we must go home at once." And she would say no more until she was seated at her elegant little escritoire.

"I am writing to my old friend Elvira. She seldom leaves her house, as she is very lame and she suffered cruelly from a chest complaint all winter, but she hears everything." And after scrawling a hasty note, she sent it off by one of the footmen and would say no more on the subject to Anne. Unaccustomed as she was to the ways of London society, even she could not escape a feeling of impending doom. Letitia Bradshaw, having taken decisive action by writing her letter, had sunk onto her daybed, vial of sal volatile in hand.

"But Aunt Letitia," Anne protested, "if you are not well, or are out of sorts, should I not tell Mayhew to say we are not at home to callers?"

"No, for I doubt we will have any," was the depressed reply.

They were not long left in suspense.

Even as Mayhew entered, murmuring, "Ma'am, Mrs. Nugent has come—" Anne could hear a strident voice calling, "Letty! I really cannot climb those stairs, even for you. Do come down."

Letitia sat bolt upright on the divan, exclaiming, "Elvira! Do tell her we'll be down in a trice, Mayhew. Quick, now!" Standing up and tucking her smelling salts into her pocket, she told Anne, "I really cannot shout as Elvira does. My mama slapped such tomboyish behavior out of me before I was ten. But I am so thankful she has come, for she will know what to do."

In the parlor, Mrs. Nugent perched upon her chair like some pet parrot, which she much resembled, being small and thin, with a beak-like nose. She was very brightly gowned in coral and blue-green. Clearly, too, however lame she might be, she did not avoid spending time in the sun, for she was as deeply tanned as saddle leather.

"I was sitting down to write you about the matter when your own letter came," she said. Her voice, when not raised to carry, was pleasant enough. "I heard the rumor but half an hour before, when the Pendleton sisters called upon me. Such gossips! But useful, of course."

"What did they say?" Aunt Letitia asked, with the air of one who expects the worst.

"Mind you, they're fools, so they're probably mostly wrong, and exaggerating, too. But—" And she cast a penetrating glance at Anne. "—if they're saying it, so will others, and it is as bad as it could be."

"Elvira, my nerves will not stand much more."

"Very well, it is best to face the worst." She sipped her ratafia. "The Misses Pendleton claim it is being said that your young friend here is Guysbridge's mistress and that she was actually seen with him in a house where assignations take place."

Aunt Letitia moaned and tossed off the last of her cordial, before reaching for the bottle of ratafia.

"Just so," Elvira agreed. "I don't suppose you did…?" she inquired delicately

Anne glanced at her aunt and bit her lip.

"I am not easily shocked, I assure you, and although Letitia affects these die-away airs, she is quite as practical as I. It is essential to know the truth in order to make plans."

The story poured out then, not only the first episode but also the second, accompanied by exclamations of "My goodness!" and "Good God!" from Letitia and Elvira respectively, and several intelligent questions from the latter. The only piece that Anne suppressed was Marianne Saltstall's involvement.

When she came to the end of her tangled narrative, Elvira regarded her thoughtfully. "I think there is more to this than you have told us. For although criminals might abduct a girl to sell into indentured servitude in the Colonies, they would not ordinarily choose a girl of the upper classes, who would be sought for with diligence. Servants or country girls vanish, and their families have not the resources to hunt for them, or to rouse the law on their behalf. And often enough, the girl has run off with some unsuitable swain."

"I was dressed very plainly," Anne replied. "They may have taken me for an abigail."

"That might explain it, if you had not already been lured to the house of accommodation. And Guysbridge as well. If you're quite sure he had nothing to do with bringing you there?"

"Not a thing! He positively dislikes me."

"Never say so, Anne! Why, he came to visit you.

241

So naughty," Letitia said, "to pretend to be James's acquaintance."

"The two events cannot be unrelated," Elvira Nugent said. "I do not believe in coincidence. When two fashionable and rival ladies both appear in the same gown, it is the result of some scheme, and not happenstance. The same must be true here. What is the connecting thread?"

"Now, I agree with you, Elvira. When Mrs. Bracken and Mrs. Cope both attended the opera in virtually the same *toilette,* and such a noticeable orange, too, it was all Mrs. Orris's doing, to humiliate them. And why should anyone plot against you, Anne?"

So she had no choice but to explain Marianne's involvement. "Because I rather resemble her daughter, she felt I was an embarrassment."

"How foolish of her," Letitia said.

Mrs. Nugent, however, eyed her sharply, before taking up her glass of ratafia and drinking it down in one draft, in a most unladylike manner. "Do you know, although it is considered a ladies' beverage, this is really quite strong. I've often thought as much. I believe I am getting a bit tipsy."

"I am positively as drunk as a lord, as my poor son would have said," Aunt Letitia declared. "If I may use the term."

"My dear, given what we are discussing, such a piece of cant is the least shocking thing."

"Whatever are we to do, Elvira? And what if there are further rumors?"

"What else could possibly be said that would be worse than what they are already saying?"

"My niece's claim that Anne is James's by-blow."

"A bagatelle."

"I cannot believe it. We all know gentlemen will do these things but James! No, no, he would have acknowledged her, if it were true. And how on earth could Marianne have said such a wicked thing of her own father? A lady ignores these things, if she can." Letitia began to sound angry.

"She ignores them unless she can do something about them. But there! I'm glad to hear you sounding less dispirited. We shall need boldness and resolve." And Elvira refilled her glass.

"I wonder if His Grace of Guysbridge has heard the talk?"

"I wonder if he would…" Aunt Letitia's voice trailed away.

Elvira Nugent's silvery eyebrows rose. "There is no chance of it," she replied briskly. "The Anniscotes have never been known for sentiment, principle, or self-sacrifice. Though by all accounts the current duke is better-behaved than the last one. Unless he's a fool, like his brother and father."

"He is not!" Anne interjected. "The duke is very intelligent."

Letitia and Elvira exchanged speaking glances, and Elvira said, "If that's so, he will marry an heiress. Or a girl from some great family. One must be a realist."

"Yes, of course. I don't have any *tendre* for him. He is odiously overbearing."

"It's very sensible of you. If he has heard the gossip, I wonder what he will do?"

****

Jeffreys found him in Saltero's coffeehouse. Anniscote was reading a newspaper in splendid isolation, at a table apparently shunned by all the other patrons. Ordinarily, Tom would have considered it odd, as men went to coffee houses to meet their friends, converse, and learn the news, though Don Saltero's in addition possessed the attraction of curiosities both natural and manmade. He noticed, rather nervously, that the low-voiced discussion at the other tables died as he approached the duke's table.

"Well met," Anniscote greeted him. "I had hoped for some company, and here you are."

"No topics that interest you under debate?"

"I suspect there are, but I have only to join a table to cause its occupants to recall other obligations. I wonder if I display signs of leprosy, or bear the mark of Cain upon my forehead."

Jeffreys seated himself, taking some care with the arrangement of his coat. "Then you are not *au courant* with the latest *on-dits*?"

"You should visit France, Tom; your accent is barbarous. But no, London might be a wasteland, for all I have heard today of interest."

The waiter brought coffee for Tom and refilled the duke's cup.

"You are very grave. I trust your family is well?"

"Yes, they are in good health, as far as I know. But about the earl's party at Vauxhall…I did not mention it then, because we were with others, and there was no opportunity afterward, and there seemed no reason to speak of it."

"Ah! I wondered if you'd seen Hurst there."

"I did. And I thought his behavior was peculiar."

"I thought he intended some mischief."

"That, undoubtedly," Jeffreys replied grimly.

"What's he done?" Anniscote demanded, with profound misgiving.

"Why do you think everyone is keeping well out of your way, John? No one dares tell you what is being said. I have not been able to hunt down the source of the rumors, but I have no doubt they originated with Hurst."

"What rumors?"

Jeffreys lowered his voice yet more. The other patrons of the coffeehouse were carefully taking no notice of them, but their conversations were still very subdued. "About your meeting with Mistress Anne at a house of assignation."

"She was lured to that house, as was I."

"Mistress Anne's abduction seems to have gone without notice thus far, but it's a damnable coil," Jeffreys said.

"Damnable indeed. How long has this been circulating?"

"I first heard it yesterday evening."

"Why have I heard nothing until now?"

"They're all afraid to mention it, for fear you'll call them out."

"I'll call someone out, certainly."

"Killing Hurst will do no good, for only we suspect him of starting the rumor. But what to do for Mistress Anne is more than I know."

"Reluctant as I am to admit it, I fear you are correct. Never mind, I'll settle Hurst one of these days." He rose and tossed some coins onto the table. "Come, Tom. We must pay a call."

Chapter 34

"His Grace the Duke of Guysbridge has called," Mayhew announced, with a stateliness suitable for presenting the visitor to the king, "with Mr. Jeffreys. But perhaps you are not at home, madam."

Letitia cast a glance at Mrs. Nugent. "Do you think I should—?"

"Oh, yes, I believe so. Mistress Anne says he is intelligent. And he is concerned in this, is he not?"

Anne felt herself blushing furiously.

Once the duke and Mr. Jeffreys had been shown in, and greetings and introductions and offers of wine tendered, there was a sudden lapse into silence. Even Mrs. Nugent hesitated.

"You have heard the gossip, I assume," Anniscote said finally.

"My old friend Mrs. Nugent brought the news. Though I guessed there had been talk, as an acquaintance of mine and her daughter gave us the cut at the Mall," Letitia explained.

"I told Aunt Letitia and Mrs. Nugent everything, Your Grace."

He raised his eyebrows.

"Including your deductions and conclusions about the source of the trouble."

"Our deductions, Mistress Anne," he responded with a slight bow.

"It was perfectly wicked of Marianne, if it is true. I must say, I cannot dismiss the possibility or indeed the likelihood of it. She did display a…well, a very practical side, even as a girl."

"I do not wish to cause you pain, Letty, but I would call it a scheming side, myself. I met her any number of times when she was with you, and thought her at best a minx. Thank God Mr. Saltstall took a fancy to her."

"Yes," Letitia sighed.

"I don't think we need worry about Mistress Saltstall further," Anne said. "Now that she understands that I am not an embarrassment to her—"

Four sets of eyes gazed at her, pityingly, she thought.

"But you are," the duke said. "It matters little who your father was or was not, but you are obviously a connection of hers, whether through a distant cousin or some closer relationship, and so any scandal attaching to you reflects upon her."

"And your resemblance to her daughter makes it worse," Mrs. Nugent added. "However, what we must think of now is how to deal with the rumors."

"We know with whom they originated," Jeffreys said, entering the conversation for the first time. "Hurst's trouble-making tongue is well known."

"I wonder if that is what Mrs. Saltstall was thinking of, when she urged me to leave London. After all was settled between us, when I mentioned Mr. Hurst, she became agitated and urged me to go away. Although her suggestion he might try to abduct me is surely far-fetched."

"Although I have never heard of his indulging in kidnap or rape, I would not discount the possibility," the duke said. "He really has no morals to speak of."

"I wonder how Mrs. Saltstall knew?" Jeffreys asked. "I would think the circles she moves in as an alderman's wife are hardly likely to come in contact with Hurst's."

"That's well thought of, Tom. Yes, it is puzzling."

"But what are we to do?"

Seeing her courtesy aunt—good heavens, her real aunt, if James Sinclair really were her own father—so distressed, Anne took her hand and said, "I am so sorry to have caused you this distress."

"My dear, it is not your fault."

"It does not matter whose fault it is," Mrs. Nugent declared. "We must plan. I think Marianne's idea that Anne should go away for a time is sound."

"Out of sight, out of mind," Jeffreys agreed. "Do you not think so, Anniscote? Until time or some other event makes it possible to return?"

"Yes, it would be best."

"But where are we to go?" Letitia asked.

"Letty, I am of the opinion that you must remain in town. If anyone should comment upon Anne's going, or allude to any rumor, you must certainly be here to raise your eyebrows and give a chilling rebuke. You used to do it very well, and I am sure you have not lost the ability, if you choose to exercise it."

"She cannot go alone. That would be almost more shocking than what is being said. If our family does not show that we support her, everyone will think the gossip true."

"It would depend on where she went, and the alleged reason for going. Have you any elderly relatives who might need Anne's assistance, or younger ones with a sickness, or...."

"Or an *accouchement*," the duke suggested baldly.

"That is a very good suggestion," Elvira Nugent said approvingly.

"We have only my nephew, Wemley, and his family, and they are now here in London."

"I saw the announcement of the engagement. No more distant family?"

"There may be, but we have lost contact with them. We have no more relations in Scotland, and my sister and brothers are all dead. I have several nieces and nephews, but apart from Marianne, they are scattered to the winds."

"I don't think I would describe it as 'scattered to the winds,' Letty. As I recall, you have one niece living in a French chateau, one nephew breeding horses in Ireland, and another with a diplomatic mission somewhere or other on the Continent."

"Well, but they aren't here, or anywhere convenient to send Anne. Not that Gerard would be suitable at all, as he's not married, and Cuthbert's Irish manor sounds very remote and not really in good repair. Except the stables, of course. And as for poor Eleanor's *comte*...no, I really couldn't let her go there."

"Scotland," Jeffreys mused.

"You are thinking of my sister-in-law."

"I know she is sadly lacking in company, as your brother made himself odious to the gentry of the neighborhood. And as she is in mourning, she could hardly go about in society even if that were not the case."

"It's true I meant to send that girl—Prudence?—to Guysbridge. Mistress Anne could go with her."

"Your name having been mentioned in connection with Anne's, sir, it would look as if there were some truth to the report," Aunt Letitia stated.

"If there were, would I send Mistress Anne to bear Her Grace company?"

Mrs. Nugent, even less averse to plain speaking than His Grace, said, "It would be acceptable only if you were committed to an action I doubt you have considered."

Anniscote regarded her thoughtfully. "Indeed. I hardly think we need contemplate such a course. Mistress Anne, can you go to your home in Fletching? Or to friends there?"

"It is leased, Your Grace, and there is no one I could impose upon."

"My nephew and his lady can have no objection to Anne's visiting their country home, even in their absence. She is not used to the noise and bustle of town and is quite worn out by it," Letitia remarked mendaciously. "Pray excuse me while I write, asking permission for her to recover her bloom in the quiet of Wemley." She went to her little desk and took out paper, quill, and ink.

"I suppose he will have heard the talk already and understand," the duke said.

Mrs. Nugent laughed. "Nothing is less likely."

"My nephew is a retiring sort and not worldly. Even if some acquaintance hinted at scandal, it's probable he would miss the meaning."

"Wemley is scarce more than seventy miles from Guysbridge, if as much," Anniscote said. "Perhaps, if your nephew the earl gave his consent, my widowed sister-in-law might visit to provide Mistress Anne with some distraction. Someone must escort Prudence to Guysbridge. That same someone might quite easily then accompany Her Grace and her maid to Wemley."

"If you think Her Grace would wish to go visiting while in mourning. I'm sure I never could have done so, when my dear husband was taken from me."

"Time hangs very heavy on her," said Jeffreys. "The companionship of another lady, and a change of scene, must raise her spirits."

"I am sure you are correct, Tom. And while no one could object to my escorting the duchess to Wemley… "Here he gave Jeffreys a very strait look.

"I have no pressing engagements in town," Jeffreys said. "I can act as Mistress Anne's courier, to make her journey to Wemley easy. Then I could proceed to Guysbridge with Prudence and return with Her Grace and her maid."

"My traveling coach is at your disposal."

Mrs. Nugent nodded approval. "That is a very suitable arrangement. In any case, Your Grace must remain in town."

"But will the duchess be willing to visit me when my reputation is in question?" Anne asked.

"She knows from her own experience what it is to be slighted and is too kind to deny her support to another," said Jeffreys.

"May I inquire, ma'am, why you think I must remain here? For while I agree with you, I wonder if it is for the same reason."

"If you were to leave town at the same time as Mistress Anne, it must cause talk. That we have already touched upon. And someone must deal with Hurst so that she can eventually return."

"How would you suggest I 'deal with' Hurst?" Anniscote asked, gently ironical.

"As to that, I am sure you know better than I. It would be unwise to challenge him to a duel, however."

"What, because he might kill me?"

"It's far more likely you would kill him," Mrs. Nugent replied frankly. "No, even if you used some foolish pretext, such as objecting to his style or manner, it would deceive no one, and give support to the stories about Anne."

"They are not only about Mistress Anne," Jeffreys said, with an apologetic glance at Mrs. Bradshaw.

"How's this? Who else do they concern, Tom? You cannot mean my humble self. Scandalous talk has circulated about me all the dozen years since I came to town, though some of it was merely on my family's account."

"Ha! No, any supposed damage to your character is not worth mentioning. No, one of the tidbits I heard concerned—hmm!—another lady."

"I am no tooth-drawer, dear fellow. As Mrs. Nugent has said, we need all the facts."

"I am sorry, Mrs. Bradshaw," Jeffreys said. "It is being alleged by some that Mrs. Saltstall was unchaste before her marriage. No one hinted she has been unfaithful to Mr. Saltstall, only that when she was a girl, she had a lover. If she was not actually…ah, a courtesan. Though of course, no one could really believe that."

"How dare anyone!" Letitia exclaimed. "The most wicked, ridiculous—"

"Not many are repeating it, fortunately. Few are heedless enough to wish to offend a man who, if he is not a noted swordsman, is extremely influential, and may well be Lord Mayor of London in a few years."

"To spread such lies is abominable. In Anne's case, of course, it's understandable—"

Anniscote's lips twitched, and Jeffreys coughed into a handkerchief, his face turning bright pink.

"My poor Marianne lived with me from the time she was sixteen or seventeen, when she returned from the Continent. It's not only insulting to her, it's insulting to me." Aunt Letitia colored up until she almost matched Jeffreys.

"Taking a girl of that age to the Continent always seemed an odd thing," Mrs. Nugent remarked.

"When Mr. Hurst passed our supper-box at Vauxhall, I saw him notice Mistress Saltstall," Anne said reluctantly. "It appeared that he recognized her, or thought he did."

Somehow Mrs. Nugent contrived to convince them that there was little further to say about the matter, although Anne suspected that Mrs. Nugent had not shared all her thoughts with them.

When the gentlemen took their leave, Elvira Nugent said, "You are both welcome to call upon me. I do not often go visiting, for walking any distance exhausts me, but I have not cut myself off from the world. I correspond with friends who live mostly in the country, and my friends who are in town visit me. In your case, Mr. Jeffreys, I will not expect you until your return." And she gave the duke what Anne thought was a meaningful look. He made a very graceful leg in reply.

"Madam, I will do myself the favor of calling upon you in the near future."

"I am pleased to hear it," she responded with a very small smile.

Aunt Letitia told Anne to tell Sally and Prue to begin packing—"For you must take Sally with you, as it would look so strange if you did not, and Prudence must go to Guysbridge, and you should leave as soon as we hear from Wemley, which I have no doubt will be this evening, or at latest, in the morning. Which I think is just as well, under the circumstances." Anne left the two old ladies together, sure that they would be talking secrets.

Once Sally was busy filling her trunks, with Prudence helping and making up her own little bundle, Anne sat down to write a letter to Marianne Saltstall.

Chapter 35

"How this is all to be resolved baffles me," Jeffreys commented before they parted company. "We are but mopping up the tide, it seems to me, while the water yet rises."

"This is uncommon gloomy of you. Mrs. Nugent has given us our marching orders, and yours at least are more plain than mine."

"What will you do?" Jeffreys asked.

"I tell you frankly, I am damned if I know. If I cannot challenge Hurst, I must find some other way of silencing him. If I knew of some reliable cutthroats—"

"John!"

"You rise to the bait like a fish after a fly, Tom. No, there have already been too many rogues involved. But it will take some thought to know how to close his mouth."

"We can hardly have him pressed as a common seaman, or forge indentures and ship him off to the Colonies, as was planned for Mistress Anne."

"No. Though getting him out of England would certainly serve. Or discrediting him so thoroughly that no one would believe anything he said."

"I am glad my task is so simple and enjoyable. I do not envy you yours."

"I am pleased to have gratified you and alleviated the poor widow's boredom," the duke bowed.

"How will you proceed? For it seems to me that the sooner this matter is quashed, the better it will be."

"I believe I will avail myself of Mrs. Nugent's invitation. I suspect she means to give me a hint and expects me to dance to her tune."

"And will you?"

"If she has a better notion than I do of what to do, right willingly. You have sometimes accused me of pride, but I hope I am not so puffed up that I would refuse to take advice from someone more cunning than I. That lady has something of a Machiavelli or perhaps a Sir William Cecil about her."

"Think you so? She seems a pleasant, harmless old lady. Rather like my favorite aunt."

"Those are the most dangerous sort, Tom. They can have your life's history and your unuttered secrets out of you in a twinkling, as well as those of everyone else, too. And Mrs. Nugent has little else to occupy her time, but the gathering of intelligence. Now you had best be off to pack, for I hope you will be able to set out tomorrow."

****

He poured a glass of brandy but was not able to settle to enjoy it. How convenient it would be if Hurst should develop signs of madness! A Restoration dramatist would have had no hesitation in inventing a potion to mimic insanity, had the plot required it. What a pity life was so little like the theater!

At last he took down Charles Anniscote's book, hoping to divert his mind.

Charles Anascote: When he had slept for a time, and drunk of a little broth, my father continued:

I have prayed every day that your mother not be

judged for having obeyed my order to practice the new religion, but that the sin, if any, be borne by me alone. She was an excellent wife and mother and a notable housewife who made our home more comfortable than it might have been. She eased my way with our servants and tenants, for many of our folk were not pleased to have a Spaniard for a master, no, not even when Queen Mary's husband was a Spaniard. Which is perhaps not surprising, for I myself heard a nobleman of Prince Philip's entourage say that because of her lack of armament, England would be very easy to conquer. It was passed off as a jape, but it sat ill with the English.

I find myself thinking sometimes of what my life would have been had I remained in Spain. I still mislike some English ways. They eat and drink to excess. They often lack the gravity, punctilious manners, and discipline of Spaniards. But if I had not come to England and stayed, the cloud over my mother's family might have affected Francisco. Certainly it would have shadowed my life and the lives of whatever children I begot.

Do you recall I told you that when first I was presented to Her Majesty, Queen Elizabeth, I said, "I have an English heart, though I have a Spaniard's face." She was pleased to be amused, and to commend me for my wit and my bow. Because I have made myself English, the recent loss of so much of the Spanish fleet did not discompose me, though I prayed that none of the men lost were our kin. But the news you have had out of Ireland of the wreck of the Girona *grieves me. To have taken so many survivors of other ships aboard, to have had a chance to make Scotland, from which they might have reached Spain again, only to sink in a storm, seems to me a sad end. Far better to die in battle. But worst of all is that I know the names of some that are reported dead. They must have been sons or grandsons of men I knew in Spain. If I had not remained in England, I might now be mourning for my own sons.*

Odd, that Mrs. Nugent should resemble Good Queen Bess in her later years. He would seek her out at the first opportunity tomorrow. And thinking of those perilous old times—

"Mulley," he said, on reaching his chamber.

"Your Grace?"

"If I were desirous of having someone's comings and goings watched discreetly, how might it be accomplished?"

His valet pondered as he assisted Anniscote in the taking off of his coat.

"I believe I should enlist the services of some street boys. They go everywhere. And if you know one or two of the person's usual haunts, there might be an apprentice or two, or a servant, who would be glad of a douceur. Times being hard, you know, sir."

"Can you arrange it, Mulley? Discreetly?"

"Yes, Your Grace, I believe so. I would have our bootboy act as my agent."

"Have we a bootboy?"

"Certainly, sir. He is the cook's cousin's lad. A little unpolished, but a clever bantling and will shape well. Let me add, he cleans your boots, but I polish them. It takes years of practice to perfect that skill."

Chapter 36

The next day, presenting himself at Mrs. Nugent's elegant house, he found a distressed Mrs. Bradshaw closeted with her.

"Come join our council of war, your Grace. Letitia has just told me an interesting thing."

"I am sorry to be so distraught, sir, but it is the strangest circumstance." She dabbed at her eyes and sniffed mightily. "I did not know who else to consult, with Anne gone into the country, so I came to my dear Elvira."

"And very right, too. But I think you should go home and lie down, perhaps with a lavender water compress on your forehead. That is always soothing. I will explain matters to His Grace."

"I believe things progress," Mrs. Nugent remarked, when her friend had departed.

The duke raised his thin black brows.

"Mrs. Saltstall—Mrs. Bradshaw's niece, you know—intruded upon her morning cup of chocolate in a rare taking."

"She had heard the rumors herself, I take it?"

"One might think so, but in fact, she heard of it from Anne, who sent her a note this morning before departing." Mrs. Nugent made a trifling adjustment to her fichu and smoothed the skirt of her yellow-flowered silk gown.

Anniscote waited.

"Letitia, I am glad to say, drew no conclusion from this. However, she was able to repeat to me what Marianne had told her, in broken phrases and with some sobs and tears interspersed. Apart from the mere fact that gossip was circulating about Anne herself, Anne seems to have mentioned that Mr. Hurst appeared surprised to see that the earl's party included Mrs. Saltstall and Anne. Anne may have mentioned this only by way of explaining that seeing Anne, and you, was the impetus for Hurst spreading these scandalous stories."

"Which is very likely, considering the first time he saw Anne with me in a place I shall not further describe," he finished repressively.

"Oh, Lud! As if I had not heard the details from Anne! I had not realized you were so nice-minded. However, as Letty recounted Marianne's visit, Mrs. Saltstall seemed most concerned that Hurst had seen her. Marianne, I mean. Marianne repeated several times, 'He saw me. And Anne says he may be telling tales about me, as well as her.' "

"He would hardly draw the line at a falsehood, though why he should blacken Mrs. Saltstall's name, I cannot imagine."

"I wonder if it would be a falsehood," she murmured.

"I beg your pardon?"

"You have met Marianne's daughter, have you not? Did she impress you as headstrong and spoiled, to put it no stronger?"

"I hardly like to…"

"Your Grace, I have heard that she positively

stalked you, and in a manner which would shock any well-behaved lady. Did she really leap into your arms?"

"She slipped on the step of a hackney coach and fell. Really, I had to catch her."

"I suppose so, but it might have done her so much good if you had let her fall," Mrs. Nugent said regretfully. "I apologize for the digression. She is very like Marianne at that age, in behavior, if not appearance. And I always wondered why Dr. Sinclair took her to the Continent when he went there to recover his health. Particularly as I'd never heard of his ailing previously, and he came back cured. The man had a constitution of iron. I suppose it is because of his Scottish ancestors; one is always hearing of Scots sleeping wrapped in their plaids in dripping-wet heather, subsisting on oatcakes, turnips, and kale, and never so much as a cold to show for it. Letitia, too! Never a day ill in her life, and even after being delivered of her children, she was out of bed almost at once. It is a thousand pities they took after their father in their health. Though I suspect Mr. Bradshaw's complaints were mostly the result of eating too much and unwisely."

"In short, you believe Dr. Sinclair's illness was a pretext to visit the Continent."

"More to the point, to take Marianne out of England."

To remove her from contact with some ineligible suitor? Anniscote wondered. Or—?

"You see," Mrs. Nugent went on, "I believe in plain speaking, although not necessarily with everyone. I judge that you are the one most likely to be able to help my friend and Mistress Anne. Mr. Jeffreys is a good-hearted, reasonable fellow, but in an affair of this sort, that is not an advantage. This requires the subtlety of a serpent."

"Thank you, ma'am. So you think Mistress Anne is Mrs. Saltstall's natural child?"

"Oh, yes, I believe so. An unchaperoned, headstrong girl of sixteen or so, living in London with a busy father? What is more likely than that she should find herself enceinte?"

"Mistress Anne is said to resemble any number of Sinclair ancestors. She might be Dr. Sinclair's daughter, as Mrs. Saltstall told Anne."

"She might, and no doubt he would have taken her in, precisely as he did. However, I was acquainted with Marianne when she came to live with Letty, and I have known any number of similar chits. Given her father's taking her away for the better part of a year, and his subsequent adoption of a baby who has grown up to resemble Marianne's daughter to a remarkable degree, what other explanation can there be? Were there any way of proving indisputably whose daughter Anne is, I would wager you five hundred guineas that I am right."

"I think I would not take such a wager, considering your expert knowledge."

"If she is Marianne's, it explains why Marianne was distraught on receiving Anne's letter."

"As well as why she tried to remove her from London. And yet, how could she attempt to ruin her reputation and to sell her into servitude in the Colonies? Could any mother treat her child so?"

Mrs. Nugent fixed a beady stare upon him. "It would depend upon how self-centered the mother was, surely? And perhaps whether she has a close relationship with the child. Sometimes the child's nurse is fonder of her charge than its mother is. Ladies of wealth and fashion have so many claims upon their time that they often see little of their children."

His own mother had found her patience taxed to the extreme by seeing himself and Nick for half an hour in the evening. He agreed.

"She must have been desperate, as well. It must be obvious to anyone who saw both girls that they were related."

The duke objected, "But according to Wemley, their features are well known in the Sinclair family, and Mistress Anne is said to be the daughter of some Sinclair cousin. Such resemblances are not uncommon."

"And would cause no comment—if everyone were aware of those facts. Anyone who has not been privileged to see the Sinclair portrait gallery, or hear the earl on the subject of the Sinclair jaw and eyes, might well comment upon it. Though certainly it is helpful that the earl and his family have been seen in company with both girls. Nevertheless, many will not be aware of the…" Mrs. Nugent paused momentarily, at a loss for words, which the duke guessed was rare.

"Let us call them 'the facts,'" he suggested.

"Thank you. I think I shall write my friends and acquaintances, mentioning in passing how much I enjoyed meeting James Sinclair's young cousin however-many-times removed, whose guardian he was, and how I shall miss her, now she is visiting the family home." She smiled. "I do not know all of Society, but I venture to say that I am on good terms with a great many of its most important members. Those with whom

I do not have an epistolary relationship are probably friends or correspondents of one of my acquaintances."

"That should give Mistress Anne standing and an appearance of…ah…"

"Let us call it 'legitimacy,' " Elvira Nugent suggested.

"You do realize, ma'am, that if you are correct, Mistress Anne may be Hurst's daughter?"

"I fear so. But she seems to be a well-conducted girl with good principles."

"Well-conducted! The things she says—the predicaments she falls into—!"

"They are not of her seeking for the most part," Elvira Nugent pointed out. "And as an advocate of frank speech myself, I cannot fault her for that. Admittedly, she is somewhat deficient in the arts expected of young ladies. However, if a female is to marry and have children, the ability to dress a wound is of more use than skill at embroidery."

Anniscote remembered his mother fidgeting with her embroidery and tossing it aside. He could not recall her ever actually completing so much as a monogrammed handkerchief—though perhaps as a child he would not have noticed such a thing anyway. But he thought he would have recalled if she had tended to his scrapes and bruises herself.

Chapter 37

It was vexing to have to leave London before she saw all its marvels. But on the whole, Anne was enjoying her journey. The duke's travelling coach was even more comfortable than the Beatons', although it was by no means new, and seeing Sally's and Prue's pleasure at every change of scenery increased her own. Too, Anne found it a relief not to attend parties and events at which some people refused to recognize her, or were markedly cold. The number of invitations she received had fallen off noticeably, although not from those who were friendly with the Earl of Wemley's family or wished to ingratiate themselves with him. But it was humiliating, and to escape (or run away) for a little while seemed best. She also looked forward to seeing the Sinclairs' ancestral home and to meeting the duke's sister-in-law. She had no idea what to expect of Elspat, Duchess of Guysbridge. Mr. Jeffreys had spoken so warmly of her that Anne wondered if he loved her. The duke's attitude was less clear. His brother's wife had brought a very sizable dowry with her to the marriage, but many noble families looked down on the merchant class and particularly tradesmen, no matter how rich. There was prejudice against the Scots as well.

Mr. Jeffreys, riding beside the coach, proved efficient at arranging their stops and accommodations and was a pleasant companion at meals. He was the very pattern card of a gentleman: courteous, solicitous of her comfort, witty, and well-informed. What a pity he had so little interest in science! When she mentioned Lady Mary Wortley-Montague's fascinating observations regarding smallpox inoculation in Turkey, he only said it sounded most unpleasant and even dangerous and asked whether she would prefer beef à la mode or fricassee of chicken for her dinner. Perhaps he was only squeamish. When he introduced the subject of current plays and who was acting in them, she listened with at least an appearance of interest. Anne had seen too little of the theater to have many opinions and scarcely knew the name of a single actor or actress. But she made a mental note to secure a copy of Congreve's *Way of the World* to read. Mr. Jeffreys had seen it performed and had not cared for it, but Anne thought it sounded quite amusing. She did not say so, because she was sure Mr. Jeffreys would never dream of arguing with a lady. If he disagreed, she supposed he would say so and change the subject. Now, the duke was not always courteous. He was arrogant, high-handed, and occasionally bad-tempered. She rather wished he were her escort instead of Mr. Jeffreys. A lively argument could be so entertaining.

Chapter 38

As he made his way to Sinclair House, he wondered what Anne was doing. She must have reached Wemley several days ago. She would not, of course, write to him directly to let him know. That would be most improper. Mad thought! When had impropriety kept her from doing anything? No, he wronged her. She would not do something she knew was improper…unless she had an excellent reason, or what she considered one at least. Life was certainly never dull when Anne was nearby. While her path was littered with gaffes, indiscretions, and improprieties, he could not forget her face glowing with delight at the sights of Vauxhall. The man at whom she gazed with such pleasure would be lucky indeed. He sighed and recalled her pink alabaster bosom and her terrifying blend of naïveté and shrewdness.

He would inquire of Mrs. Bradshaw if she had yet received a letter, when he saw her that evening. He had been invited to dine with the earl's family, partly by way of showing that the Sinclair family and the duke were on excellent terms, and partly, he guessed, because the countess enjoyed entertaining and meant to make up for all the opportunities she had missed at Wemley.

The party was not large, consisting of his host and hostess, their son, his bride-to-be and her parents and her sister, who had recently emerged from the schoolroom, the three Saltstalls, himself, and a man of about his own age, who seemed to know Saltstall well. His bearing and appearance were polished but not those of a gentleman born, Anniscote thought. Or perhaps he had come from a well-bred but not well-to-do family, for he had something of Alderman Saltstall's manner. Marcus Easterday was introduced as a ship owner and importer; Anniscote gathered he had been at sea himself. That no doubt accounted for his air of command.

He was placed next to Mariah Saltstall, who seemed subdued.

Anniscote recalled dinners where the talk was wittier or at least livelier, but perhaps that was not to be expected when the company was made up of family and near connections, except for himself and Captain Easterday. What gave the evening interest was the demeanor of several of the guests. Mariah was not in spirits. Her mother, for all her attempts to appear calm and attentive, was playing her part with difficulty. Her eyes glittered with the feverishness the duke associated with gamblers losing heavily but too desperate for a chance to recoup their losses to stop playing. One would hardly notice the slight tightness around Mr. Saltstall's lips. A merry little family group, indeed. Wemley seemed oblivious, but Lady Wemley did her best to lighten the tone.

She asked if the Saltstalls would attend the masquerade ball she meant to give.

Mr. Saltstall replied that he and his wife would be pleased to come, but that Mariah would be visiting Captain Easterday's family in Lancashire.

"It has not been announced yet, but she and Captain Easterday recently became betrothed."

The marriage was clearly the doing of the alderman and Easterday. The latter accepted congratulations with calm courtesy; Mariah's downcast eyes and silence might have been taken for shyness by someone not acquainted with her but were probably a fit of the sullens instead. Marianne Saltstall managed a faint smile and responded to any remark addressed to her, but her thoughts appeared to be elsewhere. Anniscote misdoubted they were on her daughter's trousseau.

After dinner, he managed to speak privately with Letitia Bradshaw.

"I received a letter from Anne only today," she said. "She is full of information about farm equipment and agricultural methods. At least she seems to be enjoying herself. I fear we have made little progress here in quelling the talk."

****

He was strolling down Bond Street the following day, wondering if he should seek out a coffee house to see if he could hear some gossip relating to the odd doings of the Saltstalls—for he was almost certain that Mariah had been intended to marry a young man named Dunham—or whether to go to his club for the same purpose when something caught at his sleeve.

A grubby little hand tugged it again.

"What's this?" the duke demanded, in a voice of thunder.

The urchin released his hold and piped, "Yer Grace, sir, I'm Harry. Mr. Mulley said as you'd come this way, so I come as quick as I could." He stood at attention that would not have disgraced a Life

Guardsman.

"Harry?"

"Yer bootboy, sir. Come to make my report, like. And begging yer pardon as I couldn't do it sooner, but my...my informant, he reckoned it could wait until morning, it being late at night, then he likely stopped to play shove ha'penny or dice or watch a dog fight this morning."

"Report, soldier."

Harry was clearly determined to do the thing handsomely. "Regarding the cove as Yer Grace was wishful to have watched, he went 'round to his club and a gambling house and such, and there wasn't nothing to be learned 'til last night. He come out of his club early, afore it was quite dark, and Jem was thinking he'd get a chair and go on to a gambling hell or maybe to a school o' Venus. But he don't. He strolls along to the next street and stops. There's a hackney there, that don't belong in that part o' town. The horse is ready for the knacker, the paint's chipped, and the coachman looks a proper hedge-bird, an' he's off the box, doing something to the harness, like. Jem was put about, for it's easy enough to follow a chair, but a rattler is a diff'rent matter, if the streets isn't busy, 'less you can get up behind it, where a footman would be on a gentleman's coach. So Jem slips past, sly as a gib-cat, to be ready to jump up, if he can. The cully as he's watching gets in. But the coach don't move. The coachman takes no notice of him, just goes on fiddling with the harness.

"Jem says to himself it's odd all the way around. And then he thinks, it must be there's someone else in there, but he can't hear anyone talking. Though," Harry added, "with the coachman right there, if there was two people inside and they was talking, they'd be speaking low, so the coachman couldn't hear. He did say the coach wasn't rocking, so it wasn't a as-sig-nation."

The duke was vastly entertained but merely remarked, "Jem seems to be an acute observer."

"Ay, he is. Gets him in trouble sometimes. Well, he thought as how it would be good to hear anything he could, so he sneaked up closer, 'til he was right outside the offside door, but crouched down. The driver was on the other side, at the front, so it was safe enough. This is what he hears, but it's only bits: a woman says, pretty loud, 'You may have thought to cause mischief there, but you'll ruin others, too.'

"'I don't mind disobliging Guysbridge,' Captain Grand says.

"'It's not him I care about,' says she. 'You'll ruin me—' and he says, 'You ruined yourself years ago.'

"Out she snaps with, 'You'll ruin my daughter as well.' To which he fires back, 'Like mother, like daughter, no doubt. What concern is she of mine?' Then Jem thinks he hears a hand on the door, like someone's going to come out, and he thinks maybe he'd better make off afore he's seen." Harry paused to catch his breath, and the duke nodded.

"But Jem don't and nobody gets out. The lady says to the cove, 'I swear if you ruin my family, I'll see you and yours ruined, too.' He barks out a laugh, and Jem thinks he said, 'What can you do to me?' but he only caught part of it, so he's not right sure of that. But he heard her say, clear enough, 'It will cost me everything, but it will cost you the same.' Then she something about your daughter, and—"

"Whose daughter?"

"The one Jem's following. His daughter, 'cause she said, 'your daughter' and she's talking to the gentry-cove. And there's another long silence before he says something like, he didn't know. And there was more gibble-gabble as Jem couldn't make out. Just then, Jem thinks he hears the coachman move, so he ducks under the coach and misses a few words. When he sees all's well and the man's still up by the horses' heads, he pops out again."

"What else?"

"They were talking too soft, so he couldn't hear any more. And after a bit, the cove gets out, and he tosses the coachman a coin. Then he walks back toward the way he come, but a bit funny."

"In what way? Drunk?"

"No. Nor sick, neither. Jem said it was like the way he'd go, himself, if he knew his pa was at home, waiting to give him a whipping for aught. Or if he was worried bad about something, like the time he thought on the things the preacher said would send you to hell, and Jem figured he'd done most of them and meant to do the rest, soon as he was old enough. Said he suspicioned that intending to do them was near as sinful as doing them. He had a bad few days, before he decided that if he was damned, there was no use worrying about it 'til he was ready to die."

"I see. Did he go back to his club?"

Harry lost his brash confidence. "I don't know, Yer Grace, 'cause Jem didn't follow him. I'm sorry if he didn't obey orders, but he figured I might want to know who was in that coach, so when the coachman got up on the box, Jem got up on the platform in back. I would have, too," Harry said.

"I could not have resisted the temptation, either. So he traveled with the coach until it reached its destination?"

"No, sir, 'cause it came to a stop, and the coachman let the lady out, and she went into a house. Then the coach started up again, and Jem dropped off a few houses farther on—so as not to be seen by anyone at the lady's house—and he didn't want to go wherever that carriage was going. He took notice of which house it was and come and took me to it, first thing this morning."

"You have both done well. Er…where is the house? Can you take me to it?"

"If you want, sir. It's hard by Golden Square."

"Golden Square," the duke repeated. "Did Jem describe the lady?"

"He couldn't say particular what she looked like. She had the hood of her cloak up, and it was dark anyhow. But she moved young, not like a old lady."

****

The duke stood looking at Mrs. Bradshaw's house. He had sent Harry off with a brace of sixpences for his trouble and an admonition to share the largesse with Jem.

The butler ushered him into Mrs. Bradshaw's boudoir, where her maid had evidently been reading to her from a book of sermons. The woman rose, curtsied, and took the book with her.

"Is there any news, Your Grace?" Letitia Bradshaw asked. "Good news, I mean? For I confess my spirits are quite failing. A friend visited yesterday and hinted—in the kindest way—that Anne's going to the country was being talked of."

"Was it the lady who visited you in the evening? Soon after dark?"

"Oh, no, that was only Marianne. Poor thing, she is in a sad state. Possibly you noticed how drawn she looked at dinner the other night. One would think she would be delighted that her daughter is eligibly betrothed, but she hardly spoke of it. Why, she actually wept, but when I asked her why, she would not tell me."

"Perhaps she has some other trouble on her mind," Anniscote suggested. "Was there not talk of some other man Mistress Mariah was to marry? Perhaps the girl was attached to him and is not eager to marry Captain Easterday."

"Oh, no. For she had no opinion of Mr. Dunham, and I must say that although I am sure he will do well in business, I don't think he is old enough or experienced enough to know how to manage Mariah. Mr. Saltstall must have realized that, too, when he discovered how poorly governed Mariah has been. So he must have determined to get her a husband better capable of controlling her. Which I think is wise. Marianne may have hoped for a titled match, but still she must realize that as the tiresome child has been going on, a firm husband may be all that saves her from utter ruination. And Mr. Saltstall is not in favor of marriages outside one's social circle. Indeed, I fear that he has come to regret marrying my niece, which was not an unequal marriage by any means, for what can a grandfather or an uncle who is an earl signify when one's father is a mere honorable? And works as a physician?" Mrs. Bradshaw continued, "Or it may be

Marianne is ill. At my nephew's dinner she had circles under her eyes, and she hardly ate. I think she should go to Bath or even better, a quiet seaside town."

Privately the duke thought that any woman who had aught to do with Hurst might well weep. Fortunately, Mrs. Bradshaw's mind was so occupied with plans for Marianne's recuperation and speculations about Mariah's wedding, she never thought to ask why Anniscote had asked about her evening visitor.

Chapter 39

Mr. Jeffreys had obviously travelled at speed to Guysbridge, as he returned with the duchess sooner than expected. "I made very good time on my way, as there was no need for the duke's travelling coach, there being one at Guysbridge," he said.

Anne was prepared to like the duchess at first sight. Elspat had lovely high cheekbones, the milky skin (dusted with golden freckles) that goes with red hair, and—at the moment, being assisted to alight from the coach by Mr. Jeffreys—a rosy blush.

"Thank you for coming to keep me company," Anne said, after the formalities of introduction.

"I was glad to come. Before my marriage, I was always busy and had friends to visit and shopping to do. There is not a great deal to do at Guysbridge, and the gentlefolk in the neighborhood do not visit. They made the proper visits of condolence, of course," she added hastily, "but people don't pay calls upon the bereaved, unless they are close friends."

"Oh, I know! And it makes it so much worse, not having any occupation to take one's mind off one's loss. That's why I went to London, without waiting out a year."

"I am so glad you understand, Mistress Anne. I have missed the company of female friends."

Anne reflected that she had never had close female

friends, as she had spent most of her time at Fletching with her grandfather and had not really had time to make any in London, except Aunt Letitia who was an aunt more than a friend. A friend, she thought, would share the same interests and sense of humor. She said only, "I am delighted to have the chance to make a new friend."

Jeffreys took his leave, to stay at the inn until his departure in the morning. With no host, it would naturally not be proper for him to stay at Wemley. And Anne had to admit that they did not need additional cause for scandal. But after he left, Elspat gazed out the window abstractedly and seemed wistful.

Anne ventured, "I believe you had not long been married?"

"I beg your pardon, Mistress Anne, my mind wandered. Pray forgive me."

"Grief is very hard."

"I am not grieved. Only *thochtie*."

"Th—?"

"Pensive, I should have said."

"Or worried?"

"Ay."

"Is there aught I can do? Perhaps talking would help."

Elspat sighed. "I fear nothing will help. It's my father."

"I hope he's not seriously ill?"

"No, not he. He's strong as an ox. But I had a letter from him before I left Guysbridge that has put me out of frame."

Anne waited expectantly.

"My brothers died, and then he married again but

two years ago, and his new wife died in childbed and the bairn with her. So he arranged my marriage to the Duke of Guysbridge, even though…"

"You didn't want to marry him."

"No. Why, I'd never so much as seen him, nor he me, and if I had…well! But since my father has had such ill luck with sons, he decided that the next best thing would be to marry me to a nobleman and provide him grandsons. There'd be no boy to learn shipbuilding or inherit the foundry, but to have a grandson with a title, who owed a good deal of his wealth to my father's efforts, would have been some consolation. I imagine he'd have been quite tiresome about 'my grandson, the marquess,' " she remarked dispassionately.

"It's unfortunate, but…"

"So he has employed a writer—a solicitor, you'd say—in London to look about for another titled gentleman who's willing to marry for what my father will give him. He says it should be easier this time, as there's not only his money to recommend me but also the fact I'm a duchess. And I do not wish to be sold again."

"But you are a married lady now, and part of the Anniscote family. He can't make you do anything you don't want to."

"You don't know my father." Elspat twisted her handkerchief. "Once he's set on something, there's no turning him from it."

"I don't need to know him. I'm acquainted with the Duke of Guysbridge, who has enough resolve to deal with a half-dozen stubborn papas. You need only mention it to him, and he will make sure that your father has no opportunity to browbeat you."

"I couldn't tell His Grace!"

"Whyever not?"

"I know he thinks his brother married beneath him. Och, well, Nick did, it's true. My father's father was naught but a plowman, and for all his money, my father could not be mistaken for a gentleman. Lord John—the new duke, I mean—was very kind to me when he was here after Nicholas died, but that was just good manners. I am sure he believes I should be milking cows, not parading in silk and lace."

"He is very proud," Anne agreed. "Yet he has exerted himself to help me with a...social difficulty I found myself in, in London—"

Elspat nodded. "Mr. Jeffreys explained it a little, though not in detail. He felt it best, and the duke had asked him to do so."

"He helped me, and he thinks I'm an unmaidenly hoydenish creature. You should have seen him, Your Grace, and Mr. Jeffreys, too. They were like the heroes in an old tale of chivalry, rescuing a maiden from the stronghold of banditti."

"He said nothing about a rescue! I hope you mean to tell me all about it, Mistress Anne."

"I will, if you will call me Anne and leave off formality."

"Only if you do the same and call me Elspat. My late husband misliked the name for being Scottish and called me Elizabeth. Lord John, as he was then, called me by my right name, no matter how he may have felt about my nationality."

"So he does have some redeeming qualities?" Anne inquired with a chuckle. "Even if he isn't as nice as Mr. Jeffreys?"

"Mr. Jeffreys is exactly what a gentleman should be, I think." Elspat colored and looked away.

Anne chose not to press that matter further, and merely said, "If you like, I will mention the matter to the duke and you may enclose my letter in one of your own, for there is nothing to cause talk or speculation in your writing to your brother-in-law."

"But for a young lady to write to a man who is not a relation is—oh. Of course, if no one but the three of us know, it may still be improper but it will not cause scandal, and while it is not, strictly speaking, necessary…"

"As to that, it may be necessary, if you are not to be badgered by your father. What if he should come to Guysbridge? He sounds like a man who might be difficult to withstand."

"He wouldn't come, for he's always beset with business. And to appear uninvited at a duke's residence—" Elspat broke off in the middle of her sentence. "But he has a low opinion of noblemen. It's difficult to explain. He values the title for its status but not the holder, do you see? and would not hesitate to affront a duke or even a prince, I suppose."

"Then certainly we must enlist Anniscote… Guysbridge…oh, whatever one must call him…in your behalf."

Having won a tentative agreement from Elspat, Anne proceeded to recount her adventures in London.

"I wish I could have seen it," the duchess said wistfully. "It's like something from a novel or an old ballad."

"It was not nearly as enjoyable, I promise you. Until I recognized His Grace, I was actually very frightened. Which is odd, because I once set a boy's broken leg all by myself—except for his father holding him—when my grandfather was miles away at a difficult birth, and I wasn't even nervous. It must have had something to do with feeling I was not in control, when I was confined in that awful place."

"Och, I know I wouldn't want to have been there myself. But I should have liked to see Mr. Jeffreys—and the duke—running through the house, crying 'Fire,' and then delaying the bawd with their wits."

"Yes, I'd have liked to see that part, too. The duke told me Mr. Jeffreys should be on the stage, playing comic parts. He didn't *quite* describe how they came to be allowed upstairs, but I can guess. And he was trying not to laugh, too." Anne reflected that she had seldom seen him laugh; the duke's humor tended to be dry. It was remarkable, how a laugh changed a severe face for the better.

At all events, by the end of the evening, they were fast friends.

Chapter 40

He had scarcely stepped into his club when Hurst came up to him. It was almost as if he had been lying in wait.

"Just the man I was looking for," Hurst said with a bonhomie which almost masked the effort it cost him. "Do I not recall hearing from poor Nick that you are familiar with the old French game of basset?"

"I know not where you heard it, but it is true. Our grandfather learned it when he made his Grand Tour. He taught it to me when I was a lad, so that he had a partner with whom to play, after he was too old to be coming to London. My brother did not take to the game."

"Excellent. Someone mentioned it recently, and there was some discussion of how our English version differed from the original. If you would be so good as to teach me the French manner of play, I will be in your debt."

"I have no objection, so long as we play for small stakes."

"Your brother was used to call you a dull dog of a Puritan. He would not have hesitated to play deep."

"I do not intend to emulate Nick."

"Yet stepping into his shoes must have transformed you somewhat. Rumor now paints you as dangerous to young ladies, where before you only dallied with wives," Hurst remarked.

"Does it?" Anniscote inquired, bored, and beckoned to a servant to bring two new packs of cards.

"I would hardly have credited it, had I not seen you with my own eyes in that very discreet house."

The duke said nothing and proceeded to deal to Hurst all the diamonds from the first pack. "Each player's thirteen cards lie face up. The second pack lies before the banker, face down."

"It would be nothing to remark," Hurst continued, "had your…ah, little friend been the cast-off maidservant you represented her to be. But really, Guysbridge, to be debauching an innocent, gently bred girl only just up from the country! Is this the act of a gentleman?"

Anniscote weighed the risk of telling Hurst the truth and concluded that it was no greater than the risk of a lie. "I did not 'debauch' her. Both of us were cozened into going to that place by forged messages. Each player places a wager on any card in his own suit of cards."

"Well, well, I will not give you the lie—you are so ready to call out anyone who annoys you. But do you not think you should do the honorable thing and wed her? A shilling on the two of diamonds."

The duke stopped in the midst of turning up the top card of the second pack and stared at the other.

"Marry her? You must be mad. How many have you seduced in fact without offering any of them marriage? And I repeat, I did not seduce her. My card is a five. If you had wagered on the five, I would have won your shilling."

Hurst shrugged heavy shoulders. "I have confined

my attentions to seamstresses, tradesmen's daughters, and the like, whose loss of reputation hardly matters." His ruddy complexion might have darkened a trifle. "I don't say I may not have behaved badly once or twice when I was a youth."

The duke continued to stare while turning up the next card in his pack, which was a queen. "If it were a two, I would be obliged to pay you a shilling."

"You should reflect upon the matter. After all, Mistress Anne is related, if remotely, to a good family and has some connections which would be of assistance to any gentleman. It would not disgrace you to marry her and would certainly still the gossip and enhance your own reputation. Why do you sit staring like some bumpkin at a two-headed calf?"

"I beg your pardon. I was momentarily distracted." A two-headed bovine would be no more surprising than Hurst preaching morality. What would have caused him to champion Anne but the knowledge that he was her father? "Had you won, the banker would have paid you seven shillings or instead, you could have left your one shilling stake in place on your two of diamonds. If by some chance, the next card the banker turned up was also a two, you would win seven shillings. If you let your stake remain and the two came up for a third time, you would win five guineas. In this game, skill plays no part. Winning depends entirely on luck, and all the advantage lies with the banker."

Hurst gave a harsh crack of laughter. "As is true in life, damn the whole species," he said sourly.

The man's affairs were perpetually hovering off the reefs of ruin. If never in such dire straits as Nick's had been, they must still be desperate enough with two daughters recently engaged and their dowries to provide.

An odd meeting, he thought when they parted at last. Hurst's behavior perplexed him. Apart from his lecture on the propriety of saving Mistress Anne's reputation by marrying her, he had seemed unwontedly serious, even grim. But his financial situation could account for that. In retrospect, Anniscote almost thought Hurst's reason for seeking him out had been to urge him to marry Anne, rather than to learn the rules of an old card game. He dismissed it from his mind in favor of wondering how to reestablish Anne's reputation so she might return to London, if she wished. Perhaps Mrs. Nugent was correct, and time and fresher scandals would silence the talk. The support of Wemley and Mrs. Nugent would go far toward mending matters, but he would not blame her if she chose to make her home elsewhere, after the series of embarrassments and actual dangers she had encountered in town. London would be duller for her absence. But if Hurst himself was turned Anne's champion—ridiculous thought!—all might yet be well without the necessity for either bloodshed or kidnapping. In spite of his protest to Jeffreys, he had not entirely ruled out either.

Chapter 41

"Anne!" the duchess exclaimed distressfully, entering the morning room almost at a run, a sheet of paper clutched in her hand.

Anne looked up, startled. "Bad news?"

"The warst…worst. My father is coming."

"How did he know you were here?"

"He didn't! He went to Guysbridge. The steward wrote to warn me. Och, Glossing is clever. He told my father he could not quite recall where I had gone visiting and offered him refreshment while Glossing inquired of the head groom. And then Glossing wrote this and sent it off with one of the grooms at a gallop. Glossing said that by the time Father had refreshed himself and Glossing went back in to him, it would be too late to set out, and Glossing would suggest he should stay overnight. As fast as he can travel in a post-chaise, he can scarcely be here for two days or three days or more. Whatever am I to do?"

"We must write Anniscote—Guysbridge, I mean—and have one of your grooms carry it to him."

"But His Grace, coming from London as he would be, cannot be here before my father. Anne, I fear he has arranged another marriage for me. And he will be angry that I was not at Guysbridge, I know he will."

"I will not let him bully you, Elspat."

"'Tis very brave of you, but you don't know what

he's like. He will raise his voice and pace up and down like a caged lion and glower, and sometimes I weep when he shouts at me and berates me for being foolish and worthless and a discredit to him and my poor mother, and an expense to him and I haven't even given him a grandson—"

"You were hardly married long enough to produce one," Anne pointed out. "Unless…never mind. There is no point in working ourselves into a state. What do you think we should do?"

"Run away," Elspat said succinctly.

"How did you manage when you lived at home, if your papa puts you so out of countenance?"

"I was at school for years, then when I left the Rexford Academy for Young Ladies, I kept house for him and was useful and was no trouble to him, and all his hopes were upon my brothers. But since he paid such an amount of money on His late Grace's account, and I haven't repaid him by providing an heir for the title, he feels he has been cheated."

"Well, it's not your fault. But we must make a plan. First, write the duke, and I will write Aunt Letitia. Where shall we go?—London?"

"No, for you came here to escape London. But then, you need not come with me, if you are not afraid to remain here to face my father."

"I'm not afraid. But it would be difficult to pretend that I didn't know why and where you'd gone, for I find it difficult to conceal my feelings if they are strong."

"I own I would rather you came with me as I would not then worry about your being subjected to my father's temper."

"In any case, it would be quite improper for you to

travel any distance by yourself. That would not suit Anniscote's notions of propriety at all."

"Will he not disapprove, even if you come with me?"

"Not once he knows the circumstances," Anne pronounced. "Now, where shall we go? Lincoln?" which was the only large town she knew, apart from London. "Or perhaps Bath? And do you have enough money for the journey? I have very little, myself. I am ashamed to admit that His Grace supplied the funds for the changes of horses and for the inns."

"I am well supplied, so you need not worry about that. I would like to go to Scotland, to visit our old housekeeper. She left us to live with her brother that had lost his wife a little after I came home from the academy."

"But would two of us and our maids, or even one maid, not be an imposition?"

"Och, no. Her brother died two or three years ago, and the cottage is a fine one. He was a farmer and did very well for himself. There are three or four bedchambers. It's not a but and ben—a two room cottage, you understand—with only box beds. But I think we need not take even one maid, for we will not be dressing grandly and needing assistance, and it would be very cramped in the coach with another person."

Chapter 42

It was annoying that occupied as he was with Mistress Anne's tangled affairs, he should have to visit his banker to make certain arrangements. Most of them had to do with the improvements necessary to the Guysbridge land. Fortunately, the house, though shabby in the extreme, was sound. The duchess had somehow contrived to have the pressing repairs done; he could not imagine how. While they had not involved much expenditure, they had certainly increased Guysbridge Hall's comfort, as he had noticed during his stay following his brother's death. When he had commented upon them, Her Grace had looked guilty, and her Lowlands Scots accent became a little more pronounced.

"Ah, well…it only needed looking to see what was wrong, and some thought to decide how to make it good. Your estate carpenter-man is very obliging but…"

"He's skilled at carpentry but not at thinking," the duke said. "If you tell him what to do, he does it. It's a pity that my father and Nick could never be bothered to give him instructions. But I would not have had the slightest notion of how to fix the fireplace mantel, so I could not have told him either. I'm filled with admiration."

"I hope you don't mind that I used some things

from the attics, sir. The oak chest that provided the wood was too damaged ever to use as furniture. It appeared that there had been a fire on its top."

"The one with fat little cherubs at the corners? I believe that may have been in the house when my ancestor—Don Diego, the Spaniard—bought it in Queen Elizabeth's time, and the chest was already old, or so I recall being informed. But you are right; it was good for nothing but salvage. My brother, Philip, started the fire. He fell between Nick and me in age."

"I apprehend he is no more?"

"No. He broke his leg badly, and it mortified. My father—and Philip himself—did not want it amputated. By the time there was no denying the necessity, it was too late."

"I am very sorry," she said.

"There's no need. He was struck from the same mold as Nick and no great loss."

"And that is more pitiful yet," the duchess remarked.

It was some time later that Anniscote wondered whether she had meant Philip's death, his lack of character—or Anniscote's opinion of his brother. Or all three.

However clever at household matters—and carpentry—Elspat might be, she had not been raised in farmland. The estate agent knew what needed to be done. Anniscote's part was to provide the funds. He was approaching the bank's entrance when he saw Richard Saltstall come out and turn up the street, walking briskly. The alderman, his expression grim, did not see him.

****

"You cannot imagine how satisfying it is to find a member of one of our old families who has a grasp of economy," the banker remarked. "I trust you will not take it amiss when I say that His late Grace was a source of constant anxiety to me."

His new Grace inclined his head, acknowledging the compliment.

"Not that he was the only one; no, indeed. Many of our oldest families, titled and untitled, are sadly improvident. Why, only today I was obliged to decide that we can no longer overlook one gentleman's…ah, pecuniary deficiencies. Over the years, we have given him time to raise money to pay his outstanding obligations to us, and he has always done so— eventually. Sometimes by gambling, I fear. But I understand he is now quite done up. It's sad, very sad, particularly for his wife and family, but there it is. So you see, Your Grace," the man ended on a more cheerful note, "it is a positive pleasure to serve a gentleman who understands how to hold household. We look forward to continuing our long-standing relationship with your family." The talk turned to matters other than financial, as they finished their claret.

****

The next day being rainy and gusty, Anniscote found himself uninterested in venturing forth. Such weather made it impossible to arrive at one's destination without muddy shoes, splashed stockings, and a general air of dampness and dishevelment. If the rain stopped in the afternoon, he would go out. For now, he had a letter to write to his estate manager giving his approval of the man's proposed changes.

A stealthy movement outside the library door caused him to pause in his writing, leaving a blot at the end of "…drain the field if you think nec…" The door began to open, and an urchin slipped in and closed it quickly—but not very quietly—behind himself.

"This is quite unexpected, Harry."

"Beggin' yer pardon, Yer Grace, but Mr. Peters don't like me in the front o' the house, but Mr. Mulley that'd let you know quiet-like I had to see you is out and I've come to report."

"An urgent matter, I collect?" Anniscote wondered what new disaster had arisen. His old life, though hand to mouth, seemed peaceful by comparison, if rather lacking in savor.

"Not to say urgent. But it's funny, and it seemed like you should know, Yer Grace."

"What is it, then?"

"Well, this morning I was the one on the lookout, and it was dull work. The gentleman don't come out early as a rule, but today he was out the door right smart—middle of the morning. He walks a ways, then takes a hackney, and I follow along which was easy, as it was where the street got busy. I trotted along like I had an errand when it could move, and when it was stopped, I just idled along. But he doesn't go to his club which I knew he wasn't going to because it was the wrong direction, and soon enough, we're right in the City."

It did not seem remarkable to Anniscote, who had been in the City of London, the city's ancient, original heart, very recently himself, to see his banker. Harry, however, was clearly stuffed full of news.

"And where does he go, then?" the lad asked,

rhetorically.

"Where, indeed?" the duke murmured, as some response seemed expected.

"To a bank, that's where. An' what he did inside, I don't know, but when he came out, he were in a rage. The quiet kind, not the roaring, knock 'em down kind."

"That is interesting."

"No, 'tisn't. Banker must of not given him the gelt. I understands that much. He goes home, don't he, and he don't stir out of doors, which is not his habit. Always out, he is, at his club or at a cockfight or the like."

"Perhaps he couldn't afford to go out."

"Ha! All them gentry-coves is on tick. Owe money everywhere, they do."

"Well…many of them do, that's true."

"Don't you, Yer Grace?" Harry asked.

"Very little. It hardly seems gentlemanly of me, does it? Mr. Hurst stayed home?" Anniscote prompted.

"Ay, he did. But then a man like a Quaker come to call on him. He was dressed plain. Good cloth, but dark, no gold lacings. And he had sort o' a calm face."

"And you know he called on Hurst, rather than the ladies of the family?"

Harry shrugged. "Might be he saw them, too, but after a bit, the Quaker-cove comes out, and your cove with him, and they stood on the step."

The duke waited.

"But not friendly-like, as you might jaw a bit before parting outside the public house. Mr. Hurst, he was white as a sheet, then he flushed up. The other man, he was cool as…well, I don't know what. Then he bows a little and goes off."

"I trust you followed him?"

Harry blushed and toed the carpet. "I did, but I lost him. I'm sorry, Yer Grace, I wasn't far behind, but the streets was busy and some young hemp-seed tripped me. I get up fast as I could and didn't even stay to cuff the brat, but the black-coat was out o' sight. I run up the street and look into the next turning, but he hadn't gone that way and there was buildings he could have turned into."

Perhaps Mulley knew someone who could discreetly question Hurst's staff to find out who it was.

"It couldn't be helped, I suppose, Harry. Here's a farthing—"

Peters opened the door. "Your Grace, Mr. Hurst— you imp, Harry, what are you doing plaguing His Grace?"

"No, Peters, it's all right, I asked him to do an errand."

"Very good, Your Grace." Recollecting himself, he added, "Mr. Hurst has called, sir."

Harry grinned and made his escape.

"This is unexpected," the duke said when his visitor was ushered in. "Will you take brandy?"

Hurst ignored the first comment. "Yes, thank you. The library is much improved. It used to be that dust puffed up when I dropped into one of these chairs."

"Yes, it did when I sat down, too," Anniscote replied, pouring a sustaining amount of liquor into a pair of glasses. He passed one to Hurst, who fortified himself with a long swallow. "To what circumstance do I owe…?"

"My calling on you? I wondered if you had given thought to my suggestion."

"Suggestion?" the duke repeated guilelessly.

"That you marry Mistress Anne." Hurst glared at him, seemed to realize he should attempt to be placating, and forced his face into friendlier lines.

Really, the fellow was falling apart. He appeared not to have slept, and his skin had lost most of its ruddiness. "That? I assumed it was a jest."

"Hardly! The poor girl's reputation is ruined. I confess it freely, it was partly my doing. You know my tongue runs away with me at whiles. It came to me that as I had said some ill-natured things—and untrue, as it turns out—about her, I should do all I could to make amends. I have set it about that I was mistaken in thinking I had seen the young lady in any unsuitable company or place. Believe me, I am heartily sorry for it. But the talk continues unabated."

"Yes, once the cat is out of the bag, stuffing it back in can be difficult."

"So I bethought me to make it right by getting her a husband. And as you are the brother of my old friend, and I may have damaged your name as well as the lady's, it seemed to me that your marriage to Mistress Anne would settle all."

"Why not make a match for your son with Mistress Anne?"

His guest appeared stricken dumb. Then he uttered, "No—no, impossible—" before regaining his composure. He tossed off the rest of his brandy, and Anniscote refilled his glass. Hurst drank again, before continuing.

"My son is too young for her and must marry an heiress in any case. You need not marry money, thanks to Nick having done so. It would also allow you to secure the succession, as Nick failed to do. You have a duty to your name to marry and beget an heir. Who can number his days on earth?" Hurst inquired, rhetorically.

"Not I, certainly. However, even if I felt myself duty-bound to offer for her, she would not accept me."

"Nonsense! Of course she would. So would any woman and any guardian in the world, on her behalf. You're a duke! You have an unencumbered estate. What more could any female ask?"

"If you believe she'd have me, you little know Mistress Anne."

"No matter how capricious she may be, you need only press your suit upon Mrs. Bradshaw and Wemley, and they will do the rest."

"It is unnecessary. I think you take too pessimistic a view of Mistress Anne's situation. I do not suppose she will care to return to London, even if you manage to quell the rumors, since she is singularly unsuited to society. She is doomed to be a spinster, I fear. She is as full of learning as some Oxford don, but unlike the don, there is no place for her at a college. She is argumentative, too. She lacks charm and accomplishments, and when she is thinking deep thoughts, she trips over things. All kinds of things: footstools, spaniels, stairs, her escort's feet, her own feet. If she ever does marry, it must be to some reclusive country gentleman of similar habits, who never entertains." Anniscote stopped, aghast. Whatever had made him speak so? He rather liked Anne, and much of what he had said was exaggerated or actually untrue. He had never seen her trip over a spaniel. And while it was true that she did none of the things expected of genteel ladies, neither was she boring. Also in her favor were her pretty ankles, glimpsed once or twice when she alighted from a carriage, her rose-leaf complexion, and her waist, which fairly begged for a gentleman's arm around it. Good God, what was he thinking? But he was damned if he would retract a word before Hurst.

He noticed that the man was goggling at him. He looked almost ill.

"I did not realize you felt so strongly. There is no more to be said, then," Hurst said finally, standing up. "Well, I have done my best to make things right and failed. No doubt I deserved it, but it seems plaguey hard on the girl. And others." With a curt nod, he strode out the door.

Anniscote found he did not like himself overmuch but came near to liking Hurst. He had thought Hurst's claim that he was obligated to marry Anne was merely intended to discomfit him. Apparently, Hurst took the matter seriously. If, as it appeared, he had recently discovered that Anne was his illegitimate daughter, was he feeling a paternal interest in Anne's reputation? Even if he were, his reaction seemed extreme.

And what of his own reaction? Was he besotted, to be thinking of Anne so often and with such mixed emotions?

Chapter 43

Elspat had insisted on concealing their destination from the earl's staff, the duchess mendaciously announcing that a family crisis made their departure urgent. "Not but what it is indeed a crisis," she added to Anne.

As the rather bare statement was followed by a torrent of charmingly worded apologies and requests (and a distribution of douceurs), the steward had neither chance to ask for particulars nor inclination to do so. Anne admired the duchess's technique exceedingly.

"It is dreadfully discourteous to leave the earl's home so abruptly," Elspat murmured to her. "It would be worse only if the earl or any of his family were here. I would not do it for the world, if it were not so necessary. "

The only one entrusted with their destination was the Guysbridge coachman, and she swore him to secrecy.

"Are you sure he won't tell anyone?"

"Not he," the duchess said. "He's been a Guysbridge man all his life, and very loyal to the family. When I mentioned that my father might come to force me into marrying again and therefore I must stay out of his way until His Grace was able to discourage him, all he said was, 'Ah! Your dad'll have to find you first, Your Grace, and I'll not let it come to that.' But I did not tell him more than that we were going north. When we're well on our way, I'll give him exact directions."

"Did you let His Grace know where we'll be?

"Ay, I felt obliged to tell him."

Chapter 44

Afterward, Anniscote could not understand how it had come about. Neither could Tom, except in the most general way. They and several others at Saltero's coffeehouse were discussing the sporadic rioting.

Anniscote remarked that the rioters probably worried about starving when grain was in such short supply and the price of bread so high.

"Your father and brother were in the right of it," Hurst said contemptuously. "You have the soul of a clerk. You would incite a mob against its natural betters, like Cromwell's damned Roundheads."

The accusation was so ludicrous that there could be no reply but, "Really, Hurst, you should have another cup of coffee. Or several. This habit of drinking strong spirits in the morning—"

One of their group barked a laugh, quickly cut off. The others looked uncomfortable. Several countrified-appearing gentlemen who had come in more to gawk at the cases of curios and freaks than to drink coffee suddenly moved away.

He did not see the glove until it whipped across his face.

"You insult me, sir! Name your second."

"My dear fellow," someone said and broke off as Hurst wheeled to glare at him.

"I think the boot is rather on the other foot,"

Anniscote drawled.

"Ay," Sir Hugh Morris said. "Guysbridge had the right to issue his challenge first, as undoubtedly Hurst insulted him first."

"I don't give a curse for that. If Guysbridge is too much a coward to challenge me, I've a right to challenge him."

All eyes except those of Anniscote fixed on Hurst at this improper sentiment. Anniscote was removing a bit of fluff that clung to the left sleeve of his coat. "I will not stand on ceremony."

"There are forms to be followed," Sir Hugh opined, and Jeffreys added, "Anniscote, you have no choice but to challenge him. Unless, of course, he chooses to retract. "

Hurst snarled something which all took to be a refusal.

"As Hurst has challenged me, it hardly seems necessary for me to challenge him, for no doubt the matter will be settled in our first meeting."

"While I am not entirely comfortable with the way in which this affair was commenced, as a practical matter, I tend to agree with Your Grace that a second meeting is unlikely to be required. If it is, Guysbridge can issue his challenge then. Mr. Hurst, does this meet with your approval?"

"It does," Hurst answered through clenched teeth.

"Tom, will you act for me?"

"Of course." Sir Hugh agreed to represent Hurst. The two retired to another table to discuss the arrangements, while Hurst moodily retreated to examine a stuffed crocodile mounted upon the wall some distance from Anniscote's table.

"Tomorrow," Jeffreys told Anniscote later, in the latter's library. "Five in the morning, Tothill Fields. A doctor is engaged, and Sir Hugh and I discussed ways of settling this deplorable matter without bloodshed. But Hurst will not retract, and you cannot refuse to meet him. Not after he called you a coward. One would think he set on deliberately to make you challenge him."

"So it seemed."

"And when you did not…why the devil did he do it? He cannot be unaware of your reputation. You might easily kill him."

"I shall endeavor not to do so." His Grace smiled. "I've given orders for my coach. I'll call for you in the morning."

"Talk of it has already spread like fire."

"Has it. How did that happen?"

"Some of the other patrons of the coffee house saw what passed. No one could misunderstand the meaning of the exchange. I daresay several repeated it to friends, who repeated it to their friends. This has been a mismanaged business."

"Well, there's nothing to be done about it now."

"Except get a good night's sleep," said Jeffreys. "I trust you don't intend to go out tonight."

"No, indeed. I've already sent my regrets to Lady LePage, pleading urgent family business. A night of drinking and cards, followed by a duel, might have been my idea of entertainment when I was new come to London, but I protest I am grown sedate. My evening will consist of a light supper, a little reading, and my bed."

****

Charles Anascote: I and my brother Francis and sister Lucy sat by our father's bed. All of us respected and loved him, but I perhaps mourned our coming loss the most, for I knew him the best, he having spent so much time with me, teaching me the Spanish language and preparing me to be his heir. I believe I understood him the best, having learned to understand the Spanish character.

He was, as I have said, reserved and punctilious even to a fault. However, he was not a harsh father, and while he would never have let any of us make imprudent marriages, he did not force my sister Margaret to wed the man he had originally intended for her husband, when he learned she disliked him.

His several natural sons and daughters were not summoned to his deathbed, but he had written letters to each some months previous and entrusted them to me to deliver after his death. I do not know whether the others knew that we had half sisters and brothers. My father considered it a point of honor not to cause our mother pain or humiliation. Many women accept their husbands' informal dealings with indifference, for indeed, such things are not uncommon. Being of a retiring disposition and devoted to my father, my mother could not have done so. The knowledge that he sometimes had a mistress would have wounded her.

Don Diego made excellent provision for his other children when they were of age to be on their own, as he was well able to do. His brother had given him money with which to establish himself in England, and my father had husbanded it carefully, purchasing the Guysbridge manor. After marrying our mother, he invested some of it with merchant captains and in agricultural improvements to our lands. One of my half brothers has a ship, the other is secretary to one of Her Majesty's privy counsellors. Don Diego arranged suitable marriages for the girls.

My father spoke with my brother and sister, and dictated letters to my other sister and brother who were unable to be at his bedside. He was calm and, I think, at peace.

Toward dawn, he said, "It is well." Don Diego Anascote, son and brother of dukes, slipped out of life soon thereafter. He had as good a death as any man can hope for.

A suitable topic for bedside reading the night before a duel, Anniscote thought wryly.

Chapter 45

Surveying the garments Mulley had laid ready for him, the duke said, "Do you really consider these suitable for a duel? Put away the red suit. I will have the black cloth instead. And I will not require wrist frills."

"No frills? But, Your Grace—"

"I am to fight a duel, Mulley. I would have to tuck them up."

"But afterward, if you are seen in public in such a shabby suit and with no frills, it will be thought you have no valet, or one who is incompetent."

"Oh, your professional pride is suffering! Very well. To gratify you, I'll tuck them up. They will of course be wrinkled afterward—if they have not come untucked and killed me."

Mulley suppressed a moan. "No, no, Your Grace. I was not thinking. One of the plain shirts, then."

"An old one, if you please. For if I should be pinked, there is no sense in ruining a good shirt."

The chaise stood at the door in the misty pre-dawn light. The duke had anticipated leaving before most of the staff were on duty; however, he found himself seen off not only by Mulley but also by Peters, Davy the groom, and Harry the bootboy, whose expressions were somewhat more apprehensive than Anniscote felt warranted.

Peters actually said, "Take no chances, Your Grace."

"Do you know how many times I've been out, Peters?"

"Several, I believe, sir."

"And never took any harm, bar a scratch or two."

"It's different now, Your Grace."

"Well, admittedly, I am now Duke of Guysbridge."

"Yes, sir, and with no heir."

"I'll see about remedying the situation—but after this morning, if you don't mind."

"Not at all, sir," Peters replied, impervious to irony.

As he was stepping up into the chaise, a man muffled almost to the eyes in a roquelaure stepped out of the darkness, almost at Anniscote's elbow. The coachman exclaimed, "Here, you!"

"A word," the stranger said, and Anniscote thought the voice and the visible portion of the face seemed familiar. Certainly they were those of a gentleman. "It's all right," he said.

Low-voiced, the man said, "I've come to ask that you not kill Hurst. Or, I suppose, injure him seriously enough that he might subsequently expire."

"It was not my intention, but what's your interest?"

"My own? Very little. I am acting as a messenger for another party, who may provide you an explanation later."

"I will look forward to it," the duke said grimly.

The other gave a slight bow, hardly more than an inclination of the head, turned and strode away. "Let's be off," Anniscote called up to the box. The duel itself would be an anticlimax, he thought.

****

Hurst and his second were already present. Hurst, who had removed his coat, waistcoat and wig, was white-faced and sweating despite the cool morning. Sir Hugh, standing near him, was speaking earnestly into his ear.

"Perhaps I had better have a word with Sir Hugh," Jeffreys said. "Mayhap there is yet a possibility of settling the matter."

"As you will," Anniscote said. He cared not how it was resolved, whether by an apology from Hurst or by his shedding a few drops of Hurst's blood. The man was not known for dueling. He might have fought once or twice when he was younger, but while he was frequently rude and sometimes quarrelsome, it seemed not to lead him into challenges. Until now.

He set about pulling off his own coat, and saw a plainly-dressed fellow with a case clambering down from a gig. On approaching, he proved to be young, with a Scotch look about him. He gave the parties a brusque nod, stated, "Ferguson, surgeon," and took a position off to the side. Trust Tom to secure the best. No doubt the man had studied at Edinburgh.

Jeffreys and Sir Hugh exchanged a speaking glance and walked aside to confer. Unbuckling his sword belt, Anniscote drew his blade and cast belt and scabbard aside. Hurst made a show of inspecting his own blade, as if he expected to find either blood or rust upon it. Jeffreys and Sir Hugh parted.

"Hurst will not withdraw his challenge. If you apologized, he would of course have to accept it. But that is not to be thought of anyway, I know, as no one believes you insulted him. Sir Hugh informs me that he reminded Hurst of your skill and your past duels, but it made no difference. Although," he added, "he certainly appears to be nervous."

"He appears to be afraid," the duke corrected. "Well, I had best pink him quickly, before he goes off in an apoplexy."

They took their places, and the signal was given. Hurst lunged, suddenly but without skill. Anniscote parried his blade easily. If he himself had been a less practiced swordsman, he might have been killed, or he might have reacted by running Hurst through. Or, of course, both at once.

Hurst had scarcely regained his balance before Anniscote left a trail of blood on his left upper arm.

"Is honor satisfied?" the duke asked.

"Damn you, no!"

Jeffreys stifled an exclamation, and Sir Hugh grunted disapproval.

Hurst lunged again, his face that of a man looking into Hell. Anniscote fell back. *By God, he means to kill me if he can*, he realized. It was a task for which Hurst's ability was inadequate. But his bull-like attacks might force the duke to kill him.

No. He must disable Hurst without killing him outright. As he parried yet another brutal thrust, he wondered how his mysterious messenger this morning had foreseen some such outcome.

Hurst's face was now red with effort. He was panting, and Anniscote could see drops of sweat among the red-brown stubble on his head as well as on forehead and cheek. There were half-a-dozen scarlet patches on his shirt where the duke's point had pricked him. None of them were deep but with the exertion, they must begin to sap his strength. Hurst's blade was beginning to waver, and the duke expected him to collapse momentarily, bringing this clumsy business to an end.

"For Heaven's sake, Hurst, have done," Sir Hugh cried.

Instead, Hurst charged straight at Anniscote, his sword levelled at his heart.

What the devil was Hurst about? the duke wondered as he leaped to one side. Hurst fought as if battling for his life, when Anniscote had given him no indication that his life was in danger. He had only defended himself against Hurst's onslaught.

The blades clanged and slithered. Hurst's lips drew back in a snarl, and his chest was heaving. He threw himself at Anniscote once more.

Hurst could not believe himself capable of slaying him, or even of wounding him seriously, and though the duke now had several oozing cuts, none were deep. The point of Hurst's weapon sliced the air inches from the duke's right eye.

Give over thinking of why, Anniscote warned himself. *That pass might have cost me dear. Why is of no consequence.*

Jeffreys shouted, "Hang the rules! Enough of this!"

"It must stop," Sir Hugh agreed. "I say, Hurst, surely honor's satisfied?"

Anniscote heartily agreed but could not spare breath or attention to say so, or to ask how it could be stopped while Hurst continued to slash at him.

"Fight!" Hurst spat. "Fight or die." He stumbled toward the duke.

As Hurst raised his wavering blade to strike,

Anniscote struck a blow to the base of the smallsword that sent it flying out of his opponent's hand. Then he cast his own aside and sprang forward to punch him squarely on the chin. Hurst fell back full length on the grass.

"I do not think that was quite consistent with good dueling practice," Sir Hugh observed. "One should not change weapons in the course of a duel—unless, of course, one of the blades should prove defective, or break, in which case, I suppose one might substitute another."

"Oh, never mind that," Jeffreys said, moving to collect the fallen blades while the doctor examined Hurst and Anniscote, panting, sucked his skinned, bruised knuckles.

The Scots surgeon closed his case. "I can find no dangerous wound that will not wait for his own doctor's attention. I could administer sal volatile, but I think it unwise at this point, as it appeared to me this gentleman's mind was disordered, and he may still be violent upon reviving. That was a very fine, punishing blow, and just what was needed, in my opinion," he remarked in the duke's direction. "It will be best if he is taken home as he is and given a composing draft. His own doctor should see him and, most important, be advised of his patient's behavior this morning. You are his friend, I think?"

"Ay," Sir Hugh said. "My coach is just there—the blue one. Jeffreys?"

Between them, and with assistance from Sir Hugh's coachman, they wrestled Hurst's inert body into the coach.

"I do not think that was entirely a suitable end to a

duel," Sir Hugh announced. "I could not wish to see Hurst slain—or, indeed, anyone else—but it would not surprise me if he wished to continue it after he recovers. Gentlemen do not settle their differences with their fists, like drunken laborers."

"Better, perhaps, if they did," the Scotsman remarked, and Jeffreys, speaking at almost the same moment, said, "Does the code of honor permit a man in the grip of temporary insanity to fight?"

"That is a question," Sir Hugh agreed. "I shall give it thought. Though I suppose it is up to the parties involved, and if Hurst's convalescence is prolonged…"

The surgeon glanced at Anniscote's cuts and stated, "You'll do, sir. Have them dressed; no doubt your valet can do it well enough. There's no need for any special diet. I would suggest you not undertake any strenuous exercise for a day or two and limit your use of wine and brandy. A glass of port, which is a strengthening drink, would do no harm. "

"Thank you, Mr. Ferguson."

****

At Guysbridge House, they breakfasted on slices of rare beef and tankards of ale, for as the duke said, "I really cannot drink port at this hour of the morning."

"Whatever caused Hurst to act as he did?" Jeffreys asked.

"One would think he was trying to make me kill him. But why I have no idea. And here is an odd circumstance, Tom—" and Anniscote related the strange incident of the mysterious messenger. They were still pondering the meaning of it when Peters entered.

"Your Grace, a gentleman has called. He requests

an interview with you, although he has declined to present his card. I have asked him to wait in the morning room."

"This may be the visitor I was expecting," he said, with a significant glance at Tom. "Do you wait in the library, if you have no pressing business elsewhere, while I speak with him."

"I would be glad to hear the denouement if you can share it with me."

Chapter 46

The visitor was gazing at the landscape painting over the fireplace when the duke entered.

"It's a terrible piece," Anniscote remarked casually. "My grandfather brought it home from the Low Countries, as you can see by the presence of a windmill and a cow."

The man turned, and the duke exclaimed, "Alderman Saltstall!"

"I take it you did not guess it was I who sent you the message this morning, Your Grace. I thought you might have recognized Captain Easterday."

"He was swathed in a wrap-rascal. I thought I had met him before but could not be sure."

"He must have greater powers of dissimulation than I thought. I had hoped to manage matters without revealing my involvement, but things have gone too far."

Anniscote gestured wordlessly to a chair, and Saltstall took it.

"I have come to believe that if I must confide in someone, you are no bad choice. You were dragged into this affair, so you have some interest in it. After meeting you at Vauxhall Gardens, I formed the opinion that you are both intelligent and discreet. And I was born a clergyman's son: my conscience would not permit me to let Hurst kill himself on the point of your

313

sword."

"It begins to be an embarrassment that I have such a reputation."

"It is never too late to amend," said the clergyman's son. He went on, "It was partly my fault, and I fear I have some soul-searching to do. I am not in the habit of acting out of anger but gave in to it in dealing with Hurst."

"As he was traducing the reputation of Mrs. Saltstall, few would blame you overmuch."

"So you had heard of that? However, I am ashamed to admit my anger was not solely on that account. It has been suggested that I might in time be Lord Mayor of London, and I am vain enough to think I might be of benefit to London in that capacity. However, I must first serve as a Sheriff of the City. It is possible there has already been enough talk to destroy my chances of election as Sheriff, for while such bibble-babble as there has been may not be enough to ruin a reputation among the nobility or even the gentry, the Guilds may take a sterner view. I was therefore anxious to quell the gossip." Saltstall fell silent. He drummed his fingers upon his knee.

At last he said, "I think I must tell you the whole. I trust you will not divulge it—except to such persons as have a material interest in the matter and will not spread it further, as reputations are at stake."

Anniscote inclined his head in agreement.

"You were drawn in by my very foolish and wayward daughter, who wanted to marry a nobleman. Your brother's death and your inheriting the title—and your unmarried state—were much talked of, and she thought it would be a fine thing to be a duchess. I am sorry to say that my wife has not reared Mariah with such firm principles as I would have wished. I am to blame for that, for I was well aware that my wife was…was perhaps more ambitious and concerned with worldly success than I might have wished, but at the same time, her charm and skill as a hostess have been of great assistance to me. Welladay! Mariah set her cap for you, and because she had no access to the circles in which you move, she resorted to various stratagems to attract your notice. I am exceedingly sorry to say that through a connection of her maid's, she was able to hire the services of a set of persons she would never otherwise have known of," Saltstall said grimly.

"I see."

"I have come to the point that I must admit to you that my daughter and wife both acted in a manner which I find indescribably embarrassing. My wife learned that our daughter meant to meet you in a place which would so compromise her virtue that she believed you would feel bound to marry her. Marianne realized that the possibility of success was slight, though mind you, I am not saying she would have approved of it even if it were sure to succeed." He flushed.

The alderman might not say it, or think it, but Anniscote felt sure that if Mrs. Saltstall believed the plan would succeed, she would have felt little reluctance to let it go forward.

"Mariah had already dispatched a billet to entice you to the meeting. Marianne decided that she must take some action to divert attention from our daughter by sending someone else in Mariah's place."

"And she chose Mistress Anne Sinclair because she

shares the Sinclair resemblance, in the hope I would not notice the difference and would ruin Mistress Anne. No doubt she worried that the resemblance would be commented upon, but perhaps she believed that Mistress Anne would leave London so quickly that it would come to no one's attention," Anniscote commented.

"You are substantially correct, sir." Saltstall hesitated. "There was another factor of which I think you are unaware, which shows my wife in a very unflattering light. She did not panic and make use of Anne Sinclair's convenient likeness to my daughter merely to deceive you. She feared that Mistress Anne's presence in London would endanger her own reputation, as in fact it has, though more by her own machinations in trying to avoid ruin than by unlucky chance."

The duke said nothing and gazed out the window to avoid the sight of the man's humiliation.

Saltstall continued, "I married for love. At the time, I knew that some of Marianne's views were more worldly than my father would have approved, but for a man in business, that is not a disadvantage. She had only a small dowry, but I was already comfortably situated, so that did not matter to me. I was not aware that she had been seduced."

"By Hurst, of course."

"Yes. Dr. Sinclair took her to France to prevent the seduction's unfortunate sequel becoming known. Marianne gave birth to a daughter there. On their return, Doctor Sinclair raised the child as the orphan of distant relations. You will have guessed by now that it was Mistress Anne."

"One or two things made me suspect it," Anniscote said. "I am glad to hear my suspicions confirmed. If 'glad' be the correct term."

"My daughter's folly and Mistress Anne's presence combined to cause my wife to take the unwise measures that have led to our problem. With great luck, Mistress Anne might have escaped the Cantwells' house of accommodation with her reputation unblemished. Having been seen by Hurst, however, it was almost certain that he would meet her sooner or later and, given his troublemaking tongue, that he would blacken her name. Mrs. Saltstall's first effort having failed due to you, she had Anne kidnapped, intending that she should be shipped off to the American colonies. That plot failed as well. There was a little talk, servants' gossip, yet it might have been weathered but for that ill-starred party at Vauxhall Gardens, where Hurst happened to see my wife, my daughter, and Marianne's illegitimate daughter."

"Hurst could hardly have resisted the temptation to talk," Anniscote remarked.

"No. The lady he had seduced years ago, now married, must have seemed amusing to him." Saltstall roused himself. "I began to notice some time ago that my wife was not herself. Her aunt thought she must be ill, and I thought she was uneasy about something, but unfortunately, like many men, I am not very perceptive about the feelings of ladies. Finally, she came to such a state that I realized her bouts of weeping were more than megrims and insisted she tell me the whole.

"As you can imagine, I was not well-pleased to learn that my daughter was so inadequately chaperoned and so light-minded, and that my wife had entered into a plot worthy of an Italian Renaissance prince to distract attention from Mariah's and her own misdoings. At length Marianne confessed that the young lady she had chosen to sacrifice in Mariah's place was her own natural daughter. I was angry, of course, but I was at a loss to account for my wife's extreme discomfiture, as while I found there had been some talk, it hardly seemed serious enough to ruin either girl's reputation or my wife's. At last she admitted that something Mistress Anne had told her suggested that Hurst meant to seduce her—not realizing the girl was his own daughter, you understand, for Marianne had never told him she was with child and never encountered him again until the Vauxhall Gardens visit." Saltstall's lips thinned. "Why the possibility of unwitting incest should utterly overset her, when attempting to ruin her own daughter or having her sent to the colonies as an indentured servant did not, is something I will never understand. However, I believe she has paid for her crimes with her own tears. I had to mend matters as best I could."

The duke rose and went to the cabinet in which he kept a bottle of brandy and glasses, and poured out a measure, which he passed to Saltstall.

The alderman went on. "My efforts had unintended results. I spoke to a banker of my acquaintance at the bank which enjoys—if that is possible—Hurst's patronage. I then spoke with Hurst and made it clear that unless he stopped all attempts to blacken my wife's name and those of my daughter and of his own illegitimate daughter, he would find his financial situation far more difficult than it had been. I know that he has complied and attempted to stanch the flow of talk, but he now seems to be as distraught as my wife was. When I heard that he had forced a duel upon you, I was thunderstruck and concluded he intended to die. My next visit must be to Hurst to let him know that I consider he has done all he can to rectify his actions. Captain Easterday is willing to marry my daughter in spite of her faults. My wife must endure the consequences of her own actions. I fear they will fall most heavily on Mistress Anne, poor girl."

"Hurst did his best to undo it, for he pressed me in the liveliest terms to wed her."

Saltstall looked up, startled.

"Did he? I do not suppose…"

"I declined. Not from any defect in Mistress Anne, who is—" The duke paused to consider how to describe her. "She is intelligent and has a lively wit. Her manners are those of a lady. She is very pretty, especially when she is not wearing spectacles. Admittedly, she sometimes speaks her mind very freely. There is nothing to dislike in her behavior or appearance, and a good deal to admire." *And to love.*

"She is not quite what one would expect in a duchess, perhaps," said Saltstall.

What does one expect in a duchess? the duke wondered. Then he remembered his mother. "No," he agreed.

****

After explaining the matter to Jeffreys, whom Anniscote deemed an interested party, both because of his assistance in Anne's difficulties and because the duke expected him to be a sort of brother-in-law in the next year, Anniscote decided that he must also visit Hurst. The duke found him reposing in his chamber less

319

because of injury than because he was still groggy from whatever his doctor had dosed him with. The patient seemed no more glad to see Anniscote than the latter was to be there.

"May we consider the quarrel between us settled?" Anniscote inquired after the briefest exchange of civilities.

After clearing his throat and sipping from a glass on the stand beside the bed, Hurst muttered, "I would be glad to regard it as closed. Why did you not kill me?—I meant you to do so, and we have never liked one another."

"As I set out, someone approached me to request that I not kill you, which I had not intended to do in any case. It would have caused so much talk. There's already been enough of that commodity. And I really could not deprive your wife of your company. Besides, your death would have cast a pall over your eldest daughter's wedding, or postponed it."

"My daughter's wedding…damned waste of money. Too bad it's not respectable to elope. You may have wondered…I have been under some strain which caused me to act rashly."

"Alderman Saltstall paid a call upon me at a perfectly unreasonable time of the morning, and I understand your reasons for pressing a challenge on me."

Hurst drank again. "I hoped if I died, Saltstall would not carry through with his threat, which would have ruined my family. Letting you run me through seemed an easy way of accomplishing the matter. My wife is a twittering fool, but I thought I could spare my family the double shame of poverty and my being refused burial by the church."

"Well, you have done so, and without dying, so all's well that ends well. The talk will die down in time, and I suppose we will see Saltstall become Lord Mayor presently."

"I should have liked to see you wed Mistress Anne," Hurst replied dreamily. "It would have been so entertaining." Had anyone else been present, it might have seemed a non sequitur. "…so deliciously ridiculous and scandalous…"

"I trust you are now relieved of your trouble?"

Hurst managed a death's-head grin. "I believe I am past the greatest part of it. Now if my wife will control her tendency to shed tears when she looks at me, and my daughters to tiptoe about, I may be tolerably comfortable. Though part of that comfort may be traced to whatever that fool of a doctor has given me," he added reflectively.

Anniscote wished him a speedy recovery and turned to go.

"I can't decide," Hurst murmured, "which I wanted more: to annoy you or to benefit the girl. Both seemed worthy aims." He was still choking with laughter when Anniscote left.

Chapter 47

Under the duchess's generalship, the maids packed their trunks in an amazingly short time, while she composed a missive to the duke and Anne wrote to Aunt Letitia and the earl. As soon as the letters were given to the steward to be dispatched and they had put on gowns suitable for travelling, they mounted the coach.

They were well away from Wemley before Anne asked, "How far are we going?"

"As to that," Elspat replied, "I am not quite certain. From Glasgow to Guysbridge was a matter of something over four days, but the roads were good, and my father's travelling coach is new, with the latest improvements."

"Improvements? Can you tell me—no, never mind. I'll ask later. But we are some way south of Guysbridge, I think."

"Not so far. His Grace's coach is old, but well-made and well-sprung. It was two days' easy travel to Wemley. So it is about six days to my old housekeeper's home or a bit more, for she lives a little way north of Glasgow. Seven or eight days, perhaps, if the roads are bad, and naturally we will not travel on Sunday."

Anne hoped that they would not have to spend Sunday in some Scottish village—or that if they did, it would be a town of some size. Few things could be more depressing than enforced idleness, when one had nothing to do, nothing except the Bible to read, and was disbarred from any frivolous pastime. In one's own home, one might do as one pleased or as one's religious sentiments permitted, and Dr. Sinclair's disregard of the Sabbath was of such long standing that Mrs. Bowman had given up remonstrating with him. Anne usually read, but they had departed so hurriedly that she had failed to provide herself with books. Sally had packed the thin volume of poetry Anne had last been reading, but it was not enough to occupy many hours. If only she had had her copy of Sir Thomas Browne's *Religio Medici*, she might even have passed it off as devotional literature.

However, they made good time to the Border. Anne thoroughly enjoyed the new views, and in the evenings both she and Elspat were too tired from the coach's rumbling, shaking progress to do more than eat supper and go to bed. Once in Scotland, the villages they passed began to have foreign-sounding names.

The roads worsened and the locals' knowledge sometimes extended little beyond the next ten or fifteen miles. They stopped often to inquire the way, and the duchess sometimes had to interpret the Lowlands Scottish dialect for her coachman.

The road turned into weedy ruts, and Jenkins halted the coach. "Your Grace, I'm thinking we must have gone wrong. Mayhap we should turn the coach and go back—while we still can turn it," he added significantly. The lane had become very narrow.

Elspat popped out and stood among the nettles, weeds, and thistles, to the detriment of her skirt, and stared around. Anne followed her.

The countryside was more empty of habitation than any Anne recalled in England. She imagined vast expanses of the Americas must be this frighteningly isolated, with no neat fields and cottages, no farm laborers to be seen.

"Look there," Elspat said. "Do you not see a wisp of smoke, to the left of the way?"

Jenkins squinted doubtfully. The postilion exclaimed, "Ay, 'tis close by that wee hill."

"We will go a little farther. There must be some dwelling there, or an inn, and we can try to get some word of our route."

A little farther on, past the shoulder of the hill, they saw with relief that there was a habitation of sorts.

The sound of their coach brought a woman out of the hovel. She wore a ragged skirt, from behind which two small children peered with wide eyes. On a bench beside the door slouched a man wearing travel-stained breeches and a sort of long shawl around his shoulders. His hair was clubbed back under a flat knitted cap like a dinner plate. At intervals, he drank from a mug while he watched with the interest of one enjoying a theatrical performance. A scruffy brown and white dog lay at his feet.

There was a burst of speech from the woman as they drew up. While Anne was still trying to puzzle it out, Elspat said, "Jenkins, you were quite right. This lane ends a little farther on."

The ragged woman made a hesitant inquiry, to which Elspat responded, "Och, ay. Do you ken someone?"

The woman grinned at her, showing missing teeth

and gestured at the man, who placed the mug on the bench and said in accented but understandable English, "You'll be wanting a guide."

Which was how they came to travel with Andrew.

Anne had asked, rather timidly for her, if he knew the roads well in that part of Scotland.

"I do. I'm a drover, you'll ken. I've taken herds all over Scotland, and even across into England."

Elspat asked his price for seeing them to their destination.

"Droving, I am paid by the mile. But it is not so many miles you are going, though it may take several days as there's no way to go straight to it. So I'll take six English pence a day and my food."

"And lodging of course," Elspat said.

"Nay, why? When I am taking the cattle to market, I often sleep out. Wherever you stop for the night will have a byre or some outbuilding to keep the rain off me."

Chapter 48

Back at Guysbridge House, after taking his hat, the footman ventured, "There's a letter come for you, Your Grace. The boy as brought it last night swore it was urgent, but Mr. Peters had said you wasn't to be bothered by anything, because of the, ah…hrumpf!…this morning, and I'm sorry to say it was forgotten when Your Grace returned."

"The ah…hrumpf!…was no great thing, I assure you. Peters was unnecessarily concerned."

"We all knew as much, Your Grace, and Hutchins won a tidy sum, wagering on you."

"I believe I am flattered."

"Not at all, sir," said the footman, returning to formality. "There's a letter come from Wemley, too, by one of Her Grace's grooms."

Anniscote stared at the two missives. One was addressed in a shaky hand which he suspected was that of Elvira Bradshaw, the other was the rigidly correct script of his sister-in-law, the duchess. He opened the latter.

Moments later, he stretched an arm to reach for the bell pull, and halted in midreach, recalling that Mrs. Bradshaw's letter was said to be urgent.

Written in a shaky hand, with many underlinings, Elvira Bradshaw begged his attendance upon her at his *very earliest Convenience* the following Morning, even as early as ten of the Clock, so that they might discuss the Odd and disquieting News she had received from Anne.

He knew what its substance must be, and the duchess's brief, formal letter had been quite enough to raise his apprehensions, even without Anne's enclosed note. She wrote concisely and in an admirably legible hand, requesting that he do something to prevent the duchess's father from harassing her.

He inked his pen and scribbled a hasty sheet, sprinkled it with pounce, and folded and sealed it. Then he rang for Peters and issued a string of instructions.

****

"Your Grace!" Elvira Bradshaw exclaimed tremulously. "I was monstrous worried when I received no response to my letter—not that I blame you in the least, for you must have thought it an old woman's foolishness—and then of course I heard from Mrs. Nugent and understood why you hadn't come, and worried twice over." Overcome with emotion and lack of breath, she sank onto a settee.

The duke turned to the butler, who was still present and eying his mistress apprehensively. "Send for Mrs. Bradshaw's maid—if she be discreet—and a restorative."

"At once, Your Grace."

But with a deep breath, Mrs. Bradshaw composed herself.

"I received a letter from Anne yesterday which fills me with dread." She took a folded sheet from her pocket and passed it to Anniscote.

"I imagine it informed you that she and the duchess intended to go to Scotland," he said. "I received the

327

news from my sister-in-law only this morning." Unfolding the much-creased sheet, he scanned it briefly. As he had apprehended, the matter was worse than Elspat had cared to disclose.

And he could not even blame Anne for it, unless he held that she should have restrained the duchess. Which, from what she described, might have been beyond even her abilities.

"You see why I am overcome, thinking of Anne and the poor duchess travelling among those bare-legged Highland savages. Why, they might as safely travel among Red Indians in the Colonies! Except that would involve a long sea voyage which might equally be fatal."

"You need not worry about Highlanders, Mistress Bradshaw, for she says they are bound for a Lowlands village. Not but what—" He broke off, tardily realizing that what he had been about to say about the state of civilization in general and inns in particular even in the Lowlands of Scotland, might not be reassuring. He had heard that country referred to as "Itchland."

"What?" Letitia demanded.

"The roads are not likely to be good—not as good as in England." Which would make them very bad, indeed. "But she and Her Grace are not alone. I do not imagine the duchess will have set out without the coachman, a postilion, at least one footman, and their maids."

"Servants! What use will they be, if there is danger? What if the Highlanders raid? Or rebel as they did in '15? What if the natives do not speak English? I feel a presentiment that some danger will befall them. What am I to do?"

The duke had no great regard for the presentiments of excitable ladies but said, "There is no need for you to take any action. I will see to it. I cannot permit my sister-in-law either to be hounded by her father or to wander in Scotland. Or Mistress Anne, either," he added. Who knew what difficulty might overtake her, let loose on her own in such a place? There could be little real danger, surely. Yet extricating Anne from scrapes had become a habit which he would be loath to give up.

He was addressing a few soothing words to his hostess when the butler opened the door to Mrs. Bradshaw's boudoir, and Thomas Jeffreys burst through it immediately behind him, like champagne after a cork.

"I beg your pardon, ma'am, but Anniscote having sent me a message about—" He paused in mid-spate and glanced at the scandalized butler. Mrs. Bradshaw waved Mayhew out.

"I felt I had to come at speed, although I am taking advantage of our acquaintance."

Mrs. Bradshaw, partial to handsome, well-mannered young men, replied, "It is most kind of you, and I am sure you will be of assistance."

"May I take it you are not unwilling to make a tour of North Britain?" Anniscote inquired, with a slightly satirical lift to his eyebrows.

"Try if you can stop me," Jeffreys retorted tersely.

****

"How long would it take a coach to travel from Wemley to the duchess's destination—whatever it is?" Jeffreys asked. They had left London at midafternoon, both of them feeling that they could ride some distance on their journey, given the long summer days.

"According to Her Grace's letter, it is a village called Knockahoo, or some such name. From her description, I estimate they would be five or six days on the road. Depending on the roads. And the weather." He cast an eye at the clouds gathering.

"And we are coming from farther away yet. I hope the rain does not delay us. Though I recall my tutor saying that the news of Queen Elizabeth's death was brought from London to Edinburgh in only sixty-two hours."

"I have read the same—but the messenger had good horses stationed along the route, and I believe stopped only to change them. We do not. But we can yet make progress when a coach might stick fast in the mud, even on the stumbling nags we will have to hire along the way. But cheer up. Think how glad Duchess Elspat will be to see you."

With an effort, Jeffreys concealed his anxiety. "And no doubt Mistress Anne will be pleased to see you."

"I really have no idea whether she will be pleased or not. She is so unpredictable." The duke decided to ignore Jeffreys's suppressed smile.

Taking another tack, Jeffreys remarked, "I thought our purpose was to escort them on the journey, but on reflection, given when the letters were written, we cannot hope to find them still on the road. They will have arrived at this…er, Knockahoo, before us. Surely they will have reached the place safely? The Lowlands are not the deserts of Araby, after all. Not that I am at all averse to riding forth like a knight on a quest."

"Mrs. Bradshaw has had a premonition of disaster

befalling Mistress Anne and Her Grace."

This appeared to reassure his friend. "And you believe in such things?" Jeffreys asked with a grin. "For the only premonitions I trust are those which tell me that I should avoid the card table."

"No…but I cannot like the idea of my sister-in-law fleeing from her father. She is my responsibility to protect, now that she is a widow. And this sudden flight from Wemley might be thought odd behavior in Mistress Anne, given her reputation in town."

"But then our pursuing the ladies—"

"Would cause more talk, if it were known. I trust it will not become common knowledge. Did you tell anyone where you were going or why?"

"No, of course not. Merely that I was off on a tour of scenic places and would be absent for perhaps three weeks or a month. Or less, depending on the weather."

"I told Mulley much the same. Mrs. Bradshaw's servants seem a close-lipped lot, and I warned her not to enlighten them."

****

"This road appears little travelled," Jeffreys remarked.

"Both sheep and cattle have passed here, but I admit it hardly looks suitable for a coach. But I have paid close attention to the directions Her Grace supplied, and I do not see how we could have gone wrong. "

But when they came to a tumble-down hut and a few outbuildings with half a dozen ragged children playing around the largest, the duke said, "A coach cannot have gone farther than this—the lane ahead is too narrow."

The children had vanished inside the dwelling, calling, "Mam! Mam! More gentles!"

A frowzy woman with a good-humored face emerged wiping her hands on her apron. From the dusting of flour on her skirt, Anniscote deduced she had been baking. Of greater interest to him was the children's cry of "More gentles!" Though given the state of his body linen after several days' wearing, he did not feel like gentry, much less nobility. But they had brought only one change of linen in their valises, and that must not be resorted to until they were within a ride of their quarry, or in a place they might stay long enough to have their small clothes laundered.

Thomas Jeffreys asked urgently, before she could even greet them, "My good woman, have you seen a coach with two young ladies come this way?"

"Och, ay," she said placidly.

"Can you tell us where they went from here, mistress?" The duke feared the answer would be only, "Back the way they came."

"Ay, sir. Andrew Raburn that's my gudeman's cousin undertook to guide them on their way."

"Would he know the way?" Jeffreys inquired dubiously.

"He knows every road and path in Scotland, and in England as well. The north part, at the least."

"Then we must go back to that branching of the road and try if we can follow their movements from there," Anniscote said to him.

"No, why, masters? If you but go on this way, you will come out on the road they took, maybe ahead o' them, if they meet with mud or some setback. Forbye it's the shorter way for onyone that's riding or afoot.

And there's a change-house where this track meets the main road. You'll get word of them there, if they are before you."

"I wonder the directions our friends were given sent us this way, if a coach cannot pass," said Jeffreys.

She bent a pitying look upon him. "Why, sir, who would come this way in a great coach? Those who have business in these parts go on foot or on horseback, or perhaps in a wee cart."

They accepted her offer of home-brewed ale and a bite of cheese, and then left her with an English pound for her trouble, an amount which clearly staggered her.

"I hope the posting inn has better beasts than these," Jeffreys murmured. Anniscote agreed; the horses they'd hired at the last stage might have been good in their prime but both were now stricken in years and bored by travel.

Riding at a slow pace to save their horses, they came at evening to what the woman had called the change-house at the meeting of two main roads, where their lane ended. The Red Thistle's size and bustling appearance promised accommodations, a decent meal, and possibly even good horses. They bespoke rooms and dinner before the duke asked the innkeeper if a coach with two young ladies had passed. "There cannot be many pairs of young gentlewomen travelling by coach in these parts, and they would be likely to change horses here."

"There's been none like that come this way," their host said. "Certainly they'd have stopped, to eat or to stay the night, even if they did not change horses. Would they perhaps have come by another way, sir?"

"They were given directions by the friend they

proposed to visit, although it directed them to come by this road we travelled, which they could not do, in a coach. They acquired a drover as a guide after their instructions failed them, who is said to have meant to take them by way of a road some way to the east of this."

"I ken the road. It ends at yon highway that leads to Glasgow. A drover, is it? That's lucky, then. They are a canny lot, the drovers, and honest as a rule. Men will not trust their cattle to a cateran or land-louper. Not more than once."

The duke asked, "Do you know many of the drovers? The ladies met with him down the lane, just where it becomes impassable for a large carriage."

"Och, do ye ken what drover?"

"One Andrew Raburn, I was told."

The innkeeper laughed. "They are as safe as bairns in their mothers' arms, then. Andrew will not lose them or lead them astray. And if some blackguard should try to rob them, he will be more use than many coachmen or postboys."

Anniscote chose to ignore the last part of this statement, seeing from Jeffreys's expression that he did not find it as reassuring as the publican had intended it. "Is the road so much longer than the lane we took? I know they must have re-traced their way to get to it, yet from what we can learn, it must be two days since they met with Raburn."

"'Tis longer than I would expect. Even a heavy coach should make it in a long day's travel. Unless it rained, or the bridge over the stream washed away—but I do not suppose it did, as there's been no rain I know of. Or a wheel might ha' broken or some other part have failed."

"Would they not have sent one of the servants or the postboy to the nearest smithy? Or the nearest harness-maker, if the harness broke and they could not make the repair themselves? This man Raburn would know where to go for assistance, surely," Jeffreys said, and glanced out the open casement at the sky.

"To be sure, he would, and if there was some mishap of that sort, it's an odd circumstance that we have not heard of it, for this is the closest town with all they might need in any calamity on yon road."

"It is too late to set out to find them now," Anniscote said. "If they have met with some difficulty, it must have been at least a day ago, if not more. But we will set out early in the morning, if you will have us woken as early as may be, and fresh horses saddled."

As they climbed the stairs to their chambers, Jeffreys remarked, "Do you recall what we ate for our supper?"

"Some sort of soup, I think? And saddle of mutton?" Whatever it had been, it must not have agreed with Jeffreys, for Anniscote heard him pacing back and forth until Anniscote himself fell asleep at some late hour. Both were dressed and ready to leave before the kitchen maid knocked to wake them. Neither had much appetite for breakfast.

"I am not easy about this," Jeffreys admitted as they mounted. The sun was not over the horizon, and the air was cool.

Nor was Anniscote, but he said only, "It is odd that they have not arrived, but there may be a number of explanations. The drover, Raburn, may have taken them by some other road he knew of. They might have stopped for a day to rest the horses. One of them may have felt ill from the motion of the coach, and they have stopped so that she might recover."

"They may have been robbed and murdered. Or abducted. Or the coach may have gone over a precipice, and their bones are scattered at the bottom."

"Really, Tom, Mistress Anne would be the first to inform you that so few days would not have reduced them to skeletons. She probably could tell you exactly how long it would take, given the weather and the local predators," he added, smiling at the thought. She would not hesitate to discuss the phenomenon over breakfast or at a ball. Imagining the hearers' reactions kept him from envisioning what real dangers Anne might have encountered.

"John, such remarks show a lack of sensibility on your part."

"I beg your pardon. However, I don't feel we need despair yet. Both Mistress Anne and Her Grace are sensible young women, and they are accompanied by my servants and a drover who is said to be reliable."

"That is what worries me most. I cannot think of any minor mischance which would prevent one of your servants, or Raburn, from going for assistance."

As the duke could not think of any reason either, he had nothing to say upon the subject.

"And what servants did they have with them? The coachman, of course, and the postboy. Their maids, I suppose, and a footman. I know she only brought two from Guysbridge, and one she sent to London with the letters."

"Ah…" Anniscote belatedly thought of a line in the duchess's letter that he had not previously considered.

"They cannot have a footman with them, because she mentioned sending the second footman to accompany both maids to Guysbridge."

"Good God! It's worse than I thought, then. They are in a strange country—yes, I know Scotland and England have been united for decades, but it's like a foreign country, and English people seldom have any reason or inclination to visit—with only a coachman, for who knows how reliable the postilion is?"

"The duchess is a Scotswoman herself, Tom. I don't like the idea of two ladies wandering so far with only Jenkins, but he is an excellent coachman. I will say for Nick that he chose the best to work with his horses."

Anne's maid being sent to Guysbridge presumably meant that Anne meant to go there herself, after the visit to Elspat's former housekeeper. Which, if it became known, would suggest a degree of familiarity between himself and Anne that might seem to support whatever rumors were current. *Which might work to my advantage*..."She is said to be visiting the duchess, to cheer her in her bereavement," the gossips would say. If a lady, the response would be, "She was never acquainted with the duchess previously, was she? She met Guysbridge after she came to London, I think." If a man, there would be a wink and a satiric "Ho-ho!"

"It's odd that this road is so little travelled," Jeffreys remarked when they had ridden for a while.

"I think I recall hearing something about a newer road that is longer but goes around hills rather than straight up and down again, and avoids some boggy areas."

"I don't remember seeing another road, do you?"

"No—but we know Raburn intended to bring them

by this road. And this seems a rather barren district. What would bring anyone here?"

Chapter 49

A few sheep grazed on the rolling land, with here and there a copse. Once they saw a cottage but far off.

"I cannot think a coach could get up that rocky little path to it," Jeffreys said. "And if it had, we would be able to see it. That hut is too small to conceal it."

They had gone some distance farther when the duke exclaimed, "So ho! There's a fine lot of cattle in that field."

"A cow, some sheep—and half a dozen horses—and a scrawny fellow watching them. And a stable or the like."

"I think that is a cottage, not a stable. See, there's a little stone wall around it, and a chimney."

The horses' attendant, seeing them, waved wildly and seemed to be beckoning to them. A dog stood up and barked.

"Those cannot belong to this place."

"He seems to be dressed like a postilion," Jeffreys said. By then, they had nearly reached the fellow, who called out, "Thank the Lord."

Before Anniscote could rap at the rough wooden door, a voice creaked, "Enter and welcome, sir." With a start, he saw a beady eye and half a wizened face peering out through a narrow gap where one panel of the shutter had been left ajar. The interior seemed too full to admit two more persons, but as his eyes adjusted to the dim light from the window, he saw that the impression came from the furnishings the room contained: a table, a bench, a wooden chair with arms for the man of the house, two settles, several stools, a spinning wheel, a cabinet with shelves above it, a wooden chest, and an enclosed bed, its doors open, occupied by a motionless form. A mongrel dog lay beside the box bed.

Someone, slouched on one of the settles, straightened up and made as if to rise. "Your Grace!"

"Jenkins?"

"I beg Your Grace's pardon for not rising, sir, but my right knee's wrenched so bad it's a job for block and tackle, almost, to get me up. We've had mortal bad luck, and what to do about the ladies was more than I knew."

The old woman who was sitting on a stool by the window, advised him, "Dinna fash, now." To Anniscote she said, "It's not such a hurly-house as it looks."

The duke saw Jeffreys glancing around dubiously. "I don't think it can mean what it sounds like," he replied very softly.

A faintly Scottish voice came from the open door behind them. "Hurley-house means a tumble-down, untidy place, which this is surely not. Why, it has a good fireplace that does not smoke, and the thatch does not leak, and there is a loft above. And Mistress Brown keeps a neat house. It's only that there are so many of us here."

Turning, Tom Jeffreys started toward her before noticing she had a plucked, headless chicken in one hand and a large knife in the other and stopped.

The duchess realized it at the same time and tried

to hide the corpse and the weapon behind her skirts, then gave up the attempt as futile. "I am making soup," she said.

"Can I be of any assistance?"

"I do not like to ask it…but if you could carry in some peat? The peat-neuk is empty. Poor Jenkins and Raburn need to be kept warm, and there is the cooking to do, as well." She smiled shyly. "I'll show you where the peat stack is."

"If you can make soup, I can certainly carry peat," Jeffreys said.

"Ah…may I ask where Mistress Anne is?" the duke inquired.

"She is out in the kale yard behind the house, if you wish to speak with her."

"I would not want to interrupt her labors, as I suppose the kale will be needed for the soup. Perhaps Jenkins will tell me what happened. And why no one thought to send to the town."

As Jeffreys followed her out the door, Anniscote noticed she was still carrying the knife and chicken.

"I'm terrible ashamed, Your Grace," said Jenkins before Anniscote could make any further inquiry. "Your coach, that your grandsire bought and was so proud of—so I was told, for I wasn't born then—is likely ruined. If it hasn't been stole," he added.

"There's no land-loupers hereabouts," their hostess interjected. "And if there was, what use is a great thing that needs four horses or more to pull it?"

"Never mind about the coach, if it can't be used. Why did no one send to the nearest town for assistance?"

A voice from the box bed gave a crack of laughter.

"Yon fool postboy would not leave the horses."

"But someone else—"

Mistress Brown said, "There is no one else. Your Sim Jenkins, here, is lame as a three-legged dog. Andrew Raburn, there, has a broken arm. I'm too lame to be hobbling up to the crossroads, and I hope a gentleman would not be expecting either of the young leddies to go. And I do not know how we could make do if either of them were gone."

"Certainly it would be improper for one of them to go out on such an errand, but surely you do not live alone in such an isolated place?"

"Och, no, but my granddaughter that lives with me is awa' to help her sister that's delivered of a bairn. My son comes every week to bring me what I need. He will be back in three days, and Jean with him, after her month in town."

"But the sheep and the cow must need tending."

"My old dog brings them to fold every evening when I call him, and the cow follows along. I can hobble along to the cow byre to milk her. The rest I manage well enough, though it's true I'll be glad to see my Jean come back. She'll marry her lad soon, and they'll live here."

"I wish them both joy and prosperity," Anniscote said, and reflected that his London friends would stare to see him now.

"They will be the better for your good wishes. You'll be the great duke the young leddies have mentioned, without doubt. You'll set things right, now you've come."

Something erupted through the door, taking him by surprise before he could add, "I certainly hope so."

"Ah, Mistress Anne," he said, turning to make his bow.

"I am so glad to see you, Your Grace! I am a little concerned about Raburn's arm, and—"

He took in her glowing face, wind-blown hair, the basket of—kale, was it?—clutched to her bosom, bedraggled skirt, and shoes an English maidservant would have scorned. He was amazingly happy to see her.

"—I don't want to have to amputate it—"

"I will lose my arm over my dead body," Raburn said.

"That's exactly what I hope to avoid. But I need some things from the nearest apothecary."

"Perhaps it would be sensible for Jeffreys to ride back to the change-house and hire a coach and horses to remove your…ah, patients…to the nearest doctor."

"Och, nay, a doctor would have my arm off for sure."

"I fear the jolting would do Raburn no good. I've set the bone, but mortification can so easily set in when the bone has broken out through flesh and skin. If he is kept quiet and lying down," she added, with a significant glance at the drover, who had managed to raise himself up a little in the box bed, "and if I can get some benzoin, laudanum if it's available or else opium, lint, and alcohol, I can try to save the arm. Mistress Brown has only a little whisky—"

"We must save that for drinking. I came near to greetin' when you wasted some of it on the outside of my arm. It is too good a whisky to use except for drinking."

"That is why I want some alcohol from the

apothecary," Anne assured him. "And more whisky, too. Oh, and a length of linen for Mrs. Brown, for I had to use a sheet of hers for dressings. And candles. Do you have any paper and ink so I can write out a list, Your Grace?"

"I left them back at the inn. It hardly seemed necessary to bring them on this excursion."

"Well, no matter. I can write it on a piece of the sheet with a burnt twig."

Most young ladies would be in hysterics or fainting, Anniscote reflected. Or sulking furiously, like his mother. It was too bad the army had no female regiment. One couldn't permit them to fight, of course, but judging by Anne, Elspat, and even the old woman, the world was failing to make use of a reservoir of calm, brisk efficiency.

"I'll write my list. Perhaps you would tell Mr. Jeffreys we require him to do an errand."

"Unless you would prefer that I do it?" Anniscote inquired to see how she would answer.

She bit her lip and seemed to consider. "No, I think he should go. For as Her Grace's brother-in-law, it is perfectly proper for you to stay and chaperon her, and she will be my chaperon, and then, of course, Mistress Brown is here, too."

"And so are we," Andrew Raburn volunteered.

"Yes, but that doesn't make it any better," Anne said frankly.

Raburn, whose face was pale under his sun- and wind-reddened skin, managed a laugh.

"The lad needs a stowp of whisky," Mistress Brown said.

It might have been a good long time before the

duchess started the soup, if Anniscote had not gone out to find Jeffreys. His sister-in-law and friend were deep in conversation beside a mound of dark brown brick-like objects, presumably peat. They both started a little when Anniscote cleared his throat. The duke supposed he would be bringing in the peat himself.

"I must start the soup," Her Grace said hurriedly. "Excuse me, please."

When she had vanished around the corner of the house, Jeffreys said, "John, I think we must talk about how to prevent any further scandal."

"Yes, yes, but first you must ride back to the crossroads and find an apothecary. Or someone who sells what Mistress Anne requires to tend to Raburn's arm."

****

The peat-neuk by the fireplace was filled, the soup was simmering, and Mistress Brown was making oatcakes at the table when Jeffreys returned with two hampers and a coarse bag.

"It was the devil of a chore, riding with these slung over the saddle. If I'd known, I'd not have bought so much."

"It seems a great deal," Anniscote admitted. "I had no idea Mistress Anne required such quantities."

"Oh, it's not all her supplies. It seemed wise to bring a few other things, as well. Necessities, you know: a ham, bacon, brandy, claret, sugar, some rice, in case she wishes to make rice pudding for the invalids. When I was a child, my nurse always made that for me when I was ill. Beef, a few other trifles to make the ladies more comfortable. Lavender water, hartshorn, and the like. The inn sold me a roast chicken and a loaf of bread."

While Anniscote was still rubbing down the rented hack with a wisp of hay, Jeffreys came out to the cow shed, where the two riding horses were stabled with the cow.

"I thought I had best talk to you here. There's no place to be private in the house. I know I said I'd wait a year before asking Elspat for her hand, but in the current circumstances, I think I must do so at once. Or at least, very soon."

"Have circumstances altered so much?"

"The innkeeper knew we were searching for the young ladies so when I returned, he naturally asked if we had had any success, and what was I to say but that we had found them? There were several local men present, all listening with their ears pricked up, and then, too, I had to buy Mistress Anne's medicaments, and food, so I fear word is gone all over town. Worse, as I went out, who should arrive in the inn yard but a party of young Englishmen who are making a tour of the Lowlands. I believe these Scots are great gossips."

"I suppose it will be a nine days' wonder, and everyone who passes through will hear of it," the duke said.

"You are very calm about it. If this business is heard of in London…"

"Yes, I've thought of that. You should speak to my sister-in-law as soon as you can get her alone," he added with a smile.

"Thank you, I shall. Besides, there's her father to be thwarted. But what of Mistress Anne? Her position is even more difficult, given the unfortunate events in London."

"Believe me, Tom, I am well aware of it. Some solution will present itself, I'm sure." He counted upon the force of public opinion, or her desire to spare Mrs. Bradshaw embarrassment, to outweigh Anne's objections to himself. He did not flatter himself that she had forgotten his arrogance at their first meetings or his critical comments on her behavior.

****

The gudewife had stowed away the provisions and exclaimed over the linen, which she said was much finer than the old sheet Anne had used, her dog had brought the sheep to fold, the cow following docilely, the postboy had tethered the coach horses nearby for the night, and Raburn's dog had been set to watch the sheep pen. The postboy would be sleeping in the cow byre.

"Where we are to put you and Mr. Jeffreys, I cannot imagine," the duchess remarked, though she did not sound particularly worried.

"The loft," the old woman said. "It has not been muckle used since my bairns all marrit. Nane o' them cared to stay here, and acause o' they all made good matches, nane o' them needed to stay, except my poor daughter, Maggie, that died a few years syne."

They ate a surprisingly good supper, though His Grace could tell that Anne was somewhat distracted and was watching Andrew Raburn closely. He apparently had little appetite, and his face looked flushed—or perhaps it was only the red glow of the burning peat. No sooner had Her Grace and Mrs. Brown cleared away the remains of the meal and put the dishes in a bucket of hot water to wash, than Anne said, "I want to inspect your arm, Andrew."

"You won't cut it off?"

"Not unless there's no other way to save your life."

"One-armed, I'll have no life."

"We'll talk about amputation when there's no other hope. But now I may have to, ummm, clean the wound out a bit. Elspat, would you pour out a measure of laudanum, please?"

The sun was still well up in the sky but the east-facing window did little to light the interior, so Jeffreys held a pair of candles for Anne, without looking at Raburn's injury himself. Anniscote did not blame him; after one quick glance, he also found somewhere else to gaze.

"It's bad, ay?"

"Not as bad as it could be," Anne replied. "Just drink that down now, if you please." She whispered to the duke, "You'll have to hold him while I work."

Chapter 50

"There, that's done," Anne said. Raburn had either fainted or fallen asleep as a result of the laudanum. She covered the wound lightly with linen, and Anniscote noted that her hands were shaking. The duchess and the old woman began tidying up, collecting the basin of water, the soiled linen bandages, and the blood-stained knife.

Jeffreys set one of the candles down, and asked, "Will he be all right left alone?"

"No, I'm sitting up with him," Anne replied.

"But…" Jeffreys glanced at the duke, who said, "I'll stay up with Mistress Anne."

"It's not necessary, Your Grace."

"All the same, I will remain. If the poor fellow should become delirious, you might need assistance."

The duchess cast an inquiring look at Anne, who raised her eyebrows and gave a little shrug.

"Then I accept your kind offer, sir."

Elspat, Mrs. Brown, and Jeffreys retreated into the other room, the women to go to bed in the sleeping room or "ben" as Mistress Brown called it, Jeffreys to climb into the loft. Jenkins lay on one of the settles, with a rough bench pushed up against its edge to keep him from rolling off. Anne seated herself on the second settle, glancing rather shyly at the duke. He took the chair.

"It really isn't likely that I will need help with Raburn, but thank you for thinking of it," she said.

He cocked his head and listened for a moment, then moved to join Anne on the settle. At last! An opportunity to converse without chaperons. When he heard Jenkins snore, he said, "It may not be necessary for that purpose, Mistress Anne, but I assure you it is essential."

"What, for my reputation? How should that be in jeopardy?"

"You are a young lady sitting up with a coachman and a Scottish drover. Would your grandfather have permitted you to remain all night with a male patient?"

"No—but it was never necessary."

"But if it had been, in the absence of a family member or servant?"

"Well...no, I suppose he would not. He would have sent for one of the elderly women who sometimes acted as sickroom or lying-in attendants. Or stayed himself."

"And why would he do so when you were there and had received the benefit of his training?"

"Oh! Are you thinking it might have caused talk? You may be correct, but here that cannot apply."

"No? Do you think the Scots never talk?"

"Perhaps they may, but this is not England, after all. Why, it's almost a foreign country, and very isolated."

"Yet there is a busy crossroads a few miles away. Jeffreys tells me that a party of Englishmen were there when he went for your supplies. Nothing is more likely than that the innkeeper will regale them with the tale of the missing English ladies and their accident. And no doubt at least one of them will mention it to a friend or family member in a letter or in person. We can hope that none of them will, or that if they do, the recipient will be a recluse who will not pass it on, but we cannot count on it. Only think of Mrs. Nugent, whose net of correspondents covers all of England."

Anne inclined her head, conceding the point, but objected, "Still, even if it became known I had sat up with Raburn, what could anyone make of it? He's full of laudanum, and his arm is broken. Your coachman is asleep, having drunk off a quantity of whisky, which I trust will ease his knee somewhat, but I don't look for him to wake before morning."

"My dear Anne—"

"Sir!"

"I beg your pardon. We have shared so many adventures that I feel we are old friends. Remember how gossip passes from one to another: the facts are lost, and what remains is your spending a night in the company of a male servant and a drover, in a country most English people regard as rather uncivilized, even if it is not as wild as the Highlands. You have no maid with you. How would this sound if you heard it?"

"You make it sound very improper." She stifled a sigh before she continued, "I can always remove from London to live retired in some town where I am not known."

This was not the conclusion he had wished her to reach. "You need not despair," he said. "This imbroglio may not become known. Even if it does, your friends will continue to rally 'round you. And now, will you tell me how the accident occurred? We have been so occupied, I had no time to inquire of either Jenkins or

Raburn."

****

"And so when the side of the bridge gave way under the wheel and the coach tipped into the stream, Jenkins was jolted off the box, and the coach hit Raburn a glancing blow. It was the sheerest ill-luck that his arm was so badly broken. And thank heaven the water was no deeper," Anne finished.

A chill ran through him in spite of the warmth from the hearth, imagining Anne (and Elspat, too, of course) trapped in a coach in a cold Scottish river. "I fear you and the duchess must have been bruised and shaken up, if no worse, and I apprehend wet as well?"

"We were not even discomposed, except by the injuries to the men, as we had stepped down from the coach to lighten it when we encountered the boggy part of the road just short of the bridge. And that is the story of our adventure."

"Not all of it, surely. Where did this occur? How did you manage to transport two injured men?"

"The postilion, Carson, and the duchess and I managed to mount Raburn and Jenkins on two of the horses, and our necessities on another. Then he unhitched the team from the coach, and we led them until we came to Mistress Brown's cottage, about a mile farther on."

"I am heartily sorry you should have had such an experience," he said. She and Elspat must have waded into the water to help the men. Not one lady in a hundred would have managed so well. "And I am glad that you were here to support the duchess, even if her flight to avoid her father was unnecessary."

"Your Grace, women are not typically as shielded

from difficult or dangerous experiences as you seem to think. As for Elspat's desire to escape her father, I think it was not unreasonable. How many young ladies do you know who have perhaps married against their own wishes at their papa's command?"

"Well…but one expects that a daughter will be guided by her parents' greater knowledge of the world. A giddy young girl may think of nothing but a handsome face and ingratiating manners."

"Whereas to marry a fool or an inveterate gambler or a roué or a man who is drunk to falling down half the day is desirable if he possesses a title or fortune?"

"No, certainly not. At least, I would never require a child of mine—if I had one—to marry solely for the sake of a title or fortune. I would not consider a suitor who lacked good character." Might she overlook some of his own failings?

"That seems not to have been a consideration for Elspat's father. And to have risen from poverty to wealth as he has done, he must have great determination. The duchess is more sensible than any young lady I have met in London, but I can understand that between her habit of obedience to her father and his temper, she feared to face him."

"But if she had sent to me, I should have come and prevented his forcing her into any action she disliked. It is my duty to protect my brother's widow until she remarries."

"Her father might have arrived first. And she did not say so, but I believe she thought you might be glad to have her removed from your family. You often seem very proud, you know. Even haughty."

He wanted to say *I hope I have not wounded your*

feelings recently. But the conversation that should follow such a beginning did not belong in this stuffy little room. Better to reserve the tête-à-tête for a more suitable setting.

"I confess I was not well-pleased with Nick's marriage at first. However, on acquaintance with Her Grace, I find her admirable. Far better than my brother deserved. One is not necessarily condemned to be no better than one's father or mother. You, Mistress Anne, are worth a hundred of your father and mother together."

Even in the gloom, he saw her start.

"Sir, you did not have the benefit of knowing my father, but I cannot imagine a kinder, better-informed man. Any virtues or abilities I may possess I owe to him."

Too late, Anniscote realized that while he and several others were aware of her parentage, there was no reason to suppose that Anne knew that Mrs. Saltstall had lied to her.

"I beg your pardon," he said, wondering how to extricate himself. Evidently she believed that Dr. Sinclair was her father; was it better to let her think so? But what if Hurst should say something to her when she returned to London? As rational as she was, she might still be hurt and humiliated. She might decide to leave town. He felt Anne turn toward him on the settle. A faint gleam from the fireplace outlined her cheek as she stared up at him.

"I think you were not referring to Dr. Sinclair," she said at last. "Who did you suppose to be my father, sir?"

"May I ask first why you thought he was your

father?" he countered.

"Why, Mistress Saltstall told me. When they lived in France for a time, my grandfather—my papa, that is, that I used to think only my guardian—had a liaison with a—a woman of low birth. Rather than abandon me, he chose to take me in."

The duke gazed into the peat's red embers, trying to decide how best to respond.

Anne said, "Do you know something more of the matter?" He could hear the unease in her voice. Best to do it quickly, like an amputation, to spare her further pain.

"I am sorry to say Mrs. Saltstall was not truthful. Given her previous behavior to you, it can be no surprise that her character does not match her father's."

"It's true she acted very rashly," Anne admitted. "But when one is afraid, it is easy to make a bad choice."

"Very true, and it is high-minded of you to put the best construction on it, but there is no reason to suppose she would not lie as readily as she attempted to have you ruined. I am sorry, but the truth can only cause you distress, and yet it is best you hear it from a friend. I hope you consider me a friend?"

"I do," Anne said rather shyly.

Come, this is encouraging. "Then I must tell you what Mrs. Bradshaw, Mrs. Nugent, and I pieced together of your ancestry. While there is no proof of it which would be accepted at law, the sum of the parts is convincing, and it was subsequently verified by information received from Alderman Saltstall, who had it from his wife." He took a deep breath of peat- and whisky-scented air.

****

The burning peat gave too little light to show much of Anne's face. He heard her sniffle and caught the rustling of fabric as she fished for a handkerchief in her pocket.

"I'm sorry."

"Mrs. Saltstall and Hurst!" she muttered. "It could hardly be worse. As though my difficulties in London, most of them brought on by her scheming, were not bad enough. I suppose everyone will soon know. Perhaps I had best go to the American colonies."

"I am convinced you would not care for the colonies. They cannot be nearly as amusing as even a provincial town in England. And there is no reason to think anyone will learn of it. Your family, Mrs. Nugent, Jeffreys, and I are your staunch friends. You have other supporters as well."

"I suppose Mrs. Saltstall—I cannot call her my mother—will not speak of it lest she damage her own reputation, but Hurst will hardly scruple to blacken my name and hers, too."

"Oh, he'll be mum. He won't risk Richard Saltstall's enmity. Or even mine."

She sighed.

"My dear girl, you are in no worse trouble than you were before, and we will weather that." He hoped she would notice his use of "we."

"It's much worse," Anne said despondently. "With such parents, I hardly know myself anymore."

"It's unlike you to be poor-spirited."

"Would you let a son marry a female like me? If you knew about her parents and illegitimacy?"

"Yes, if she were like you. And I refuse to compete

with my son—if I had one, which I do not. Yet. Though I have some hopes in that direction."

"Thank you for trying to cheer me, sir. I used to have a good opinion of myself, but how can I maintain it now?"

"You are the same person you were before. Your mother's waywardness must be the result of her upbringing, of which Mrs. Nugent was very critical. Yours, however, was excellent, if a little unconventional. As for Hurst, I can only say that you need not be like him, as I was not like my father." There was no sound but the wind whistling around the eaves and Jenkins's snores for several minutes.

"It is very kind of you, but yours is not the common view, I fear." Another sniffle punctuated this pronouncement.

"Perhaps not, but many of my views are unconventional, like your own. And as no one outside your circle of friends will know, your own opinion is all that matters. I have but recently come to realize that my being unlike my father and brother is no reproach to me."

"How could it be? Forgive me, but if all I hear is true, your brother did your family no credit."

"None at all," His Grace agreed cheerfully, "and my father was not much better, though he drank less. Nor was my grandsire, or my late uncle. My father considered me an embarrassment."

Indignant, Anne demanded, "How could he count it against you that you are not a sot or gamester or…or whatever else the rest of your family may have been?"

"Very easily. Would you care to hear how my ancestor, Don Diego Anascote, came to live in

England?"

"If you would like to tell me. I had heard that you were descended from some noble Spanish family but no more than that."

"I discovered the whole story only lately, in a handwritten account in our library. Are you warm enough? Let me put another peat or two on the fire."

"Yes, yes, do. The room should be kept warm for Raburn."

When he returned to the settle, he managed to mistake his former position, so that he sat down so close to Anne her skirt lay against his thigh and he caught an enticing scent of Eau de Cologne. She seemed not to notice, or at least did not mention it.

"And now, pray tell me."

"In Spain, a little before the time of our Queen Mary, there was a very bold and provident duke…"

****

"Don Diego had to leave Spain because his many times great-grandmother might have been Jewish? Or a Mohammedan, or some such thing? Not that I'm not glad he did, but how unfair!"

The duke laughed a little. "Thank you for being glad he came to England. I will take it as a compliment."

"Well, I should think so! How was it his fault, whatever his ancestors may have been?"

"It wasn't, of course. Oddly enough, his lady's response to the tale was very much like yours."

"And yet—oh!" This time Anne laughed. "You mean me to apply the lesson to myself."

"It fits, does it not?"

"But having a forebear of the wrong religion is not

quite the same as having one whose character was…well, sadly unsteady."

Anniscote's shoulders shook with suppressed laughter. "What a delicate way of phrasing it. My dear, I have no doubt everyone's family tree bears some rakes, profligates, women of…er, obliging habits…traitors, murderers, thieves, cowards, liars, fools, and the like. We may pretend otherwise, but if you read any history, it is clear that some of the foremost families in the land had their share of persons we would hardly care to know."

Anne turned her head to gaze up at him. "That is very true, I know, but somehow one never thinks of it as relating to their descendants. As bloodlines count for so much in the breeding of animals, it's a pity—"

"Oh, my love!"

"I beg your pardon! That is the sort of thing I was able to discuss with my grandfather…and to think he actually was my grandfather!"

He heard her sniffle again. As she had raised no objection to his addressing her in such familiar terms, Anniscote slipped his arm around her shoulders. "And you may certainly discuss it with me. In fact, I hope you will."

"Thank you. It's so tiresome, not being able to talk about important things and having to pretend to be interested in fashion and gossip. I was going to say that what is successful in breeding dogs and horses should pertain to humankind as well. But as you have pointed out, in families there may be intelligent, well-behaved members and also others who are neither. What can account for the difference?"

"Even in animal husbandry, all the pups from one

litter may not be equally good." The duke prepared to take possession of her hand. He was optimistic that she would permit it.

"Ye maun kiss her," a thick voice from the box bed advised. "If she's talking of breeding, I ken she's weakening."

Damnation.

"Sound advice," Anniscote said, thinking to take advantage of the interruption. Anne stood up abruptly. In rejection of the suggestion? Or merely because she was concerned for Raburn? He hoped it was the latter.

"How do you feel, Raburn?"

"Not so bad." A yawn. "But you should marry His Grace. It would be a fine thing to be a duchess. And I could aye boast I'd been waited on by twa duchesses then."

"We are not discussing marriage," Anne said repressively.

"Go back to sleep, Raburn," the duke added, exasperated.

"Could I not have a tass of whisky to help me forget my troubles and sleep sound?"

"Yes," Anne replied, "I suppose a cup will do you no harm."

"Nay, I'll get it," Anniscote said. "Then Raburn can boast he's been waited on by a duke, as well as a duchess."

A series of snortings and snufflings came from the settle on which the coachman was sleeping. "Either there is a wild boar nearby or Jenkins is waking."

"A little more whisky would do him no harm either," said Anne.

****

"I think by tomorrow when Mrs. Brown's son comes, we may be able to move Raburn," Anne said, after examining Raburn's arm.

Anne had not felt it necessary to sit up with Raburn after the night of her surgery on his arm. Anniscote had even asked if they should not do so the following night, but she felt it safe to leave him to sleep, well dosed with laudanum and whisky. There had been no opportunity for further private conversation.

"Would you abandon me to some doctor with a saw, mistress?"

"Certainly not. But it will be easier to care for you at an inn. I won't leave you until your arm is past any danger of infection."

With an internal shudder, the duke imagined the sensation they would make at the Red Thistle. It was the sort of scandalous situation that would set tongues a-clacking. If there had been any hope of suppressing the story of Anne's and Elspat's adventure, a stay at an inn to nurse a drover—and Jenkins, too—unchaperoned except by the duchess, and with himself and Jeffreys present, would put an end to it. But he would not have wanted her to go back on her word, even if he could have asked it of her. And really, how much worse could the gossip be? Selfishly, he hoped whatever talk there was would tip the balance in his favor.

Chapter 51

Anniscote emerged from his room at the inn, blissfully clean, in fresh linen, with his suit brushed and his sword belted on. He had ridden ahead to tell the innkeeper to prepare several bedchambers and make the kitchen aware that invalid foods and barley water would be required. He had arranged for the coach and luggage to be retrieved—if it had not already vanished. Now sounds of activity in the yard suggested that the rest of the party had arrived.

Two of the inn's menservants were preparing to carry Raburn upstairs on a litter, while Anne stood by, peering under the blood-stained linen on his arm.

"The jolting caused the wound to open a little, but I do not regard it as dangerous. See, the bleeding has already stopped and is clotting," she was saying to the duchess.

An English voice from the taproom observed, "I don't know what the world is coming to, that women play at being physicians."

Another replied, "And in such company, too. We might hazard our luck with them, for they'd both be passable if cleaned up."

Anniscote came down the last three steps in one bound, hand on the hilt of his sword.

"You insult the ladies," he said to the two bumptious cubs standing in the door to the tap.

The fair-haired one drawled, "Really, one could hardly be expected to realize that these…ah…ladies…were…gentlewomen."

His companion, a stocky man with eyes set too close together and an unfortunate marmalade-colored waistcoat, said, "Belford, you are too credulous. In a gentleman's house, one might assume a fellow with a decent coat and a sword was a gentleman, and even that a female, however draggle-tailed, might be a lady. But this is an inn and open to whatever Captain Hackum has some gelt. And his—"

Whatever he had meant to say was cut off by Anniscote's back-handed blow.

Jeffreys came in just in time to see Marmalade Waistcoat reel back. Elspat drew him aside to whisper an explanation to him, one hand on his arm.

"Your name?" the duke inquired with deadly calm. The one called Belford looked as if he would like to edge away from his companion.

"Harlow. Geoffrey Harlow, damn you," Marmalade Waistcoat muttered thickly. His nose was bleeding, and Anniscote noted with satisfaction that the horrid waistcoat was showing scarlet spots, in spite of Harlow's handkerchief.

Anne said, "Guysbridge, I think—"

"Mistress Anne, you and Her Grace should escort your patients to their rooms."

Her attention turned to Raburn, who had raised his head and was staring fixedly at the two Englishmen, and Jenkins, leaning heavily on a crutch-handled cane and glowering.

"Yes, just what I was about to say," she replied. "And…ummm, Duchess?"

Anniscote caught the slight hesitation before she addressed Elspat. Oh, these social dilemmas! She was in the habit of calling his sister-in-law by her first name, as neither of them was overburdened with concern for social niceties (and under the circumstances of the past week, formality would have been ridiculous), but to do so in public would have been extraordinarily improper. Even the informal "Duchess" might be considered overly familiar by a stickler, given the difference in their rank. His challenging a man in front of ladies was also a social lapse, but again, under the circumstances…She had called him by his name, too, like a close friend. Well, it had taken long enough.

"Yes, I'll come up with you," Elspat responded, with a quick glance at Jeffreys.

"I'll remain with His Grace," he said.

"Guysbridge?" Fair Hair repeated stupidly.

The ladies had vanished upstairs before Anniscote spoke again. "Yes, I am the Duke of Guysbridge. I have the honor to inform you that one of the ladies is my betrothed, and the other my sister-in-law."

"And Her Grace, the late duke's widow, is my intended wife," Jeffreys added, thin-lipped.

The appalled silence was broken by Belford's stammered, "I beg your pardon most sincerely, Your Grace. I—we—misunderstood the situation. I am unfamiliar with…mmmm, the customs prevailing in Scotland."

"If you mean to challenge me, I am glad to oblige," his friend, whose handkerchief was still pressed to his nose, uttered.

"I am pleased to hear it, for I rather thought I had already challenged you," His Grace replied silkily.

"But our meeting must be postponed until my eyes have stopped watering."

"Of course. I would not wish it said I had taken unfair advantage. Perhaps by tomorrow morning, Mr. Harlow?"

"Ah…yes, of course. Belford, will you act for me?"

There was a perceptible pause before Fair Hair answered, "Certainly. But there are significant differences between English and Scottish law. Should we not first inquire how the Scots view affairs of honor?"

Jeffreys growled, "A gentleman—"

Anniscote interrupted, "My friend would say that the period of Mr. Harlow's full recovery should allow an opportunity for whatever research into Scots law you may wish to undertake. Though if Scottish attorneys are no quicker than the English sort, it may take a little time."

"Of course, your friend and I, as seconds, must also seek to resolve this unfortunate misunderstanding, sir," Belford continued.

"Thomas Jeffreys, at your service." Jeffreys bowed.

****

"Harlow has no wit, no manners, and more impudence than ten common harlots," Jeffreys remarked. "But I believe his friend will persuade him that the state of his health makes a duel unwise at this time. That young sprig has obviously heard of your reputation."

"Good. It's my hope the whole business may be postponed indefinitely."

"This is not like you, John."

"I'm grown less hot-headed. Have you not often claimed I am too quick to take offense? But what befits a younger son with no prospects is unsuitable for the head of a ducal house. Most especially one without an heir. Besides, the affair with Hurst was bad enough, and only think what a twittering it must cause if I were to fight a duel on behalf on Mistress Anne and Duchess Elspat. There will be talk enough as it is. Why did you think I afforded those pups every chance to put off the meeting, preferably forever?"

"Zounds! I had not thought of that. Ay, it must be prevented at all costs. I have written to my father about Her Grace."

"When is the wedding to be?"

"As soon as possible," Jeffreys said. "She would like to be married before she sees her father. It does not seem quite proper to me, but on the other hand, to be visiting him together when we are not married and have travelled all that distance in each other's company—and she not out of mourning yet, too—would be even worse. I don't suppose you and Mistress Anne would care to visit Glasgow? Assuming he is there, and not hunting through England and Scotland in pursuit of her?"

"If necessary, I will accompany you, and I am sure Mistress Anne will not abandon her at this stage. But she won't leave here until Raburn is out of danger. I think you should accompany Elspat back to England, either to Guysbridge Hall or perhaps to stay with your parents, and then make your way to Glasgow to make her papa's acquaintance and give him notice of your intentions."

"I fear he will not be well pleased, if he has another noble suitor in mind for her."

"Perhaps not, but what can he do? She is of age, after all, and she will not be present to be browbeaten."

"That is a point, indeed, and I give him leave to rail at me as he pleases." He laughed. "We must hope this business with Harlow never comes to light. I can only imagine what Sir Hugh would say about our handling of it."

"I misdoubt he will ever hear of it. Harlow and Belford appear to be provincials, and even if they should visit London, is it likely they will talk of this, unless Harlow and I have had our meeting?"

"Anniscote...I could not but notice that you called Mistress Anne your betrothed. Are...er... congratulations in order?"

"My dear fellow, what could I say? Not to do so would have made the situation seem even more unsuitable than it already was." And he must persuade Anne before he could announce their betrothal even to a close friend.

"Ah. Well," said Jeffreys.

****

It was not quite as easy as it sounded. Elspat did not want to leave Anne, pointing out that Anne should not be staying at an inn with Anniscote and no maid present. Anne pointed out that Elspat meant to travel post with Jeffreys.

"But not unaccompanied," the duchess protested. "I will hire a local lass to come with me and send her back once we reach Guysbridge."

"The publican has a niece who can act as Mistress Anne's maid while we remain here."

"After that…" Anne began doubtfully.

"I have already made a plan, if it does not miscarry," Anniscote said. "An' it does, I will make other arrangements."

"Oh!" How admirable it was that the duke was never at a loss. He had thought to have their luggage brought to the inn, too, while the coach was being repaired. She quite looked forward to the return trip.

Elspat and Jeffreys departed the next day, feeling that it was best to set their affairs in motion at once. Laughing and blushing at the same time, the duchess begged Anne to return as soon as she could leave Raburn. "We mean to marry as quickly as possible, though I suppose even with a special license it will be a month before the marriage can take place. It is a week's travel to his parents' home, then another week to go to Glasgow to see my father, then a week back again, if all goes well! I wish I might go to my dear old Janet, as we are so close now, but Thomas says we will visit her when we return to see my father after our wedding, for he will not wish to travel all the way to London to attend it. But it would be very strange of me to be traveling with Thomas when we are not married yet. Janet does have very strict notions of morality, too," Elspat added.

It might have been awkward if Mr. Belford and Mr. Harlow had been staying at the inn, but they had removed to a smaller (and less comfortable) hostelry which was, as Belford explained, in the next street from the local doctor's house. This made it more convenient for him to attend Harlow, whose broken nose was said to have brought on a series of headaches, nausea, and dizziness.

"With his health so low and with Mr. Jeffreys gone off, it is impossible to attend to any arrangements either for a meeting or to negotiate an apology," Belford explained. "And it may be necessary to remove Harlow to his home in York where he may be examined by his own doctor."

Anne, having heard Harlow's name, shamelessly lingered outside the taproom to eavesdrop on the conversation. She would have inquired if such a journey would not be very taxing to the patient, but the duke accepted the excuse and merely suggested that when Mr. Harlow was recovered, his second might contact the duke either at Guysbridge House in London or possibly at Guysbridge Hall. "I am not quite certain where you will find Mr. Jeffreys," he added. "He is travelling at the moment on family business."

Before Belford or the duke left the room, Anne had whisked out of sight. She was not in the least surprised that a duel had been in contemplation. The duke's evident unconcern did puzzle her until she realized that he must consider Harlow too callow to warrant his attention. That was forbearing of him. She had no doubt at all that so accomplished duelist as Anniscote would be the victor in any meeting with Harlow. Not that she wished him to fight a duel on the duchess's or her behalf. If he were injured, she would never forgive herself.

The following day, the duke invited her to take a walk. Anne had told Raburn he might walk around his room a little and even venture down to the taproom if Jenkins accompanied him. It would be good for the coachman to start exercising his knee, if he did not try to do too much. Exercise would do her no harm either, as she had not strayed far from her charges since the accident.

Chapter 52

The day was pleasantly warm, and they strolled for some distance without finding the solitude Anniscote had hoped for. Just when he thought they had come to a suitable place, they would meet with a woman with a market basket, or half a dozen children, or a man leading a Galloway to the smithy to be shod. At last, they turned back and on reaching the Red Thistle, Anniscote suggested they have a cooling beverage in the private parlor he had engaged for their party's use. It was pleasantly dim, and the window sashes were open, letting in the air and the soft drone of a bee in the straggling rose bush below and occasionally a voice from the stable yard.

The waiter brought ale for the duke and lemonade for Anne and left.

"Finally!" Anniscote said, setting his tankard on the table and going to join Anne on the window seat. He took her glass and set it aside also.

"Finally?" she echoed.

"I have been wishing for a tète-à-tète with you ever since that night we sat up with Raburn and he awoke and made his very sensible suggestion." He slipped his arm around her shoulders.

"I cannot think why," she said, with a revealing blush. "You cannot be taking that nonsense of Raburn's seriously. He was clearly delirious."

"I thought it was remarkably good sense." His arm being already around her, it was easy to pull her toward him and answer her with a kiss. After a moment's hesitation, she melted into his arms.

"I had no idea it was like that!" she said when he released her. Evidently realizing that the comment might seem unmaidenly, she went on hurriedly, "That is, I don't know what to say, sir."

"Your first response was perfect. Will you do me the honor to marry me? And may I kiss you again?"

She blushed. "I was absolutely unaware of your sentiments, if they are your sentiments. Our places in society are so far apart that it must be a shocking misalliance on your part."

"Anne, my dear, what does Elspat call Jeffreys?"

"Why, she calls him Thomas. Although she does pronounce it more like 'Tammas.'"

"Then do you not think you should call me John? Not that I object to 'Guysbridge,' for I was charmed when you referred to me so, but first names are so much more intimate, are they not? And I mean to continue to call you 'Anne.'"

Anne averted her face. "That might imply a degree of intimacy which…which…"

"Which does not exist? Which you prefer not to encourage? We are surely better acquainted than many couples are when they marry. And your patient advises marriage."

"You cannot be serious?"

"Why not? Only think of the advantages: neither of us would be bored, I would be able to gratify my butler's desire that I provide the family with an heir, and no one looks askance at a duchess."

"I would not care for a marriage of convenience. Not for a marriage only of convenience," she amended.

"Anne, if marriage for merely practical purposes was what you preferred, I would offer it—and try to persuade you to, er, reciprocate my feelings after the wedding, because for me, it would be a love match. Please marry me. I love you, and it's been deucedly hard to find an opportunity to tell you so."

She was staring at him in amazement. By way of a further inducement, he added, "Think of the experiments we could do."

"I didn't realize you were interested in scientific matters. What sort of experiments?"

"We might breed some children and see how they turn out."

She was surprised into a burst of laughter, which seemed promising.

"I should, of course, have addressed myself to your nearest male relative, but since you are of age, and I refuse to ask permission of your papa, I thought I would petition you instead. Although Hurst did say that he would be pleased if I married you."

"He did? However did he come to say so? It seems quite unlikely."

Realizing that an explanation would be fraught with difficulties, he said airily, "We men must have our little secrets, even as ladies do."

"You cannot really want to marry me. Besides, it's not necessary for you to save my reputation."

"Of course not. But I cannot resist the prospect of a bride who thinks people should be bred like spaniels."

"I do not! I merely—"

He kissed her again.

"Ay, that's the way!" he heard a Scottish voice call out from below.

Swiveling to look out the window, the duke inquired, "Jenkins, do I pay you to stand there grinning?"

Jenkins immediately assumed the bland expression of a good servant. "No, Your Grace. I'm very sorry, sir, and I wish you both happy. I'll just help Raburn here back inside, sir." Raburn continued to grin, but by the time Anne could collect herself enough to lean out the window and admonish him for venturing out of the inn, he and Jenkins were out of sight.

"There you have it," Anniscote remarked. "A Scots drover, my coachman, and Hurst all think we should marry. So too does Thomas Jeffreys, and I shouldn't be surprised if my sister-in-law and Mrs. Bradshaw agreed. And I suspect Mrs. Nugent foresaw it. Can such a number of persons—and so diverse!—be mistaken?"

"I would not make a good duchess," Anne said in a small voice. "I'm not in the least stately. In fact, I'm clumsy. I have no ladylike accomplishments. I'm tactless, and I get into difficulties. I have no dowry worth mentioning, and my family connections are…irregular. You know there was talk about me before I left London. What would the fashionable world say now?"

"I don't greatly care what they say, and they won't dare say it of my duchess in any case. My own reputation this ten years has not borne repeating in polite company—not that that kept the gossips silent. I missed you when you left town. I won't try to tell you how glad I was to find you unharmed. And can you really tell me you do not reciprocate my feelings?"

"N-no. I missed you almost before I was out of London," she confessed. "If you're really sure you want to marry me…"

"That is a relief. I believe it used to be the custom here to abduct the lady one wished to marry, if her family objected to the match, or she did, but even I hesitate at such an impropriety. Though it might be very romantic."

He thought Anne looked a little cast down. "It would be very improper. I suppose we must go back and have the banns read and send out invitations."

"Certainly, we must go back eventually, but I think, if you do not object, it would be better to marry at once, here in Scotland."

She gazed up at him. "Can we? I know one hears of elopements to Gretna Green, but is it really so simple?"

"The particular attraction of Gretna is that it is just over the border from England and there is no residence requirement in Scotland. We can stroll over to the church here and ask the minister to marry us. When the coach is ready, we will go to Guysbridge. After you have seen our home, we can proceed to London to receive the congratulations of our friends. By the time we arrive, the notice of our marriage will have appeared in the newspapers, and the surprise will have worn off."

"You think of everything, John."

"And the further advantage of a runaway match like this is that the guest list for our wedding might be awkward," he continued. "For we would have to invite all of our friends and connections, which would mean including Mrs. Saltstall and Mr. Hurst—"

Anne visibly recoiled.

"She is your former guardian's daughter, and we could hardly not invite her when we would certainly invite Mrs. Bradshaw. And Hurst was a good friend of Nick's, and Mrs. Hurst is related to the Sinclairs' son's bride-to-be, so common civility would require it. I'm sure all concerned would prefer any other relationship to be forgotten."

"Oh, in that case! May we be married as soon as possible?—for I am quite curious—" Anne said as the door opened.

"Excuse me, Your Grace, but the coachmaker wants to know—"

In the background, they heard Raburn's burr, "You heard the leddy, Jenkins. They mean tae marry. I kenned it was that road with the pair o' them."

A word from the author...

I earned a master's in English literature at the University of Washington, focusing on pre-1850 fiction. I subsequently worked in several fields, including a longish career as a paralegal and a shorter stint as a security officer.

My short stories have been published in *Psycho-Paths and Monsters in Our Midst* (both edited by Robert Bloch), and *Over My Dead Body Magazine* (overmydeadbody.com). I have also self-published a novel, *Getting By*, and a short story, *Minor Miracles*.

I've always been interested in history, particularly English history, and more recently in New Mexico's history.

Hobbies: reading, writing, costume, cooking, spinning wheel repair.

Thank you for purchasing
this publication of The Wild Rose Press, Inc.

If you enjoyed the story, we would appreciate your
letting others know by leaving a review.

For other wonderful stories,
please visit our on-line bookstore at
www.thewildrosepress.com.

For questions or more information
contact us at
info@thewildrosepress.com.

The Wild Rose Press, Inc.
www.thewildrosepress.com

Stay current with The Wild Rose Press, Inc.

Like us on Facebook

https://www.facebook.com/TheWildRosePress

And Follow us on Twitter
https://twitter.com/WildRosePress

www.ingramcontent.com/pod-product-compliance
Lightning Source LLC
Chambersburg PA
CBHW050026030726
47506CB00001B/142